MORE BY I

THE HALL OF FAITH

The Praise Singer
A Disciple of Melchizedek

The Oak of Weeping
The Story of Isaac, Rebekah, and Deborah

The Epistle
A Story of the Early Church

ROBERT CURTIS MYSTERIES

Called Into Service

Soldiers of the King
The Bramshill Affair

Lords and Ladies
The Banqueting House Plot

A LITTLE GOOD BOOK

Huldah and the Last Righteous King

WWW.BLUEFORGEPRESS.COM

To Sofía, Alina & Joel

A Light
IN THE DARKEST NIGHT

SIXTEEN STORIES OF LOVE AND REBIRTH

David Marty

DAVID MARTYN

BLUE FORGE PRESS
Port Orchard, Washington

Blue Forge Press is the print division of the volunteer-run, federal 501(c)3 nonprofit company, Blue Legacy, founded in 1989 and dedicated to bringing light to the shadows and voice to the silence. We strive to empower storytellers across all walks of life with our four divisions: Blue Forge Press, Blue Forge Films, Blue Forge Gaming, and Blue Forge Records. Find out more at: www.MyBlueLegacy.org

Blue Forge Press
7419 Ebbert Drive Southeast
Port Orchard, Washington 98367
blueforgepress@gmail.com
360-550-2071 ph.txt

To all who have overcome and can sing with David

The LORD is my light and my salvation;
whom shall I fear?
The LORD is the stronghold of my life,
of whom shall I be afraid?

When evildoers assail me to eat up my flesh,
My adversaries and foes,
It is they who stumble and fall.

Though an army encamp against me,
my heart shall not fear;
though war rise against me,
yet I will be confident.

Psalm 27: 1-3

ACKNOWLEDGMENTS

I thank God for all the wonderful brothers and sisters who have blessed me and contributed to my writing. These sixteen stories are the fruit of sermons I've heard, Bible studies I've attended, conversations with family and friends, chats with Christians at book signings, and everyday contacts. Truly iron sharpens iron, and Christ's Church is a community of disciples gifted by the Holy Spirit for the building up of saints to the glory of God!

TABLE OF CONTENTS

A Light

IN THE Darkest Night

Sixteen Stories of Love and Rebirth

David Martyn

STAND FIRM, ELIJAH

*H*e awoke to a beautiful morning. The sun was rising, sending orange and golden rays of light to shimmer and dance across the waters of the Mississippi River. Elijah Parish Lovejoy stood at his boarding house window admiring the beauty.

Only God above can bring beauty to the muddy brown water of that river. His goodness cannot be blotted out by my sins or the sins of any man. And today, Lord, I begin a new chapter—you have called me to this work! I know it is your doing.

Thank you, Lord, and thank you, Reverend Potts!

I must write to my father. Oh, how he has waited and prayed. Yes, I must share with him my good news.

Elijah planned his day as he walked to his first appointment: *Hire a helper. Someone diligent and trustworthy. See to uncrating the press. Get another set of keys to the shop for Miller and then, yes, lunch with the Gamble brothers. A weekly newspaper; what day should we publish? The Gamble brothers will want to know when the first edition is published. What will I write? Ideas, so many, but news too. Am I to be a reporter as well as co-editor?*

A crowd had gathered in front of the courthouse.

A LIGHT IN THE DARKEST NIGHT

Elijah heard a loud shout: "Sold! Now, who will start the bidding on the fancy girl? A rare one she is! Fifteen years old. See how the sun highlights her light curls to blonde! Yes, her eyes are blue, and you can see her beauty both of face and figure. You will not find a lighter mulatto in Saint Louis. Why a man could double or triple his money on her in New Orleans. Who will give me one hundred and fifty dollars?"

Elijah stopped and stared. He saw a row of mostly dark-skinned people—slaves—lined up on the top of the courthouse steps. There were men and women, children, too. The adults all with heads bowed, their eyes cast down at their feet. Even the children knew not to look out at the crowd. Occasionally, something would stir within one of them, and a quick glance would reveal dead eyes, their humanity hidden inside. Elijah watched as, one by one, God's precious creatures, made in His image, were auctioned off.

In his two years in Saint Louis, Elijah had seen many slaves. He knew it was evil. Every morning he awoke to the sun rising across the river in Illinois, a free state. His Presbyterian church-going friends, well-connected in the city, assured Elijah that it was the way of the world.

"Yes," they would argue. "Slavery should be abolished. Gradually. It will take time. But rash action would only lead to disorder, riots, even rebellion. Gentle persuasion and prayer is the only solution."

Elijah's joy and optimism left him. He closed his eyes and shook his head. *This cannot be God's will. Sin. Only sin could so coldly blind us to such an evil injustice. Yet I am off to hire a slave.*

It was Archibald Gamble who recommended Elijah see James Walker, a slave trader. Walker bought slaves in Saint

Louis; many were captured runaways (as determined by the police and the courts) that Walker resold in New Orleans. But slaves needed to be fed and housed and cost money until they could be sold again. Rather than allowing them to languish in his holding pens, he hired them out.

Elijah found Walker waiting in his office. "My name is Lovejoy. My friend, Archibald Gamble, recommends—"

"What services do you require, Mr. Lovejoy?"

"I'm co-editor of the new *Saint Louis Times*. We start publishing soon and I need help setting up the press and printing; someone diligent and able to learn. Someone who can be trusted to work alone when I am called away. Someone—"

"You won't find one like that in my trading pens. But I personally have such a boy. He is quick to learn and will not run; the boy will never leave his mother, my cook. I have taken him with me on the river. He has had his chances. You can use him for a while, but he travels with me when I travel. A dollar a week."

Walker went to an interior door, opened it, and shouted, "William!"

"Yes, Massuh! Coming, Massuh."

A small, wiry teenager with dark brown skin and large, inquiring brown eyes stepped into the room. He was dressed as a house servant, with black slacks and a white cotton shirt. He was privileged to wear blackened shoes and socks; most slaves went without.

"William, you will go with Master Lovejoy. You will do as he says. Work hard, and you can visit your mother."

William said nothing by voice or body language as they walked past the slave auction still in progress on the courthouse steps.

Nonetheless, his spirit troubled, Elijah asked, "It is just you and your mother, William?"

"Oh no, Massuh Lovejoy. I have five brothers and a sister. But they're all gone—sold off—every one of 'em. Massuh Walker, he keeps Momma and me together."

"I'm not your master, William. Call me Mr. Lovejoy or Elijah. And yes, you may call me Elijah. What about your father?"

"He's in Kentucky. A white gentleman. We're all mulattos: My brothers and me and my sister. Different fathers but we don't care none; not momma, not any of us. Doctor Young sold them off. Promised my father, Doctor Young's cousin, that he would keep Momma and me... but he just sold us off last."

"Mr. Walker tells me you travel with him. Do you like traveling?"

"Traveling is easy work. Mostly just waiting on the boat. Not much to it. Eat and sleep easy! I miss my momma. But I...."

Elijah recognized the hesitation and said, "Now that we are going to be working together, I expect you to do your best. I will never ask you to do anything I won't do or haven't done myself. I grew up poor, on a farm in Maine. Did you ever hear of Maine, William? I reckon not. If I am to trust you, you must know that you can trust me. I am going to teach you the newspaper business, and you can teach me."

"Teach *you*, Massuh—I mean: Mr. Lovejoy? What can *I*

teach a gentleman?"

"You have stories to tell me, William. I will listen to your stories."

"Stories? Why, I can tell you stories, all right. Whew, the stories I can tell!"

Elijah stopped going to church. He never wrote that letter to his father, the Reverend Daniel Lovejoy, a Congregationalist preacher in Maine. The Reverend Potts visited once. Elijah listened politely as the pastor asked after his Christian walk.

Elijah shook his head. "My Christian walk? You ask: Do I sin?! If there is a righteous God, then I sin. This world—this city—is filled with unredeemable sin. Your church is not a block away from the courthouse, the seat of justice in our city. Justice? It's where men, women, and children are sold on the steps! My walk, you ask? I walk alone in anger. Anger with them... but also with you and all the hypocrites in your church! I have learned more from the slave boy I hired out than from you and our upstanding citizens."

Elijah's anger waned. "Forgive me, Reverend. You are no worse than any other, perhaps even better. I am jealous of your faith—and of your hope—because I see neither."

Reverend Potts smiled. "Slavery. So many have become accustomed to its presence that they no longer smell the foul odor of injustice. But you are right to call it sin. You are right to say I walk a fine line with our city leaders; I try to provide them with a conscience rather than outright admonition. You must not be too hard on them. They are slow learners."

"Slow learners? Their well-rehearsed line is slavery must end *gradually*. Hypocrites! They're all slave owners themselves! They'll let it end only when it comes at no cost from their purses!"

"As I was saying, Elijah, there is another pastor, a Presbyterian brother, who sees as you do. He believes he is called to preach against this sin of our time. His name is David Nelson. He has opened a school, Marion College, upriver in Palmyra in Marion county. Visit him; hear what God has to say through him."

After the Reverend Potts left, Elijah thought: *An abolitionist in Missouri? And a college as well. There might be a story there.* Elijah convinced his friend and co-editor, TJ Miller, that the founding of Missouri's first college, not in bustling St. Louis but in tiny Palmyra? Now that was newsworthy.

The overnight riverboat trip to Palmyra was the first of many to come. Elijah lay in his bed, unable to sleep. Loneliness brought on by the strange surroundings fed memories of home and the sacrifices his father forced upon the family in order to send Elijah away for the education and opportunities his parents never had. Even the comforting sounds of the river, the methodical splashing of the water from the paddlewheel, and the muted voices of other passengers enjoying their evening in the main salon did not lull him to sleep.

Slowly the outside sounds faded into a dream: Elijah was in the barn with his father. It was a Saturday evening.

"Elijah, that broom will not push itself. Hurry Son. Mother has dinner waiting then a bath. Tomorrow is the Sabbath. You can rest after church."

Elijah pushed the broom slowly. "Father, why did you name me Elijah? It's... I don't...."

DAVID MARTYN

The Reverend Daniel Lovejoy looked at his son. "You don't like your name, Elijah? It's a fine name. Do you know what it means? It means Jehovah is God. You are my first-born son, a gift from God above. He gave me your name. I prayed for a son who would be a great witness to the Lord. The Sunday before you were born, I preached on Elijah, the great prophet of God. What an example he was for us: A prophet to an evil king in a land that had forgotten—no, *forsaken* God. Wicked Queen Jezebel persecuted him but four hundred fifty priests of Baal could not stop him. And God loved him so much that He took him into heaven alive. Never be ashamed of your name, Elijah. Let it inspire you to live up to that great prophet."

"Father, what if I can't be like Elijah? What if I don't want to be a preacher like you? It's unfair to carry a name that I haven't chosen. It's my name. It should be my choice."

Daniel knelt beside his son and hugged him. "Ah, there's the rub. We don't choose our names. They are chosen for us by our parents who love us. Names don't change who we are. Molly, our cow, would give milk no matter what her name. No one is limited by their name. It is your character and the gifts of God above that make you who you are. And in naming you Elijah, I intended a gift—perhaps, more my hope—to remind you to boldly proclaim your love of God and every brother and sister in all His creation. Now, let's go in. Mother made biscuits tonight; I know that is one thing you do love!"

The week Elijah spent with David Nelson changed his life. Nestled in the woods outside Palmyra, Marion College was just a log-building at this point. He found a close friend and kindred spirit in the older Reverend Nelson.

Here is the man for whom my father prayed! Fearless! Righteous and bold! It is all so clear—pray yes, never cease to pray—but act! Do something! Preach the Word. Proclaim the truth! Confront the evil! Confront the priests of Baal, the apologists of slavery and bigotry. Surely, they will fall in judgment before our Righteous God!

On their last night together, Nelson asked Elijah, "The Lord speaks to you, Elijah. Have you heard His call? His Spirit speaks to your heart. What do you hear?"

Elijah bowed his head. "I haven't loved Him with all my heart, soul, and mind. I have not loved my neighbor as myself. I condemn others but do nothing to change it." Elijah looked up. "I repent. I truly repent. I want to serve Him. You have been a great blessing. You have made the prayers of my father come true. I will serve the Lord!"

Elijah found himself singing the Old Hundredth Psalm as he strode to the office of the *Saint Louis Times*. TJ Miller, an early riser, was sitting at his desk when Elijah came through the door. Tossing a folder to his friend, Elijah said, "The story. Ready for the next edition."

Miller looked up at his friend. "Did I hear you singing? I sent you for a story; sounds like you went to a revival meeting." Miller opened the folder and read the headline aloud: "'Rev. D. Nelson Opens First College in Missouri.' A mundane headline if I ever read one."

"Read on," Elijah urged.

Miller read the sub-heading: "'Nelson's Marion College in Palmyra: A Voice in the Wilderness. Make Straight the Pathway for the Lord!' What?!"

"Read on!"

Miller read the article and set it on the desk in front of him. "Missouri is damned to 'rioting, looting, murder, and mayhem' unless slavery is abolished? Our border with free Illinois makes us a 'refuge for bigots, ruffians, outlaws, and slavers?' We can't publish this! It's the most radical abolitionist tirade I've ever read."

"Now, it might not be something you would write in an editorial position of the *Saint Louis Times*, but it's news. It's not *our* words; they are the unvarnished, true words of the Reverend David Nelson. Lord knows, he is not alone in this view. We print the words of our politicians and leading citizens. It is only fair we print the other side. Put my name on the by-line. You can write some self-deprecating disclaimer in an editorial."

Elijah picked up the article and began to walk away. "The nation has been arguing this since independence. This is 1831. Fifty years! Isn't that long enough? We're publishing it. I will do the front page layout myself."

Response to the published article was immediate and heated. Any citizens of Saint Louis in agreement kept their views private. A prominent surgeon, Doctor Horace Beall, accompanied the mayor on his visit to the newspaper. Ever the politician avoiding an embarrassing quote, the mayor allowed the hot-headed Beall to speak.

"I demand a retraction of this scurrilous article! This is nothing less than an incitement to riot! This rag you call a newspaper can be closed, never to be reopened! And if the city doesn't close you down, I expect a mob will!"

Miller rose to the paper's defense. "You would send a

mob to close us down? For what? Printing bad news? You read bad news every day: Robberies, fires, even murder! We printed news, not our opinion. Didn't you read the editorial disclaimer? Shall I be telling a judge you threatened to destroy this establishment?"

The mayor saw Miller's point and calmly reasoned: "Our city is growing. It has a great future if we maintain peace and order. You told the story once; it has been told and need not be told again. Do not think giving a voice to radicals relieves you of your duties as editor and publisher of this newspaper. Let it go. The story will die in a few days. Learn from it. Good day, gentlemen."

Elijah spent the night in Bible study, prayer and meditation. The following morning, he sat beside Miller in the office. "TJ, I'm resigning my position as co-editor. I've decided to sell my interest in the paper. I hear the call to ministry, to preaching the Word of God, like my father and my friend—"

"Your friend David Nelson?"

"Yes, Nelson, but also Reverend Potts, who chides but does not offend. The proceeds could pay for seminary. Princeton. I count you as my close friend. I'm making my offer to you before all others."

Miller nodded. "Someone or something is calling you. You certainly have the fire of a preacher. Yes, I will buy your share. Let me talk to my backers. I will pay a fair price,"

"You must agree to keep William. He is a good young man. I have been teaching him to read. He is a fast learner. Oh, and feed him here. No telling what scraps James Walker leaves him. William can operate the press alone."

"I, too, hold William in high esteem. When will

you leave?"

"The day you pay me is the day I depart."

Several days later, Elijah went to the office to collect his money. Watching him secure the bills in a money belt, Miller asked, "Aren't you going to count it?"

"No need to, my friend." Elijah reached out his hand. "Well, I guess this is goodbye."

TJ pulled Elijah into a bear hug. "Come back, brother. Missouri needs men like you."

"Maybe, Lord willing. I want to say goodbye to William."

"Of course. I am not the only one who will miss you."

William was running the press on the next edition when Elijah came in. "Mr. Lovejoy..."

"Will it never be Elijah, my friend?"

"I heard you are leaving. I am honored you stopped by. It is a rare thing for a slave to be permitted goodbyes."

Elijah nodded. "I wanted to hear one more story before I go."

"Well now, Mr. Lov—I mean, *Elijah*—you have heard all my stories."

Elijah sat down. "Your friend Cynthia. How is she doing?"

"She's gone from his house."

"Please, William, from the beginning?"

William smiled. "Massuh bought her in Saint Louis. She's beautiful. A quadroon, they would call her in New Orleans. You know, they pay well for fancy girls in New Orleans. We took her aboard the steamboat then Massuh went about business. He told me to put her in a stateroom, not the slave quarters with the others. I knew what that meant and it was no good for her. Sure enough, he went in that stateroom up to no good. I listened outside the door and heard him make his no-good offer: Give him his pleasure and stay in Saint Louis as a housemaid... or else. She would hear none of it! No, sir. She was a good girl and God-fearin'. She sure stirred him one, she did. He said: 'Agree to be my pleasure girl or I'll sell you as a plantation slave to wither like dried corn in the August sun.'

"I spoke with her the next day, Elijah. What could she do? She knew he could force his way. She stayed with him in Saint Louis and had four of his children. But when Massuh decided to marry, he sold 'em all and shipped 'em off. I heard she's workin' the fields now somewhere in Louisiana."

Elijah nodded slowly. "The Bible says—William, promise me you will read the Bible I gave you—'What does the Lord require of you? Do justly, love mercy and walk humbly with your God.' You remember that, William. Never accept slavery as God's will. It's always man's sin."

"I'll remember that, Mr. Lovejoy."

Elijah stood up and said, "Come here, my young friend."

Elijah hugged the surprised William and smiled as the young man wiped tears from his eyes. "I want you to do something else for me, William. Something important. I want you to write down your stories. Don't leave out the pain or the joy. I can argue with logic and Scripture, but you have the real thing: Authenticity. You speak straight to the heart."

"Will you come back, Mr. Lovejoy?"

"I don't know. If the Lord wills, I will come back to my friends."

Not a year had passed when Elijah received a letter while studying at Princeton Seminary:

Brother Elijah Lovejoy,

We pray this letter finds you in good health. Several of your brothers and sisters in Saint Louis have urged the leadership of First Presbyterian Church to offer you a ministry position. As you have boldly written and spoken in the past, our city and county are beset by sin in all of its malignant manifestations. Only changed hearts can overcome the will to sin. How can a sinner repent unless the Word is preached?

After prayer and discussion, the session, with the support of community leaders, has endorsed the founding of a Presbyterian newspaper. If you will accept the position of editor and additional duties as circuit evangelist to the outlying towns and settlements of our county.

Yours in Christ,

Reverend William S. Potts

Pastor

Lovejoy was ordained in Philadelphia on April 18, 1833. On November 22 of that year, the first edition of the *Saint Louis Observer* was published. The preacher who returned had left all doubts and thoughts of compromise behind. The Reverend Elijah Parish Lovejoy was steadfast in his faith and determined to call sin what it was. He began a campaign for repentance, righteous living, abstinence from alcohol and tobacco, and the end of slavery.

Anxious to get started, Elijah called upon TJ Miller at the *Saint Louis Times*, "TJ! You look well, my friend. You must have heard how I am now editor of the *Saint Louis Observer*. I have come to you hoping you will allow my employ of William in setting up my press."

Miller greeted his friend. "I have heard, and congratulations, my friend. I hear it is to be a church publication. Probably the better for you. But as for William, he is gone."

"Gone? Where? Traveling with Walker?"

"No, it is good news. Walker took William and his mother with him on a trip to Cincinnati. Well, the story is they escaped and traveled north with the help of the Underground Railroad. No one knows their whereabouts; of course, if they did, they would surely say nothing."

Elijah smiled. "Hallelujah! Escaped to freedom! God bless his soul!"

An early issue of the *Observer* brought Reverend Potts and the financial backers to Elijah's office. The ever-diplomatic Reverend Potts spoke for the group, "Elijah, we meant the *Observer* to be a forum for the improvement of our city, a voice of reason to call our citizens to righteous living."

"That is my heart as well. It is why I accepted your generous offer. Why do you come to me? Complaints? Who complains to my pastor and the board?"

"French fur traders founded our city. Catholic French fur traders. The Mississippi was a French Catholic thoroughfare through the heart of the continent. They brought Christianity here and have never departed. Do you think our Catholic brothers and sisters have less desire for righteous living than Presbyterians? Your recent writings against heavy drink, tobacco, gambling, prostitution, and all the vices that trouble our city—including slavery—rail against Catholic tolerance and false repentance for these sins. Do not

Protestants, including Presbyterians, commit these same sins? Would you divide those who seek the same faithful ends and open yourself to a charge of hypocrisy? The religious wars are over; thank God above, we have put them in the past. We live in a new city and we must unite all citizens of goodwill in a crusade against sin and lawlessness that threatens peace and justice."

Elijah's head fell back against the heavy blow he felt. "You are right, Pastor Potts. I repent of my sin, and I offer my resignation."

"We haven't come for your resignation, Elijah. We have come to encourage you. Your passion and boldness are great gifts. But sometimes, you stray from the goal. Learn from this. The board and I will advise you." Potts paused and then added, "Prophets and reformers may draw many followers but find few friends. Their words and warnings are harsh. Their zeal and commitment to God's calling on their life go beyond what most good people can imitate. It would be wrong to judge others less committed; they weigh other commitments: Family and worries of the day. You must accept this and love them for doing what they can."

Preaching the circuit was a tonic to Elijah's soul. Sharing the Gospel brought him boundless joy. He ceased all attacks on other Christian faiths and turned his attention to the unchurched or Christian families longing to be disciples and find fellowship with other believers. At a church in Saint Charles, Missouri, Elijah met an earnest young woman, warm to the faith. As Elijah listened to her questions, he watched her intelligent eyes sparkling with enthusiasm and pondered her sweet smile.

A LIGHT IN THE DARKEST NIGHT

"And how would you answer, Pastor Lovejoy?"

Elijah's jaw dropped. His mind failed him. Her questions hadn't interrupted his fixation on the beautiful creature sitting across from him. He hadn't heard a word she said. All Elijah could manage was, "Ah, well, yes. Let me think. Perhaps we can talk more of this, you and I, after... I mean... if no one else has any other questions, perhaps we should close in prayer? I'm told refreshments have been prepared."

Elijah Lovejoy married Celia Ann French on March 4, 1835. The happiness Elijah found in his home life did not shield him from the increasing hostility brought against him for his abolitionist views. A brick through his window carried the threat of tar and feathering if he did not cease publishing his anti-slavery message. Elijah was sure of his calling and would not relent. But the threats did not stop; they grew louder and graver. New threats of burning him out: Threats of murder and threats against the church could not be ignored by First Presbyterian, Reverend Potts, and the newspaper board. In October of 1835, Elijah resigned from editing the *Observer*. Celia was pregnant with their first child.

Elijah was at home when visitors came to his door. Cautiously looking from behind his curtain, he recognized old friends: His backers from the *Saint Louis Times*. Elijah welcomed them into his home. "Elijah, you are the only newspaperman in town still willing to challenge the slavers. We have a proposition for you."

"Friends, Celia and I have work. We will continue to ride the circuit, preaching the Good News of Christ's salvation and pastoring our rural brothers and sisters."

"By all means, Pastor, continue preaching but hear us

out. We have purchased the *Saint Louis Observer* from its mortgage holder. We will resume publication, and we want you to be the editor."

"You understand, gentlemen, I will stand by the abolitionist cause."

"We expect it. Do you accept?"

Elijah turned to Celia. Her smile was enough, but she spoke, "Husband, it is your calling. The Lord told me you were set apart for His work before I married you. Be bold, Elijah, and brave. Know that I love you and will never doubt your calling."

That night Elijah dreamt he was sitting in his father's church. Pastor Daniel Lovejoy was standing in the pulpit, his open Bible balanced in his left hand, reading from I Kings, Chapter 18. "Now it came about when Ahab saw Elijah that Ahab said to him. 'Is this you, you troubler of Israel?' And Elijah said, 'I have not troubled Israel but you and your father's house have, because you have forsaken the commandments of the Lord, and you have followed the Baals. Now then, send and gather to me all Israel at Mount Carmel together with four hundred and fifty prophets of Baal and four hundred worshippers of the Asherah, who eat at Jezebel's table.'"

Elijah dreamt of the battle of prophets. The hapless rantings of the priests of Baal, their prayers all unanswered. His mind's eye watched as the great prophet Elijah taunted his enemies: "Perhaps you should cry louder. Perhaps your god is busy with others or off on a journey."

The prophets of Baal cried louder. They cut themselves with knives but their god did not answer. All day they prayed from morning until evening. Finally, Elijah called the people near. He repaired the altar to the God of Abraham,

Isaac, and Jacob. He dug a deep trench all around it. He placed wood on the altar, sacrificed an ox, cut it into pieces, and laid it on the altar. He called upon men to pour water over the altar again and again until the water overflowed from the trench around it. Only then did Elijah pray, 'Oh Lord, the God of Abraham, Isaac and Israel, today let it be known that Thou art God in Israel and I am Thy servant. I have done all these things at Thy word. Answer me, oh Lord. Answer me, that this people may know that Thou, oh Lord, art God; that Thou hast turned their hearts back again.'"

Reverend Daniel Lovejoy's voice rose and thundered, "The fire of the Lord fell and consumed the burnt offering and the wood and the stones and the dust and licked up the water that was in the trench!"

His voice softened, "And when all the people saw it, they fell on their faces. They said, 'The Lord, He is God! The Lord, He is God.'"

Elijah awoke. He looked at Celia asleep beside him. "In the morning," he whispered and fell back to sleep.

Elijah waited until breakfast to share this vivid dream with his wife. "What could it mean?"

"You know what it means. Stand firm, Elijah. God is with you."

The threats against Elijah resumed with the first publication of the *Observer* under the new ownership. If Celia was afraid, she kept it between herself and the Lord, never discouraging Elijah from his calling.

In April of 1836, Elijah printed the story of a free black man arrested for stabbing two Saint Louis police officers, killing one. Never one to condone killing, Elijah was struck by the injustice that led to the tragedy and raised the issue to his readers that slavery was the root cause of these and many other injustices.

Elijah reported that the free black man, Francis McIntosh, was about his business when he witnessed two constables chasing a slave. The officers called for McIntosh to take chase in their place. Mister McIntosh did not see it as his duty to chase slaves and continued his business. The two officers were incensed. They ceased chasing the runaway and arrested Mister McIntosh, swearing that he would be sold into slavery for refusing their order. As the police dragged him off towards the station, McIntosh pulled a knife from his pocket, slashed at his two captors, killing one and wounding the other, then escaped only to be recaptured.

McIntosh was in jail, awaiting trial when the story ran in the *Observer*. Doctor Horace Beall, the wealthy Saint Louis surgeon and outspoken supporter of slavery, formed a committee of five to denounce and silence Elijah Lovejoy. But Beall's hatred did not end with Elijah. Francis McIntosh escaped or was conveniently released from jail before trial. Beall's mob soon recaptured him, tied him to a tree, piled wood around him to his chest, and set it on fire. Mockers called out to him as he burned, "Ain't you dead yet?"

McIntosh cried in anguish, "I'm as alive as you. Please, the pain! Save me!"

The mob paid a boy to tend the fire all night until the body was entirely burned.

County Judge Lawless put the death of McIntosh solely on Elijah Lovejoy for inciting the riot. The judge's condemnation convinced Elijah it was time to leave Saint Louis. He could continue his work with his wife safe across the Mississippi in Alton, Illinois.

A LIGHT IN THE DARKEST NIGHT

After shuttering the newspaper and plastering a large 'Closed' sign across the storefront, Elijah crated the printing press and moved it to the ferry crossing by wagon. He missed the last ferry of the day but was assured his cargo would be safe until morning. No sooner had Elijah gone home than one of Beall's informants called for a mob to destroy Lovejoy's press.

As the mob gathered and made its torch-lit way to the ferry dock, an alderman on his way home saw the crowd and sent for the police. Alderman Bryan Mullanphy pleaded with the men to go home and waited in vain for the police to restore order. "Is this the action of civilized men? You have driven a man from our city. Isn't that enough? Let him go! Do not become lawbreakers! Go home; I've sent for the police. You have families. Would you have your children witness your arrest?"

"The police won't come. Trust me, boys." It was Beall. "You know what to do. Get on with it."

The printing press was destroyed and the broken pieces were thrown into the river. In the morning, Elijah, Celia, and baby Edward Lovejoy rode the ferry to Alton, Illinois. Elijah never again set foot in Missouri.

The first night in bed in a strange room in Alton, Elijah lay awake, depressed and exhausted. He fought to be quiet and hold back his tears, trying desperately not to disturb Celia, pregnant with their second child, asleep beside him. Sometime before dawn, his painful consciousness slipped into a dream. He was in the same small church in Maine. His father was preaching.

"Now Ahab told Jezebel all that Elijah had done and

how he had killed all the prophets with the sword. Then Jezebel sent a messenger to Elijah saying, 'So may the gods do to me and even more, if I do not take your life as the life of one of them by tomorrow at this time.'"

Daniel Lovejoy's voice boomed: "And how did Elijah receive this news? How did the man who witnessed the power of God—who had answered his prayer, sent fire from heaven, and given him a miraculous victory—react?"

The preacher paused and in a softer voice said, "Let me read: 'And he was afraid and arose and ran for his life. He went down and sat under a juniper tree. He requested to die, and said, 'It is enough, now, oh Lord. Take my life, for I am not better than my fathers.'"

Daniel Lovejoy was a simple man. A simple farmer, not well educated, but he knew his Bible, and he knew people. He continued his sermon to his tiny congregation. "The strongest of men is weak. Saint Paul says in Corinthians, 'We have this treasure in hearts of clay to show that this all-surpassing power is from God and not from us.' But God never abandons us. Listen to how God attended to Elijah. He sent his angel, who prepared food and drink and told Elijah to eat, for a man of God needs his strength.

"For forty days, God sustained Elijah in the wilderness and, after he was nourished and refreshed, sent him on a journey to Horeb, God's mountain. At Horeb, God asked the strengthened Elijah, 'What are you doing here?' Elijah still did not understand the strength and power of God. Elijah complained, 'I have been zealous for God. Israel has forsaken Your covenant, torn down Your altars, and killed Your prophets. I alone am left, and they seek to take my life.'"

The preacher continued, "God does not argue with us.

A LIGHT IN THE DARKEST NIGHT

He shows us His love. God said to Elijah, 'Go, stand at the mountain before the Lord.' And the Lord God was passing by! A great and strong wind was blowing across the mountain and breaking in pieces the rocks before the Lord. But the Lord was not in the wind. After the wind, an earthquake; but the Lord was not in the earthquake. And after the earthquake? A fire."

The preacher paused and scanned his congregation. His eyes fell on young Elijah. Elijah felt his father's eyes. He tried to stare back but he could not. He closed his eyes and bowed his head. His father continued, "Quiet. Everything was quiet, silence. Silent before the Almighty. And then... Ssh! Listen! Do you hear it, my friend?"

Daniel Lovejoy held his hand behind his ear and looked up, his eyes searching in anticipation. He did not move. His voice soft, he continued, "A gentle blowing. When Elijah heard it, he wrapped his face in his mantle and went out and stood at the entrance of the cave. A voice came to him. It did not scold him but gently asked, 'Elijah, what are you doing here?' God would not hear his excuse. He sent Elijah off on a mission. Elijah was sent to do God's work. But as Elijah departed the mountain, God told him one more thing: 'I leave seven thousand in Israel, all the knees that have not bowed to Baal and every mouth that has not kissed him.' He reminded Elijah that he was not alone. There is never one of us left alone. Like Israel, there is always a remnant.

"Take heart in the lesson of Elijah. Find that still peace of God in your heart. Be nourished and strengthened in your faith and do the work God asks of you, knowing you are not alone and the victory has been won."

Elijah shared his dream with Celia. She looked through Elijah's eyes into his soul and said only, "God is not through with you. Didn't God send the prophet Elijah to anoint his successor, Elisha? Who is your Elisha?"

Celia thought but dared not say aloud: *And then God took Elijah to heaven above.*

Lovejoy was called to pastor the Upper Alton Presbyterian Church where he joyfully preached the Word and was bathed in the love of his congregation. He opened another newspaper, *The Alton Observer*, and championed the abolitionist cause. He maintained regular correspondence with his friend, the Reverend David Nelson, forced to flee Missouri for Quincy, Illinois. Nelson tirelessly supported the Underground Railway in Quincy and encouraged Elijah to remain steadfast in his campaign for abolition.

Elijah sat in his office on the fourth of July 1837 and penned an editorial: *Bitter mockery! On this, our Independence Day, we gather to thank God for our freedom. We eat and drink with joy and gladness of heart. We celebrate freedom while free American feet are on the necks of nearly three million of our fellow men. Be sure of this: Our shouts of self-congratulation can never drown their groans. The very flag of freedom that waves over our heads is sewn from cotton cloth cultivated by slaves, on a soil moistened with their blood.*

Two days later, Lovejoy was summoned to his office. The building had been ransacked; the printing press destroyed. Elijah silently vowed: *Doctor Beal, neither you nor your friends shall ever silence me!*

Returning home to Celia after visiting the destruction, Elijah said, "I will continue; God help me, this is not over."

Elijah wrote to David Nelson seeking his help in forming an Illinois chapter of the American Anti-Slavery

A LIGHT IN THE DARKEST NIGHT

Society. Soon Elijah scheduled an American Anti-Slavery Society Congress to meet at Upper Alton Presbyterian Church on October 26, 1837. But before the congress could meet, Alton and the rest of the nation were caught up in an economic crisis.

A friend wrote Elijah, urging the congress be postponed:

My dear Elijah, your desire for a congress of the American Anti-Slavery Society in Alton is indeed noble. But I urge you to delay until our people's minds are fixed on the cause and not distracted by our current circumstances. Must I remind you of the facts? President Jackson's refusal to renew the charter of the Second National Bank, add to that the credit defaults of American cotton barons, taken together, have led to a run on the nation's banks. Banks no longer cover their deposits with gold or silver. Loans cannot be had. Western expansion has stopped. In our great heartland, the loss of loans for farming is worsened by the Hessian Fly, which devastates our wheat crop. The crop in the field is lost, and there is no capital for seed for the next crop. Panic grips our land. People are frightened. How will they feed their families? Concerns for others give way to a struggle for survival. Wait. There will be a more propitious time.

Elijah slapped the letter down on his desk. "Wait? Wait for a more propitious time? Will the condition of the slave improve with time? Times are hard—hard for the free? I say: Even harder for the slave. No, I will not wait!"

When the congress opened, organizers were surprised to see Illinois Attorney General Usher Linder and Congressman John Hogan registering. Both politicians were well known for their pro-slavery views. When approached, Elijah told the staff to admit all who would listen. Rumors spread through Alton that Lovejoy's congress would antagonize southerners. They feared Saint Louis would close its markets to Alton produce, and the attorney general would investigate ways to sanction the city.

The congress concluded without incident and many residents of Alton were determined to do more in the cause of abolition. Encouraged by the congress, several prominent merchants called on Elijah. Winthrop Gilman and Benjamin Godfrey, both grocers, were their spokesmen.

"Pastor, isn't it time *The Alton Observer* resumed publication?"

"*The Observer*? How many times can it be resurrected?" Elijah asked.

"Friends. Your friends, Elijah, want to buy another press. We have considered both the risk and the reward. We'll keep the location of the press a secret. Only trusted men will know. I own a warehouse for the grocery store. It is large, stone, and secure; it's near the river, away from prying eyes and with few windows for the curious. We have found a printing press as well."

Now Godfrey interrupted: "The hearts of the people have been warmed; there was money raised at the congress. What do you say, Pastor?"

Elijah took the idea to Celia. She smiled and kissed Elijah. "It's your gift and calling." Yet she thought: *And, I fear, the beginning of the end.*

On the sixth of November, a barge delivered a press consigned to Gilman and Godfrey's Grocery. Elijah was summoned to the warehouse. But word of the delivery was leaked; Doctor Beall and his pro-slavery committee dispatched a mob, mostly Missourians but men from Alton as well, to seize the press. Gilman arranged for eleven armed men to move the printing press to his warehouse across the street from the wharf. The mob arrived just as the doors of the warehouse were closed.

Henry West, an Alton pro-slavery man, walked forward to negotiate. "It's the printing press we want. Surrender the press, and all you men can walk home. No harm will come to you. Just the press!"

Someone shouted, "You'll not be taking this press or putting so much as a finger on Pastor Lovejoy unless you step over my dead body!"

Shots were fired from both sides. A man named Bishop, one of Beall's mob, fell dead. More shots. Bullets pierced the wood doors. And then silence. Elijah found a sack of flour and sat down. He closed his eyes. He heard the murmurs of his protectors as they talked and planned their defense. The voices grew quieter, softer, and soon he could no longer hear them. He tried to pray. But neither his words nor any sound or sense heeded his painful cries. Winthrop Gilman sat down beside him. But Elijah did not see or hear him. His mind was lost in the silent blackness.

Then came a gentle wind.

Elijah listened intently. Yes, he heard a soft wind blow... and a voice: *Elijah, are you ready to come home?*

From deep within him, he replied, *I haven't laid my mantle on Elisha, Lord.*

The voice answered: *Your mantle has indeed been laid on others.*

"Celia?" Elijah murmured aloud.

Celia knows. She will follow when her work is done.

Elijah opened his eyes. He now heard Winthrop Gilman whispering, "The walls will hold. The roof. They will certainly try to burn the roof...."

Elijah stood up and walked towards the door.

"Don't be fooled, Elijah. Just because it's quiet out there doesn't mean it's safe."

Elijah said nothing. He unbolted the door and swung it open. It creaked as it swung. Shadows crossed its path and light dissected the room. The door stopped, and silence returned. Elijah took one step forward.

Boom, boom, boom, boom, boom. Five loud rifle shots shattered the silence. Five bullets found Elijah's body. He fell back and through the blood flowing from his mouth, he said, "My God, I'm shot!"

Elijah Parish Lovejoy was dead.

Elijah was buried on his thirty-sixth birthday. His grave location was kept secret. Celia Lovejoy was twenty-four years old.

Without ever fully realizing it, Elijah had indeed laid his mantle on the shoulders of so many others. His words and actions created a ripple of effects that touched far more than just his own life.

The runaway slave, William, took the name William Wells Brown. He married and, for a time, worked steamboats out of Buffalo, New York. Self-educated, William went to Europe and lectured extensively for the abolitionist cause returning to America with his two daughters only after the passage of the Fugitive Slave Act when a British couple purchased his freedom. He was an equally active and popular speaker on the abolitionist circuit in the United States and recruited African Americans for the Union cause during the civil war. William is the first published African American playwright. He also wrote fiction and drama. After the civil war, he wrote a history of African Americans in the Revolutionary War. Later in life, he studied homeopathic medicine and opened a practice in Boston.

Elijah's brother, Owen, became the leader of the Illinois abolitionists. While running the Underground Railroad in Quincy, he wrote a memoir about Elijah published in 1838, distributed widely among abolitionists uniting them in calls for action.

Edward Lovejoy was raised by his mother, Celia, in nomadic poverty. Finally settling in California. After successfully defending a man wrongfully accused, Edward studied law and was admitted to the bar. Edward was elected District Attorney of Trinity County in the mountains of northern California. He was active in the defense of Asian Americans, whose poverty and mistreatment he believed would end only in slavery. He was the only voice for Asians and African Americans in Trinity County. He served as a judge and opened a newspaper, like his father. He cared for his mother until the day she died.

The Sunday after John Brown read of Elijah Lovejoy's death, he proclaimed in church, "Here before God, and in the presence of these witnesses, from this time, I consecrate my life to the destruction of slavery."

A young Abraham Lincoln, in his 1838 address to the Young Men's Lyceum in Springfield, Illinois, warned, "Whenever the vicious portion of our population shall be permitted to gather in bands of hundreds and thousands, and burn churches, ravage and rob provision stores, throw printing presses into rivers, shoot editors, and hang and burn obnoxious persons, at pleasure and with impunity, depend upon it: This government cannot last. By such things, the feeling of the best citizens will become more or less alienated from it, and thus it will be left without friends, or with too few, and those too weak to make their friendship effectual." Historians write that this reference to Elijah Lovejoy, and the freedman Francis McIntosh, awakened Lincoln's oratory career.

Lovejoy's friend, Winthrop Gilman, the grocer who defended his property, was tried for inciting a riot. A jury found him not guilty after fifteen minutes of deliberation. Charges were dropped against the eleven other defenders. Two doctors from Alton, who fired the shots that killed Elijah Lovejoy, were tried and found not guilty in a separate trial. One of the gunmen taking part in the assault was a jury foreman in the murder trial. No one was ever convicted of Elijah's murder.

The Beall house in Saint Louis is a museum open to visitors. It remembers the life of Elijah Lovejoy, the man Doctor Horace Beall persecuted.

Stand Firm, Elijah *is based on actual historical events.*

THE CINDERS OF
PLINY THE YOUNGER

*G*aius Plinius Caecilius Secondus, Imperial Governor of Bithynia and Pontus, walked onto his palace portico overlooking the Black Sea. The chilly morning air matched the overcast sky and mist lying over the water. Only the echoes of fisherman, readying their boats enshrouded in the fog, disturbed the silence. Most of the city was still asleep, recovering from yesterday's festival of Lunuariaeum honoring Anna Perenna, goddess of the new year. The whole Roman world celebrated the festival on the first of March, the first day of the year on the Roman calendar.

Not the view from my villa on beautiful Lake Como and none of the comforts of my estate at Tiberium in Umbria, but better than that hellish Syria posting, the governor thought.

Two weeks until the Ides of March and word of new Imperial postings. No, I will hear nothing. It has only been a year. And Bithynia is a governorship. It is peaceful and quiet, except for complaints about these Christians. But it seems there is no escaping the turmoil they bring. If I am to stay, I will send for my wife. But now, to work!

Governor Plinius walked to his front door and removed the greens set out for the festival. He saw black soot spotting his white woolen tunic as he stretched out his arm. Brushing at it only smeared the inky sludge. He mumbled, "The temple of Janus. Ironic that his embers fall on my house this first working day of the new year."

Plinius called for his slave, "Quintus! Another tunic. And the toga pulla. There is soot in the air."

From another room came the reply: "The toga pulla is for funerals."

Plinius shouted back, "It's black. No one but you would question my toga. Besides, this fog and dreary weather have the air of a funeral. I will not soil my fine red toga trebea. Clean this tunic. And bring the sweet gifts—the honey—for my officers."

Quintus came in with a clean white tunic with broad vertical purple stripes and the long, black toga. Plinius changed his tunic and stood still as Quintus draped the heavy black wool toga over his master's shoulder and around his body, carefully arranging each fold. When he finished, Quintus said, "The sweet gifts were all delivered yesterday, Master Plinius. As your officers came yesterday with their gifts, I sent each home with a gift from you.

"As for the soot: I have asked the priests of Janus to take care when the mist and fog appear. The smoke of their sacrifice does not rise to the gods; rather, it falls on their governor. Do not stay too long. You work too hard, harder than all your officers. Come home for supper and rest. Remember the promise you made to your wife."

Plinius smiled. "Sometimes, I think your loyalty rests with her more than me."

Quintus replied, "Master Plinius, you know my fidelity to you."

Plinius climbed the hill, passing the temple of Janus with the two faces of the god, one looking back on the past and the other looking forward to the future. *I refuse to believe the superstition foretold by our weather. The year ahead cannot be as dark as the past. Not so dark as those days I shall never forget!*

He walked into the Agora, through the square to the far end where the tall columns topped with a pedimented roof covered the comitum, the Roman court. Lucius was waiting for Plinius when he arrived. "It is good you celebrated judiciously, Lucius. Connections alone will not make your career. Hard work and competence. Ambition and a cautious tongue alone will serve you no better. Now, what do you bring me this morning?"

Lucius knew better than to comment on the governor's black toga. He replied, "Wise words, Governor. More complaints. Accusations against the atheists."

"Names published in the anonymous list, no doubt. You call the Christians atheists? They have a god."

"But they do not bow before the known gods. They do not worship the emperor. They do not buy meat sacrificed at the temples. They have no temple, so where is their god? Can there be such a god?"

"They show amazing devotion to their Christ and their formless god. Atheist does not describe their persistence against all threats. How many today?"

"There remain three arrested before the festival, and likely more before day's end."

Plinius snorted. "Neighbor accusing neighbor. Why?"

Lucius replied, "The fishing has been poor, and the

spring is late in coming. The fields are too wet to sow. Sacrifices are made in the temples, but nothing happens. Few people go the priests, and the priests blame the Christians—"

Plinius interrupted. "So, blame your enemy whether he is truly a Christian or not. This is not justice, Lucius. Well, don't delay. Bring the first one before me."

Plinius removed his black toga pulla, slung his magisterial bright white, purple bordered toga praetexta over his shoulder, and entered the judgment hall. He sat in the judgment seat and sampled a fig from the table of fruit and wine by his side. An old, white-haired man, stooped with age, leathery, wrinkled skin, and blackened hands, was brought before him. Without looking up, Plinius asked, "Name and charge?"

Lucius replied, "He goes by the name Portus. He is charged with atheism—refusing to honor the gods and the emperor. He is accused as a Christian."

Plinius asked, "He is accused? Who accuses him?"

"The accuser asks to remain anonymous."

"Anonymous?" Plinius glanced at the prisoner. "Tell me, Portus, are you an atheist? Do you refuse to worship the gods?"

Portus lifted his head, "I worship, Magistrate—"

"I am Governor Plinius."

"My pardon. Yes, Governor. But my work? It is not our habit to worship at the temples."

"What is your work that prohibits temple worship?"

"I am a seaman, Governor."

"Can one so old pull an oar or trim a sail?"

"Governor, I served the emperors aboard many galleys, though now I spend most of my days at the shipworks working in pitch. Your pardon, Governor, but are you nephew to Admiral Plinius? I remember a nephew. We met some years ago."

Plinius sat back and studied the prisoner. "You knew my uncle? He adopted me as his son, and I bear his name. Yes, I remember you. You were with my father when he died. You told me his story, how he gave his life to rescue the good citizens at Pompeii. Yes. Many years ago, I was recording the account of my uncle's bravery. I wrote what I saw that day Pompeii was destroyed and sought out survivors from among his men. It is you. You told me all that he encountered."

The room was quiet. Plinius' thoughts went to the uncle he loved who had raised him and adopted him as son and heir.

Lucius interrupted. "Governor Plinius, how do you judge?"

Plinius tuned to Lucius and snapped: "We have had this discussion. The accuser is anonymous. What proof is presented of this man's guilt? Who has been harmed? The two women anonymously accused last month; they would share no information on others or bend their knees before the gods. Even under torture, they held stubborn to their god. Must we torture every man, woman, and child anonymously accused? To what benefit? No, Lucius. I will withhold judgment and write to Emperor Trajan for instructions."

Lucius nodded. "As you wish, Governor. But what should I do with the accused? If he is freed and the emperor determines.... The man is a seaman; he may try to—"

Plinius did not let him finish. "He shall be held in prison. But he shall be treated well like a Roman citizen awaiting passage to Rome for trial."

A LIGHT IN THE DARKEST NIGHT

Portus was taken back to prison. Plinius adjourned court and retreated to his chambers to write his letter. Plinius relied upon his training in rhetoric and political skill which allowed him to rise in the empire through the tumultuous reigns of three emperors. He wrote:

It is my practice, My Lord, to refer to you all matters in which I am in doubt. For who better can give guidance to my hesitation or inform my ignorance? I have never participated in trials of Christians. I, therefore, do not know what offenses to punish or investigate. I have been hesitant as to whether there should be a distinction on account of age and whether pardon should be granted for repentance.

In the case of those denounced to me as Christians, I have proceeded to interrogate as to whether they were Christians. Those who confessed, I interrogated a second and a third time, threatening them with punishment. Those who persisted, I executed, for I had no doubt that, whatever the nature of their creed, stubbornness and inflexible obstinacy surely deserves to be punished. Those found to be Roman citizens I ordered transferred to Rome.

Soon accusations spread and an anonymous document was published containing the names of many persons. Those who denied they were or had been Christians, when they invoked the gods, in words dictated by me, offered prayer with incense and wine to your image, and cursed Christ—none of which those who are really Christians, it is said can be forced to do—these I thought should be discharged.

Others named by the informer declared that they were Christians but then denied it in past years. They all worshipped your image and the statues of the gods and cursed Christ. They asserted that the substance of their error had been to meet on a fixed day, before dawn, and sing responsively a hymn to Christ as god and to then bind themselves by oath, not to some crime, but not to commit fraud, theft, or adultery, not to falsify their trust or refuse to return a trust when called upon to do so. When this was over, it was their custom to depart and to assemble again to partake of food. I found nothing else but depraved, excessive superstition.

I, therefore, postponed the investigation and hastened to consult you. For many persons of every age, every rank, and also of both sexes are or will be endangered. The contagion of this superstition has spread to the cities, villages, and farms. The contagion can be checked. The temples, once deserted, have begun to be frequented. Hence, it is easy to imagine what a multitude of people can be reformed if an opportunity for repentance is offered.

Portus lay in his bed entrapped by walls and bars unseen in the blackness. A lightwell was too far from his cell to allow the faint light of a dark, overcast night to wander the distance to his cell. Somewhere water dripped, and the cadence of soft splashes in a puddle below marked time. He could measure minutes and hours with concentration and estimate time until dawn. Two hours after total darkness, a guard made his rounds. The light of the lantern and the sounds of his footsteps reminded Portus that he was not dreaming, that he had not crossed the river Styx or fallen into hell. As he listened, he discerned two men, not one. The hard footsteps of the iron-studded sandals of the guard and the softer footsteps of a man in leather shoes.

The light came closer. It stopped. An arm raised a lantern close against the iron bars. And then a voice: "Prisoner

A LIGHT IN THE DARKEST NIGHT

Portus, you have a visitor."

Keys rattled, and the lock clanged against its intruder. A click of the mechanism and creaking hinges urged Portus to sit up and then stand. A table and chair were now visible in the cell. A candle was set on the table and lit from the lantern.

"That will be all. I can find my way out. I wish to inquire of the prisoner alone." Governor Plinius was now visible and sat in the chair by the table. The guard left, the cadence of his iron-studded sandals confirming his retreat. "Did they feed you? And give you a warm blanket? It's a dry cell and the air is not foul. I shall see that you are exercised and well cared for while I await word from Emperor Trajan. Before we begin, I remind you to say nothing as to the charges against you. Do not make me an accuser."

Portus sat on the bed. "Far drier and warmer than the emperor's galleys. And the food is no worse."

Plinius nodded. "Good. I would like to recount our discussions from my uncle's service. You were with him. Tell me, had you served with him before?"

"Admiral Gaius Plinius Caecilius was a good and noble man, respected and honored by those he led. Yes, I served with him for three years. I was a trusted man on his galley but also crew on his barge as we rowed him from ship to ship or ashore. He knew the names of his trusted men. He knew my name and the name of my wife, my village, and my father. He listened as well as commanded. Yes, a good man."

Plinius stared through the lantern, his gaze boring through the table, the stone floor, and deep into the past. "I will never forget that day. The noise. The sky. The cloud rising from the volcano. It was like a giant umbrella pine—you know, like the trees that line the via Ostia from the port of

Ostia Antica the whole distance to Rome. It rose to a great height like a trunk and then split into branches. I imagine it was because it was thrust upwards by the first blast and then no longer supported by the pressure or borne down by its own weight. It spread out and then dispersed. In places, it looked white but then blotched and dirty. No one knew what to make of it."

Plinius paused and then added, "I was seventeen years old. Such a very long time ago, yet I remember it as yesterday."

Portus softly replied, "Yes, it was just as you say. Then just the cloud hanging over the mountain. A few people began leaving Pompeii. They went to the beach and found boats across the bay."

Plinius was looking up now but his eyes remained focused on his thoughts. "The second day, I was with my mother. We were across the bay from the mountain. Ashes were falling, though not yet very thickly. I looked around. A dense black cloud came up behind us, spreading over the earth like a flood. I said to mother, 'Let us leave the road while we can still see.' We had scarcely sat down to rest when darkness fell. Not the dark of a moonless or cloudy night, but as if a lamp had been put out in a closed room. You could hear the fear, the shrieks of women, the wailing of infants, and the shouting of men. Some were calling to their parents, others their children or their wives, trying to recognize them by their voices."

Plinius paused then shook his head and continued: "There were some who prayed for death in their terror of dying. Many begged the aid of the gods but still more imagined there were no gods left, and that the universe was plunged into eternal darkness forever."

Portus answered, "Yes, the second day. As you say, the falling ash and the darkening sky bought the admiral to the harbor. The earth shook. No one knew whether it was safer inside away from the ash or outside so the house would not fall upon you. Everyone was running, moving farther away from the bay and the growing black cloud. The admiral came down to his boat and called for his crew to take him across the bay for a closer look, to see if there were others seeking to escape Pompeii.

"We hurried and steered a straight course for the volcano. He was fearless and called out to his officer to record each new movement or phase as he observed them. Ash was already falling, hotter and thicker as the boat drew near. Bits of pumice and blackened stone charred and cracked by the flames were driven down on us. We were engulfed in blackness, unable to see ahead or behind.

"Then suddenly, we were in shallow water, and the shore was blocked by debris from the mountain. The air was foul and burned my throat. I was bent over, coughing, on the lee side of the boat, when a hot wind blew hard against us. The boat lurched as if to capsize against so strong a wind, and I tumbled into the water. It was the last I saw of the boat, the crew or the admiral."

Plinius answered, "My uncle—my father—suffocated on the toxic ash and the foul air. He and the rest of the crew were found floating on the debris of broken boats and rooftops. The beach was buried in debris. Not one soul remained alive. Dead fish lay far inland, and the city of Pompeii lay in silent ruin, buried under blackened ash and pumice. But you lived. How did you, alone among many, survive?"

"I prayed. I prayed to the only god with ears to hear. I fell deep into the water. I was entangled in debris and caught in a strong current. I felt heat rush over me. And finally, breaking free but still in total blackness, my head broke the water and hit an object above me. I could breathe, though the air was hot. The sound of my breathing echoed as in a chamber. I felt around me and determined I was under a capsized boat, half-sunken but the bow still afloat. I determined to stay inside the hulk until silence returned, and the sea beneath me began to grow lighter. When I finally ventured out from under the hulk, I found myself near the island of Ischia and I swam ashore."

"You say the only god who hears. Do not tell me it is this Christ. If Emperor Trajan agrees, no man can be tried on an anonymous complaint. I am a man of honor and will do my duty as my emperor demands. But I share thanks for your service to my adopted father and sharing your good report of his bravery. Now, I must be going. I will speak to the guards. You will be treated better now that they know I have an interest in your case."

Plinius got up to leave. As Plinius closed the door behind him, Portus spoke, "I have heard it said of men like Admiral Plinius: "Greater love has no one than this: To lay down his life for one's friend.""

The door closed, and the light faded. The footsteps of Plinius faded away. Portus laid down on his bed and clutched the blanket. Once again, in silent blackness, he listened to the sound of his breathing. Slowly the sound began to echo its confinement. The air was fit to breathe, but the wrecked hulk again entrapped him.

A LIGHT IN THE DARKEST NIGHT

It was weeks before Governor Plinius received a reply from Emperor Trajan:

You observed proper procedure, my dear Plinius, in sifting the cases of those who had been denounced to you as Christians. It is not possible to lay down any general rule to serve as a fixed standard. They are not to be sought out; if they are denounced and proved guilty, they are to be punished, with this reservation: That whoever denies that he is a Christian and really proves it by worshipping our gods—even though he was under suspicion in the past—shall obtain pardon by repentance. But anonymously posted accusations ought to have no place in any prosecution. For this is both a dangerous kind of precedent and out of keeping with the spirit of our age.

Plinius visited Portus again. Portus had been moved to another cell, above ground with a window and fireplace for heat. He was provided water to wash, good food, and comfortable furnishings.

Plinius smiled as he entered the small room. "I see you have been made comfortable in your wait. Well, friend, I come with good news for you and many others. The emperor has agreed that all anonymous accusations are of no merit or cause for trial. You are free to go. But I caution you to beware. If you confess to anyone that you are a Christian, and that person makes an accusation against you, you will be brought before me. Then, only if you repent and worship our gods will you be pardoned. But if you do not repent, you will be punished."

Portus rose and bowed. "Governor Plinius, I thank you as a man of wisdom and seeker of justice. You do honor to the name of Admiral Plinius who adopted you."

Plinius paused, then, "Since our last meeting, I have considered our bond to my uncle—my father by his gracious adoption. I remembered the first time you shared the account of his death. I remembered a younger you, with hair still black and strong, proud eyes. You wore a cross that day. Like some found on the beach at Pompeii. It would trouble me to sentence you to death. But, be warned, I will do my duty to Rome."

Portus smiled. "As always, the punishment of Rome is death. Do you know why the Christians you bring to trial, like the two deaconesses tortured some months past, do not repent? You have heard my story. My prayers were heard, and I, alone of your uncle's crew, was saved. And what great salvation that was! But I will still taste death, like all men. The Christians do not fear the judgment of Rome. They fear God who can kill the soul and the body but loves them for their faith. Having died and risen again victorious, Christ promises the same victory for all who believe. If the gods of Rome are powerless in life, how can they save us in death?"

"Be careful what you say, Portus...."

Portus continued boldly, "A great apostle of Jesus once said to a Roman King, 'I would wish to God, that whether in a short or long time, not only you but also all who hear me this day, might become such as I am, except for these chains.'"

Plinius replied, "Even now you try and convert me to this Christ? I will hear no more. Go quickly before I change my mind. I do this only to respect your service to my uncle." Plinius turned around and left the cell.

But Portus called after him: "You're a man who knows honor and integrity. Do not try the patience of God. Do not trust in riches or titles. I beg you listen to the voice of God who speaks to you."

Plinius stopped and stared one last time at Portus before turning and leaving.

Portus shouted, "Jesus said, 'It is easier for a camel to pass through the eye of a needle than for a rich man to enter the kingdom of God.'"

Two months later, a solemn Portus stood and watched the body of Governor Gaius Plinius Caecilius Secondus as it burned on its funeral pyre. He watched the black smoke rise and the soot fall back to the earth. He closed his eyes and silently prayed. The acrid smell, the soot burning in the back of his throat, took his mind back to another time and place, the place of his assurance of salvation. He opened his eyes and watched the body of a good man turn to cinders.

ZIPPORAH
IN THE WILDERNESS

ipporah walked to the front of the black goat hide tent and lifted the flap. Dawn's light was an opaque red, diffused through the dark cloud that enshrouded Mount Sinai. Weeks had passed since Moses and Joshua went to the mountain, leaving strict orders that no one should climb or even touch foot to the base of the Mountain of God until they returned.

Zipporah hunted for the slightest glimpse of the steep, craggy, red granite peak or any signs of life. Like each day before, she could see nothing through the ominous, ever-swirling, ever-changing cloud. Three days after Moses climbed Mount Sinai, wisps of white appeared diffused in the clear blue sky, darkening and drifting together, thickening en masse above the ragged peak. What was small and separate became one great turbulent impenetrable smoky black vapor that descended, unfurling a fierce lightning storm and smothering God's holy mountain. The cloud seemed alive, possessed with uncanny intelligence, searching, scouring, and penetrating every rock, pebble, and grain peering into every crevice on the mountain; it was an unworldly presence at once revealing and mysterious. It still held its firm, unrelenting grip against the wind, weather, and sun.

All Zipporah could find was a lone figure at the base, Joshua keeping watch, warning any visitor away.

Who is he going to warn? Only a fool with no regard for his life would approach the mountain, Zipporah thought.

A tail of the cloud circled and hovered over the brave and faithful Joshua but never obscured him from view as he stood in his steadfast watch.

God called them to His holy mountain; surely, they are safe. God shields Joshua. I must believe God preserves Moses, His very servant chosen to lead Israel to His promised land. Zipporah's thoughts swirled with worry nonetheless. *What delays them? The people are restless. Sweet water and manna from heaven are not enough! Even Aaron is worried.*

"Gershom! Eliezer!" Zipporah called. "Bring the baskets. It is time to gather the manna for the day. Soon the sun will be above the Holy Mountain, and the manna will stick to the ground and spoil. If you expect to have bread this day, we must go now."

The young men appeared in front of the tent. Gershom groused, "Again, manna. Always manna."

Eliezer gazed off to Mount Sinai and added, "No word from father yet? He could be anywhere on that mountain. Suppose he fell among the rocks? In all that fog and darkness, no one would know. How long should we wait?"

"I shall hear no such talk," Zipporah cut off her son's queries. "Your father is a holy man of God! He would never fall from a ledge! God would not permit such a thing!"

Eliezer replied, "Everyone speaks of it. Surely, Mother, you hear it as well when you gather manna or go for water.

Did not God send his angel to slay father on the road to Egypt? And only when you cut me did the angel return to from where he came?"

Zipporah snapped, "God does not punish without warning! He is merciful as well as just. It is His nature to warn before He punishes. You are sons of Moses; you should permit no such talk among the people."

The family of Moses joined the many others walking outside the camp filling their baskets with manna, which lay like white flakes of frost on the ground. They'd learned to gather only enough for the day, knowing that it would spoil overnight except, mysteriously, when it carried over for the Sabbath day when new manna did not fall. When they returned to their tent, pitched alongside the tent of Aaron, they saw Korah, Dathan, and Abiram speaking with Aaron in the open area of Aaron's tent.

Zipporah whispered to Gershom, "Go to Aaron and inquire after your father but listen to what Korah and his friends say to your uncle. Hurry! Listen but do not interrupt."

Gershom stood behind Dathan and Abiram as Korah spoke, "It has been weeks since Moses went up the mountain. We have waited long enough. The people have had enough. It is time to act. I say we return to Egypt and offer our services to the Pharaoh at fair wages. He will surely negotiate to have us return."

Aaron replied, "I will wait for Moses. He speaks to God. Do you forget it is the Lord who took us out of slavery? And you wish to return? Return to making bricks of clay for the Pharaoh? Is that more honorable than living in a land of our own? A land promised to us—flowing with milk and honey?"

A LIGHT IN THE DARKEST NIGHT

Korah snapped in angry retort, "Wait for *Moses*? I am the rightful leader of the tribe of Levi! I am the firstborn son of the firstborn son for generations back to Kohath, Levi's firstborn son! I speak for the family of Kohath, and the Kohaths speak for Levi. And my friends, Dathan and Abiram speak for the tribe of Judah."

Aaron looked to Dathan and Abiram and asked, "Would you disobey Moses and the Lord who sustains you with cold sweet water and manna for bread? Have you forgotten that the Lord delivered us from the Amalekites? Has the Pharaoh forgotten the pain of the death of his firstborn son? Has any Egyptian forgotten the loss of their firstborn sons, the firstborn of their cattle and sheep and livestock? All of Egypt reeks with the smell of death! Have the Egyptians lost their desire for vengeance? This is madness. Go back to your tents!"

Korah kicked dust at Aaron's face. "The people will speak. They have lost patience with you and Moses. Baking under the sun in this wilderness has never been their choice. We are here because of Moses and his God! It is not by our will or our doing. Our people, Israel, want more. They demand more! You shall see."

Korah turned around and stomped off, pushing the bewildered Gershom aside as he left.

Gershom managed to ask meekly, "Any news, Uncle, from my father or Joshua?"

A shaken Aaron replied, "No, Nephew. There is no news." And Aaron retreated into his tent.

When Gershom returned to Moses' tent and told Zipporah all he had heard, she closed her eyes and shook her head. She whispered, "Moses, Moses, they don't understand.

You must return soon."

Zipporah sat down, lost in the memory of the last months, the upheaval of forty years of marriage. She remembered her dissatisfaction and the hard lesson she had learned. It all began that late afternoon when Moses returned to her father, Jethro's camp in Midian, two days late....

Zipporah remembered the view of the late afternoon blue sky that drifted to orange and then red as her eyes followed the sun's descent, shining through the cloud of fine red dust. The sound of bleating sheep disturbed the muted voices in the camp. She saw a servant bow as he entered the goat hair tent of Jethro. "My Lord, your son-in-law, Moses, returns."

Jethro stood up and walked outside to Zipporah, waiting. She said to her two sons, "Gershom, Eliezer, go help your father water the sheep. Tell him supper will be ready in an hour. There would have been a fine roast if he had sent word ahead, but as he has no consideration for any other, he will share what little lentil and lamb stew I have made for his sons."

The young men walked to the well to help their father. Jethro called to his daughter. "Zipporah! Is that how a wife honors her husband? You shame him in front of his sons? That is not how your mother raised you. You disgrace her and me. You do not want for food or any good thing. Moses works hard and is an honorable man. He gives you all that you ask. Who knows why he returns late? Thank the God of Abraham that he returns safely, and you are not left a widow before your time."

Zipporah bowed before her father. "Forgive me, Father. As you say, my husband is a good man." Zipporah sighed deeply.

Jethro studied his daughter and said, "You have all you need but are not happy. You want something else. What is it you want, my daughter?"

Zipporah looked into the loving face of her father, shook her head, and replied, "Yes, something else—something more."

Father and daughter stood looking at each other for a moment before Jethro said, "Go prepare for your husband and wash up. Put on a clean robe and perfume. Go, do as I say. I will hear from Moses all that he has to say."

Nearly an hour later, Moses came to Jethro's tent. "The flock is fine, and none are lost. The grass was thin. I moved the flock to the west of the wilderness near the Mount you call Horeb—"

Jethro interrupted, "The Mountain of God, yes. Some call it Sinai. I know the place. Go on."

"I saw the most amazing sight. High on the mountain, I saw fire. Well, you know the danger of fire in the dry wilderness. As I gazed at the fire, I saw a burning bush within it. It kept burning but was not consumed and the fire did not spread. As I stared at the fire, I heard a voice call to me, 'Moses! Moses!' And I said, 'Here I am.'"

Jethro stared at his son-in-law. He saw a good man, a steady worker not given to tall tales of bravado or drink. Despite his royal Egyptian upbringing and education, Moses was a humble man.

Moses continued, "The voice said, 'Do not come near here; remove your sandals for the place where you stand is holy ground.' Then He said, 'I am the God of your father, the God of Abraham, the God of Isaac, and the God of Jacob.'"

Jethro asked, "The God of Abraham? The God of my fathers by Abraham's son Midian? What did he look like?"

Moses shook his head. "I hid my face. I was afraid to look at God. He said to me, 'I have seen the affliction of My people who are in Egypt, and I have given heed to their cry. I am aware of their suffering.' He sends me to bring His people out of Egypt. I must go. You have other sons to care for the flocks. I must go as the Lord commands me."

Jethro's face reflected his shock. "The Lord God spoke to you and now sends you to Egypt? What is His name? And why you? You are a wanted man there. It is not safe for you to return to Egypt."

"God told me those who sought me are dead. He told me, my people, His people—I am to tell the Pharaoh that Israel is God's firstborn son, and He has called them to Himself. Israel will hear my voice and follow to a land God promises—a land of milk and honey! And yes, I asked Him His name and He said to me in a great booming voice, 'I Am who I Am!' and He told me to say to the sons of Israel, 'I Am has sent me to you.'"

"But the Pharaoh holds the sons of Israel as his slaves—"

"Yes, of course. But God has prepared me with signs and wonders. He has given me this staff."

Moses threw the staff on the ground and it became a live snake! But Moses calmly said, "Do not fear." And picked up the snake by its tail... and it was again a staff.

Moses continued: "I must go soon. My brother Aaron will meet me. He will be my voice to the Pharaoh. Now I must go to Zipporah and tell her and my sons. We shall leave as soon as we can pack."

A LIGHT IN THE DARKEST NIGHT

Jethro stood silent.

Moses said, "Are you not also called Reuel, a priest, and friend of God? Will you not offer a sacrifice and seek God's blessing on your son-in-law's family?"

Jethro nodded. "Yes, of course. Now go to your wife and sons. Take with you all that you will need. You have my blessing."

Two days later, Moses had packed tents, clothes, food, cooking pots, and everything necessary for the long journey to Egypt. At the first light of morning, Moses loaded his belongings, his wife Zipporah, and his sons, onto donkeys that his father-in-law, Jethro, gave him and they followed the road to Egypt.

They came to an inn several days later, and Moses decided to spend the night there. While Moses slept silently beside her, Zipporah dreamed. They were on the road to Egypt and a figure, like a man, approached as if walking out of the sun. She could not see the man for the brightness. A voice came from the man in the sun, "I have come to slay Moses, who has not remembered my commandment. He has not circumcised his son according to My will and law."

Zipporah, dreaming, replied in fear, "Do not slay my husband! It was my will. I did not desire my son to be circumcised—why such pain for my little one?"

"The penalty for sinful disobedience is death. This day blood will flow."

Zipporah passed the night awake in fear. She said nothing to Moses. Moses arose at dawn and woke his family. "We must go. It is better to travel early before the heat of the day bears heavily upon us."

As Zipporah, Gershom and Eliezer were waiting to mount the donkeys, Zipporah looked east at the rising sun and saw a figure approaching them. Quickly she took her younger son aside and said, "Come with me!"

Zipporah took a flint knife and circumcised her son. She left him in pain in the inn and hurried outside as the man walking out of the sun approached Moses. Zipporah threw the foreskin at the feet of Moses and said, "You are a bridegroom of the blood to me!"

The stranger never left the brightness of the sun. He stopped in front of Moses, turned around, and walked back into the sunlight.

Moses turned and saw the terror in Zipporah's eyes. Shivering with fear, she said, "The Lord came to slay you. I had a dream last night. He spared you because I said, 'You are the bridegroom of the blood—because of the circumcision."

Moses embraced his wife. "Our son, he is in great pain. Take our sons and return to your father's house. It is better I go on alone."

Three days later, when Zipporah, Gershom, and Eliezer rode back into his camp, Jethro ran to meet them. "Is all well? Where is Moses? What has happened?"

Zipporah replied softly. The redness of her eyes told Jethro she had been crying. "Moses is safe. He travels to Egypt alone. Eliezer must heal, and we are to wait here."

Jethro stared at his grandson. "Eliezer must heal? Heal from what? What has happened?"

Zipporah began to sob. "Father, I almost lost him. The Lord came to slay Moses because I would not permit him to circumcise our son. A dream, I was warned in a dream, and it happened just as I dreamt. So, when I saw the angel of the Lord coming out of the rising sun, I circumcised Eliezer. I threw the foreskin at Moses' feet and said, 'You are the bridegroom of the blood—because of the circumcision.' The angel turned around and returned into the sun. Moses sent us home. He travels to Egypt alone."

"What did the angel of the Lord say when he saw you throw the foreskin?"

"Nothing. He just turned around and returned from where he came."

Jethro reflected a moment and said, "The bridegroom of the blood—you bought back your husband. God warns us and warms us. The God of Abraham is righteous and holy but also loving, ever merciful and gracious. He has called Moses from exile to his home, not the royal palace of Egypt but to Israel, God's people, a nation in exile. God has chosen Moses as his instrument. Should Israel follow a man who refused to have his son recognized as a son of the promise, a son of Jacob? For that is what circumcision is."

Zipporah replied, "But he came to me at night, not to my husband."

Jethro said, "You and Moses are one flesh. You have both sinned. Moses knew of God's command, but he put the desires of his wife above the law of God. And you, Zipporah, placed your will above your husband's duty. But you are not a daughter of Jacob and place no value on their law. Perhaps the Lord chose you to dream so that you may see that in becoming wife to Moses, you join him under God's command to the children of Israel. The angel of the Lord came by night in love. He came in the morning as a righteous judge but turned away in mercy."

Zipporah looked into Jethro's eyes and asked, "Will I ever see my husband again?"

Jethro nodded. "Moses will send for you and his sons in God's time. My daughter, you begin to see what your heart desires."

Four months. She waited four months with no word of Moses. Then a caravan of traders passing through Midian to Egypt stopped by Jethro's camp. A trader told Jethro of the Hebrews they'd passed, encamped at the valley of Rephidim in the wilderness. "We have heard of these Hebrews, escaped slaves from Egypt. We were warned to stay well away, but nothing prepared us for what we saw. So many people! Far too many for any man to count—like the grains of sand in the desert! How they can survive, I do not know. Yet they thrive! What they eat and where they find water—only their God knows!"

When the caravan moved on, Jethro called for Zipporah and said, "Moses and his people are camped at Rephidim. The God of Abraham has freed the sons of Israel. They have become a great multitude, and God sustains them with food and water. Let us go! You and your sons should see this great thing the Lord has done for your husband."

Jethro sent a servant ahead to Moses with the message: "Jethro, your father-in-law, is coming to you with your wife and two sons." When Moses heard the message, he went out to meet Jethro, bowed down, and kissed him. Zipporah and her sons followed and were reunited with Moses in tears of joy. Moses brought his family into the camp, and Jethro pitched his tent.

Many hours were spent as Moses told of all that the

A LIGHT IN THE DARKEST NIGHT

Lord had done in Egypt. He recounted the hardness of the Pharaoh's heart, the plagues, and the Passover. Moses spoke of the hardship the people faced in the wilderness. He told of the parting of the Red Sea and how the Lord provided water from the rock and how the Lord gave them a great victory over the Amalekites who attacked them as they passed peacefully through the land. The next morning, his family accompanied him as they gathered manna and ate.

Jethro rejoiced for all the good the Lord had done to deliver Israel. Jethro asked to address the elders. He said, "Blessed be the Lord, who has delivered you out of the hand of the Egyptians, and the people out of the hand of the Pharaoh. Now I know that the Lord is greater than all gods because, in this affair, the Egyptians and their gods have dealt insolently with the people." Jethro brought a burnt offering and sacrifices to God. Aaron, Joshua, and all the elders of Israel came to eat bread before God with Moses' father-in-law.

The next day Moses sat to judge the people. Jethro watched the people congregate around Moses from morning to evening. That night Jethro said to Moses in private, "What is it you are doing for the people? Why do you sit alone, and all the people stand around you from morning until night?"

Moses replied, "The people come to me to inquire of God. When they have a dispute, they come to me, and I decide between one person and another, and I make them know the statutes of God and His laws."

Jethro said, "What you are doing is not good. You will certainly wear yourself out, for this thing is too heavy for you alone! I will give you advice, and God be with you! You shall represent the people before God and bring their cases to God, and you shall warn them about the statutes and the laws. You shall make them know how they must walk and what they must do. Moreover, look for able men from all the people, men who fear God, who are trustworthy and will not take a bribe, and place such men over the people as chiefs of thousands, hundreds, fifties, and tens. Let them judge the people at all times. They shall bring every great matter to you, but they shall decide any small matter themselves. It will be easier for you, and they will bear the burden with you. If you do this, God will direct you, you will be able to endure, and these people shall go to their place in peace."

Moses listened to Jethro. He chose able men and made them heads over the people. His appointed chiefs judged the people and brought only the difficult cases to Moses. After some time, Jethro said to Moses, "Let me kiss my daughter and my grandsons and return to my home. They shall go with you where the Lord leads and receive His blessings. The Lord has blessed me and comforted me. But I have other sheep in Midian."

Moses wept, for he loved his father-in-law.

Jethro kissed Zipporah and said, "Daughter, you must bring strength to your husband, not weakness, for a multitude of this great nation will bring their troubles, doubts, and unhappiness to Moses. Just as you have seen the God of Abraham warn you, even in love, so too has this great nation witnessed the power of God but did not understand their return from exile to a promised land. Yes, they have heard the promises of milk and honey, of bounty and blessings. But the land God promises is a garden where God's chosen people walk with Him, each man, woman, and child, Reuel—a friend of God."

Jethro kissed his grandsons and said, "Obey your father and mother, for this is pleasing to God. Do not forget your sacrifices to the Lord! Pray—always strive to become friends of God. May his blessings follow you on your journey to the promised land."

Then Jethro mounted his donkey and returned to Midian.

The memory of her father's words kept repeating in Zipporah's mind, "A multitude of this great nation will bring their troubles, doubts, and unhappiness to Moses. This nation does not understand their return from exile to a promised land."

Zipporah's daydream was interrupted by the shouts of an angry crowd.

"Aaron! Aaron! Make us a god to lead us out of this place. We must leave this wilderness before we die of thirst or starve!"

Aaron raised his arms to quiet the crowd then said, "Have you forgotten the oath you made to the Lord God before Moses? When the Lord said, 'If you will obey My voice and keep My covenant, then you shall be My possession among all the people of the earth, for all the earth is Mine; and you shall be to Me a kingdom of priests and a holy nation.' And each of you replied, 'All that the Lord has spoken, we will do.'"

But then some among the crowd shouted back, "This Moses, we do not know what has become of him!"

Another shouted, "Surely the great cloud has swallowed him up and he is no more!"

Others cried out, "Moses is dead! Perhaps his God has taken him. We are abandoned in this wilderness! Make us a god to lead us!"

A chant arose among the people, "Make us a god! Make us a god! Make us a god!"

Aaron looked out at the sea of angry faces and feared. Again, he raised his arms and called over them, "Tear off the gold rings from the ears of your wives, your sons, and your daughters and bring them to me."

The people took off their gold rings and brought them to Aaron. Aaron asked, "What god shall I fashion?"

Some cried out, "Apis! The bull god of Egypt who bears the dead. He can lead us from this dead wilderness."

Others called out, "Baal, the strong bull god of Canaan whose land is promised to us!"

Aaron fashioned a mold and made a molten calf, and when the people saw it, they called, "This is your god, Oh, Israel, who brought you up from the land of Egypt!"

The next day, the people rose early and offered burnt sacrifices on an altar that Aaron had built for the golden calf. They brought peace offerings and sat down to eat and drink before they arose to play. But their drinking, dancing, and laughter ended when Joshua sounded his shofar, and Moses appeared at the foot of the mountain!

A great anger burned in Moses' eyes. Words failed him, so he lifted two stone tablets he carried off the mountain and threw them down, shattering them against a rock.

Moses walked to the altar, took up a stone, and broke the golden calf apart. He gathered wood and burned the altar and idol. The people ran off to their tents. Only Aaron remained. Moses ignored Aaron's weak excuse for his sin and the people's sin. When the fire burned out, Moses told Aaron to crush the remains to a powder, scatter it across water and make every man, woman, and child of Israel drink it.

Moses challenged the people saying, "Whoever is for the Lord, come to me." All the sons of Levi gathered with him. They strapped on swords, went through the camp, and slew as Moses instructed. About three thousand people fell that day.

Afterward, his anger spent, Moses spoke again to his people: "You have committed a great sin in making a god of gold for yourselves. But now, I am going to the Lord. Perhaps I can make atonement for your sins."

After Moses sought the Lord, he assembled the people and said, "We shall leave this place and go to the land which the Lord swore to Abraham, Isaac, and Jacob. The Lord will send an angel before you, and the Lord will drive out the Canaanite, the Amorite, the Hittite, the Perizzite, the Hivite, and the Jebusite. Go up to a land flowing with milk and honey. But the Lord will not dwell among you as you travel because you are an obstinate people, lest He destroys you on the way. The Lord says, 'Put off your jewelry and any adornment, that I may know what I will do with you.'"

When the people heard this sad word, they went into mourning, and none wore any jewelry. Moses' own heart was broken. He recognized that the people had repented and mourned God's word to withdraw His presence. Again, Moses interceded for his people and prayed to the Lord: "You say to me, 'Bring up this people,' but You have not let me know whom You will send with me. Yet You have said, 'I know you by name,' and 'You have found favor in my sight.' If I have found favor in Your sight, please show me Your ways, that I may know You to find favor in Your sight. Consider, too, that this nation is Your people."

The Lord answered Moses, "My presence will go with you, and I will give you rest."

Moses asked, "Is it not in Your going with us so that we are distinct, I and Your people, from every other people on the face of the earth?"

Moses returned to God's holy mountain and brought back two new stone tablets written by the finger of God—the ten commandments. And Moses brought down the law and God's plan for His priests, His altar and sacrifices, and His tabernacle—a place for His presence among His people.

In the privacy of his tent, Moses shared with Zippora all that God spoke to him. Snuggled close beside him in the still darkness of the night, she said, "The Lord leads beyond Canaan, beyond a land flowing with milk and honey. He leads us into His very presence. He lives among us, with us that we shall never want for peace and rest."

Moses leaned over and kissed Zipporah. Zipporah smiled in the darkness and curled her black hair around a finger. "Husband, I recall you and my father discussing God's creation, the garden, how everything was good. Are not all of us exiled from the garden called Eden?"

"Yes, that is true. And the garden was washed away in the great flood because of the sin of man."

"Moses, is it wrong to hope that the Lord will call all of His people out of exile into a new garden? Even sweeter than the promised land, where there are no bandits, doubters, and lawbreakers?"

A LIGHT IN THE DARKEST NIGHT

Moses laughed gently. "Truly, the Lord has given me a wise wife! It is my very hope that all of God's people walk with Him in His garden, a new Eden, free from harm, free from mourning, with tears only of joy, knowing His love forever."

SOLOMON AND
THE SHULAMMITE MAIDEN

*A*wake. His eyes open to the dusky morning. Misty droplets of dew stand in line, waiting their turn in the procession. Slowly, one by one, they coalesce into firm round droplets and slide down the lily in freefall from the snow-white trumpet petals onto the verdant leaves, slowing, meandering down along the pale tubular stem. The grass beneath his head is moist and fragrant. He tips his head and looks up at the apple tree, its boughs outstretched, a lacey canopy against the indigo blue sky losing its nightly grip against the few, slow to flee, dim stars. A deep breath disturbs the arm lying across his chest and he quivers at the delightful tingling of his back caressed by the soft, warm body snuggled tight against him.

Carefully, he rolls over and gazes at the young woman still asleep beside him. A gentle smile confirms the perfect peace he feels as he drinks in her beauty. *I am Adam and this is the first sight of Eve. Can any sight be as wondrous? Could peace and joy be more full? Could Father Moses find no better proclamation to woman, this final and most remarkable creation of God, than very good? What a great gift to me! A taste of Eden, a living memory of the love God intended. Rightly she is named Tallah, Dew from God. If not by God's perfect plan, where could this power to bind my soul to another, forever, come from?*

Somewhere above him, hidden in the soft folds of the apple tree, a bird sings a sweet morning song. The woman stirs and awakens. Her eyes open to the smiling face watching her. She breathes deeply and returns his smile of contentment. Eyes and hearts lock in a silent embrace until, at last, she sits up and says, "My brothers! What will they think? I must return home. They will be angry!"

"I have asked them to give you to me in marriage. They know of our love. Are we not betrothed?"

"Yes, they know of our desire, but they have given no answer. I hear them speak in whispers, thinking I do not hear. They find you, a shepherd, unworthy. And now we fall asleep. They will find shame in this!"

"I feel no shame, only love."

"And I love you as well. But you must go. Your flock is not far. I will say I stayed in the vineyard watchtower, too tired to return home."

The shepherd stood up and helped his love to her feet. "I will go now. As you say, I must show myself worthy and must not neglect the flock. But I will not be put off! You will be my bride. We are bound together. Your heart is mine, and my heart is yours—always!"

The young shepherd gently squeezed his love's hand and kissed her cheek. "Until this evening. I will come to the vineyard again this evening." The happy young man merrily skipped off towards the sheep fold. She lovingly watched him hurry off and sang to herself:

"May he kiss me with the kisses of his mouth!

For your love is sweeter than wine. Your oils have a pleasing fragrance,

Your name is like purified oil; therefore, the young women love you.

Draw me after you, and let's run together!"

Tallah walked into the small village of Shulam of the tribe Issachar, rising from the Jezreel Valley in the shadow of Mount Gilboa. She walked past the well to the humble house she shared with her brothers. Three horses and a donkey were tied outside her home. She slipped quietly to the door, stood outside, and listened to a stranger inside.

"As you say, King Solomon is the wisest of kings. God blesses him with power and wealth beyond any ruler. Should he not have the most beautiful women of Israel to comfort him? If your sister is indeed as beautiful as you and the elders insist, we will take her to the king. Who knows? Solomon may marry her if she pleases him. Is it not a good thing to be brothers to a wife of the king? Now, bring her before us that we may judge her."

Tallah opened the door and stepped inside. Her oldest brother spoke, "Sister, back from the well at last! Go, wash your face, and put on a clean robe. Then return and show hospitality to our guests."

Worried about what she'd heard, Tallah said nothing and walked face down to her room. She returned a few minutes later with a bowl of wine and wooden cups. She ladled the wine and gave a cup to each visitor, trying to be hospitable but not making eye contact. One of the men said, "Thank you, sister. Is this some new custom? You cover your head in your home?"

A LIGHT IN THE DARKEST NIGHT

Her elder brother said, "Yes, take off your scarf. Grace our friends with your sweet smile. They have come from Jerusalem and the palace of King Solomon. It is a great honor and joy to our house!"

Tallah removed her scarf and slowly lifted her head. The steady, deliberate grace of motion highlighted the shine of her black hair and the wellspring of her eyes. She felt the stares of the strangers studying her. She smiled bravely, and said, "You are welcome in our home. We have flour, oil, raisins, and honey. Shall I make sweet cakes as well?"

The stranger looked at his companions, who nodded their assent. Then he said, "Indeed, your smile welcomes the weary traveler with peace and grace. Your beauty is a blessing from God. You will find favor with your king. Your brothers have consented. Your future awaits you in the palace of the king's wives. Go, prepare a simple bag for the journey. But you will be clothed befitting a queen in Jerusalem."

Stunned, Tallah turned to her brothers and spoke softly, "My brothers, but another has asked—"

The eldest did not let her finish. "This fulfills our duty. Our sister is blessed and honored. Say no more. As the King's servant says, pack lightly and depart with our blessing!"

The door to the palace of Solomon's wives and concubines closed behind her. Women, many extravagantly dressed, their hair and skin fragrant with oil and perfume, watched her enter and stand confused and disheveled in her peasant's robe. Finally, she broke her silence: "The King has brought me into his chambers." She felt every eye of the beautiful women of Solomon's harem study her closely.

It seemed an eternity, but only moments later, in

unison, their answer mocked her: "We will rejoice in you and be joyful; We will praise your love more than wine; Rightly do they love you."

Tallah recognized the cold sarcasm in their voices and took a few steps toward them. And in pain and loneliness, she said softly: "I am black and beautiful, you daughters of Jerusalem, like the tents of Kedar, like the curtains of Solomon. Do not stare at me because I am dark, for the sun has tanned me. My mother's sons were angry with me; they made me caretaker of the vineyards, but I have not taken care of mine own vineyard."

Tallah's heart longed for her beloved shepherd. What must he be thinking? The words gushed up from within her: "Tell me, you whom my soul loves, where do you pasture your flock, where do you have it lie down at noon? For why should I be like one who veils herself beside the flocks of your companions?"

Solomon's wives and concubines, laughed and again mocked her: "If you yourself do not know, most beautiful among women, go out on the trail of the flock, and pasture your young goats by the tents of the shepherds."

King Solomon stepped from behind a screen. The harem became silent as every eye went to him. The King walked slowly towards the young woman and spoke: "To me, my darling, you are like my mare among the chariots of Pharaoh. Your cheeks are delightful with jewelry, your neck with strings of beads."

The women of the harem bowed as the king walked past and offered: "We will make for you jewelry of gold with beads of silver."

Tallah watched the king approach, bowed, and told

the king of her lover, the tender shepherd of Shulam from whom she was taken. "While the king was at his table, my perfume gave forth its fragrance. My beloved is unto me a pouch of myrrh which lies all night between my breasts. My beloved is to me a cluster of henna blossoms in the vineyards of Engedi."

Solomon slowly circled around her. He pondered to himself: *She is beautiful, like no other, yet she pines for another lover. I shall make her pine for me!* Enchanted by her beauty and purity of soul, he listened as she continued with her eyes closed and a sweet smile of remembrance on her face.

She sang from her heart:
"How beautiful you are, my darling,
How beautiful you are!
Your eyes are like doves.
How handsome you are, my beloved,
And so delightful!
Indeed, our bed is luxuriant.
The beams of our house are cedars, our rafter, juniper.
I am the rose of Sharon, the lily of the valleys."

Solomon stopped in front of her and interrupted her song. "Like a lily among thorns, so is my darling among the young women."

The memory of her last night with her beloved refreshed her. She ignored Solomon's comment and continued her song:
"Like an apple tree among the trees of the forest,
So is my beloved among the young men.
In his shade, I took great delight and sat down,
And his fruit was sweet to my taste.
He brought me into his banquet hall,

And his banner over me is love.
Refresh me with raisin cakes, sustain me with apples,
Because I am lovesick.
His left hand is under my head,
And his right hand embraces me."

Solomon studied her beauty from head to toe. *She still speaks of another. I will not be dissuaded! Her oaths of love to this past lover, a mere shepherd, cannot abide. Yet I am drawn to her boldness. The riches of my palace do not charm her. How rare and magnificent she is! Yes, I am challenged to win her heart!* His eyes met Tallah's. He smiled, then looked to the women of the harem and sang:

"Swear to me, you daughters of Jerusalem,
by the gazelles, or by the does of the field,
that you will not disturb or
awaken my love until she pleases."

Solomon called for the keeper of the wardrobe and matron of beauty. "See that the Shulammite maiden is bathed, and her extraordinary beauty complemented with the finest oils and perfumes. But do no harm to her complexion—her color radiates the sun, moon, and stars. Her wardrobe shall be the finest linen, bejeweled but not gaudy. She is the perfect jewel. Let her adornment be her setting. I shall not call for her until she is perfection. And permit no other, not wife or concubine, to show her disrespect."

Left in the charge of the matron of the palace wives to be bathed and groomed, the young Shulammite woman sang to herself:

"Listen! My beloved! Behold, he is coming,
Leaping on the mountains. Jumping on the hills!
My beloved is like a gazelle or a young stag;

A LIGHT IN THE DARKEST NIGHT

Behold, he is standing behind our wall;
He is looking through the windows,
He is peering through the lattice.
My beloved responded and said to me,
Arise up, my darling, my beautiful one,
And come along.
For behold, the winter is past,
The rain is over and gone.
The blossoms have already appeared in the land;
The time has arrived for pruning the vines,
And the voice of the turtledove
has been heard in the land.
The fig tree has ripened its fruit,
And the vines are in blossom
And have given forth their fragrance.
Arise, my darling, my beautiful one, and come along!
My dove, in the clefts of the rock,
In the hiding place of the mountain pathway,
Let me see how you look; let me hear your voice,
For your voice is pleasant, and you look delightful.
Catch the foxes for us,
The little foxes that are ruining the vineyards;
While our vineyards are in blossom."

Sitting alone in her bath while the women of Solomon's harem watched and teased her, Tallah again worried about her young shepherd. *What must he think? He must know I have not abandoned him. I will seek him out and find him. Our love cannot be broken.* Her thoughts welled up from her heart, and she sang sweetly:

"My beloved is mine, and I am his;
He pastures his flock among the lilies.

Until the cool of the day, when the shadows flee.
Turn, my beloved, and be like a gazelle
Or a young stag upon the mountains of Bether.
On my bed, night after night,
I sought him whom my soul loves;
I sought him but did not find him.
I must arise now and go around in the city;
In the streets and the public squares
I must seek him whom my soul loves.
I sought him but did not find him.
The watchmen who make the rounds
In the city found me,
And I said, 'Have you seen him whom my soul loves?'
Hardly had I left them,
When I found him who my soul loves;
I held on to him and would not let him go
Until I had brought him to my mother's house,
And into the room of her who conceived me."

Solomon was lingering beyond the screen, hesitant to leave the sight of the mesmerizing beauty. He sighed and slowly made his way to his secret door. Halfway out, he stopped as his harem sang the Shulammite maiden's refrain:

"Swear to me, you daughters of Jerusalem,
By the gazelles or the does of the field,
That you will not disturb or awaken my love,
Until she please."

The day arrived when a loud knocking was heard against the great door to the palace of wives. Shofars sounded, trumpeting a royal visit. Singers, Levites from the temple, lifted their voices in exultation. The door was opened, and

A LIGHT IN THE DARKEST NIGHT

King Solomon sat in his gilded litter borne by eight tall, strong young men. A company of palace guards surrounded the king, their burnished helmets and bronze swords flashing in the sun. The singers, all sons of Asaph, led the great men of Israel, seasoned warriors all, followed by the priests and courtiers, each noble robed in rich embroidery; they were a great company, all in a joyful procession.

King Solomon reclined on his sedan, a gold wedding crown on his head. He was resplendent in a white and purple robe with golden borders and silver trimmings. Behind him stood a beautiful servant girl, her head veiled and her body adorned only in jeweled rings shimmering as they danced dangling from her ears, nose, fingers, and toes. The jewels followed in rhythm, a slow and sensual movement as she gently fanned the king with large, bright peacock feathers.

The matron whispered to Tallah, "The King has returned from his pleasure house of cedar in Lebanon. You have been summoned. You will accompany the King to his palace. It is a great honor—today, you alone, among all of his wives and concubines, go. He judges you as the most beautiful of all. The sound of the Shofar and the songs of the sons of Asaph announce that the King comes as a bridegroom. Rejoice: Today you are to be married!" The matron joined the singers in the joyful chorus:

"Who is this coming up from the wilderness
Like columns of smoke,
Perfumed with myrrh and frankincense,
With all the scented powders of the merchant?
Behold, it is the traveling couch of Solomon;
Sixty warriors around it,
Of the warriors of Israel.

All of them are wielders of the sword, expert in war;
Each man has his sword at his side,
Guarding against the terrors of the night.
King Solomon made for himself a sedan chair
From the timber of Lebanon.
He made its posts of silver,
Its back of gold and its seat of purple fabric,
With its interior lovingly inlaid
By the daughters of Jerusalem.
Go out, you daughters of Zion,
And look at King Solomon, with the crown
With which his mother crowned him
On the day of his wedding,
And on the day of the joy of his heart."

The young Shulammite woman stepped out of the palace of wives. Her raven black hair rested on her pure white linen gown. Her head was crowned with a golden grapevine tiara over a sheer white veil. Earrings of pearls and a ruby necklace played against her suntanned skin. Only the lightest of blue accentuated her eyes lids and her thin lips were delicately reddened. Folds of sheer Egyptian linen enrobed her perfect figure, barely shadowing her tawny skin. The sheer robe was clasped over her shoulder with a jewel-studded gold shell.

Solomon smiled when he saw her. His eyes drank in her motion as he watched her approach. The singing continued:

"How beautiful you are, my darling,
How beautiful you are!
Your eyes are like doves behind your veil;
Your hair is like a flock of goats

A LIGHT IN THE DARKEST NIGHT

That have descended from Mount Gilead.
Your teeth are like a flock of newly shorn sheep,
Which have come up from their washing,
All of which bear twins,
And not one among them has lost her young.
Your lips are like a scarlet thread,
And your mouth is beautiful.
Your temples are like a slice of pomegranate
Behind your veil.
Your neck is like the tower of David
Built with layers of stones
On which are hung a thousand shields.
All the round shields of the warriors.
Your two breasts are like two fawns,
Twins of a gazelle that graze among the lilies,
Until the cool of the day when shadows flee.
I will go my way to the mountain of myrrh,
And to the hill of frankincense.
You are altogether beautiful. My darling,
And there is no blemish on you.
Come with me from Lebanon, my bride,
You shall come with me from Lebanon.
You shall come down from the summit of Amana,
From the summit of Senir and Hermon,
From the dens of lions,
From the mountains of leopards.
You have enchanted my heart, my sister, my bride;
You have enchanted my heart
With a single glance of your eyes,
With a single strand of your necklace.
How beautiful is your love, my sister, my bride!

How much sweeter is your love than wine!
And the fragrance of your oils
Than that of all kinds of balsam oils!
Your lips drip honey, my bride;
Honey and milk are under your tongue,
And the fragrance of your garments
Is like the fragrance of Lebanon.
A locked garden is my sister, my bride,
A locked spring, a sealed fountain.
Your branches are an orchard of pomegranates
With delicious fruits, henna with nard plants,
Nard and saffron, spice reed and cinnamon,
With all the trees of frankincense,
Myrrh and aloes, along with all the finest balsam oils.
You are a garden spring,
A well of living waters,
And flowing streams of Lebanon."

Tallah only thought: *Someday, I will again share my garden with my lover. I will share it with no other. He shall find me and take me from this place!*

She sang as she walked to Solomon's chair:
"Awake, north wind, and come wind of the south;
Make my garden breathe out fragrance
May its balsam oils flow.
May my beloved come into his garden
And eat its delicious fruits!"

A voice sang from the crowd of observers. A clear, bold voice, strong and beautiful. The voice of a young shepherd from Issachar:
"I have come into my garden, my sister, my bride;
I have gathered my myrrh along with my balsam.

A LIGHT IN THE DARKEST NIGHT

I have eaten my honeycomb with my honey;
I have drunk my wine with my milk.
Eat, friends; drink and drink deeply, lovers!"

The sound awakened hope in Tallah's heart! Surprise turned to joy as Tallah searched the crowd for the face of her beloved.

Solomon, his face flushed red with anger, also looked for him but could not find the singer. Who dared to sing a love song to one chosen to be wife to the king—on his very wedding day?! But the shepherd had slipped away in the throng. Incensed, Solomon commanded his guards to carry him to his palace. Tallah was ordered back into the palace harem. The great doors to the wives' palace were closed, and the iron-strapped heavy oak doors were barred.

The women of the harem looked with pity on the Shulammite maiden. She had no desire for the riches of the palace, no schemes to become a Queen Esther to Solomon and win his heart against all others. Her heart was wholly given to another and she put love above riches.

Tallah woke from a restless night and shared her dream with the women of the harem: "I was asleep but my heart was awake. A voice! My beloved was knocking:

"'Open to me, my sister, my darling, my dove, my perfect one! For my head is drenched with dew, My locks with the dewdrops of the night.'

"'I have taken off my dress, how can I put it on again? I have washed my feet; how can I dirty them again?'

"My beloved extended his hand through the opening, and my feelings were stirred for him. I arose to open to my beloved and my hands dripped with myrrh. And my fingers with drops of myrrh on the handles of the bolt. I opened to my beloved, but my beloved had turned away and was gone!

"My heart went out to him as he spoke. I searched for him, but I did not find him; I called him, but he did not answer me. The watchmen who make the rounds in the city found me: They struck me and wounded me; The guards of the walls took my shawl away from me. Swear to me, you daughters of Jerusalem, if you find my beloved, as to what you will tell him. For I am lovesick."

Intrigued, the wives and concubines asked: "What kind of beloved is your beloved, oh most beautiful among women? What kind of beloved is your beloved, that you make us swear this way?"

Tallah closed her eyes and sighed. A sweet smile graced her face. "My beloved is dazzling and reddish, outstanding among ten thousand. His head is like gold, pure gold; his locks are like clusters of dates and black as a raven. His eyes are like doves beside streams of water, bathed in milk and perched in their setting. His cheeks are like a bed of balsam, banks of herbal spices. His lips are lilies, dripping with drops of myrrh. His hands are rods of gold set with topaz. His abdomen is like panels covered with sapphires. His thighs are pillars of alabaster, set on pedestals of pure gold: His appearance is like Lebanon, choice as the cedars. His mouth is full of sweetness. And he is altogether lovely. This is my beloved, and this is my friend, you daughters of Jerusalem."

The daughters of Jerusalem repeated their question. "Where has your beloved gone, oh most beautiful among women? Where has your beloved turned that we may seek him with you?"

Tallah wondered: *Do they mock me in my love-sickness?*

A LIGHT IN THE DARKEST NIGHT

But then she sighed. *It was only a dream—a bad dream. But yesterday, I heard his voice! My beloved has found me. Our reunion is only a matter of time.* Her tears now gone, Tallah smiled as, one by one, she looked at the women in the harem and sang:

"My beloved has gone down to his garden,
To the beds of balsam.
To pasture his flock in the gardens and gather lilies.
I am my beloved's, and my beloved is mine,
He who pastures his flock among the lilies."

Solomon's anger eventually cooled, and he was more determined than ever to win the heart of the beautiful Shulammite woman. He was Solomon the wise, the wealthy, the powerful. What woman could resist him? He entered the palace of his wives and called for the reluctant maiden. He had offered marriage, not the lesser honor of being his concubine. His pride was wounded. He must win her heart!

Tallah stood before the king and listened as he sang:
"You are as beautiful as Tirzah, my darling,
As lovely as Jerusalem,
As awesome as an army with banners.
Turn your eyes away from me,
For they have confused me;
Thy hair is like a flock of goats
That have descended from Gilead.
Thy teeth are like a flock of ewes
Which are come up from their washing,
All of which bear twins,
And not one of them has lost her young.
Your temples are like

A slice of pomegranate behind your veil.
There are sixty queens and eighty concubines,
And young women without number;
But my dove, my perfect one, is unique:
She is her mother's only daughter;
She is the pure child of the one who gave birth to her.
The young women saw her and called her blessed,
The queens and the concubines also
And they praised her saying.
'Who is this who looks down like the dawn,
As beautiful as the full moon, as pure as the sun,
As awesome as an army with banners?'"

Tallah remembered the last night with her shepherd lover and how she was taken from her village. She spoke softly, "I went down to the orchard of nut trees to see the plants of the valley, to see whether the vine had grown or the pomegranates had bloomed. Before I was aware, my soul set me over the chariots of my princely people."

Her sister wives and concubines of Solomon urged the young woman to follow her heart back to her shepherd lover and her simple village life, singing as if they were back there already: "Come back! Come back, oh Shulammite. Come back, come back, so that we may look at you!"

Solomon raised his voice in frustration and anger: "Why should you look at the Shulammite? As at the dance of the two armies?"

His wives and concubines dared to cast their eyes scornfully on Solomon in reproof.

They had heard his fawning words and knew they were meant only to charm. They turned their voices to the brave Shulammite maid and boldly praised her in song:

A LIGHT IN THE DARKEST NIGHT

"How beautiful are your feet in sandals,
prince's daughter!
Thy curves of your hips are like jewels,
The works of the hands of an artist.
Your navel is like a round goblet
That never lacks mixed wine;
Your belly is like a heap of wheat surrounded by lilies.
Your two breasts are like two fawns,
Twins of a gazelle.
Your neck is like a tower of ivory,
Your eyes are like the pools in Heshbon.
By the gate of Bath-rabbim;
Your nose is like the tower of Lebanon,
Which looks towards Damascus.
Your head crowns you like Carmel,
And the flowing hair of your head
Is like purple threads;
The king is captivated by your tresses."

Solomon saw that even his wives and concubines tired of his pursuit of the beautiful maiden. He stepped forward, drinking in her beauty one more time. His fingertips gently caressed her face. His eyes poured themselves into hers, and the humbled king made one last entreaty: "How beautiful and delightful you are, my love, with all your delights! Your stature is like a palm tree and your breasts like its clusters. I said, 'I will climb the palm tree, I will grasp its fruit stalks.' Oh may your breasts be like clusters of the vine, and the fragrance of your breath like apples, and your mouth like the best wine! It goes down smoothly for my beloved, flowing gently through the lips of those who are asleep."

Tallah closed her eyes and bowed her head for a

moment. "Oh good and wise King, you are blessed with many wives and concubines who long to comfort you. Why pursue a humble servant? For you know: I am my beloved's and his desire is for me.

She spoke then as if speaking to her love, "Come, my beloved, let us go out to the country, let's spend the night in the villages. Let's arise early and go to the vineyard. Let's see whether the vine has grown and its buds have opened, and whether the pomegranates have bloomed. There I will give you my love. The mandrakes have given forth fragrance and over our doors are all delicious fruits, new as well as old, which I have saved for you, my beloved.

"Oh, that you were like a brother to me who nursed at my mother's breasts. If I found you outdoors, I would kiss you; no one would despise me either. I would lead you and bring you into the house of my mother who used to instruct me. I would give you spiced wine to drink, from the juice of my pomegranates. Let his left hand be under my head and his right hand embrace me."

Solomon shook his head and said to all in the room: "Truly, her love is greater than my wisdom. For such love is wisdom. It binds her in a most agreeable union that no power can undo." Then he smiled, turned to the harem, and sang:

"Swear to me, you daughters of Jerusalem,

Do not disturb or awaken my love until she pleases."

Solomon sighed and stepped back from the Shulammite maiden. "If not your husband, would that I was your brother, that I would be permitted to kiss you in the market and or in the square. I have acted foolishly. My love for you is not returned. If my love be true, I must say: Go. Go, return to your village and your poor shepherd lover."

A LIGHT IN THE DARKEST NIGHT

The gate was barely closed and barred behind her when her shepherd love sprang to her side. "Is it true? Has the King released you? We are free to marry?"

At the Shulam village gates, the elders and Tallah's brothers watched them approaching. "Who is this coming up from the wilderness, leaning on her beloved?"

The lovers walked past the vineyard and the apple tree, where they'd spent their last night together. The shepherd sang:

"Beneath the apple tree, I awakened you;
There, your mother went into labor with you,
There she was in labor and gave birth to you."

Tallah stopped and turned to her young man. With face aglow and smiling brightly, she exclaimed, "Put me like a seal over your heart, like a seal on your arm. For love is as strong as death; jealousy is as severe as Sheol. Its flames are flames of fire, the flame of the Lord. Many waters cannot quench love, nor will rivers flood over it. If a man were to give all the riches of his house for love, it would be utterly despised."

Tallah's selfish brothers mocked her and called from their seats at the gate: "We have a little sister, and she has no breasts. What shall we do for our sister on the day when she is spoken for? If she is a wall, we will build on her a battlement of silver. But if she is a door, we will barricade her with planks of cedar."

Tallah had no use for her brothers' words. Her face became iron, her will as a tall and insurmountable mountain. She spoke for herself: "I was a wall, and my breasts were like the towers. Then I became in his eyes as one who finds peace.

Solomon had a vineyard at Baalhamon; he entrusted the vineyard to caretakers. Each one was to bring a thousand shekels of silver for its fruit. My very own vineyard is at my disposal. The thousand shekels are for you, Solomon, and the two hundred are for those who take care of the fruit."

The Shulammite bride and her betrothed shepherd walked to her mother's house. Her beloved picked her up in his arms and carried her in. He sang joyfully:

"You that sit in the gardens,

My companions are listening for your voice:

Let me hear it!"

Tallah, the beautiful Shulammite woman, smiled and replied: "Hurry, my beloved, and be like a gazelle or a young stag upon the mountains of balsam trees!"

All the songs and the majority of the dialogue itself in "Wisdom of Love" are actual scripture quotations taken from the New American Standard Bible (NASB), copyright 2020 by the Lockman Foundation. Scripture quotations are used by permission. All rights reserved.

DEATH COMES TO EILENBURG

The full moon cast its light upon the tall black figure moving down the street. Mud, straw, and manure silenced its footsteps. The head of the figure bobbed as it moved, prying eyes cast down, occasionally looking about. Searching. Methodical in movement like a raven or vulture hungry for carrion. The figure moved through a shaft of light showing through an open window. Its ebony face was clearly seen in silhouette, a long black beak protruding below two darkened, encircled white eyes. An erect creature over five feet tall, head to foot, its coat, black as a moonless night, falling from narrow shoulders to the ground. Wings (or were they arms?) swung at its sides as it walked. Yes, it was arms. Black claws clenched tightly around something in its grip. The figure did not linger. It walked past the church, past the trench—unconcerned with the stink of death—unmoved by the blackened hand of a child frozen as if it had clawed its way up from the depths of the lime-strewn earth.

The silent figure stopped at the door of a small house, the parsonage of Saint Nicholas Church. Its breathing labored, it cocked its head from side to side, listening to voices inside. It rapped loudly on the door with the object in its claws. The door creaked as it slowly opened, spilling light outside and spotlighting the ominous coal-colored creature. A weary voice was heard from inside. "Herr Doctor, it is good that you come. I fear she has grown worse. Come in."

The man in black stepped inside and replied, "I fear I have disturbed your prayers, Herr Pastor. Please, return to your dear wife and finish your prayers. You are my last call of the night. I can wait."

"We pray for the families of the dead. Funerals, my day is spent with funerals. But come in, we have more time for prayers, and I would hear your list of new sufferers that we may pray for them."

Standing in the full light of the parsonage, Doctor Mueller, dressed in his plague mask, great coat, and black leather gloves, stepped into the house. "How many funerals today, Pastor?"

"Forty and fifteen of them children. I do not know which is worse, to see your children die or to leave them as orphans, condemned to die alone."

"You spend more time with the sick and dying than I. Why not wear a mask? Protect yourself from the deadly air. It is well established among physicians the plague is carried in foul air. The beak of the mask is filled with healing herbs and spices. Pleasing aromas that will protect you. Doctor Jacobs has died. You can have his mask."

"Who am I to be more deserving than any other? I dare not risk frightening my flock or have them believe I fear ministering. No, I leave it in God's hands."

"We have spoken of this before, Pastor Rinkart. If not

for yourself, then for those who need you—the flock you minister. Would you leave our city without a pastor? Pastor Schultz is ill. I say this in confidence, Pasto Rinkart, I fear he will soon succumb. Pastor Schwarzkopf is dead, and Superintendent Pastor Schmidt—well, who knows where Pastor Schmidt is? He left at the beginning of the outbreak and was to return with help but it's been months."

Pastor Martin Rinkart nodded. "Perhaps highwaymen or an accident along the way...."

"More likely his knowledge of Latin: *Cito, longe, tarde.* Gallic advice from the Hippocratic sayings on the plague: *Leave quicky. Go far away. And come back slowly.*"

The pastor shrugged, then turned and called to his wife, "My love, the doctor is here. Let me help you sit up. Son, there is beer. Bring a cup for the good doctor. Darling daughter, put the little ones to bed."

The teenage girl stood up. "Papa, you haven't eaten. While the doctor sees to mamma, have some bread at least and cheese; we still have a little cheese."

"You and your brothers and sister eat. I have enough."

The young man looked to his sister and said, "I have found more grain below the floor where the sack is kept. Please, Papa, eat a little bread."

Martin followed the doctor to his wife's sick bed, knelt down beside her, and lifted her to a sitting position. "She grows weaker, Doctor, and her mind wanders when we talk."

If the doctor smiled, it was hidden behind his beak mask. "Were you able to stand today, Frau Rinkart? Let me see your buboes."

He gently lifted the banket from the shivering woman. Large bulbous growths circled her neck and swelled in her armpits. Leeches clung to her skin across the largest boils. Lifting further, he commented: "I see those around your groin have grown. Let me see your fingers. And your toes."

The poor woman's fingers were black from the tips to the knuckles. Her toes were black. She coughed; blood covered her hand as she tried to cover her mouth. The doctor instinctively turned away. Her teeth chattering and her body shivering, she clutched the blanket tightly around her again. "So cold. So tired but I cannot rest for the cough. Tell me, Herr Doctor, I am a dead woman. How long?"

Martin stroked his wife's head and whispered, "You are loved. You will not leave us—not me, not your children. Some survive. Some get well and strong again. Is that not true, Herr Doctor?"

"Yes, of course. There is more treatment. The leeches are not strong enough. I will lance the buboes, drain away the bad blood. And there is medicine. Yes, I brought medicine. Good things, tree sap mixed with roots of white lilies, quicksilver, mineral clay, and a special paste. It is good to use once the boils are lanced, and Martin, cool rags on her forehead for the fever. We shall get you up and well, Frau Rinkart, and all will hear your sweet voice praising God in church."

The doctor drank the mug of beer the lad had set beside him. Then he opened his bag and took out a lancet caked in blood. One by one, he cut open the large dark buboes and let the blood run into the mug. After letting the blood flow for some seconds, he wrapped a used bandage around each. When he finished, the cup was filled.

The woman's head was bobbing and swaying. "Dizzy. Lay me down, please! So tired. So very, very tired."

Martin gently laid his wife's trembling body down on the bed and covered her with another blanket. "The medicine, dear, my love, you must take the medicine."

Doctor Mueller opened a vial and retrieved sticky balls of medicine. The smell of human excrement, the special paste, was overwhelming. Martin took one of the balls and placed it in his wife's mouth. "Swallow, my love."

"It tastes wretched but I will try."

She swallowed and then began to cough. Martin held her in his arms and gently rocked her back and forth. "I am here, my love, I am here." His tears mixed with her spittle and blood on his worried face.

The following day, the Burgermeister found Pastor Rinkart at the church. A long line of dead bodies was laid out in the aisle. Two more carts of dead awaited outside. "How many today, Pastor?"

"Twenty-eight so far but there will be more. Funerals will begin in an hour."

"I'm afraid I come with bad news. The refugees—there are more today and a soldier among them carries news."

The pastor turned to his friend and said, "You must warn them. The plague—it is dangerous."

"We warned them. The signs of plague are everywhere, yet they come. They are starving, Martin. They come for food and what shelter we can offer. How can I turn them away?"

Pastor Rinkart sighed. "You say a soldier, with news? Bad news?"

The Burgermeister stared at the bodies lying before

him. "The Swedes are coming. The Imperial Army has retreated to Bohemia. The army of our Duke John George is no more. They were crushed at Wittstock. Those not killed were captured. Now the Swedish Field Marshall Johan Baner and his generals move south, pillaging all of Saxony. It was foolish for Duke John George to make peace with the Emperor on his own. Now our allies return to pillage what they once preserved."

Martin stood up and stared in thought. "Duke John Georg was given assurances that all Saxony is free to worship in our Lutheran faith. It is not his fault other princes and rulers continue the war for lands and titles. But as for the refugees, they think our walls will protect them. Walls did not save the people of Magdeburg. And food? There is little food in the market and none will say what they have hidden away. I pray that the Swedes will remember the great respect and mercy Eilenburg bestowed upon their King Gustav Adolphus when he fell in battle. Why the King, first laid out in the Red Deer Inn, was memorialized in this very church before his body was returned to Stockholm. Queen Christina would never permit her army to wantonly pillage and plunder our city."

"Yes, he left his daughter, Christina, as Queen. Too young to rule, a privy council and regent rule for her. And why would the Swedish nobles tax themselves to pay their army? Always, the problem of paying soldiers what they have been promised! It is the way of war today: They pillage for pay!"

Pastor Rinkart looked down. "You must gather every animal, every kernel of grain, piece of fruit and vegetable into the city...."

"I have already given the order. Martin, you are the last pastor. I need the church—all the churches, barns, and public buildings—for the refugees that keep coming and those sure to follow."

As the men spoke, Rinkart's eldest son ran into the church. "Father, you must come home! Mother...." The boy began to cry.

Martin hugged his son. "I will come home with you."

"She's gone, Papa."

Pastor Rinkart knelt beside his son. "Gone?"

A deep sigh pulled all the air from his lungs. His shoulders slumped and his head dropped. He replied softly, "Yes, to the very bosom of our Lord. Cry, Son. We shall all cry but we are not without hope. The resurrection will come. Have faith. Even in pain, we must have faith."

Martin was numb as he tried to comfort his children. Their question, the same question he heard from hundreds of others, haunted him. "Why, Papa? Why did God let her die? We prayed so hard. She loved God. She was good, always kind, and so sweet. Why did God take Mamma? Didn't God love her?"

Martin stroked the matted hair of his dead wife. He gently slid her eyelids closed, kissed her forehead, and fought back tears. His forehead resting against hers, he prayed silently: *Oh Lord accept the soul of your servant, my dear wife. Love her, Father, even more than we have loved her. Be merciful and gracious and comfort our children. Even so, I will praise you. In the name of the Father, the Son, and the Holy Ghost. Amen.*

His daughter helped him wash and clothe her. His words to his grieving children could not answer his own pain. They seemed mechanical but he replied, as all good pastors reply: "Who can know why? I only know that God loves us and will call each of us to Him someday. A day of rejoicing will come. In the meantime, we look to Jesus and our heavenly Father, who sent the Holy Spirit to comfort us in our sorrow. Pray for faith, children. God never denies a prayer for faith."

Numbed and trembling, Pastor Rinkart stood up. "I must return to the church. The others. So many others. Funerals. I will come for mother after the others. She shall be last today. We will bury her and mourn her together."

Pastor Rinkart insisted on separate funerals for each family. He faithfully followed the liturgy and committed the dead to the Lord. They were gently laid in the trench in the churchyard. The kind pastor offered comfort and prayer for each mourner before repeating the rite for the next victim of the cruel plague. A full moon was rising when he began the funeral of his wife. His body fatigued, his eyes swollen red but too dry to shed any more tears, he recited the liturgy slowly, his mind lingering on every word, every promise, and every hope. When her body was laid in the mass grave, Martin paused, not ready to turn his back and walk away. He looked at his children sobbing at the edge of the pit. His heart aching, he said, "Children, sing with me our table song. From this day forward, we will sing this song in remembrance of God's blessings. What better way to remember your dear mother as a blessing sent from God."

"The song you wrote, Papa?"

"Yes. It brings me comfort." Martin began to sing in his strong baritone voice, "Now thank we all our God…."

One by one, the children joined in:

"With hearts and hands and voices.

Who wondrous things has done,

In whom the world rejoices."

When the children sang the next line, their voices cracked and turned to sobs:

"Who from our mother's arms
Has blessed us on our way,
With countless gifts of love
And still is ours today...."

Martin stopped singing. Unable to continue, he gathered his children in his arms and cried.

Only after Pastor Rinkart escorted his grieving family home did the grave digger emerge from the shadows. He slowly made his way along the trench, spreading a shovel full of lime over each corpse. He then made his way to a wagon filled with earth and sprinkled just enough dirt to cover the bodies. At the end of the row, the stubborn blackened hand of a child still reached out to the living.

Weeks passed, and Pastor Rinkart struggled on, mourning with the mourning and grieving with the grieving. The deaths continued. He conducted as many as fifty funerals a day. His heart ached for the families of the dead. He knew their pain, and it somehow blunted the stabbing heartache in his soul. Refugees continued to pour into the city, and many soon succumbed to starvation or the plague. To the Eilenburgers, the refugees were nameless so they had only Pastor Martin to mourn for them and pray for their souls.

The humble pastor brought comfort to his city. The dead were constantly replaced by refugees. He was kind to all he encountered, those who sought solace in their faith and the Church, and those who blamed God and renounced the Church. He prayed for those who sought refuge in witchcraft.

A LIGHT IN THE DARKEST NIGHT

It must have been a refugee who convinced many to tie a live chicken to their body and keep it healthy until either the chicken or the wretched soul perished from the plague. It was never Martin's desire to scold or ridicule. He pursued mercy for all. The enemy was the devil, and the war was spiritual. Rinkart's weapons were faith, compassion, and prayer.

Martin was reluctant to eat. He insisted his children have enough, but he took his portion to the homeless souls sleeping in the church or the Rathaus. He was thin and pale. His black robe hung from gaunt shoulders and dragged through the dirt as he walked hunched over through the city, visiting the sick and the lonely.

It was in the Rathaus where the Burgermeister approached Martin. "They have come. A Swedish army is in view of the city walls. A messenger approached the gate. Come with me, Herr Pastor. Let us hear the terms."

The Burgermeister and Martin went through a small gate in the heavy iron strapped city gate now closed and barred to the outside world. A young officer in filthy clothes and the half-armor of a Cuirassier waited on horseback. The Mayor stepped forward. "Our gates are closed. It is not safe for you to enter." He pointed to a sign. "Plague. Our city is cursed with the plague. It would be un-Christian to quarter soldiers here."

The young officer looked at Martin. "You are the bishop or a pastor of Eilenburg?"

Martin nodded. "We are Lutheran. I am the last pastor. It is true what the Burgermeister says. The plague has taken my fellow workers in Christ. Thousands have died within our walls. Can't you smell the foul odor of death?"

The officer's horse sidestepped nervously as if the

words and the appalling odor spooked him. "We have seen your warning signs and heard from others of the plague. I will confirm your report with my General and say this is not a fit place to quarter our soldiers. But a tribute must be paid. Twenty thousand gold florins."

The Burgermeister replied, "Is there twenty thousand florins remaining in all of Saxony?"

"If there is, we shall find it and take it," the officer replied.

Martin asked, "Who is your General?"

"The Scotsman, General Leslie."

Martin nodded. "I am acquainted with General Leslie. A great soldier and a good Christian. I would like to speak with him. Would you tell him Pastor Martin Rinkart of Saint Nicholas Church—the church where King Gustav Adolphus was honored—asks to speak with him?"

"You ask that my General come into a city blackened by the plague?"

"I will go with you or meet him where he decides."

"Take off your robe. Let me see if you're clean."

Martin removed his cloak and his clothes. He lifted his arms and turned slowly before the young cavalry officer. "A bit gaunt from hunger, but as you see, the good Lord has kept me free of the plague."

The soldier nodded. "You may follow me. I will tell the General of your request."

Martin dressed and followed the mounted officer on foot. Two miles from the walls of Eilenburg, a Swedish army commanded by General Alexander Leslie was camped. A regiment of Scots was on one side, and two regiments of Swedes and German mercenaries were camped on the other side. The General's tent was pitched between them. Martin waited outside as the cavalry officer made his report.

Five minutes later, General Leslie emerged from the tent. "Pastor! It is you. How good it is that the Lord has preserved a righteous man! Come in. I was about to eat. Join me."

Martin followed the General into his tent. Leslie said, "Our rations are short: Bread and cheese and a little cured meat. But please, sit and eat."

Leslie pointed to a chair. Martin sat down, and the General sat across from him. "The plague, I'm told Eilenburg suffers. I'm sorry for you and your city. But my men fare little better. This war—crops have not been sown, and there is little food anywhere. The Swedish crown has been late with pay for my soldiers. Your Duke John George and the Imperial Field Marshal Melchior von Hartzfeld recover and fatten their soldiers in Bohemia. They will regroup and return to fight another day. So, you see, we wait here, but I must see to my men."

Martin stared at the food before him but did not touch it. Leslie said, "Guilt should not lead to an empty stomach. Eat, Pastor. You, too, must be strong to lead your flock."

Martin laughed. "You sound like my children. They say the very same words."

Rinkart took a piece of bread but spoke before eating. "Eilenburg has nothing to give, General. The plague has killed thousands, yet refugees come daily looking for food. Will not the Queen of Sweden remember the kindness and the honor Eilenburg showed her late father, King Gustav Adolphus?"

Martin ate the bread and waited.

Finally Leslie replied, "I cannot speak for her highness,

Queen Christina, or her privy council and regent. But because I remember and would reward your kindness, I will not break down your walls or destroy your city. But, like you, I serve my men. You must give us something."

Martin nodded. "There is the church silver. And my wages; I can go to the moneylenders to garnish my wages. I will buy all the grain in the market today."

Leslie asked, "That would help. And what will become of your people, Pastor?"

Rinkart's jaw clenched, and his brow tightened. "It will force the hoarders to sell."

Leslie smiled. "Eat, my friend. And listen to your children. There is wisdom in their words."

When the Burgermeister heard the terms that Martin had arranged, he commented, "You would give away the church's treasures, the property of Christ our Lord?"

Martin replied, "Christ suffered and died on a wooden cross, not silver. He ate and drank from plates and cups of crude clay or wood. He seeks our hearts, not our treasure. But I ask you to come with me to the market and see the purchases are made safely. I have given General Leslie my word, and he has given his."

General Leslie accepted the tribute offered by Eilenburg and marched his army past the city. Slowly, the toll of the plague relented, but the meager crops would not feed the countryside, and refugees continued to pour into the city.

Within a year, events in Scotland drew General Leslie home. The Chancellor of Sweden, Axel Oxenstierna, gave leave of Leslie, three hundred of his officers and thousands of Scottish soldiers to return to Scotland. The chancellor gave Leslie his army's artillery in return for back pay owed to his men. General Alexander Leslie returned to Scotland and led the Covenanter's Army in the First Bishop's War under the banner, "For Christ, Crown, and Covenant." While Leslie defended the Presbyterian Kirk of Scotland, a new Swedish General occupied Saxony.

The spring of 1639 brought signs of hope to Eilenburg. The plague was losing its deadly grip on the city. Food was scarce, but young shafts of grain began to emerge from once barren fields. With God's providence and careful rationing... perhaps, maybe, by fall... all would be well.

The last pastor of Eilenburg continued his daily rounds, consoling, comforting, and against the better judgment of his children, giving his meager rations to others. His friend, the Burgermeister, the only surviving alderman, did his best to administer a city drowning in despair.

"They keep coming—they see our fields are green and well-guarded. But they are too many. What can we do? Our people say bar the gate. Save what we have. But many—if not most—were once refugees. How can I say no to others?"

"My friend, you have done more than any man can. I will support you. We are in God's hands. He will provide."

The conversation was interrupted: "Burgermeister, an army approaches. Shall we bar the gates?"

"How far? From where? Yes, bar the gates. I shall hear their demands."

A Swedish officer rode to the city's gates and called out, "Open the gates for the army of Sweden, General Georg Dorfflinger, Commanding General."

The Burgermeister and the pastor stepped outside through the small man-gate. "Our city is stricken by the plague and filled with starving refugees. It is not safe for your army to quarter or, indeed, for even an officer to enter. There are signs posted."

The officer replied, "We have seen your signs. They are old. It is said the plague has run its course in Eilenburg. And your refugees—many are soldiers, deserters. We have come to arrest them. Have no fear; we shall permit you to bury their bodies once they receive justice."

The Mayor replied, "The only men at arms are the city militia who guard our walls and fields. They belong to no army and fight no war."

"It is well known that Eilenburg refuses no man entry. The deserters are among you. Will you open the gates?"

"Tell your General, with respect for his safety and the good of his men, we will not open the gates."

Martin followed the Mayor back into the city and bolted the door behind him. Behind the closed gate, Pastor Rinkart asked, "Isn't General Dorfflinger in service to our Duke of Saxony?"

The Burgermeister replied, "Not since the Peace of Prague. Now he serves the Swedish crown. I hear he is a hard man, a cruel drunkard, but most capable in battle."

Not three hours later, an advance team of the Swedish army of General Dorfflinger set up camp in the greening fields beyond the walls. Columns of soldiers marched by the gate to the growing city of tents and wagons. Artillery arrived. An enormous siege cannon was placed in front of the main city gate. Many more artillery pieces were deployed around the city wall. By evening, every trace of green grain stalk was ground into the mud. Campfires were lit and men could be seen settling in.

At sunrise, the blast of the great cannon awakened the city. Guards on the wall blew trumpets and took positions on the parapet. The same young officer rode to the gate and called out, "Herr Burgermeister, open the gate by order of General Georg Dorfflinger."

The Burgermeister sheepishly stepped outside and looked at the badly splintered but still standing main gate. "The danger of plague is real. I will see your General and hear his terms, or I will let an officer enter and see for himself that what I say is true."

The officer replied, "Your walls still stand. Your wharves are solid for river travel. Eilenburg is a good place for our headquarters. We prefer to take your city undamaged, but it is your decision. Open the gate. I will see for myself if what you say is true and report to my General."

"Come with me through the man-gate. You may inspect the city and report what I say is true."

The officer looked at the strained hinges of the main gate and the damage made by the cannon. He dismounted and followed the Mayor. He was led to the Rathaus, through the empty stalls of the market, past the mass graves and the still open trench by the Saint Nicholas Church. Only the clouds of flies showed energy for life. The air was foul, the faces of the people dulled and wan. He noted refugees, peasants from the countryside, huddled in every church and public building. They were lying in fetid straw in the alleys, under crude awnings of old clothes taken from the dead. The young man pulled a handkerchief from his coat sleeve and held it over his nose and mouth. Finally, he muttered through his crude mask,

"I have seen enough."

At the gate, the officer saluted and said, "Wait here while I give my report."

When the Burgermeister was summoned to meet General Dorfflinger, he asked his friend Pastor Rinkart to come with him. They were led to a large tent where the General met with his staff officers. Dorfflinger was waiting, a large jug of schnapps on the table in front of him. The General's half-armor was hung behind him and his armored gloves were on the table, their blackened steel fingers pointing out like claws waiting to rip open prey.

General Dorfflinger did not wait for an introduction. He looked up and said, "It is your city I want. I have no need for you or your people. Surrender your city, pay my men, and you will be free to go. Thirty thousand thalers and your people may all leave with what goods they can carry. No livestock or foodstuffs, of course. They are now the property of my army. Tomorrow. You shall pay the money tomorrow, or the terms grow harder."

Martin replied, "General, there is not such wealth in all of Saxony. As a Christian who has served Saxony, we beg you...."

Dorfflinger stood up, turned his back, and walked away, saying, "Thirty thousand silver thalers tomorrow."

The following morning the young officer appeared at the gate. "Bring the tribute!"

The Burgermeister called back, "We need more time. We are collecting what money we have. Even so, thirty thousand thalers? Impossible."

The officer turned around and said to an orderly,

"Send up the prisoners."

One hundred and fifty filthy peasants were herded to the city gate. The officer called out. "City of Eilenberg, your neighbors require food and shelter. In one hour, any of these waiting outside your gate will be cut down and left to rot."

Martin came through the man-gate. "We struggle to feed our citizens. You would condemn innocent people to starve?"

The soldier replied, "General Dorfflinger sends this message to Pastor Rinkart. 'Pastor, feed your lambs.' Thirty thousand thalers." And he rode back to camp.

Martin led the huddled mass of men, women, and children through the small gate into Eilenburg. A riot ensued when a dead crow was found in an alley inside the gate. A child was trampled by two men fighting over the dead bird.

The Mayor stopped Martin. "How will we feed them? The market stalls are empty. Only food hidden away in houses remain. Who will take from his family to feed strangers?"

Martin asked, "Food is more dear than money. Can we raise such an amount?"

"Three hundred thalers, that is all I could raise. But, yes, soon everyone will agree. Their silver will do them no good if they starve."

Martin nodded and began to walk away.

"Herr Pastor, where are you going? The refugees...."

"Take them to the church. I am going for food. I cannot ask others to give if I will not give from my own meager larder."

Martin took half of his remaining food and brought it to the church. He and the Mayor went door to door collecting food and silver for the ransom.

The following morning, the officer led what seemed to be a regiment of soldiers to the main gate of Eilenburg. The armored officer called out, "Open the gate and bring out the tribute."

The Burgermeister replied, "I collected every thaler in Eilenburg. We offer the money as a ransom for peace."

The officer replied, "Open the gate and bring the thirty thousand thalers before me. Anything less and these five hundred prisoners from the Duke John George's army of Saxony will be released to pillage Eilenburg for food, goods, and women until they are dealt with in three days by the army of General Dorfflinger."

The Burgermeister shouted, "Two thousand thalers! We have found two thousand thalers. Please!"

From his position astride his war horse, the officer drew his sword and shouted, "Pastor Rinkart, the General commands: *Tend your lambs!*" Turning to his soldiers, he shouted, "Cannoneer, prepare to fire on the gate!"

Martin rushed through the man-gate. "Wait! Open the gate. Guards! Open the gate of Eilenburg."

The Burgermeister called out, "Open the gates. Do as our good pastor says."

Chains could be heard as the guards struggled to turn the heavy winch lifting the massive bar. And then the groaning of bent iron hinges as the great doors began to swing open. Voices were silent. General Dorfflinger was drawn to see the living hell waiting behind the gates. Martin walked slowly towards the General's tent.

The General walked towards the gates. As they opened, the smell of death rolled out like a cloud onto the army outside. Georg von Dorfflinger had witnessed many battlefield deaths and the acrid smell of fire and powder smoke, but the putrid stench of the city of death overwhelmed his senses. He froze where he stood.

Martin Rinkart stopped in front of the General and pleaded. "Accept the two thousand thalers. It is all that we have. As for food? Look! Look at our city. What do you see? Starvation is our companion. Our hope was for a meager crop but your army is camped on our field. Take our money and leave us in peace. If you stay, your future is no better than ours."

Von Dorfflinger stared at the city inside the gate. Everyone was waiting. He took a breath, straightened his body, and answered so that every ear could hear, "The ransom is thirty thousand thalers." Then he turned to return to his tent.

Pastor Rinkart walked back to the gate and cried out to the people of Eilenburg, "Come, my children, we can find no hearing, no mercy with men. Let us take our refuge with God!"

He fell to his knees and prayed. The people of Eilenburg fell to their knees. The soldiers and prisoners outside the gate stood silently and listened as the pastor poured out his heart to God. When he finished his amen, he stood and began to sing, "Now thank we all our God...."

The villagers of Eilenburg slowly joined in:
"With hearts and hands and voices.
Who wondrous things has done,
In whom the world rejoices.
Who from our mother's arms
Has blessed us on our way,

With countless gifts of love
And still is ours today...."

The sound of the people singing, following the confident voice of Pastor Rinkart, stopped General Dorfflinger in his steps. He stood motionless, his eyes closed, and his head bowed. He shook his head slowly, turned around, and walked back to the gates. He stopped in front of Martin and spoke: "Eilenburg will surrender to Sweden and quarter five hundred soldiers for my garrison. They shall eat from the provisions I leave for them and be accorded respect within the city. I will accept the two thousand thalers and move on."

The Commanding General turned to his officer. "See that the standard is raised on the city wall and from the Rathaus. Take the ransom the Burgermeister has collected to the quartermaster. Prepare the army to decamp in the morning."

The young officer saluted the general and repeated the orders to the assembled soldiers. Martin Rinkart held back tears and said, "Thank you. May God bless you, Georg von Dorfflinger."

Von Dorfflinger stared at Rinhart and said, "Herr Pastor, shepherd your sheep."

The war continued for seven more years, thirty in total. The victory over death secured, the green shoots of grain stretched forth again towards the heavens after the Swedish army marched off. Shoots became stalks, stalks grew full heads, and heavy grain developed. There was vigor in this grain, a determination to bring new life to a diseased and starving city that could not be deterred. The doctor put away his plague mask, and the devil moved on to ply his evil trade somewhere else. Soldiers of the garrison worshiped alongside their neighbors, behaving like good citizens. Eilenburg prospered.

In 1649, less than a year after the Peace of Westphalia, his work complete, Pastor Martin Rinkart went home to be with the God he loved. All his children survived and lived to see their father honored at Saint Nicholas Church. A beautiful garden grows over the graves of eight thousand victims of plague and starvation. The once rising hand of the dead child is now at rest. Christians throughout the world sing his hymn of praise:

> Oh, may this bounteous God,
> Through all our life, be near us.
> With ever joyful hearts,
> And blessed peace to cheer us.
> And keep us in His grace,
> And guide us day and night.
> And free us from all ills,
> Protect us by His light.

Death was defeated at Eilenburg. But Martin Rinkart reminds us that whatever darkness overshadows us, this truth remains:

> Streams of mercy, never ceasing
> Call for songs of loudest praise
> Here's my heart, take and seal it
> Seal it in Thy courts above.

Death Comes to Eilenburg *was based on a true story.*

THE DEAD DOG
OF LO DEBAR

*B*arnabas opened the door and followed the shaft of sunlight into the small room. He stomped the dust off his feet and sat down on a bench by the door. Wearily, Barnabas took off his sandals and poured water from a pitcher over his hot, suntanned feet into a small basin. He took the small towel from the table and looked at the young man watching his every movement.

"Well, Uncle," the younger man effused. "Did you talk to him? What did he say? Am I to go along?"

The short, middle-aged man stared silently at his nephew who waited anxiously for news. Barnabas shook his head and sighed. "No. Paul said no. We argued. I insisted you come along but he refused. I'm sorry to say we agreed to part company. Silas will journey with Paul to the churches of Asia. I thought, perhaps, you would accompany me to Cyprus?"

"You and Paul argued? And parted?" John Mark was clearly shaken. "After all these years? After all that you have done for him? You befriended him—trusted him and encouraged him when no one else would. None of the Disciples dared even be seen with him; they sent him away!

Only you saw Jesus working in him and went with him. And now you have parted...? It can't be!"

John Mark shook his head then sobbed. "Though you pleaded my case, Paul will not forgive or forget my failure; the way I deserted you both. I know I was wrong. I have begged for forgiveness. I will never forgive myself. How can I? After seeing the Holy Spirit work in Cyprus—the joy of the new believers! After we sailed to Perga... I gave up. I was homesick and exhausted. Not even your encouraging words could persuade me to stay. I have repented and prayed. It is my constant prayer, but still, Paul says no... and you separated because of me. Guilt upon guilt! Will I never be given a second chance?!"

Barnabas shook his head. "Paul will always be my brother and ever in my heart and prayers. John Mark, I'm sure he forgives you. Brother Paul knows of the dangers and hardships to be faced. He relies on men of mature faith, like brother Silas—a good man."

"You said you argued and parted company and you are sorry. You had words, hard words, because of me. I have failed you twice, Uncle. First when I ran home from Pamphylia and today when you and Brother Paul parted company. It's all my fault."

Barnabas stood and walked across the room. He sat down beside his nephew and put an arm around his shoulder. "John Mark, listen to me. I want to tell you a story. Are you listening? Good.

"A young man about your age lived in a small village—hardly a village—a collection of crude huts built around a cistern that caught the winter rain. There had been a well but it had gone dry and the cistern could barely supply water for the few lost souls who called it home. You hear the name of this place in the marketplace—a name synonymous with desolation—Lo Debar: 'No Pasture.'

"But No Pasture does not fully describe the desolation of the place. A village of no value, never to be fought over by ambitious kings. It lies at the end of a narrow valley of rock and sand. All that is beyond is the same desert wilderness or worse. It is fit only for the most miserable of God's creations, those simply awaiting the end that comes to all men."

The young man interjected: "I have heard the curses directed at those to be exiled: 'Send him to Lo Debar.' Or 'He's off to Lo Debar!' Is there truly such a place?"

"Truly, there is." Barnabas couldn't help but smile at the widening of John Mark's eyes in shock. Barnabas returned to his story. "This young man awoke every morning and slid from his bed to a mat. He was lame on both feet and could not walk. I ask you: Can a man lame on both feet even walk with crutches? Every day was the same. Simple meals from the family that protected him and sitting on a chair shaded from the scorching sun, watching. Hours, days, weeks, months, and years were spent watching, wondering, and worrying if this were the day his pursuer would find him. You see, Lo Debar was less a place of exile as it was a place of hiding."

Barnabas took a breath and stretched his neck before continuing. "The young man was a prince of Israel, the son of Jonathan, son of King Saul. His name was Mephibosheth...."

John Mark interrupted his uncle. "Of course! I know his story. He was crippled when his nurse dropped him. They were running for their donkeys, fleeing his house after the death of Saul and Jonathan. Yes, he was a young lad, only five years old. Why do you tell me this story, Uncle?"

"If you must ask, it is all the more reason for you to listen. Now, where was I? Yes, the young man was Prince Mephibosheth." Barnabus paused to collect his thoughts. "Now, it is the way of the world that when a king is killed and a new king from another family takes the throne, the surviving sons and all of the heirs of the dead king are put to death. Normally, the new king does this to secure his lineage's claim to the throne. And indeed, when Saul and his firstborn son, Jonathan, died in battle against the Philistines, David was proclaimed King of Judah and Saul's second son, Ishbosheth, rose up to challenge David. It came to pass that Ishbosheth's army was defeated, and his great general, Abner, was slain by Joab. All Israel gathered at Hebron and declared David King. Ishbosheth had fled but was treacherously murdered by his servants seeking favor from David. Of course, King David never countenanced such treachery and put the evildoers to death. By this time, the young lad, Mephibosheth, of the same lineage as Ishbosheth, was hiding at Lo Debar."

Barnabas looked up and sighed. "With all of his relatives dead (I don't know what became of his mother; perhaps she had died earlier), Mephibosheth was forgotten. David never meant any harm to the boy. Indeed, David had made an oath with Jonathan, a man he loved more than all of his brothers—no two men were closer—"

"Like you and Brother Paul, Uncle?" Mark interrupted.

"Perhaps even closer. David had vowed never to harm Jonathan's family. So Mephibosheth grew up waiting for his capture and execution... which David never intended. Can you imagine that distress and fear?"

John Mark nodded solemnly as he listened. His head bowed in contemplation.

Barnabas continued. "Many years went by—at least ten, maybe even twenty. David's throne was secure. He had driven off the Philistines, defeated all his enemies, and made Israel a great nation. Kings from the River of Egypt to the Euphrates paid tribute to King David. Sitting at his table, feasting with his great men—warriors all—David asked, 'Is there anyone still left of the House of Saul so that I can show him kindness for Jonathan's sake?' Someone remembered one of Saul's servants, a man named Ziba. Well, of course, they immediately sent for Ziba to make the inquiry. Did any soul remain? When brought before King David, Ziba answered, 'There is still a son of Jonathan, lame on both feet.' When further questioned, Ziba told the King that Mephibosheth was living in the house of Machir in Lo Debar.

"Now King David was not slow about doing good. He sent messengers to Lo Debar and had Mephibosheth brought to David's city." Barnanas paused. "Nephew, consider how Mephibosheth must have felt. All his fears were brought to bear. The journey to Jerusalem—each stride of his donkey brought him closer to a judgment he had so long feared.

"At last, they entered the city, and the young man was carried into the palace of David. Mephibosheth was set down on a mat spread before David's throne. Unable to face King David, Mephibosheth fell on his face and prostrated himself before the king. David looked down from his high throne and I feel certain his heart felt broken. Then David said softly, 'Mephibosheth?' The young man did not look up. He replied, 'Here is your servant.'

"John Mark... imagine King David rising from his throne and rushing to the frightened young man! He takes hold of his arm, helps him sit up, and says, 'Do not be afraid for I will show you kindness for the sake of your father, Jonathan. I will restore to you all the land of your grandfather, Saul, and you shall eat at my table always.'

"At last, Miphiboseth raised his eyes and looked upon King David. He said, 'What is your servant that you should show regard for a dead dog like me?' Dead dog. That is what he called himself. After all those years of waiting in fear, loneliness and despair, he saw himself as no more than a dead dog!"

Barnabas shook his head and sighed. He straightened up and gently squeezed John Mark's shoulder. "King David did not answer. Instead, he acted. He called for Ziba, Saul's servant, and said to him, 'All that belonged to Saul and to all of his house, I have given to your master's grandson. And you and your sons and your servants shall till the land for him and bring in the produce so that your master's grandson shall have bread to eat. But Mephibosheth shall always eat at my table.'

"Ziba bowed and said, 'According to all that my lord the king commands, so will your servant do.' When Mephibosheth heard this, he again prostrated himself before David. Ziba had fifteen sons and twenty servants and they all served Mephibosheth from that day forth. And Mephibosheth ate at the king's table, like one of the king's own sons."

John Mark looked up into Barnabas' face. "I still don't understand why you tell me this story. Of course, David's mercy to Mephibosheth speaks of God's mercy for us, that He calls us from sin and despair as if calling us from Lo Debar. But I have repented and I have the hope of God's forgiveness. I know I have been redeemed by the blood of Jesus, the lamb of God, who takes away the sin of the world. Why remind me of Mephibosheth, the Dead Dog of Lo Debar?"

Barnabas sighed. He lifted his arm from John Mark's shoulders and his open hand gently rubbed the young man's back. "Yes, you have been released from Lo Debar. But you are more like Mephibosheth than you allow yourself to see. Like Jonathon's young son, you fled not Judah but Pamphylia in fear. His flight in fear crippled him in his feet. John Mark, your flight from the mission journey has crippled you with doubts, discouragement, and guilt. Don't you see that God does not pursue you to judge you? Do you not have a seat at the Lord's table, where you can eat the bread of His body and drink from the cup of wine that is His blood worthily? Let go of your guilt. Let your faith and obedience speak louder than words. Come with me to Cyprus. Visit again the churches in Cyprus. Come, encourage, and be encouraged. Share in my labors to bring the Good News of Jesus to others in Cyprus. Be amazed by what God's Spirit can do! I give you my pledge to encourage you and teach you as an evangelist to open your soul to share the Word that the Spirit brings to your tongue. As for Brother Paul and Brother Silas—are not two mission teams better than one?"

John Mark nodded and wiped a tear from his eye. "I am blessed to have so gracious an uncle who chooses me above service with his great friend, Paul the Apostle."

Barnabas smiled. "Perhaps God works for the good in this. Brother Paul no longer needs my help. I see someone even closer to me who may hear the words of encouragement from one who has walked longer with our Lord. And I believe that one day Brother Paul will value your service and call upon you as a fellow worker and servant of our Lord."

A LIGHT IN THE DARKEST NIGHT

John Mark accompanied Barnabas to Cyprus. Remembered now as Mark the Evangelist, he wrote the Gospel that bears his name. He continued as a missionary to North Africa, planting churches and serving as Bishop of Alexandria. Paul's letter to the Colossians confirms Mark was with Paul during his first imprisonment in Rome. And in Paul's second imprisonment, he called for Mark, saying his presence was helpful for him and a comfort. Perhaps Mark mastered the gift of encouragement from his mentor and uncle, Barnabas.

An Island in the Sun

lack smoke appeared where the azure blue waters kissed the light blue western sky. The smoke came closer; all the while, its unwelcome aerial invasion was fought off by the northeast wind, which dispersed the noxious intrusion to ever lighter shades of gray. Soon the source of the plume was visible across the shimmering water. A steamship was making its way through the outer reef towards the village of Uma. It was a dangerous maneuver. The island, a high plateau atoll, was surrounded by reefs. There was no navigable lagoon safe for anchorage. A shift in the prevailing wind and the island's shelter would be lost.

"Pastor Solomon, a ship, off Uma," a young man said, entering the thatched hut of the Banaba Congregational Church.

Pastor Solomon was cleaning small chalkboards, preparing for another day teaching reading and writing to his small congregation. "I'm not expecting the *Archer* or the *Hiram Bingham* for another month," he replied, still busy with his task.

"No pastor. It is not the *Archer* or the *Hiram Bingham* of the mission society. It is not a whaler. You must come and see. It is like a transport ship, only smaller. The Elders will need you to speak for them, to ask why they come to our island."

Solomon looked up and smiled at the young man. "Yes, of course. We will greet our visitors on the beach."

The two men made their way through the coastal rainforest of bright red flowering flame trees, mangoes, guava, and tapioca, along the shore choked by saltbush and fry sheltering mangrove, to the small, cleared beach lined with fishing canoes. When they arrived, two elders were waiting on the beach, watching a small boat being lowered into the water from the small steamship now anchored offshore.

"Good morning, Elders," Solomon said, smiling brightly.

The Elder of Uma replied as he watched two men climb into the boat and row towards them, "White men. Find out what they want. We have nothing to trade. We have no water to spare. They are not whalers or traders, perhaps another missionary—we have you and have no need of another."

The Elder of Taokira nodded. "Extend courtesy and hospitality. The Elders will listen to their words."

"I will do my best. But whites have many languages from Europe. I know only English and a little German from my mission school days on Kosrae."

The Uma Elder replied, "If we do not understand his words, he can leave as he comes today."

The bow of the boat ground into the sand alongside a large black rock. The man at oars jumped out and pulled the boat onto the beach. The second man, seated at the stern, stood, walked forward, and stepped onto dry land. The man did not stop. He walked confidently forward to the islanders waiting. He removed his hat, nodded, and said in his distinct Australian accent, "Gah'day, friends. My name is Mister Ellis, Albert Ellis. I would like to speak with your king."

Solomon turned and translated Mister Ellis' words into Gilbertese.

The Elder of Uma replied, "Tell him we have no king."

The Elder of Taokira replied, "Say, we are ruled by Elders of the tribes. We shall hear what he has to say. Tell him he can wait in Uma while we gather the Elders. Offer him food and hospitality."

Solomon replied, "I will tell him. Perhaps, I can show him the church and the school and learn from him discreetly until a proper supper can be prepared for him and the Elders at sunset."

Both Elders nodded and walked away.

Solomon turned to Ellis and said in English, "Welcome, Mister Ellis. My name is Solomon. We have no king. Judgments are made by our tribal councils led by the Elders of our tribes. They will hear your words at a meal prepared in your honor at sunset. In the meantime, I will show you our church and our school. We are good Christians and happy to be blessed by God who supplies all our needs on our island home."

Ellis turned to the oarsman and said, "Leave the box with me. Return to the ship. I will signal when you are to return for me."

"Aye, Mister Ellis. I will give your orders to the captain."

"And tell the captain, no one is to leave the ship until I return and give permission."

"Aye, but what say you to fishing? Can we fish…?"

"Only from the ship where she lies. We are good guests and shall not impose upon our hosts."

The crewman brought a small wooden box with a leather handle and set it on the sand. He shoved the boat from the beach, jumped in, and rowed back to the steamer.

Ellis retrieved the box and said to Solomon, as the good pastor led the way inshore, "Who taught you English? You speak as an educated white man."

Solomon smiled. "Mister Walkup at the mission school and seminary on Kosrae. He is a fine gentleman, an excellent teacher, and man of God."

Ellis replied, "I met Captain Walkup—met him on the Morning Star in New Guinea years ago. I remember Walkup and his friend, the ship's master, Captain Fred Snow."

Solomon flashed a toothy smile and answered, "Indeed, Captain Walkup is known throughout all the islands. He brought the Word of God to this island. But it is his son who teaches at Kosrae and ordained me as minister to the Banaba people."

Solomon was happy to find a companion who spoke English and knew the family that gave him faith in the one true God, an education, and a purpose for his life. He happily chatted on, "I was a young boy, eager for adventure. I had heard stories of the world—of far-off Nantucket—from a Banaba man who sailed with the whalers. When Captain Walkup offered to sail his ship to New Guinea to recover brothers and sisters, refugees there, and to take an islander named Isaac to Nauru, I begged my father to let me go along. My father saw the wisdom in learning the language and skills of the whites and allowed me to leave on the promises of Captain Walkup of my safety."

Ellis smiled. "My friend—yes, he would allow me to call him a friend—and my employer is a pious Christian man. He would say our meeting is of God. He sends me here to find something—I have already seen evidence it is here. Something that will bring prosperity to Ocean Island."

"The box you carry is to help you find what you search for?"

"Yes, of course. I will show it to the Elders. Tell me, Solomon, or should I call you Reverend Solomon?"

"Our people call me Pastor Solomon, but titles make me feel uneasy."

"Tell me, Pastor Solomon, how many people live on the island? There were reports some years ago that you all perished in the Three-year Drought."

"Yes, the drought. The rains are not consistent. They usually come but not always. The same report brought Captain Walkup here to rescue any survivors. Well, we were two hundred then, but in the fifteen years since, we are many more, nearly four hundred! The water cave sustains us. There is no other water on the island. And the forest, well, as you can see, the forest along the shore survives, but the trees inland have died, and only brush grows there now."

Ellis nodded. "And perhaps rocks? Hard, dark, nearly black rocks?"

"Yes, of course. They are good for carving, but God commands us not to make graven images. Your box is heavy. We can leave it at the church. I will take you inland and show you the rocks."

"The box is dear. I am a stranger. Will it be safe?"

"We do not steal. It is the teaching of the church and the Elders. No one will touch it."

A LIGHT IN THE DARKEST NIGHT

The men entered the thatched-roofed hut with a small altar supporting a Bible and a wooden cross. Straw mats were spread before it. "You may leave the box here."

Ellis set the box down and picked up a small slate board with chalk letters. "You teach your people to read and write?"

"Yes, so they may read the Bible and understand God's promises."

Ellis stared at the slate. "Do you think you could teach your people English?"

Solomon cocked his head. The thought had never occurred to him. "If that is their desire. We hear many languages. Yes, we could learn English if the Elders wish it."

"You are very clever, Pastor Solomon. Now, show me the rocks."

The noon sun was at its zenith as they left the shade of the coastal forest. Its rays burned on the back of Mister Ellis' neck. He stopped to put a handkerchief over his head and held it in place with his hat. It supplied some relief to his parched neck. "Perhaps we should have brought water," he said softly.

"We're here," Solomon said. He swept his arm across the horizon and pointed to a rocky outcropping. Between the skeletons of two dead trees was a dark rock. "The entire center of the island is just as you see here. The trees died in the drought. We have an ancient story as to why the land has spikes of rock jutting out from the old forest floor. The fingers of the god of the cave reached up from beneath the earth to catch his daughter eloping with the son of the water god. I know it sounds foolish, and I do not allow the myth to be told in church, but there is some truth—God is sovereign. He is our creator and sustainer and works His purpose on our island and on all the earth."

Ellis dropped to his knees and took a knife from inside his belt. He chipped at the rock with the hilt, gathered the fragments, wrapped them in a small cloth, and put them in his pocket.

"The whole island is just as this, you say?"

"The rock of the water cave is different. It is not dark, but white. It is our life, and we protect it. We do not take outsiders to the water cave."

Ellis stood up. "No. That is wise. I do not ask to see it. But some cool water in the village? I am very thirsty. We can return now."

Back at the church, the wooden box sat untouched. Solomon said, "The afternoon rain will come. Rest at my hut. I will call for you when all is ready."

Solomon lived in a comfortable one-room hut. A hammock was strung near an open window. A small table held a washbasin and a clay pitcher of water. A large table with a chair was placed at the far end. The table was covered with books, writing paper, and a glass oil lamp.

"Let me pour you water, and then you may rest in the hammock. A breeze will accompany the rain. You will find it most refreshing."

Ellis took the water and drank. He set the cup down and wiped his brow. "There is no Missus Solomon?"

Solomon blushed. "No, not yet, though I pray to God that I find a good Christian woman to walk beside me in love and service."

"There must be unmarried women on the island?"

Solomon sighed. "Yes, of course, but I cannot show favoritism among the tribes. Elders have presented young women to me, hoping to use it to some advantage. There is always jealousy, you see. So, I remain single until the good Lord shows me the answer. Now, I shall leave you."

The Elders of Uma and Taokira were waiting in the church when Solomon returned from his hut. The always blunt Elder of Uma asked, "What does he want?"

The Elder of Taokira added, "You led him into the island. Why?"

Solomon was not surprised by the visit. "Elders, he seeks the black rocks. I do not know why. White men use another black rock, coal, to burn in their boilers. But our black rocks are not this coal."

"What else have you learned?"

"His English is of an Australian. He has asked about our numbers. He knew of the drought and was surprised that our numbers had recovered. And then, well, he asked if I could teach our people English. Oh, and there is this: He claims his employer and friend is a pious Christian—a good thing. But he did not speak for himself."

Alone in Solomon's hut, Albert Ellis opened his box. His fingers worked through the straw around a large black rock. He found a smaller box, placed it on the table, and opened it. Inside were several small vials and a mortar and pestle. Ellis pulled the sample from his pocket and ground it into powder. He poured the powder into a vial of clear liquid then used a dropper to add a liquid from another vial, inserted a stopper, and shook the mixture vigorously. After a minute, he lifted the vial and examined it carefully. He smiled as he returned the vials to the box and settled into the hammock.

As Solomon predicted, an afternoon rainstorm swept through and went its ordained way. As sunset approached, the now cool air carried the scent of earthy vegetation with sweet hints of tropical flowers and fruit.

A soft voice called to him: "Mister Ellis? Are you awake? It is time."

Ellis was led to the village of Uma. The embers of a fire flickered out over the tranquil waters from a well-established fire pit in front of the council house. Ellis was invited to sit on a mat across from the tribal Elders. Twenty more men, heads of family clans, were seated outside the center ring. Solomon sat beside Ellis. Following words of welcome by the Elder of Tabiang, home of the ancient Te Aka clan, the first tribe of Ocean Island, trays of food were brought forward by women wearing long, shapeless Mother Hubbard-style dresses.

The men feasted on fresh fish, crabs, taro paste, roasted breadfruit, and mangoes. Ellis was surprised his cup held only water. Solomon whispered, "We allow no alcohol or vile tobacco on our island. If the water does not satisfy, I suggest the mangoes and guava."

When the Elders finished eating, they washed their fingers and sat back on their mats. The Elder of Toakira spoke: "You have come to our home and asked to be heard by our Elders. We have shown you courtesy and hospitality. The Elders have gathered, and we would hear your words."

Albert Ellis was energized. He knew what he needed to do. "Elder and leaders of the Banaba people, I am honored to sit and feast in your presence. You are truly a noble people given to hospitality and faithful Christian living. It was by grace that God saved your people from the drought, and by grace, you have received God's Good News of Salvation. Today, I believe it was God's grace that brought me to your island. And I can promise you that my coming will bring great blessings to your people. I, too, serve under another, an Elder, the grandson of a missionary of the same faith. He is a good and pious man who will bring you prosperity."

Ellis paused to bend over and picked up the black rock beside him. "I have come looking for this stone. I saw one on the beach when I first came ashore. Pastor Solomon showed me others inland among the dead trees. You have no use for these stones, but in Australia, where the rain is infrequent and few trees can grow, where grass and grain are all that can be seen from horizon to horizon, these stones are of great use."

"The stone is not coal. Why do you want it?" asked the Elder of Uma.

"No, you are wise. It is not coal. The man who brought this to me thought it was petrified wood—ancient wood that turned to stone over thousands of years of rain and water. This stone is petrified, but not wood, guano—the droppings of seabirds. It is rich in a substance called phosphate, and like the droppings of chickens and birds, it can be made into fertilizer. The farmers in Australia need your stones to help grow food for their families."

The Elder of Tabwewa spoke, "They will buy our stones, these farmers?"

Ellis smiled. "Someone must gather the stones and take them to Australia where they are cleaned, crushed, and mixed with other crushed stones and then sold to the farmers. My Elder is the man who makes this happen. He brings blessings to you who have the stone you do not need and makes them into food for the grain to feed Australia. Is it not a Christian thing to do? You will help Christian brothers in Australia and receive a blessing in return."

The Elder of Te Aonanne asked, "What will you pay for each stone? Your ship is small, but I will sell you enough to fill it before you leave."

Ellis replied, "My Elder offers you, the Elders of the Banaba, fifty pounds sterling every year to spend as you decide for the good of your people in return for all the stone that we can carry away. And what is more, we will pay your people to remove the stone and carry it to our ship."

Pastor Solomon interrupted, "You intend to mine the island—to make our people do your mining? It is very hard labor!"

The Elder of Uma spoke, "What is fifty pounds sterling? English money! Paper that we do not need."

"Perhaps you do not need paper money to buy things on this island, but there are many fine things we can bring you to purchase from Australia. Things like lanterns and cook pots, shovels, axes, fishing nets—many wonderful things. The Elders can decide how to spend the lease money. We shall build a store to sell these wonderful items to all those who work the stone."

Solomon shook his head. "We have a good life. We don't need these things he offers."

A clan leader from the back shouted, "Pastor, you have these things. You have your lamps and your books and writing things. Why should you have them and not us?"

"I agree. We do not need the things of the whites in Australia. We do well on our own," said the Elder of Uma.

Mister Ellis nodded. "Yes, you have done well. You

work hard at fishing and tending your taro and fruit. The rock I brought was found on Nauru. I can go and ask their people for the stone. I came first to Ocean Island because you are fewer, and the money will go farther among fewer people. But if that is your decision, I will leave."

The Leading Elder of Tabiang stood up and said, "We have heard enough! Return tomorrow, and we will give you our answer."

Albert Ellis nodded. "I will leave you to consider the offer. Thank you for listening and showing me such gracious hospitality. Until tomorrow."

Pastor Solomon took a torch from along the council house and walked Ellis to the beach. Solomon swung the torch until his signal was acknowledged from the steamer. He waited silently until Ellis was safe aboard his boat.

Albert Ellis took his time coming ashore the next day. From his stateroom window, he sat for a leisurely breakfast, watching the Uma council house activity. It was well after ten before the davit was swung from the steamer's side and the small boat lowered into the water. It was another ten minutes before Ellis appeared with a leather bag and gingerly climbed down a ladder into the boat.

The loud conversations among the islanders softened. The creaking of the oarlocks and the gentle splashing of the oars carried across the quiet waters. The boat landed near the same black rock on the beach, and Ellis patiently stepped ashore. The men on the beach stood silent as Ellis walked by them up to the Elders waiting at the council house.

"Gah'day!" Ellis chimed merrily. "This is a magical island; I slept like a baby!" Still smiling, his eyebrows lifted, he added, "You have made your decision, I presume."

The Elder of Toakira spoke for the group. Pastor Solomon translated: "The Elders say that the families and clans may do as they wish upon their land. Many accept your proposal for wages to work their land. The Elders also agree that the fifty pounds sterling be paid to the Council of Elders to be used for the benefit of all."

"A wise decision. May I ask how many family clans will commit to the agreement?"

Solomon repeated the question in Gilbertese. Seventeen of the twenty men present raised their hands.

Ellis nodded and opened the leather bag. "I have papers to sign. A contract. It binds my Elders, the Pacific Phosphate Company, to pay the Ocean Island Council of Elders fifty pounds sterling yearly for nine hundred and ninety-nine years in return for our right to remove phosphate from this island. Further, the company agrees to pay each islander who agrees to work the dig ten pounds per month. The Pacific Phosphate Company agrees to open a company store and import goods to be bought at a fair price in pounds sterling. I will give the first fifty-pound note once the document is signed."

A buzz of conversation began as soon as Solomon finished translating. Solomon then asked, "Did I hear correctly, nine hundred and ninety-nine years?"

"We will pay the council for as long as we work this island. Do you plan on living nine hundred and ninety-nine years, Pastor?"

"And two more of the families now agree to work. Who shall sign? The Elders do not write."

"They may make their mark. I trust you, Pastor

Solomon, to record their name by their mark."

Two hours later, the steamer weighed anchor and sailed for Nauru Island.

Less than a year had passed when Albert Ellis returned with a team of mining engineers and surveyors. Equipment was offloaded, and a road was cleared from the Uma beach inland. A small pier was built, and wood cabins to house the Australian managers and the Pacific Phosphate Company office. The year was 1900. The flag of Great Britain was raised on the flag pole in front of the office. Britain annexed Ocean Island into the Colony of the Gilbert and Ellice Islands. A month later, a second ship arrived and slowly loaded the first cargo.

The third ship delivered the stock of the company store, and eager islanders stood in line to spend the three months of earnings. But the speed in setting up the mine did not come without problems. Transporting the rich phosphate-bearing rock to the improvised, unprotected harbor was slow and loading was even slower. Improvements were needed in the operation and safety. Untrained islanders were injured, and the sight of desolation caused by strip mining alarmed many.

Solomon spoke for himself and the Elders when he confronted the manager. "What you are doing is not good. Our island is being destroyed. Good men, husbands and fathers have been injured. Who will care for them and their families? And the cost of goods—fifty pounds a year—provides little for our people. We have been cheated! All the talk of Christian brotherhood—a lie!"

"I share your concern for your people. There have

been too many injuries. The work is harder than we planned. We will pause and train the men. I will ask for a doctor to come. Yes, a doctor and a hospital. We owe you that. I will ask for the company doctor to care for everyone on the island. As for the lease payment and the prices in the store, I will report your displeasure."

The manager stood up and looked out the window. The sky was darkening. Clouds were racing towards the island. "Tell your people we are pausing work for a time of training and improvements. Tell them I am with them and seek their prayers in my duties."

Solomon stared in silence, stunned by the request. The manager turned around. "I fear this is more than a shower—a storm. I must see that the ship leaves immediately. You will excuse me." The manager made for the door.

Solomon called after him, "We will pray. The church is open to you."

The ship had slipped its lines, and black smoke billowed from its stack. The captain had seen the storm clouds and knew his vessel was in danger. The ship moved slowly astern to where it could turn and put out to sea. But boilers take time to make steam when left on standby. Despite low steam pressure, the captain chose to risk slow speed in moving or certain loss in the shallows along the makeshift pier.

The manager stood on the beach and watched as the steamer slowly turned and pointed its bow towards deep water. The wind grew, howling through the coastal forest. He wrapped his arms around a tree and hung on. His face was soaked by driving rain. He struggled to clear his eyes. He watched helplessly as the ship was driven onto the reef, pushed by the wind, and fell on its side. The wind muted the sound of grinding metal and spilling cargo. He watched men in the water struggling against wind and wave, thrashed against cutting coral, trying desperately for shore. Only those who managed to stay with the wreck survived.

Five ships were lost in the early years of operation before a proven safe mooring station was built. New loading gantries were erected. A railroad was built from the mine to the new docking station. Work continued despite heavy losses by the company. One man, company founder John T. Arundel, would not give up on his vision. He believed in what could be accomplished. The grandson of the Home Secretary of the London Missionary Society, Arundel was convinced he was doing God's work. With the financial backing of his partner, Lord Stanmore, money flowed into the Ocean Island mine.

But Ocean Island was not alone. The Pacific Phosphate Company also mined nearby Nauru Island and Makatea Island in French Polynesia. With adequate infrastructure in place, the mines became profitable. Concerned with the Elders' complaints, Arundel amended his contracts to include royalties. He began with a penny and a half a ton. He agreed to restore the land after mining and protect the freshwater supplies. Hospitals were built, and a company doctor was assigned to each island.

In May of 1909, John Arundel, his wife, Eliza, known as Lilly, and their two younger daughters proudly greeted his eldest daughter, Lillian, as she arrived in Sydney harbor from England. It was the maiden voyage of a modern steamship built expressly for the Pacific Phosphate Company's trade. The

SS *Ocean Queen* was built in West Hartlepool, in the far Northeast of England. The ship was owned and operated by Captain Christian Johanessen on charter to Pacific Phosphate. Lillian Arundel christened the steamer as it slid down the shipway in December 1908. The young woman made the long voyage to Sydney, stopping to load mining equipment in Antwerp and twelve hundred tons of coal in South Africa.

Johanessen may have owned the ship, but it was built to Arundel's specifications. In addition to phosphate, the ship included first- and second-class staterooms for passengers. The *Ocean Queen* was three hundred and thirty-eight feet long and powered by a three hundred and forty-eight horsepower, triple expansion steam engine. She was admeasured at three thousand eighty-eight gross tons and drew just over sixteen feet draft when loaded. The *Ocean Queen* was equipped with refrigeration and electricity to the staterooms, pilot house, and engine room.

By all accounts, the adventurous Lillian Arundel enjoyed the cruise, and John agreed that he, Lilly, Lillian, and younger daughters, Dorothy and Sydney, would make the first company voyage. The plan was to load two thousand tons of phosphate at Ocean Island, off-load in Hawaii, steam to Polynesia to inspect a new project, sail to Makatea to load phosphate for Hawaii, and west to Nauru to load phosphate for Sydney.

The proud Arundel instructed Captain Johanessen to dress ship and parade around Ocean Island before docking. With signal flags strung from the masts, draping to the bow and stern, it appeared the King of Ocean Island had arrived. The European employees waited in their Sunday best to greet the boss and his family.

A LIGHT IN THE DARKEST NIGHT

"Welcome to Ocean Island," the General Manager called out as the Arundels appeared at the gangway. "If you will come with me, I have scheduled a small reception in your honor at the club, where you can meet your staff. This evening, after the ladies have had an opportunity to rest and refresh, the elders have arranged a feast in the village. I'm sure you will find it most entertaining."

The GM's plan was upended when the party encountered Pastor Solomon waiting at the door of the Company Club. "Excuse me, Mister Arundel, it is the pastor of the Banaba Congregational Church. I will deal with him."

The Manager did not wait for a reply. He faced Solomon and said, "Pastor Solomon, this is not the time. Mister Arundel has just arrived with his family. He is a very busy man. Perhaps tomorrow after he tours the mine...."

John Arundel interrupted, "Pastor Solomon? The man who sends me letters? I will make time to sit down with you, Pastor, for I am enheartened by your love for God and your people." Arundel then turned to Lilly. "Dear, you go in from this sun with the girls. I shall join you shortly."

The GM could not hide his displeasure, but he smiled and held the door for the Arundel women.

Pastor Solomon replied, "Sir, I shall not keep you from your wife's company and the fine reception planned for you. But I shall wait in the church. Perhaps after the reception we could talk?"

Arundel smiled and held out his hand. "I am pleased we meet at last. Yes, I shall come directly from this reception."

John Arundel walked to the new, freshly painted, cedar-planked church. He entered through a beautifully carved door

144

beneath a steeple topped with a cross. A man was on his knees praying before the altar. Pastor Solomon heard the footsteps, got off his knees, and turned to greet Mister Arundel. "I asked God for wisdom, and still I do not know what to say or how to explain.…"

Arundel walked to the front of the church and sat in a pew. "I have found that God meets us in our time of need. I have longed to meet you for some time. Your letters—I have kept them and read them—they question the good that I intend for your people and the people of Australia. I, too, have prayed. I know now that the rights given to the company were not understood and have led to regret. But I have partners and shareholders who will not allow us to give up those rights and leave this island."

Arundel glanced around the church. "There is a hardness to business where men risk money, often borrowed money, hoping for a good return. Little more could have been offered in the beginning because it could not be afforded. Remember the wrecks? The derailments? The injured workers? We saw no profits for several years. Since then, I have arranged for royalties and done my best to bring good things to your people—the doctor and hospital, the plentiful pigs and goats, and this church, a place to praise and worship God."

Solomon replied, "You gave things we did not need. We wish to return to our life before Albert Ellis came ashore with his black rock."

"So, you have told me time and again. But there can be no going back. The world knows the phosphate is here. If not Pacific Phosphate, then someone else. Therefore, I have made it my calling to give you a better life—better care, better education, better houses. Your people are paid a fair wage for their work, and the company store does not cheat you. In England, where I was born and raised, miners are a neglected people. Your people fare better than the miners of Wales."

Solomon looked into Arundel's eyes and asked, "Sir, you say you are a Godly man and seek only God's blessings for us. Answer me this: When the apostle Paul wrote, 'There is neither Jew nor Gentile, neither slave nor free, nor is there male or female, for you are all one in Christ Jesus.' do you, Mister Arundel, see the Banaba people, as 'children of God in faith, and baptized in Christ'?"

"Of course, I do. We shall sing praises together in glory."

Solomon shook his head. "Yes, in glory. But now? Saint Paul finishes the chapter by writing, 'If you belong to Christ, then you are Abraham's seed, and heirs according to the same promise.'"

John Arundel nodded. "Yes. All that you say is true."

"But we are not granted the same promise. You have made us slaves to the Pacific Phosphate Company. And now you would ask me to believe you are a slave to the same merciless master."

Arundel lowered his head.

Solomon continued. "The miners in Wales have a choice. I accept it is a difficult choice, but a choice to leave the mines. We have no choice. We are wholly dependent on the company. And we have no voice in our affairs."

"I will think on your words, Pastor Solomon. I can extend my visit and worship with you on Sunday,"

"I will not turn you away. But many will not welcome

you. Perhaps it is a good thing you would not understand our words. Our language is a freedom as few Europeans trouble themselves to learn it."

John Arundel rose. "I inspect the mine tomorrow. I will look at it with new eyes."

"I will pray for you. But I raise a new issue now: The water cave; Europeans do not enter the water caves. It is our custom. Only women may enter. They begin to go dry, and some water has turned foul."

"Then allow my daughter, Lillian, to view the cave on my behalf. The partners and shareholders will respect her word."

The next morning, while John Arundel was led on an inspection tour of the mine by the General Manager, Lillian Arundel was greeted at the church by Pastor Solomon and two young island women. Solomon introduced them, "Miss Arundel, these young ladies, Mary and Martha, have agreed to show you our water cave. This is a great honor, as I am sure they will tell you. They both studied hard and learned English. Only women may enter the cave. You will be the first outsider woman not born on Banaba to learn our secret."

Lillian smiled and reached out her hand. "Mary, Martha, I am honored." After shaking both women's hands, she added, "Thank you, Pastor Solomon, for arranging this outing. I feel I am about to find two new friends."

Mary commented, "Your dress is beautiful. I have seen none finer."

Lillian was immaculately attired in a purple dress with a high neck, puffed shoulder, double-buttoned front, long cuffed sleeves, and a billowing skirt to her ankles covered by high-top laced black leather shoes. She wore a matching wide-brimmed purple hat to keep the sun off her head and neck.

"How very kind. It is the latest fashion. Mother and Father insist I always look my best. I hope it is not too much. Your dresses look far more comfortable and practical."

Mary and Martha led Lillian down a well-worn path through the coastal forest. After twenty minutes, they turned onto another path inland. They came to a tall rocky outcropping where the forest met the interior brushland. Mary took a torch from the entrance to a cave, lit it, bent over, and ducked through a four foot high opening. Martha gestured for Lillian to follow. Lillian removed her hat and entered. The torch lit a small cavern. The air was cool and dank. Water could be heard dripping all around. "You must stay close to us. The cave is quite large, with many tunnels. You do not want to get lost in here," Martha's voice echoed.

Mary led them to the right. "What is the English word? Honeycombed? The passages interconnect, leading in every direction up and down. You will see. But first, we must undress."

Martha continued. "We leave our clothes in the next chamber, well out of sight of the entrance cavern, though Banaba men will not disturb us, we worry about the Europeans."

Mary added, "The General Manager heeds Pastor Solomon and has made the cave taboo. The company sends married men with families to manage the mine. They want, no.... What is the word? Frater... fraterni—no lovemaking between them and us."

The women stopped in a small chamber with a table

and bench. "It is very wet; we must pass through the water. We cannot ruin our Christian dresses."

Martha added, "Now we must buy them at the company store. White for church on Sunday and color as we desire for walking in the village or the store."

Mary chatted, "Of course, we wear our grass skirts at home. They are easy to make and much more comfortable."

Lillian stood and watched.

Mary said, "You are safe. You must not ruin your fine dress. It is the most beautiful dress I have ever seen. And such fine shoes."

Lillian nodded and set her wide-brimmed purple hat on the table. She began to unbutton. "You still wear grass skirts? Just a grass skirt? You do not find that immodest? What does Pastor Solomon say about this?"

"Modesty?" Mary asked. "A grass skirt is all the modesty we have ever needed. Our fathers and brothers know we are women and accept us as we are. Is it wrong to nurse a baby among your family? No, only Europeans must cover women from head to toe. European men look at us in a grass skirt and see lust."

Martha added, "We wear the dress when Pastor Solomon visits. But when he marries, he will learn. I intend that he marries me."

Mary gently pushed her sister, "You know, sister, it is me he will marry."

As the women made their way into the cave, passing through shallows and pools of clean, fresh water, Lillian asked, "The taboo, you hold to the old beliefs—only women may come here. You are Christian, yet you honor an old god?"

Mary answered, "We honor our ancestors, not the old

gods. Does not the commandment say, 'Honor your father and mother that your days may be long in the land that the Lord God is giving you?' We keep the taboo to honor all the mothers who brought the water from this cave before us."

Martha added, "This cave is a special place for our women. Our safe place. Here we can speak freely as women, sisters, and mothers. It is a precious thing we shall never surrender—"

Mary interrupted, "We still come. We say it is to move the pipe. We no longer must carry heavy buckets. A pump lifts the water to a tower outside. Well away from the women's cave. We are almost there. You will see."

Lillian followed the torch, and the cave opened into a large cavern around a bend. Water dripped from the ceiling. A vast pool lay before them. "Careful, Miss Arundel. It is very deep. There, see the hose? It attaches to a pipe through an airshaft. This is one of many deep pools. They change with the years and the season. There is one—we will show you—that is now foul with the black rock. We can never drink from it again."

The women retraced their steps and followed a new tunnel to another pool. The chamber smelled of garlic. "It is the water—it smells. If we take this water from the pool, it will not last. Very soon, scum will grow in it. Who could drink from such water? It is the mine above. I am certain of it. The mines will destroy our water cave."

John Arundel joined his wife and daughters in the passenger salon on board the *Ocean Queen*. "You must tell me how you spent your day," he asked.

Lilly replied, "We could not sit here and choke on the

phosphate dust. There was simply no fresh air, so while you and Lillian went your ways, I took Sydney and Dorothy ashore with me to the club."

Dorothy added, "The cook gave us a large bucket of ice to take with us for cool drinks in the shade of the island."

"Please, dear, do not tell me you took gin ashore. It would speak poorly of me to break the rules," John replied.

"No, John, the gin was in one of the lemonade jugs. The cabin steward carried the drinks for us."

Lillian stood and kissed her father's cheek. "Papa, they are such sweet people. And what Pastor Solomon says is true. There has been contamination. I saw a pool of water—it smelled of garlic. They say the water grows green scum when taken outside."

"The odor is phosphate gas and the scum is algae. What else did you learn?"

"Even the cost of clothes is too dear. They remember their history, their ancestors. They are Christian, but they honor their past. Sadly, they fear they have lost their home. They need a voice, Papa. You must give them a voice."

John Arundel sat down. "Pastor Solomon is their voice. His letters—and now that I have met him—I must acknowledge him before the General Manager. The water must be protected. The store—the cost of clothes…."

Sydney said, "Can't you give them sewing machines? One for the church and one for each tribe? I read that in America, country stores sell grain in cotton sacks printed with patterns. When they buy their flour or rice, they also receive fabric for clothes."

Eliza Arundel shook her head. "Clothes from sackcloth? How dreadful!"

Lillian said, "Mother, they would prefer grass skirts to what we sell them, yet they show us respect wearing those shapeless gowns. The mission society of our church provides better to the Aboriginals in the Outback."

John walked to the bar, dropped ice cubes into a glass, and poured a drink. "We finish loading tomorrow. I will speak with the GM before we sail. Pastor Solomon seeks an open door so the Banaba voice is heard in protecting their people and their island. From the beginning, I was convinced that this mine was good for Australia and good for the islanders. But now I learn I have made them healthy slaves."

Arundel walked to a window and stared out towards the island. "It really is a hellish place, good once only for nesting seabirds and now the guano they left behind. Its elevation is its only advantage against typhoons and unreliable rain. The people would be better off somewhere else—another island—fertile with good water, a lagoon filled with fish, and a safe anchorage. A place where never again would they nearly all perish from starvation or thirst. They could live on the fish and hogs, tend their taro and fruits, preserve their traditions, and protect their heritage in peace."

Lilly commented, "You describe Eden, an island paradise."

"That is your dream, Father, not theirs. This is their home. They desire no other. They have proven a peaceful and gracious people, but they would resist what you propose, resist vigorously," Lillian snapped.

"Lillian! Don't be cross with your father!"

John replied, "Object, yes, but once settled, they would adjust and find it all the better. And they are only five or six hundred. They have no power, and it is for the betterment of all."

Lillian shook her head. "Imagine the scandal! Do not think it just a scandal in Sydney where we are known, but the flag of Great Britain flies over the island! They are subjects of the King. No, Father, a voice, respect, and generosity—the generosity of a partnership. Take what can be safely mined and protect their water cave and coastal forest. Heal the land after the phosphate is stripped away. I don't know how, but you must promise. You cannot treat them as anything less than equals, as neighbors. Remember, perhaps angels of God walk among them."

Arundel walked to Lillian and kissed the top of her head. "What a blessing you are, Lillian, strong and wise."

In the privacy of their stateroom, wife Lilly said, "Dear, I know how you love Lillian, but is it wise to give her false hope? I have always stayed away from your business affairs, but I know you added many partners and shareholders in your efforts to raise capital. You do not control the company. You have made fortunes for many men. They shall not expect anything less."

"I must convince them."

The *Ocean Queen* sailed to Hawaii and offloaded two thousand tons of high-grade phosphate. Its first cargo sold, the ship sailed for Tahiti and then on to Makatea Island. Like Ocean Island and Nauru, Makatea was a high atoll island surrounded by a reef hard against the shore. The ship arrived off Makatea on September 15, 1909. By chance, it was King Edward's birthday. At breakfast, John said to Captain Johannessen, "Captain, what better way to honor the King's birthday than by dressing the ship and parading around the island before anchoring off the village of Moumu."

"Aye, Mister Arundel. We shall do just that!"

The crew went to work draping the signal flags and raising their largest Union Jack to the top of the mast. Halfway around the island, a loud groan of bending metal rose to the pilot house through the engine room voice tube. Soon after, the whistle on the voice tube sounded, and the Chief Engineer shouted, "Captain, we've lost power! Were checking her now, but it looks like a bent eccentric rod."

"Can you fix her, Chief? How long?"

"Aye, not an easy job. Best you put her to anchor!"

As the Chief Engineer spoke, the ship shook and shuddered. A loud grinding sound confirmed the *Ocean Queen* had drifted onto the reef. The seas and trade wind drove her hard up on the unforgiving coral. The bow rose, and the ship leaned to the starboard. The steamer went dead and, like a beached whale, took time to consider its predicament. And then the grinding resumed, and the ship began to slide back off the reef into the deep water surrounding it.

"Damage report! I want a damage report! Are we holed?!"

The Mate on watch sent crewmen scurrying to sound tanks and inspect the holds. Soon the worst was confirmed: The *Ocean Queen* was sinking.

The Arundels donned lifejackets as a lifeboat was lowered from its davit. The third officer took the helm as a dozen crewmembers rowed them ashore. The Captain, Chief Engineer, and the rest of the crew safely followed. An hour later, the *Ocean Queen* rested on the bottom under twelve hundred feet of water.

The Captain managed to send a wireless SOS. The

message of the impending sinking was acknowledged in Papeete. Two days later, an island trading schooner arrived, and the survivors set off for Papeete. The schooner offered none of the comforts of the *Ocean Queen*. Palm fans were replaced by the steady breeze of the trade wind as the sails carried the schooner along on a comfortable beam reach. Gone was the methodical thumping of the massive pistons of the steam expansion engine. It was a quiet time of soothing sounds: The occasional flapping of the sails, singing of the wind through the rigging, lyrical notes of tropical water sliding against the sleek hull, and muted French voices of crewmen who knew their work.

John reassured Captain Johannessen that a charter contract would wait for him once he settled with Lloyds of London. Johannessen knew replacing his ship would take a year under the best circumstances.

Lillian viewed the events as a warning. "Papa, you are the best hope of the Banaba people. You have been spared—given an opportunity to finish a good work."

John smiled. "I thank God that my family is safe. But as to a warning, my dear Lillian, risk in business is common, not rare. The good captain would say the same. Five ships, yes, five ships sank off the reefs of Ocean Island before a proper mooring system could be built. Ship sinkings, train derailments, and catastrophes like typhoons and droughts—acts of God—all are common to man. We will continue. It is time we returned to London. I will consult with the partners as you desire. Your mother convinces me that London offers greater prospects for successful marriages for you and your sisters."

"Papa, I am not looking for a husband!"

"Of course not, dear, but doesn't the Good Lord desire helpmates for his faithful children?"

Dorothy and Sydney replied in unison, "London! We're going to London!"

In Papeete, the Arundel family boarded the steamship *Mariposa* bound for San Francisco. A cross-continent train ride to New York would cut weeks from the voyage to London. They arrived in a bustling port, the city alive with rebuilding not two years after the devastating San Francisco earthquake and fire. "You see, Lillian, a disaster does not stop the industry of men. The energy, yes, the energy to rebuild better than before. Perhaps this, too, is a gift of God. He created so we, too—created in His image—can create. Spirit and energy, Lillian. Spirit and energy!"

"Rebuild a city, Papa, but can you rebuild an island? Make it green and lush? How long? And what of the people in the meantime?"

John's energy was short-lived. He suffered a heart attack in San Francisco. By the grace of God, he lived. The doctors were emphatic: "Mister Arundel, you must slow down! You will not survive another."

"Papa, now will you listen?" Lillian asked.

In London, John Arundel called on his friend and partner, the first Baron Stanmore, Arthur Charles Hamilton Gordon, at his Chelsea home. Their partnership went back over thirty years when Gordon was the Governor of Fiji and High Commissioner of the Western Pacific. Before he was installed as Lord Stanmore, Arthur Gordon partnered with the entrepreneurial Arundel in founding the Pacific Island Company, now the mammoth Pacific Phosphate Company. Gordon provided the government approvals and licenses, while Arundel brought business acumen and capital raising ability.

The men took their drinks in the library, filled with treasures gathered over a thirty-year career that included Lieutenant Governor of New Brunswick; Governor of Trinidad; Governor of British Mauritius; First High Commissioner of the Western Pacific; Governor of Fiji; Governor of New Zealand, and Governor of British Ceylon. Cambridge educated and politically connected, he was a lifelong collector of native art. His Fiji collection was the finest in England.

John Arundel stopped in front of the black rock which for years served as a doorstop in the Sydney office of the Pacific Island Company before Albert Ellis suspected it was phosphate and took it for chemical analysis. Lord Stanmore asked, "What is so urgent that you must speak to me before the board meeting?"

John stared at the black rock. "What a journey this rock has taken us on, Lord Arthur."

"It has made us and many others rich."

"A fortune to last many lifetimes." John turned to Stanmore. "I think we could do better. We must do better for the islanders. The people of Ocean Island where I visited, and the others as well—on Nauru and Makatea. In truth, they are partners, silent partners, and poorly paid."

"So, you have become sentimental in your old age. The heart attack has you thinking of your legacy, of your grandfather's missionary zeal. We had this discussion years ago. Be rational, my friend. Answer these questions: Do the islanders eat better now than before? Their diet has been supplemented with healthy food not subject to drought or poor fishing. Are they healthier? They have access to a doctor and hospital. Childbirth is safer. Smallpox and fevers are all distant memories. They have clothes and all the tools to care for their houses—substantial houses, better than an open thatched roof. A school where they learn to read and write—"

John interrupted, "The mission society built the church and school."

"But our lease pays for improvements. John, we have improved their lives. They are far ahead of the unfortunate islanders without phosphate or copra plantations. More money? It is as Ellis quoted their Elder, 'What need do we have of more money? To paper our walls?' Tell me, John, what need have we not met?"

"The need to be heard. The need to be respected—and to be treated fairly. They seek justice and freedom."

"They are free subjects of the King."

Lord Stanmore walked to a chair and set his drink on the side table. "Sit down, John. Enjoy the brandy. It's my best."

Arundel sat across from Lord Stanmore and sipped his drink. Stanmore continued, "I am glad you came to me first. The board members—good men who look to the future of our enterprise—this is their opportunity, their reward. God knows the Colonial Office doesn't pay them enough. You ask them to give from their future, the education and opportunities for their children, to shower extreme wealth onto primitive people with no real need? And the special category—men who ensure our interests are understood in government? No, John, we must not hinder or alarm our friends."

John sighed. "I have left orders for the GM on Ocean Island...."

"I know of these orders. Protecting the island water cave makes good business sense. But the royalty will not change, and there shall be no talk of partnership. Their pastor has the open door to the GM, as you directed. Our man will listen and do what he can while ensuring maximum productivity."

Lillian was waiting for her father when he returned home. John read her face and said, "The water cave will be protected. It makes good sense for everyone. Pastor Solomon will always have an open door with the manager who will do his best to see to the general welfare of the islanders."

Lillian asked, "A voice? Justice and a fair profit for what you do to their island?"

John walked past her and sat down. "The royalty remains one and a half pence per ton. There will be no change in the lease, no talk of partnership. The board, the Colonial Office, and the government officials will abide no changes."

"The Colonial Office? What interest...." Lillian trailed off then: "They are board members and shareholders. Government officials... you pay them?!"

"It's not like that! Yes, they invest, and some are members of the board. Others are reimbursed for services, services not otherwise provided by the government." John looked at his daughter and shook his head at her dismay. "I'm tired, my dear. I'm going to bed. You must realize the islanders shall always have sufficient food, medical care, and the opportunity for education. The company stands by it. Isn't that enough?"

The next day Lillian took a cab to Whitehall, to George Gilbert

A LIGHT IN THE DARKEST NIGHT

Scott's massive neo-classical monument to the British Empire, the Foreign and War Office building. As she climbed the grand staircase, she studied the ornate mosaics of its dome. A golden sun blazed at the center, its rays piercing a dark blue star-studded sky to the twelve zodiac signs. The dome's base was appropriately encircled by twenty classically robed female figures fronted by shields of twenty great nations of the world. She thought: *Countries represented by women, if only that were true!*

Lillian went down a long corridor to the records room of the Colonial Office. A helpful clerk directed her to the Western Pacific Commissioner's records. Notebook in hand, she went to work. After some weeks, she turned her attention to Australia and New Zealand. She learned to navigate through offices, directorates, and administrative reports of the business of returning colonial money to mother England.

The strong-willed young woman would not see any of the suitors her parents arranged, so when she agreed to accompany her father to the offices of Pacific Phosphate to hear a report of a company officer returning from Ocean Island, John was delighted. He arranged for several aspiring young men to show her about to her heart's content.

The officer reported Ocean Island remained as it was when Lillian had visited. The water cave was declared off-limits to mining. Pastor Solomon was recorded as a frequent visitor to the office. After the meeting, the eager young men escorted Lillian to various offices. A tall young accountant greeted her warmly, "Gah'day, Miss Arundel."

Lillian looked into his blue eyes and asked, "Sydney?"

"No, ma'am, North Queensland, tropical Cairns."

"Well, gah'day to you, too, Mister...?"

"Thompson, Robert Thompson. Friends call me Bob."

"Well, Bob from Cairns, I want to please my father and show him some knowledge of figures. Can you help me?"

When she returned home, she had a list of the board members, special category agents, and profit statements.

Two days later, Lillian accepted a call from Robert Thompson. The couple took long walks through the park and caught popular shows, but they spent Saturday afternoons at the library. Bob always carried Lillian's book bag. Lillian never checked out a book. They found a table in a quiet corner, opened her book bag filled with notebooks, and worked. After several months Lillian and Bob took a cab to Fleet Street.

The London New Age newspaper headline read: *Modern Buccaneers in the West Pacific.* London was alerted to a scandal. Officials of the Colonial Office turned a blind eye to stealing rich resources from islanders on Ocean Island, Nauru, and Makatea in return for fifty pounds sterling a year, for nine hundred and ninety-nine years. The in-depth expose by an anonymous correspondent called out the recently deceased Lord Stanmore and many commissioners and officials of the Colonial Office for enabling the Pacific Islands Company, 'The Swindler' Albert Ellis and many others, for decades of plundering the resources of the colonies under British protection. Official documents were quoted. The quality of the phosphate, market prices, and reserves proved to be more than forty million pounds were made public. The capitalization of the initial investors was less than seventeen hundred pounds, with another two hundred and fifty thousand paid by investors seeking shares. The paper demanded an investigation. It sought a response from the

Colonial Office and action by Parliament.

The scandal was the talk of London. The international press picked up the story. It was published in the New York Times. Lillian and Robert waited. Her father was not named in the report, but he fell into a deep depression and self-imposed isolation. Time passed, and nothing happened. The Colonial Office did not respond. The officials named made no comments. Parliament took no action. Public records could identify Colonial officials and company board members, but shareholders are secret. The empire brought wealth to England. In the end, that was its purpose.

Inaccessible to Lillian and Robert, conversations took place—not in the chambers of Parliament or committee rooms of Whitehall, but in the smoking rooms of the private clubs. The embarrassment had to be dealt with painlessly and profitably. The solution was not foretold in the press or debated on the floor of the House of Commons. In 1919, after the death of John Arundel, Parliament quietly established the Board of the British Phosphate Commission, which purchased all the shares of the Pacific Phosphate Company for more than three and a half million pounds. The secret investors made good and forever hid their culpability in cheating and despoiling good Christian subjects under the Crown's protection.

The government of New Zealand was responsible for administering Ocean Island and Nauru. Each island saw a slight increase in the royalty payment. The wages of the islanders remained the same. Prices in the company store were raised. Company managers were replaced with bureaucrats, some good but with no incentive to improve life on the islands. After abandoning the islanders to Japanese occupation and torture in World War II and refusing to raise the longstanding pay of ten pounds a month, the Banaba workers went on strike in 1948. The British Phosphate Commission replaced the strikers with Chinese laborers and coerced the Banaba people into resettlement on Rabi Island in the Fijis, where most remain today.

In the 1970s, Australians and New Zealanders with a conscience aided the Banaba people in a lawsuit against the British government's Phosphate Commission. After years of litigation, the court found a trust agreement existed but claimed it was not equivalent to a modern trust, so while finding for the Banaba people, it awarded them only one pound. The Banabans were not even awarded their legal costs of over three hundred thousand pounds. A public outcry in New Zealand prodded the government to authorize seven hundred eighty thousand pounds in reparation but refused to help the islanders exiled to Rabi Island. The Banabans persevered and returned to court. In 1981, the Banabans settled with the United Kingdom and accepted $10 million Australian, far short of the billions stolen from them, in return for no future claims.

Banaba Island has never seen restoration. Over eighty percent of the island has been strip-mined. All the water caves are polluted. A few hundred Banaba people live among the abandoned buildings and derailed train cars. Rusted loading derricks lean in mourning over the reef.

Lillian and Robert never saw the final desolation of what the islanders always called Banaba Island. They married and settled down to raise a family.

In the tropical sea off the coast of Queensland,

A LIGHT IN THE DARKEST NIGHT

Australia, the magnificent, tall, namesake trees of Palm Island leaned gracefully against the steady trades, their leafy palms synchronized in an ancient dance to the timeless rhythms of wind and waves. Their thatched-roofed island home captured the fragrance of the red blossomed flame trees, mangoes, and tapioca.

Robert walked up from the beach with two giant Pacific Spiny Lobsters. Dripping wet, he stepped through the door.

"Dinner tonight, Lil," he called, holding the lobsters up for her inspection.

The swish of her skirt was heard as she turned to look, "Beautiful, dear."

Bob drank in the beauty of his wife dressed in her house clothes, a simple grass skirt, and a lei of flowers. "You promised me that a man becomes accustomed to his wife's grass skirt. My dear, 'accustomed' does not describe what I see. I am forever smitten."

Lil hugged Bob and kissed him gently. "I am so glad we returned to civilization."

THE ROOT OF TERROR

It was a warm spring day. The noon sun was shining high in the bright blue sky. The air was fragrant with blossoms. The forest floor was carpeted in the Royal Bourbon blue of wild woodland phlox. The spring flowers rejoiced in the dappled sunlight filtered by blossoming hardwood trees in King Louis' Royal Forest surrounding Compiegne in Northeastern France. Andre Le Pen came through the door of the Le Coq tavern and walked directly to his usual table.

"Beer, *garcon*," he called out as he passed the seated waiter near the bar.

"Citizen *serveur*, Citizen! I am not a boy. I am your equal!"

The innkeeper brought the beer instead of the server. "Why do you badger him, Monsieur Le Pen?"

"Equal in rights, equal under the law, *oui*, but I am paying for his service. What has become of hard work and good service in France? Offense! Everyone is quick to take offense. For paying customers there is no longer a smile, only scowls and indifferent service."

"*Mon ami*, you want service with a smile? Ask with a smile."

Le Pen sighed. "Of course, you are correct. What is his name?"

"Paul."

Le Pen raised his mug and called, "Innkeeper, a beer for Citizen Paul!"

Just then, three men entered and came to Le Pen's table. Armand D'Argonne spoke first. "Atoning for your sins, Andre? A beer for Paul? You undoubtedly offended him as you do so many."

"You must address your equal as *Citizen* Paul, Citizen Armand!"

Claude Mulot de la Menadiere pulled a chair and said, "Citizens Claude and Emile will also have beers."

"Three more beers, Henri."

Henri, the innkeeper, smiled and bowed before walking to the bar.

Le Pen turned to Emile Fallot. "Nothing to contribute to this sparkling conversation, Emile?"

"Have you heard the news? All Catholic churches have become state property. The civil constitution declares we have freedom of religion but the National Assembly targets the Catholics."

Armand D'Argonne replied, "Emile, what is that to you? We know you're protestant. We've all known it since our days at the Sorbonne. The Catholics prospered under the *Ancien Régime*. Your Huguenots were persecuted. It's time they received their due!"

Andre added, "I have heard you say that the church grows from the blood of martyrs and prospers in persecution—"

Emile cut him off. "It's dangerous. The National

Assembly turns on its own. It was the parish priests who stood against their bishops that gave us our constitution. First, the oath, requiring all clergy to put France, the state, above the church—an oath condemned by the pope. It is one thing for a priest to question his bishop but to renounce the pope? And now this! It is to say that the church is a mere branch of the government. That is good for no one."

"Le Pen looked around. Keep your voice down. Others may misconstrue your concerns. Claude, you are a faithful Catholic—your sister is a nun."

"My cousin, not my sister."

"What does she say? What will happen to the convents?"

Mulot leaned low over the table and whispered, "They dissent. They have been ordered to renounce their vows and return home. In the meantime, they are wards of the state— the churches, monasteries, and convents, all state property. The pope has issued a *charitas* proclaiming priests taking the oath as schismatic. When King Louis took communion from a non-jurring priest—well, it has come to no good."

Andre nodded. "Other voices, outside, extreme voices steer the National Assembly and force their interpretations on the good work of the constitution. Liberty, equality, and fraternity have a different meaning for the radicals among us."

Armand shook his head. "The Catholic church has had its intolerant foot on the neck of Frenchmen long enough. I won't shed any tears."

Andre replied, "Easy for you, an atheist, to say—"

Armand interrupted. "Robespierre's Supreme Being of the deists may be harmless enough. A God who never gets in my way—makes no demands. Why, I can be spiritual with a God I create...."

Andre continued: "Claude and Emile are right. First the Catholics, then who? Jews? Protestants? The Aristocracy? Anyone with wealth? Anyone who has what they want? I am not the Christian I should be, but I, too, worry."

Andre Le Pen sighed. "I must write something. Others must see the danger. But I must be careful. Claude, will you write to your cousin and ask her what the sisters will do, what we should do? I will publish their call in my newspaper, 'The Liberty,' anonymously, of course."

Claude nodded. "If it helps, I will do as you ask."

Armand shook his head. "You seek to undo all that we have accomplished? You would turn your back on the Declaration of the Rights of Man?"

"No, Armand. I stand by the Declaration. Those who steer the assembly walk away from the rights declared. Beware, any man, or must I say, Citizen, who does not speak the new language of the radicals. Liberty is not for everyone—not Catholic priests, nuns, or monks—not for any Christian who puts God before Caesar. The king is captive and denied communion by a Catholic priest! Equality is not universal. The new ruling class decides who owns the treasure of France. Fraternity? Where suspicion and judgment silence the people? We—Claude, Emile, and I—must whisper our fears."

"Where you three see conspiracy, I see new opportunity. Perhaps small mistakes will be made, but great strides are being made for all of France!" Armand stared at his three speechless friends. "It's time we ordered our lunch. I have things to do."

There was no more talk of politics as the men ate. Afterward, they filed out, back into the new order of France. Andre lingered at the door then turned to Paul. "Friend, forgive my earlier rude remarks. You are a proud man, now working as a waiter. I have time to listen if you would share your story."

Paul looked up and replied, "It is a familiar story. You now surmise I have lost employment. Yes, it is true. I was a gardener, a vine dresser, at the King's Compiegne Palace. The king is imprisoned in Paris. No one pays us. We—all the servants—housekeepers, gardeners, craftsmen, yes, artists and musicians—must make our way in the world. Gardens, the arts, and all signs of wealth are dangerous. Henri saw pity on me, though this tavern cannot support two families."

"Citizen Paul, if a vine dresser to the King's Palace were a willing learner, he could perhaps assist a newspaper publisher? Can you read and write?"

Paul shook his head and answered, "No."

"Well, no matter. A master craftsman always has an eye for only his best effort."

"I can draw. Yes, my drawings are very good."

Le Pen turned to Henri. "Henri, you cannot keep a newspaper illustrator as a waiter. Allow Paul to work for me."

"Take him. He eats like a horse."

Paul jumped to his feet. "A newspaper illustrator, yes, I can do that. I will come with you now!"

Henri shouted after them: "Wait! Do not forget your wages, my friend!"

Le Pen led Paul to the newspaper shop. Inside, Andre said, "Don't get comfortable. We have work to do." He quickly grabbed a sketchpad, notebook, and pencils. "We're going to the palace and the gardens."

They followed the main street to a wide lane through the thick forest over a mile to the Chateau Compiegne, centuries ago a simple hunting lodge, but of late the third palace of the king. The road joined half a dozen straight hunting lanes at a garden fronting the palace, where a small guardhouse provided shelter to a lone guard. "The people's Chateau Compiegne is closed by order of the National Convention. There is nothing to see. Go home."

Andre approached and said, "I am Andre Le Pen of the newspaper 'The Liberty.' I have come to report the good work that you do. All of Compiegne, all of France should know that the king's wealth is safely in the hands of the revolution! Citizen...?"

"Beliveau, my name is Jacques Beliveau. Yes! Nothing has been taken on my watch."

Andre nodded. "So the palace is filled with treasure?"

The guard replied, "Most of the furnishings remain, though some citizens liberated draperies, bed cloths, and kitchen wares before a guard was posted."

"The king owes his subjects far more. I see no funds are wasted on frivolous show gardens and fountains."

Beliveau nodded. "Better to be used as pasture. The fruit trees could stay."

"I see no gardeners to prune them. I see no workers at all."

"No, Citizen. They have been sent home. It was lucky for me to be given this job. I worked in the armory and was familiar with weapons and locks."

"What good fortune! My illustrator was also in service.

No longer a vinedresser, he draws for me. Permit him to sketch. All should know that the revolution has relieved the nation of the king's greed."

Turning to Paul, Andre said, "Draw as it is, not as it was. Show what two years of neglect have brought. And then we shall inspect your vines."

Andre watched Paul sketch. "Indeed, you do have talent! The boards across the doors and windows should be accentuated. Our readers must feel the sad state of disrepair. Do the same with the overgrown garden with dead shrubs. Enlarge the words painted over the grand entrance: *Liberté, Egalité, Fraternité*. Everyone must know this is a property of the citizens."

With the sketch complete, they walked around the palace to the opposite garden. A small vineyard was planted alongside a walled kitchen garden. The doors to the garden were gone. The beds were overgrown with weeds. Paul walked to the vineyard. "It cannot be! Look at them! Dying, all of them."

He came closer and knelt by a vine. "It is worse than I imagined. A few old clusters, dried. Of course, for lack of pruning. But the grapes have black rot, and worse, what is this? Half dead. The vine is nearly dead!"

Deadwood was piled along the rows of vines. Paul pushed some away, following the old growth vine to the root. Tall weeds encircled each vine where the root crown entered the earth. He pulled at the grass and then noticed the blood dark caps of mushrooms. "No! There is rot in the ground." The bark at the root crown was covered with thick white fans of fungus. The bark was soft and tore away at his touch. He scraped at the earth, digging down along the tap root. Black threads, like shoestrings, followed the roots from vine to vine. Vines, hundreds of years old, were infected. All would soon be dead.

Paul could not stop the tears. "My family tended these vines for generations. They produced for us, for the good and the bad. Such foolish waste!"

Paul turned to Andre standing behind him. "It's not just this vine; this garden is dying. The palace is dying. Our city, Compiegne, is dying. France is dying. Tell me, Monsieur Le Pen, has God sent a plague upon us? A plague we call the revolution?"

Andre shook his head and answered: "I fear it is a plague, and worse is to come. But do not blame God. No, my friend, the fungus growing in France is rooted deep below the ground. Satan has pushed it to the surface and seeks to spread his evil among us."

Le Pen extended an arm to help Paul up. "Come, we have work to do."

A few days before Easter, the Compiegne Liberte's headline read: *The End of the King's Extravagance*. Paul's illustrations of the palace, the weed-choked garden, and the dead vineyard filled the page. Andre's story proclaimed: "The good people of Compiegne no longer depend on the palace wages but are now freed to find other work. Why, one man is now a *chateau* guard! Your newfound freedom makes you equal to all other Frenchmen to wander the roads searching for work, food, and shelter. But this warning, do not seek help from the church as clergy, nuns, and monks have nothing to give. They are your equals! Do not submit to their works of mercy. Strength and endurance are your only path forward."

Andre was awakened by church bells calling parishioners to the early Easter mass. He turned over, covered his ears with his pillow, and went back to sleep. An hour later, the bells again tolled. *The second mass*, he told himself. But the bells were ringing differently. They were not ringing a joyful Easter celebration. They were ringing wildly, madly like a fire alarm. Andre sat up. He could hear shouting and clamor from the street below. He ran to the window, opened the curtains, and looked out. He could see a large crowd in the street. Rows of wagons driven by men with the armband of the revolution were stopped in front of Saint Jacques Church. A cordon of guards blocked parishioners from entering. Soon, other revolutionary guards appeared carrying altarpieces, statues, silver communion plates, chalices, vestments, pictures, and every kind of item from the church. As each wagon was loaded, it drove off down the main street towards the boulevard of Chateau Compiegne towards the forlorn palace in the woods.

Andre dressed and rushed down and out to the street. He saw Paul standing across from the church sketching. "Good, keep sketching," Andre told him and Paul nodded and kept working.

Andre saw the mayor standing alongside a uniformed officer near the church. "*Bonjour*, Charles, or shall I say Lord Mayor...?"

"Citizen Mayor. We are all equal. I serve the people."

"Why the wagons, Citizen Mayor? The citizens are in an uproar."

"Nothing to be alarmed at Citizen Le Pen. The state merely collects its property to safeguard it until it can be sold."

"Sold? You would sell the sacred objects of the church?"

"As I said, state property to be sold. War has been declared on Austria. Money will be needed for the army." The mayor coldly stared into Andre's eyes. "Have you not written that our citizens seek work to feed their families? The army will be paid its wages."

"Where will people worship?"

The mayor smiled. "They have freedom of religion. But the state need not grant religious preference or provide property. And, of course, all clergy must take the oath of fidelity to the revolution."

"The abbeys and the convents?"

"They, too, are state property."

Andre asked, "Saint Anthony Church, Saint Germain Church, and Our Lady of Great Hope?"

"Of course. Wagons are there as well. There is a decree—every church in France is to transport its treasures today for the state's sale."

Andre asked, "The wagons drive to the *chateau*—the palace furnishings…?"

"Yes, they will be sold as well."

Le Pen asked, "Who has money?"

"Why there are the English, Dutch, Italian and Spanish nobility. The French nobility will be quiet about it and, of course, the *nouveaux riches*. They have been waiting to use their wealth."

"You speak of members of the National Convention, new ministers, and municipal officials, no doubt."

"You should be more careful, Le Pen. Perhaps you are not aware of the Committee of Public Safety. They have little patience for enemies of the revolution."

The church bells of Compiegne fell silent. Easter would not be celebrated for years.

Andre sat in the Le Coq Tavern eating lunch with Emile Fallot, Claude Mulat, and Armand D'Argonne.

Armand said, "Andre, do not push too hard, my friend. The mayor has warned you. He is right about the Committee of Public Safety. They are quick to arrest anyone who speaks against the revolution. The accused are tried before a court of three judges by a prosecutor named Antoine Fouquier Tinville. Everyone accused is found guilty and sent to the guillotine that very day."

Emile added, "What Armand says is true. Whole families are tried together. Fifty people were beheaded in one day. Their bodies were carted to the nearby Chanoinesses de Saint Augustine convent and thrown into a large, deep pit. They plan on many executions."

Andre nodded. "Death is the great equalizer. In that alone, they are right. Tell me, Claude, have you written your cousin the nun? What does she say? Is she still in the convent?"

Claude nodded. "Yes, for now, they can stay at the convent, though it has been searched and everything but their clothes have been taken. Again, they were told to renounce their vows and go home."

"So the convent has not been shuttered like the churches, after all."

Claude added, "Even the protestant churches! Perhaps they fear the nuns that raised and disciplined them. Or perhaps they fear the people who value them; priests hold authority by ordination and position, but nuns and brothers earn respect through serving and acts of mercy so—"

"Never was mercy more needed than now," Emile interrupted.

Armand shook his head. "These things are necessary. Yes, one must be careful with his words, but a new France is being born. Those who oppressed us or stood in the way of the revolution will pay the price, but the innocent have nothing to fear."

The revolution's campaign to de-Christianize France continued. In August, the Carmelites of Compiegne were again ordered to renounce their vows and leave the convent immediately. They stayed. In September, the gendarmes marched to the Carmel of Compiegne Convent and evicted the community. They were forced to change out of their habits and don civilian clothes. The convent was boarded and shuttered. None of the community renounced their vows. All of them found secret refuge in private homes in Compiegne.

Forty-five miles to the south, in Paris, at the Place du Trone-Renverse, a guillotine was erected in the middle of a large square. From morning until evening, the most hardened Parisiens cheered the bloody executions of their neighbors. The following January, the King and Queen of France placed their necks beneath the great steel blade. Their bloodied bodies joined those of their subjects that preceded them in filling the pit. Two men were feared by every citizen of France, Maximilien Robespierre and Antoine Tinville.

Mother Teresa of St. Augustine, the prioress, led the community of sixteen: Eleven nuns, three lay sisters, and two externs. Even in hiding, there were no defections, no renunciation of vows. The many good Christians of Compiegne protected the sisters, for surely their faces were well known. The sisters, now dependent upon the charity of others, lived and served quietly.

At the Le Coq tavern, the four friends met as was their habit.

Andre was passionate. "The Declarations of the Rights of Man, the foundation of the revolution, has been set aside by the self-righteous Robespierre! Freedom of religion? Gone! He hates Christ. He hates all who worship Christ. And now that he has banned Christian worship, shuttered churches and abbeys, he establishes his cult of the Supreme Being! Yes, in Notre Dame, which he calls 'The Temple of Reason,' he has built an altar to himself and his favorite philosophers! Where are mercy and justice? I tell you, the sisters and brothers do more for the people in secret than any member of his Committee of Public Safety! And what safety? Whose safety? The usurpers, the elite bourgeoisie and self-deluding philosophers!"

"Quiet, friend. You may be heard," Armand warned.

Emile leaned in. "Our neighbors agree. Christians, Catholic and protestant alike, still meet and pray. Christ's Church can never be destroyed. Fellowship, building up one another in faith. Why, even Mother Teresa hides in a protestant house; what better protection for her identity." Emile winked as he finished.

Andre turned to Claude and asked, "Your cousin, Sister Euphrasia, you said how she corresponded with priests and informed Christians throughout France. Does she have news? Will there be resistance?"

Claude looked both ways and whispered, "She says

A LIGHT IN THE DARKEST NIGHT

God is working. Yes, He works in mysterious ways! Robespierre's Supreme Being cult is unpopular with the Committee. They have no desire to substitute Robespierre's Supreme Being for the God and Father of our Lord Jesus Christ. They would have no god at all. Also, rebellions continue. How many have there been since Vendee, or in Paris alone? There is talk that Orleans will be next. The radicals fight each other and the people. It is only a matter of time before God's judgment, His wrath, is poured out."

Armand's eyes widened. He took a deep breath and said, "Your cousin has letters? Proof of such things?"

"Sister Euphrasia has a curious mind. She writes to many seeking spiritual guidance. But she obeys Mother Teresa and gives her letters to the prioress."

Armand shook his head. "It is of no matter. Rumors, only rumors. I urge you all, my friends, take care. Stay away from these Christian meddlers. A thousand years of meddling has brought severe justice on their own heads. Now, I have an appointment. We shall meet again next week."

As Armand was leaving, Andre said to Emile, "See which way our friend walks."

Emile watched from the door and returned. "Armand went to City Hall."

Andre turned to Claude and said, "You should warn Sister Euphrasia. And speak no more of her to Armand."

Claude turned white. "You fear Armand will betray us? After all these years?"

"I think it best you say no more of the sisters to Armand—until we know."

The following day, the 22nd of June 1794, Compiegne police

searched Emile's house and arrested Mother Teresa. They recovered the correspondence of Sister Euphrasia, who was also arrested. Soon all sixteen members of the Compiegne Carmel were in custody.

Andre confronted the mayor at City Hall. "Women, harmless women. Good women! Full of mercy and compassion. All have been arrested! Where are they? What have you done to them? Who demands this evil thing and on what authority?"

The mayor stood from his desk. "Get out! Or you shall join them. Your so-called 'good women' are, in truth, seditious corruptors of the revolution. Yes, they have been accused, along with your friend Claude Mulot."

Le Pen was shocked. "Claude? Claude Mulot arrested? He is a threat to no one."

The mayor replied, "Letters! Evidence. He conspires with these unrepentant nuns to foment rebellion. He is their priest and a leader of their conspiracy."

"A priest? No. Claude Mulot is married. I have known him from our days at the Sorbonne. A good Catholic, yes. But he is not a priest. Who brings these false accusations? Let him come forward publicly and with proof!"

"It is enough for you to know they have been accused, and the evidence has been sent to the Committee for Public Safety in Paris. I caution you, Le Pen, your meddling in this affair will be noted. We know all about you. We know you have abandoned the revolution, just as Mulot and Emile Fallot have. Only fraternity and your past dedication to liberty and reason protect you. Heed my warning."

Andre was struck dumb. He stared at the man he had grown up with. Finally, Andre said softly, "Charles, it is written: 'Come let us reason together....' But I fear all hope for reasoning is lost. I have heard your warning. Tell me, if you please, where are the accused being held? Perhaps I can be of some use in comforting their families."

The mayor sat down. "They are held at the prison that was the Convent of the Visitation."

As Andre left, he thought, *No mention of Armand. Armand D'Argonne is the accuser.*

Andre found Paul at the newspaper, and together they went to the former Convent of the Visitation. The governor of the prison would not allow visitors. Le Pen persuaded the warden that he be allowed to view the prisoners to ensure they were indeed the accused. As the sisters were paraded in front of him, they spoke their names. Andre insisted on hearing both their cloister name and given family name. Paul sketched each as Andre attempted a few questions 'in the way of clarification and confirmation of identity.' The guard permitted biographical questions such as hometown, date, place of cloister entry, and family connections.

A bruised and beaten Claude Mulot was the last paraded before him. Andre struggled to hold back tears when he saw his friend. "Is that you, Claude? Claude Mulot?"

"Andre, my friend, tell my wife I love her and I always have. Always."

Andre lowered his head. "God is merciful, my friend. May you find grace and mercy. I shall tell your wife. And I promise you justice! I shall bring your accuser, Armand D'Argonne, to justice!"

Mulot mumbled, "Armand, a Judas? May he find the same fate."

Outside the prison, Andre flipped through the sketches. "Good, you captured them well, my friend. I will print these this afternoon... and tonight we move the printing press."

It was past midnight when Andre and Paul loaded his small printing press into a wagon and drove to the city wharves. At the far end in the reedy shallows of the River Oise, a small sailing barge was tied to a planked pier. A man emerged at the wagon's arrival and helped Paul and Andre carry the press aboard. The sailing barge was even less a boat than a scow. Its flat bottom and low sides bent slightly inward, forward and aft from amidships to the squared bow and stern. A folding mast a little taller than a man was fitted forward of an aft cabin. The boat, about thirty feet in length, was perfect for navigating the shallows of French rivers. The printing press was not set in the open forward hold. Instead, it was placed in the cabin, out of sight.

The captain of the boat reminded Andre, "My cargo will be loaded by noon. Be here then. I will not wait for you."

The headlines of the Compiegne Liberty announced, "Sisters of Carmel Arrested. Citizen Armand D'Argonne accuses sixteen nuns of plotting to bring down the National Assembly and insists these 'seditious sisters' tricked naive Compiegne citizens into hiding them. Married citizen Claude Mulot was arrested as a priest ringleader. Can this be justice?"

The sketches, stoic faces of the sisters, well known in the small city of eight thousand for their acts of charity, were printed below the headlines. Andre Le Pen and his illustrator Paul were not found when the mayor ordered their arrest.

A LIGHT IN THE DARKEST NIGHT

Emile Fallot escorted Claude's wife to safety to a small farmhouse along the River Oise. Within days, Armand D'Argonne was forced to flee Compiegne, his house burned to the ground. Two weeks later, after repeated violent protests, the mayor sent the sisters and Claude Mulot to Pairs for trial.

Marie Mulot joined Andre and Paul on the floating press and sailed down the River Oise to where it joined the Seine in the suburbs of Paris. The small sailing barge was soon lost among the countless barges tied three and four deep along the Paris banks of the Seine. The forward cargo hold was filled with bundles of rag paper safely covered by an ordinary black tarp. Indistinguishable among the river barges, Andre's sailing scow moved unnoticed daily along the river and canals. The cargo in the hold shrank as nightly André and Paul carried off pamphlets to be posted and distributed throughout Paris.

The headline shouted: "The Innocents!" Smaller sketches of the nuns and Claude illustrated the story. "Accused of serving God and the poor of Compiegne." The story asked, "Is it a crime in France to remain faithful to God? Is it a crime for citizens to care for brother, sister, father, and mother—all fellow citizens—when the National Convention provides no relief? Is it just for the Committee of Public Safety to persecute Christians for holding to their faith while the hypocrites and pharisees of the philosophers and the National Convention force their new secular religion on France? Maximilien Robespierre insists we need a god, but not the God of Abraham, Moses, and Jesus. Like Aaron, he casts a golden idol, a god of his own making. He demands we kneel at the Temple of Reason to his god who cares not to listen, not to see, and never to save. Is this reason? The King's crime was indifference, the very character of Robespierre's Supreme Being. God Almighty does not serve the state! God calls the church and the state to serve the people. Citizens, it is not this uncaring Supreme Being we should fear, but his high priest Robespierre and his enforcer, prosecutor Tinville! Where are the promises made to the citizens of France? Promises of 'Liberty, Equality, and Fraternity?'

"These innocents: A merchant with a wife, his only connection by family; sixteen nuns, and their servants whose only crime was to remain in the city of their convent serving the people, living on the welfare of others. If these citizens, such good people, are a threat to France, who is not? Citizen, be careful what you say. Use only the correct words. You, too, may be accused by anyone and you will not be permitted to face your accuser. The accusation is sufficient enough! Your bloodied head and torso will be tossed into the pit. There will be no grave where your family may mourn.

"Citizens, it is not too late. The hellish terror and injustice must be stopped. The new god, the great Colossus of Robespierre, the elites, the philosophers, the Convention, and its bloody Committee of Public Safety stand on feet of clay. Shatter those feet, and they all will fall!"

Night by night, Andre sat in the taverns near the Conciergerie Prison, listening to the guards. Andre and Paul did their best to sit near the tables where the conversations were hushed and the faces solemn. They followed some of these men and approached them in the darkened streets. "Can you help me, friend? I seek word of the Carmelites of Compiegne and the accused priest, Paul Mulot."

Most sent them away. Some sought money. One man

whispered, "All Christians should show such faith. But Mulot is no priest."

Andre asked, "You have spoken to him? Is there evidence he is innocent?"

The guard shook his head. "I see the spirit and the faith of the sisters, their assurance of salvation. And Citizen Mulot, well, I asked that he hear my confession. He refused, saying he was not a priest but that he and the sisters would pray for me. Tell me, would a true priest deny a repentant sinner the rite of confession?"

"I have known Claude Mulot for many years. He is married. A faithful Catholic, but no, he is not a priest. He tells the truth. You say you see the spirit of the sisters?"

"They sing! Yes, they have written a new hymn that they sing to the tune of *La Marseillaise*. A strident hymn of victory. Yes, they boldly sing that their deaths bring victory in Jesus. Spirit, friend, I have never witnessed such spirit and faith. I hear their words when I try to sleep. 'Let's give our bodies in His name. Let's climb! Let's climb the scaffold high! We'll give God the victory!'"

"Please tell Mulot that his wife sends her love. She is in Paris and longs to see him one more time. And tell the sisters they are not forgotten in Compiegne! Tell them God will reward their great faith. Tell them!"

The guard nodded. "I will tell them, but there is little time. Their trial is tomorrow."

Andre asked, "Where?"

"At the Hall of Justice in the Courtroom of Liberty."

Andre clasped the man's arm. "Thank you, brother. God bless you for your faithfulness."

The Guard replied, "Do you know a priest who will

hear my confession?"

Andre shook his head, "They are all expelled or in hiding." Andre laughed nervously and continued, "The catechism comes back to me after all these years. Saint Paul has written of a priesthood of all believers. Perhaps God will accept your confession to Claude Mulot and the sisters. And you can help. Your prayers will be heard. It is also written: 'Confess your faults one to another and pray for one another, that you may be healed. For the prayer of a righteous man can accomplish much.'"

"I am a sinner seeking confession, not a righteous man."

"You have confessed in your heart already. No man approaches the Father on his own righteousness. But your prayers will be heard. You have been made righteous by the blood of Jesus."

The 17th of July was a hot and humid day. Despite their early arrival, Andre, Paul, and Marie could not find seats in the courtroom. They stationed themselves outside beneath an open window of the court. The sisters were tried first. They were not permitted legal counsel. Antoine Tinville read the charges.

Andre hoisted the smaller Paul on his shoulders, held him beneath the courtroom window, and whispered, "Can you hear what they are saying?"

"A man speaks, it must be the prosecutor."

"Antoine Tinville?"

"Perhaps. He did not say. He charges the sisters with continuing to live as nuns in secret after being ordered to return home and renounce their vows. He charges them with seeking the services of a priest in hiding, and now he says they have conspired with others to rise up against the revolution. Something about letters. That is preposterous. Our sisters of Compiegne, conspirators? No."

Andre replied, "Of course not. What else?"

"A sister is speaking. She asks what 'fanatical' means. The man said 'fanatical, illegal practices.' The man replies: 'You are to die because you insist on remaining in your convent in spite of the liberty we gave you to abandon all such nonsense.' The sister is speaking. She says, 'Thank you, gentlemen, that is all I wished to hear. The true reason for our arrest and condemnation is because of our religious beliefs. It is for our beliefs that we are about to die. Our eternal praise and thanks to Him who has prepared us for the road to Calvary.'"

"Is that all? What do you hear?"

"It is quiet. Wait. Now another voice. Another man speaks. The judge. He pronounces them guilty and sentences them to death this very day at the Place du Trone-Ranverse. A gavel. Another voice: 'Take the prisoners away.'"

Marie asked, "And Claude? Was Claude with them? Claude is no Carmelite sister."

Paul shrugged his shoulders. "I do not know."

Turning to Andre, Paul asked, "Should we follow the wagon to the Place du Trone-Ranverse or wait to hear if Claude Mulot is tried separately?"

Marie Mulot replied, "You must go. You must tell their story. I will wait here. I will join you later."

Andre and Paul followed the mule-drawn cart through the streets of Paris for two hours. The sixteen women ignored the jeers, insults, and street garbage thrown at them. Their eyes fixed on their Savior, they sang hymns and psalms of praise. Perhaps it was Andre's pamphlets—though more likely the indomitable faith the sisters displayed—but more than a few Parisians put down their missiles and watched silently as the singing sisters passed.

The last golden rays of sunlight announced the ending of the day as the staved cart with sixteen women chained inside rolled into the Place du Trone Renverse. When the sisters saw the orange reflection of the setting sun on the great blade of the guillotine hoisted to the top of its scaffold, Mother Teresa began to sing. Each of the sisters joined. Their last song brought silence to the crowd as they listened to the words of Psalm 116, known to Catholics as *Laudate Dominum*:

> *I love the Lord because He has heard*
> *my voice and my pleas for mercy.*
> *Because He inclined His ear to me,*
> *Therefore I will call upon Him as long as I live.*
> *The snares of death encompassed me;*
> *The pangs of Sheol laid hold on me;*
> *I suffered distress and anguish.*
> *Then I called upon the name of the Lord;*
> *Oh Lord, I pray deliver my soul!*
> *Gracious is the Lord, and righteous;*
> *Our God is merciful.*
> *The Lord preserves the simple;*
> *When I was brought low, He saved me.*
> *Return, Oh my soul, to your rest;*
> *For the Lord has dealt bountifully with you.*
> *For you have delivered my soul from death,*
> *My eyes from tears,*
> *My feet from stumbling;*

A LIGHT IN THE DARKEST NIGHT

I will walk before the Lord in the land of the living.
Precious in the sight of the Lord
is the death of His saints.
Oh Lord, I am your servant,
the son of your maidservant.
I will offer to You the sacrifice of thanksgiving...
I will pay my vows to the Lord
in the presence of all His people,
In the courts of the house of the Lord,
In your midst, Oh Jerusalem.
Praise the Lord!

The crowd was silent. No one stirred. There were no jeers, only soft 'nos' as the elderly Sister Charlotte, who walked with a crutch and could not stand and walk after the lengthy ordeal, was pulled from the cart and fell face down onto the street. Forgiving the guard, she gathered herself up and joined the sisters in line at the foot of the guillotine.

Starting with the youngest, each asked Mother Teresa for permission to die before taking her place beneath the blade. Once in place, each sister again began to chant *Veni Creator Spiritus, Come Holy Spirit*, only to be cut off by the merciless guillotine. With each violent fall, the crowd gasped. The lifeless body and bloodied head were picked up and thrown into the cart. Mother Teresa watched each of her charges die before ascending the steps of the scaffold, and her blood pooled with her sisters'.

Andre watched, and Paul sketched, careful that his tears did not smudge his work. No sooner had the body of Mother Teresa been crudely loaded onto the wagon than another wagon filled with hapless victims of revolutionary justice arrived. The sight of Marie Mulot following led Andre to scour the faces and confirm his long-time friend, Claude Mulot, was among them. The sun had set and dusk found most of the crowd had silently slipped away, their morose appetites sated and replaced by guilt. First Marie and then Claude watched as the remains of the sisters of Compiegne were carted off.

Andre stepped beside the weeping Marie and held her. Claude shouted his love for her before the blade fell across his neck. Both closed their eyes, unable to watch. Marie shuddered and her sobs turned to wails. She struggled for words but managed only, "Why?"

"We must trust God. Claude is loved and will be remembered. But I have vowed that justice be done. God is not mocked. Robespierre and his abettors will face justice. Reason? Man, the creature, cannot kill God, his creator. God is the true author of freedom and the dignity of man. The best efforts of man—and I speak of the idealist whose ambitions are righteous in his eyes—lacking God will end in tyranny."

The Liberty's headline read: "The Tyranny of the Self-Righteous." The first-page illustration showed Sister Charlotte face down in the street. Another sketch showed her hands tied behind her back as she lay beneath the guillotine. Yet another featured Mother Teresa clutching a statue of the Holy Virgin and watching the blade falling towards the neck of a younger sister. "When will Robespierre's tyranny end? How much innocent blood must be spilled? Sixteen Carmelite sisters from Compiegne were executed for practicing their religion in private! Is this freedom? If godly women serving the poor and unfortunate are butchered in public for their private exercise of religion, what greater punishment awaits the rest of us? The Committee of Public Safety, its malicious informers everywhere among us, pursues all who speak against these atrocities. The life testimonies of these martyrs quelled the rowdy crowd of blood-thirsty witnesses. Learn what they begin to see. Enough! It is the duty of every Parisian, every Frenchman, to defend free speech, free thought, free worship of God Almighty or live forever in tyranny!"

In the following pages, Andre wrote obituaries for each of the sixteen and the 'unfortunate' Claude Mulot. Quotations from the trial, the hymns, the faith-filled chants, and the story of their arrest and imprisonment were recorded for all to read.

Ten days later, Maximilien Robespierre, Antoine Tinville, and other Robespierre protégés were executed by the same guillotine, their bodies buried in the same pit, now known as the Picpus Cemetery, where a plaque now honors the sisters from Compiegne. Today, the Picpus Cemetery will bury only descendants of the families of the martyred.

Andre, Paul, and Marie returned to Compiegne. The mayor had fled. They attended a memorial service for the martyred sisters and Claude. Protestants and Jews sat with their Catholic neighbors and wept together.

Afterward, sitting in the home of Emile Fallot. Emile said what all God-fearing people believed: "The attack on the Carmelite sisters and the Catholic Church was an attack against all people of faith."

Andre replied, "Amen!" Then he asked his friend, "What word of Armand? He was our trusted friend—a good man whose zeal opened his soul to the blackness of tyranny—"

"To the rot of a dying vine whose root is planted in

hell," Paul interrupted.

Emile nodded. "You have not heard? The body of Armand D'Argonne was found hanging from an oak tree along the road to the Chateau Compiegne—an overturned stool below his dangling feet. His hands were untied. A pouch that hung from his belt contained thirty pieces of silver. A note in his pocket read only: Justice."

Marie Mulot asked, "Was it suicide?"

Emile shrugged. "Who can say? But it was justice."

THE WATCHER AND THE STONES OF FIRE

The fragrance of precious oil and perfume first betrayed his coming. But soon, the soft sound of padded shoes upon the sand and the rustling of embroidered robes in the night breeze prepared the watcher for the greeting. "I thought I would find you here, Watcher."

"Where else would I be? What brings the Royal Governor of Babylon, the Prelate of the King's Counselors, outside the city this night?"

"I would watch with you and learn from you, my friend," the governor said as he sat down beside the old man. "Such beauty in the night sky. So, it was here you first saw."

"Yes. Each time they came to me here. And it is here I wait to join Him for eternity."

The young man's smile was not observed. He asked, "Were you not charged with watching our people?"

The watcher smiled into the darkness. "Sit here beside me. The cool water of the Chebar River will refresh your spirit."

The richly-robed young man sat down. The watcher

continued, "I see the works of our people and observe what is in their hearts. It is not for me to judge, but their future is known. They have a royal governor and other good men of our nation to lead them."

"You do me too much honor, Ezekiel." The young nobleman sighed. "How the stars do shine away from the city! Their numbers are too great for any man to count."

A comet shot across the sky as they spoke.

The watcher laughed lightly. "Stars? What are the stars in the night sky? It is written that the sun shall rule by day and the moon by night. But the stars, oh, what I have learned from the stars."

The young governor replied, "Your vision. That is why I come. I have dreams—most wonderful and awesome dreams—"

"Yes," Ezekiel interrupted. "And more shall come. With them, you shall know their meaning. You are a chosen vessel. My time is ending. I wait here. But you will go on."

"You wait to be taken to the stars?"

"I will return to the coals of fire burning in the night sky. They live. They watch over us. Theirs is a realm unlike ours. Living fire—flames of life. Spirits of power and knowledge and will. I have been there, and I know, somehow, I will return."

The royal governor spoke: "I have read your words. But tell me: What was in your heart when the fire descended and you were lifted to the heavens?"

Ezekiel did not turn. He kept his eyes on the beautiful night sky. "It was a night like this night. One by one, the bright stars and comets appeared until I saw four comets approaching. They grew larger and larger until the sky was filled with fire. As I watched, there appeared four turning wheels of flame spinning above me. Each wheel was a wheel within a wheel. The flames of the outer wheel took the form of eyes—probing eyes that saw through my very soul. The flames of the inner wheel took shape—living flames, I am certain. They took the form of a human—but more. Each of them had four faces and four wings. Under their wings were human hands. Their wings touched but their heads did not turn when they moved. Each came straight forward. Faces—each had four faces. The face of a man, a lion, a bull, and an eagle. Each looked straight forward; wherever the spirit was about to go, they would go without turning as they went. All the while, there was something like burning coals of fire, like torches darting back and forth—and lightning was flashing in every direction between the flames."

The young man closed his eyes as he listened. "And they came here? It all happened here. Was it a vision? You have said you were transported to the stars. I don't understand."

The watcher turned to his young friend, his night vision catching the honesty in the younger man's face. "What is real when two realms join? I was here, and I was there, just as the living flames were here and in the heavens at once. But listen and learn from me: There was something like an expanse over the heads of the living beings, like the sparkle of a crystal. Under the expanse, two of their wings touched, and two covered their bodies—"

"Like the golden cherubim over the Ark of the Covenant in the Temple?"

The watcher patiently pardoned the interruption. "Yes, just as you say. I remember the sound—the sound like rushing water as they went. It was like the most mighty voice. A voice that came from a throne. A throne like beautiful lapis lazuli. The figure on the throne was like a man. Yes, a man shining with fire, radiant and alive. When I beheld His glory, I fell on my face.

"I heard a voice speaking. He said: 'Son of man, stand on your feet that I may speak with you.' As He spoke, the Spirit entered me and lifted me to my feet. He said to me: 'I am sending you to stubborn and obstinate children. And you shall say to them, *Thus says the Lord God*. As for them, whether they listen or not—for they are a rebellious house—they will know that a prophet has been among them. And you, son of man, neither fear them nor fear their words, though thistles and thorns are with you, and you sit on scorpions; neither fear their words nor be dismayed at their presence, for they are a rebellious house.'"

The young man asked, "And so, He has preserved you to this day."

"But not without pain, Governor Belteshazzar…."

"Please, Ezekiel, to our people—to my friends—I am Daniel. And the scroll he gave you…?"

"Yes, the scroll. Written on the front and back were lamentations, mourning, and woe. He said, 'Eat the scroll and go speak to the house of Israel.' And He said to me, 'Son of man, take into your heart all my words that I shall speak to you and listen closely. And go to the exiles and speak to them, whether they listen or not, tell them: 'Thus says the Lord God.' Then the Spirit lifted me and took me away."

"So, it was in spirit that you traveled?"

"I do not know how, but I appeared among our people in the flesh and accomplished all that I was commanded."

"You said it was not without pain. Pain from not being heard?"

The watcher shook his head no. "I understand accountability. I obeyed, and I spoke. No, it was the taking of my dear wife and the hard command not to mourn her death that was the great pain."

Daniel nodded. "You speak of the parable. Your wife as Jerusalem, the pain of her loss like the Lord's pain in the destruction of the Temple and walls of Jerusalem."

The watcher nodded. "Yes, the most painful parable. The Lord said to me: 'Son of man, I am about to take the delight of your eyes away from you. Yet you shall not mourn nor weep, nor shall your tears run down. Sigh but not aloud. Make no mourning for the dead. Bind on your turban and put on your shoes. Do not cover your lips nor eat the bread of men.' So I spoke to the people in the morning, and that evening my wife died. The next morning I did as I was commanded."

Daniel lowered his head and sighed.

Ezekiel looked straight ahead into the darkness. "The people asked me: 'What do these things mean?' Then I told them the word of the Lord came to me. He said: 'Say to the house of Israel: 'I will profane my sanctuary, the pride of your power, the delight of your eyes, and the yearning of your soul—'"

Daniel interrupted. "His Temple, the walls of the His city...?"

Ezekiel nodded. "More: His people, those He loved. For He continued: 'And the sons and daughters you have left behind will fall by the sword. You will do as I have done. You will not cover your lip nor eat the bread of men. You shall not mourn nor weep, but you shall rot away in your iniquities and groan to one another. Thus shall Ezekiel be for you a sign.' Yes, it was pain I shall never forget." The watcher took a deep breath and spoke louder: "But even greater was the hope in my heart when the Lord said, 'Then, when I make atonement for you, for all you have done, you will remember and be ashamed and never again open your mouth because of your humiliation.'"

Daniel replied, "You speak of a new temple. The temple whose building details you have prophesied."

Ezekiel nodded. "Surely, we are commanded to make sacrifices for sin upon the altar of God in His temple, but my spirit envisions a greater atonement. As a priest, I know that atonement is made through blood sacrificed by a priest for a sinner. But the Lord said, 'I will atone.' This is a mystery. Is the Lord's atonement the mourning He speaks of? It is my hope this atonement is not just for past sins but a final atonement, an everlasting forgiveness. I have seen, in the other realm, the realm of stones of fire, how the fallen morning star, Lucifer, and his followers have been cast out of the heavens to do, for a season, his evil on Earth. Still, he rebels and seeks to draw men to him. Could this final atonement be the hope and the help He has promised through all the prophets?"

Daniel asked, "You have seen? What have you seen?"

The watcher closed his eyes, exhaled a deep breath, and softly answered, "I was in the starry realm. Coals of fire filled the heavens—angels of the Lord, as flames of fire, darted about doing as the Lord commanded, and as I watched, the word of the Lord came to me: 'Son of man, raise a lamentation over the king of Tyre, and say to him, 'Thus says the Lord God:

DAVID MARTYN

"'You were the signet of perfection,
Full of wisdom and perfect in beauty.
You were in Eden, the garden of God;
Every precious stone was your covering,
Sardius, topaz, and diamond,
Beryl, onyx, and jasper,
Sapphire, emerald, and carbuncle;
And crafted in gold were your settings
And your engravings.
On the day that you were created,
They were prepared.
You were anointed guardian cherub.
I placed you on the holy mountain of God;
In the midst of the stones of fire, you walked.
You were blameless from the day you were created,
Till unrighteousness was found in you.
In the abundance of your trade
You were filled with violence in your midst,
And you sinned;
So I cast you as a profane thing
From the mountain of God,
And I destroyed you, O guardian cherub,
From the midst of the stones of fire.
Your heart was proud because of your beauty;
You corrupted your wisdom for
The sake of your splendor.
I cast you to the ground;
I exposed you before kings,
To feast their eyes on you.
By the multitude of your iniquities,
In the unrighteousness of your trade

You profaned your sanctuaries;
So I brought fire out from your midst;
It consumed you,
And I turned you to ashes on the earth
In the sight of all who saw you.
All who know you among the peoples
Are appalled at you;
You have come to a dreadful end
And shall be no more forever.'"

Daniel scratched his beard. "Certainly, Lucifer is the fallen cherub, but why is the saying addressed to the king of Tyre? And the jewels, are they not the very jewels of the priest's ephod?"

"The jewels of a high priest and servant of the Lord, and so Lucifer once was. He was a chief servant of the Most High before he set himself above the Exalted One. Even priests are slaves to Lucifer's false glory and must atone for their sins before making sacrifices for the sins of others.

"Apart from the Lord God, are not we all slaves to the master, Satan, and sin? The king of Tyre chose riches and peace with the enemy of God and God's people. The fallen star entices with pride, wealth, worldly power, and pleasure. But the Lord's fire—an all-consuming fire, has consumed the life fire of Satan, and his fate is sealed. And the Lord protects us with stones of fire—mighty angels. But more, He sends forth his flames of life to fill us with His Spirit—Spirit, and power to overcome—so that we never without hope."

Daniel nodded. "Your words remind me of the burning bush of Moses and the law and of our people in the great exodus from Egypt. I remember how the Spirit of the Lord descended over the Tabernacle in flames of fire by night and a great cloud by day. Such a great comfort and assurance of His presence and protection as He led them to their future, to the land of His promise."

"And so He will lead them back again. Just as the Lord raised up Joseph to rule over Egypt, so has he raised you up as a shepherd to watch over His sheepfold in Babylon."

"My visions, they come from the Lord...."

"His fire consumes you, your heart, mind, and soul. You will obey every command. You will endure every pain and face every trial because you love Him. You can do this because He has placed His stone of fire in your heart. And His sheep, like their shepherds, shall each receive the flames of His Spirit. They will wait with me for the chariot of fire to be carried off to another realm, an immortal realm, their home forever, the starry realm of His eternal presence."

Daniel nodded. "You wait, like the prophet Elijah, carried off in the fiery chariot, and faithful Enoch of old who walked with God and was no more. Your vision, Ezekiel, the valley of the bones. You see more than Israel being restored as a people—God's people. You hope in the resurrection of the faithful, perhaps in the heavenly realm, but Enoch and Ezekiel are only two people in all creation."

"The Lord interpreted the vision of the valley of bones to His people Israel—all Israel. And for certain, the hearts of His people will be made new and turned to their creator. But I ask you, Daniel, do you not trust the Lord? There are other witnesses to an immortal realm. The righteous Job proclaimed, 'I know that my redeemer lives, and in the end, He will stand on the earth. And after my skin has been destroyed, yet in my flesh, I shall see God; I will see Him with my own eyes—I and not another. How my heart yearns within me.' And then there is Isaiah who wrote, 'But your dead will live; their bodies will rise, you who dwell in the dust, wake up and shout for joy. Your dew is like the dew of the morning; the earth will give birth to her dead.'"

Daniel replied, "The other realm, your starry realm— an immortal realm of which the psalmist sings—where the faithful are received into glory. The promise of eternal blessings. As it is written, 'God will redeem my life from the grave. He will surely take me to Himself.'"

Ezekiel smiled. "How else could David sing, 'Surely goodness and mercy shall follow me all the days of my life, and I shall dwell in the house of the Lord forever.'"

"Yes, promises of hope—the Lord never leaves His faithful without hope. His reward will wipe away every tear and overcome every trial. Wait in peace, old friend. But now, I must go and do the work the Lord has set before me."

Daniel hugged his friend, stood up, and walked slowly into the darkness. As he reached the gates of Babylon, he saw a comet shoot to earth alongside the Chebar River. He smiled and continued to the palace and his prayer closet.

Years later, after his victory in the lion's den, his interpretations of royal dreams and his godly counsel to Nebuchadnezzar, Belshazzar, and Darius—near the end of his life. After a life overcoming trials and despair and a vision of the end times, Daniel wrote of the flaming stones of the immortal realm:

At that time Michael, the Great Prince who protects your people, will arise. There will be a time of distress such as not has happened from the beginning of the nations until then. But at that time, your people—everyone whose name is found written in the book—will be delivered. Multitudes who sleep in the dust of the earth will awake; some to everlasting life, others to shame and everlasting contempt. Those who are wise will shine like the brightness of the heavens, and those who lead many to righteousness, like the stars forever and ever.

There is Always Someone to Burn
The Bamberg Witch Trials

Snow mixed with sleet betrayed the longed-for late-May sunshine. Three boys moved slowly through the dim light, creeping past the smoldering dump fire toward her garden. Spying them through her window, the small, white-haired woman quickly threw a scarf around her neck, grabbed the broom by the door, and made her way outside as quickly as old knees and gaunt legs could carry her.

"I see you, ye scoundrels. Come to thieve me, did ye? Come no closer, or I will curse ye. Yes, a terrible curse. Now go before I give ye the Evil Eye and turn my broom on ye." Unable to lift her head above her slumped shoulders, she raised her broom and waved it at the frightened boys. "That's right, run, lads, run," she cackled as the boys ran across the frosty ground toward the city gate.

Alone again in the chill, she slowly walked to her garden. The young cabbage plants were green and leafy, the ground around them cold but soft and moist. She surveyed her plot, a narrow strip of land between the south wall of the city shielding a forge and steel oven on the other side and the city dump where a continuous fire burned the waste. She laughed. It was the only frost-free plot in all the fields of Bamberg.

After dark, the old woman was surprised to hear a heavy pounding on her door. Before she could make her way there, it burst open and three men rushed in.

"Seize her," said the last man to enter. One man stood before the frightened woman as the other stepped behind her. The man behind drove his knee into the small of her back while grabbing both wrists and quickly tied her hands together. After a sharp scream, she dropped her head and stared at the fresh muddy snow her attackers had tracked into her tidy house.

"Who are you? I have no money. Take you what you will. Leave me in peace!"

The third man, the officer, replied: "Kundigundt Kretzin, you are accused of witchcraft. Are you alone?"

"Yes. I am a widow. I live alone."

The officer commanded his men: "Put out the fire and take her. Check the outbuilding. Tomorrow, return and make the inventory."

A staved cart was waiting outside. The two guards lifted the widow, threw her into the wagon, and locked the stave door behind her.

It was a short ride to the new Malefizhaus, the Maleficent House, a witches' prison built by the Prince-Bishop. Trembling with fear, the feeble woman was led to a small room with a table. She was pushed down onto a stool. A wooden shaft was pushed down her back between her spine and bound arms behind her. The base of the rod went through a hole in the floor. She could not move from her position.

Fifteen minutes later, a man in black robes entered the room. He stared at the old woman before sitting down at the table across from her.

"I am Friedrich Forner, the Auxiliary Bishop of Bamberg. Frau Kretzin, you will confess to me your unholy witchcraft and name the witches of your coven and all that follow Satan in this—" The Auxiliary Bishop's last words were drowned out by screams from the buttlestube, the torture chamber, at the end of the hall.

"It is all a terrible mistake. I am no witch. I am a simple widow with no husband or son to care for me. Thieves! Yes, scoundrels steal what little I grow. Who will help me? I cannot fight them, so I scare them off! Witch? No. I am a good Christian. Ask the priest. I attend mass and light candles for the souls of my husband, God rest his soul, taken in the plague, and my son, my precious only son, killed in service to the Emperor. Is this how I am repaid?"

"You curse with the Evil Eye. You cast spells to injure and to seek favor with the devil. We know your field, alone in all of Bamberg, was spared from the frost. Confess and it will go easy for you."

The old woman shook her head. "I have nothing to live for. I am ready to die. Take my home and my plot. Take all that I have. Kill me if you must but bury me in consecrated ground. I am a Christian and deserving of last rites and Christian burial."

"Confess your witchcraft and all of your sins. Name all the others and perhaps we will take your head before you are burned. But do not think you can bargain with me. All that you own has already been taken from you. But a witch you are and therefore unworthy of Christian rites or a consecrated grave."

"I will not confess to what is not true."

Auxiliary Bishop Forner sighed. Turning towards the door, he called out, "Guard, take her to the buttlestube. Report to me when she confesses."

Friedrich Forner was surprised when the guard rapped on his study door fifteen minutes later. "Enter! Has she confessed? That was quick."

"No, Excellency. She is dead."

"Dead? You were too harsh! But surely, she confessed?"

The visibly shaken guard shook his head. "No, Excellency. We had just begun. From the moment we took her, she began reciting the rosary—"

"You allowed her rosary beads?"

"No, Excellency. She counted them off as she recited. We put her feet in leg irons and laid her on the table. We were securing her wrists in the irons and she kept repeating the rosary. And then she lifted her head and her eyes opened wide. She saw something and shouted, 'Save me, Jesus!' Then she fell dead on the table. We shook her and prodded her. She has no breath. The old woman is dead!"

The cleric folded his hands and sighed before mumbling softly, "So then."

"Excellency, what should we do with the body?"

Forner snorted. "She is a witch."

The guard just stared with a puzzled look on his face.

Forner laughed. "You think Jesus saved her? No, but if it was Jesus, He saw through her trickery and rejected her. Jesus judged and condemned her. She will burn as a witch with the others!"

In the council room of the Prince-Bishop's palace, Auxiliary Bishop Forner gave his report to the aldermen and Prince-Bishop. "The property confiscated from Frau Kretzin includes a field half the length of the south city wall and one hundred elle wide, planted with a healthy cabbage crop. Also there is a hut, a covered pigpen, one sow, six suckling pigs, one rooster, and six laying hens. I seek permission to sell the property and add the proceeds to the Prince-Bishop's holdings."

The Prince-Bishop's vice chancellor, Georg Haan, interrupted. "Bishop Forner, there is no report of the trial of Frau Kretzin."

Forner replied, "No trial was necessary, Doctor Haan. The witch died before trial."

Georg Haan was not put off. "The Emperor's law permits seizure of property only from criminals convicted in court of a capital offense—"

"Yes, Georg," Forner interrupted. "Witchcraft is a capital offense."

Haan rebutted, "But there was no trial."

"Our Lord judged her. He took her life before the interrogation was finished. She was judged a witch."

Georg Haan shouted, "Our Lord judged her? Did He?! Did our Lord reject Saint Stephen and his prayers when he was brutally martyred?"

Forner shouted in reply, "Don't mock me, Haan!"

"Your words and your deeds mock you, Auxiliary Bishop Forner!"

Prince-Bishop Fuchs von Dornheim slammed his fist on the table. "Enough! Auxiliary Bishop Forner is a trained theologian. He has made a great study of witchcraft and has experience in these matters. That is why I brought him here from Würzburg."

Georg Haan composed himself and lowered his voice. He turned to the Prince-Bishop and said, "Excellency, the Constitutio Criminalis Carolin is clear. In every trial for a capital offense, the accused must be permitted a defense. They have the right to be represented and to question and call witnesses in their defense. Only after such a trial can a judgment be made. I must object to the Auxiliary Bishop's crusade contradicting the Emperor's law."

The Prince-Bishop raised his hand. "Vice Chancellor, I have heard your complaints before. Witchcraft is not just a capital offense but one against the Holy Roman Catholic Church. The Emperor's law does not restrict canonical law."

Haan thought, *Does the pope give a bishop authority to execute someone without a trial? Canonical law moves even slower than civil law.* He bit his tongue and said nothing.

The Prince-Bishop continued, "Auxiliary Bishop, proceed with the sale. Vice Chancellor, you shall be more careful to stay within your authority over civil matters."

Doctor Schwarkonz lifted his hand and said, "If I may speak, Excellency. Doctor Haan's pleading for accused witches sends a dangerous message to our citizens. I do not say for certain that the Vice Chancellor is a denier but he gives aid to their cause. I propose a commission. I humbly agree to lead it: A commission to save Bamberg and the Hofstift principality from witches and those who seek to protect the witches who have brought dreadful calamity upon us. Permit the commission to enforce a ban on criticism of the witch trials under penalty of whipping and exile."

The Prince-Bishop replied: "You have your

commission, Doctor Schwarzkonz."

Turning to Georg Haan, Prince-Bishop Fuchs von Dornheim said, "If you are not a denier, Vice Chancellor, you will give your full support to the witch commission."

In the privacy of his surgery, Georg Haan discussed the council meeting with his friend and fellow council member Georg Heinrich Flock. "It was good you were not there, my friend, or you, too, might have been reprimanded and branded a denier in this ugly business."

Herr Flock shook his head. "You know I support you and the rule of law. There seems no end to this madness! This time it was a helpless widow using her only weapon against injustice. Two weeks ago, it was the refugee who survived the burning of her house and the death of her parents in this endless so-called 'Christian War.' The poor woman refuses to sleep under a roof and chooses to sleep beneath the stars, and for that, she is a witch and burned alive? New accusations are made every day. If this madness is not ended soon, I fear every last citizen will be accused and brutally murdered."

Haan replied, "I hear whispers that Christina Morhaubt will be arrested."

"The burgermeister's wife? He wouldn't dare!"

Haan lowered his head and whispered: "He has everyone believing, or at least everyone *saying*, that witchcraft is rampant in Bamberg and the cause of every misfortune. Imagine, my friend, how rich our Prince-Bishop can become by seizing the property of the merchants. I tell you, no one is safe. Everyone arrested eventually confesses under torture, and they are tortured again until they name others. How can it end?"

Georg Flock nodded. "What can we do? We must stop the mad witch hunter Forner."

Doctor Haan looked up and replied, "Forner is not the true problem. He is only the hired henchman. No, the madman is our Prince-Bishop who brought the witch hunter here. He answers only to Emperor Ferdinand II and the pope. And it is the Emperor who gives him authority in Bamberg. I will sue in the Imperial Diet at Speyer."

Georg Haan arrived in Speyer in December 1627. Even though the Imperial Army of the Emperor and the Armies of the Catholic League and Spanish Netherlands were in winter quarters, the war to rid Europe of the protestant faith took priority with the Emperor and his councilors.

Georg filed his case and waited. Word of his suit reached Bamberg and Würzburg, two cities suffering through witch trials whose councils sent secret messages to the Diet demanding delay or outright rejection. Haan found surprising support from Elector-Duke Maximilian of Bavaria. As the suit languished in court, Duke Maximilian recognized the threat to Georg Haan's life.

Doctor Haan received a letter from his friend Georg Flock in late April:

Georg,
Come home soon. Christina Morhaubt's confession led to many more. The wives of the council members, their maids, sons, and now our fellow aldermen. It is a cancer eating its way through our city. Dissent is forbidden, which makes waiting for the inevitable accusation all the more fearful. As you predicted, the Prince-Bishop enjoys confiscating the wealth of the city. He sells

off the properties only to seize them again. There is no safety in silence. We all wait in fear. There is always someone to burn.
Georg Flock

Doctor Hann returned to Bamberg and found his wife, Katharina, and their eldest daughter had been arrested, tried, and burned alive in his absence. His remaining daughter and four sons were not permitted to mourn their loss. His eldest son, Adam, scolded his father: "This is your doing! Your complaints, suing the Prince-Bishop before the Imperial Diet—you bought this upon us. You shall pay, Father. You shall pay. If you have not been condemned yet, I will go myself. Yes, I will testify against you!"

That evening, a rider carrying the standard of Bavaria appeared at the gate of Bamberg. The gate guard called down from the tower: "What is your business?"

The rider replied, "His grace, Elector-Duke Maximilian of Bavaria, requires the service of a Bamberg citizen, Doctor Georg Haan, in his court. I am to escort the doctor and his family to Munich."

The guard opened the gate and led the messenger to the palace of the Prince-Bishop. At the palace, the messenger was shown to a room and told Doctor Haan would be brought to the palace.

As the Bavarian messenger waited, Georg Haan was arrested and taken to the Malefizhaus. Immediately, he was put in thumbscrews and vices. Bones were crushed, fingernails pulled. He was stripped and dumped into a cold bath, followed by a scalding hot lime bath. Doctor Haan knew his fate, and while being whipped, he cried out, "Forgive me, Lord Jesus, I confess! Stop! I confess!"

A LIGHT IN THE DARKEST NIGHT

A document was set before him to sign. His eyes were too swollen to read, so he made a blind mark on the paper. He knew what was coming next. A new round of torture and naming his accomplices. His racked body was burned with feathers dipped in sulfur. He endured the pain until he slipped into unconsciousness.

Awakened when his head was shoved in a bucket of water, he coughed himself awake. Struggling to breathe between repeated dunking, he pled, "Yes, I will name him. I was brought to witchcraft by Johann Junius. It was Junius who discipled me!"

The following morning, the messenger sent from the Duke was told, "Doctor Haan was not at home. Perhaps he is attending the sick. Please, have breakfast. Wait while we make further inquiries."

As the Prince-Bishop's servant was speaking, a fire was being lit. Doctor Haan's flesh was being torn from his body with red-hot pincers as he was dragged to the pyre to be burned alive. The prosecutor, Johann Junius, had sealed his sentence. It was Junius' last prosecution before his own arrest and execution as a witch.

With Bamberg's only opposing voice silenced, the accusations and trials increased. Within weeks, the ashes of Haan's daughter Ursula and son Adam joined their parents in the ash heap outside the city wall. Haan's three surviving sons fled the city and found refuge in a Dominican abbey. The Haan property passed to the Prince-Bishop. Prominent citizens, officials, and wealthy merchants became the target of Auxiliary Bishop Forner, though no one was too poor or humble to burn.

The loud knocking awoke Georg Flock and his wife, Apolonia, from their sleep. Knees knocking, Georg barely had the strength to open the door. Three armed guards burst in. "We have come for Apolonia Flock. Where is she?"

"My wife is in bed. If you wait, I will ask her to dress and come out."

"Which room?"

Georg struggled to lift his arm but managed to point to the bedroom door. Two guards rushed into the bedroom and pulled Apolonia from bed. Barefoot and wearing only her night frock, she was dragged away screaming. Georg recognized the captain of the guard and asked, "Is she accused?"

The captain replied, "Councilor Flock, you are forbidden to leave Bamberg," and left.

Five days later, Apolonia was burned as a witch. Georg Flock waited for the guards to return. A week passed, and no one came.

My Apolonia would not condemn me—God rest her sweet soul. Recriminations, yes, recriminations by those condemned feed this madness. I must offend no one. I must not threaten the witch hunters or those accused. It is my only hope of survival. I will return to my duties, careful not to offend.

At the next meeting of the Bamberg council, Georg was shaken from his thoughts when the Prince-Bishop spoke, "You were here then, Herr Flock. What was the decision on the matter? Was it recorded?"

Georg replied, "Decision? Oh, yes. All decisions are recorded. The records are kept by year and locked in the archive, in the vice...." Georg hesitated. Looking around the room, he realized he was the only member surviving from before the witch trials began. *I am the corporate memory. These new members know nothing of government matters before this madness began. Undoubtedly, the Prince-Bishop knows this. It is my protection.*

"As I was saying, Excellency, following your ordained determination to bring righteousness to Bamberg, every boat and every wagon passing through the Hofstift must swear allegiance to the Holy Church and pay a cathedral toll or purchase a waiver for the year. The decision was to accept a tithe of food in lieu of coin. And, if I might add, Excellency, with so many new members of the council, it would benefit our service if you would again share your God-given calling to wipe away all that is evil, to make Bamberg the shining city on a hill that cannot be hidden for the light of its righteousness!"

Prince-Bishop Johann Georg Fuchs von Dornheim stirred at hearing the words. "Well said, Georg. Learn from this man, all of you who are new to service. Yes! Righteousness and Godliness shall bring light to Bamberg, light that will be seen throughout the empire! We will burn every witch so that the light of the Lord will shine!"

Georg felt a pang of remorse. *What have I said? Am I a coward? Only a fool would expect Godly results from ungodly means.*

A year passed, and Georg's survival strategy of parroting support for the Prince-Bishop's vision of a Godly Bamberg, never condemning and never defending anyone suspected of witchcraft, allowed a semblance of normality to return to his life. He felt safe—a forgotten member of the old regime. His feeling of cautious security turned to joy when he met a beautiful young woman from Nuremberg. He married Dorothea, convinced he had found a second chance in life.

The carriage stopped in front of a tall gabled stone townhouse on Lange Strasse in the wealthy merchant district of Bamberg. The wrought iron guild sign identified the first-floor shop as a cloth merchant. An old, carved granite stone in front bore the crest of the Flock family. Georg smiled at his young bride and said, "We are home." He told her: "These are troubled times in Bamberg. It is best not to leave the house alone. But be certain of this, my darling, I shall give you every desire of your heart."

Georg and Dorothea enjoyed a year of happiness, discovering each other in safe seclusion within the walls of their home.

The pounding on their door came as a shock.

The officer shouted, "Dorothea Flock!"

Dorothea's knees buckled. Georg shouted back: "Why are you here? I am the Hofstift Chancellor to the Prince-Bishop!"

The officer replied, "Dorothea Flock, you are charged with adultery." Turning to his guard, the officer commanded: "Arrest her!"

Alone, his old fears returned, stronger than before. *The charge is not witchcraft but adultery. She should be afforded a trial under the Emperor's criminal code. And the baby, our baby—yes, she is showing. Her pregnancy should earn her better treatment in the city jail. But these are not normal times. Someone may accuse her of witchcraft. We have no future in Bamberg. Somehow, we must escape.*

Late at night, Dorothea lay in her cell, moaning. Her cries grew louder and she began to scream between cries. A guard appeared at her cell door.

"Quiet!" he bellowed.

"The pain, my baby," she cried. "My baby is coming! A doctor—it's early—a doctor and the midwife!"

The guard held his lantern over her and stared. She cried out and then screamed at him: "Unshackle my legs! I cannot deliver my baby with my feet shackled!"

The guard knelt, took a key from his belt, and unlocked Dorothea's shackles. As they rattled against the stone floor, another prisoner shouted, "Quiet that woman! There are others here as well!"

A second prisoner began to bang the bars of his cell with his waste bucket.

The guard stood up and yelled, "Quiet all of you! Have you no respect for the birth of an innocent child?"

The whole prison erupted with shouts and banging. The guard stomped out of the cell and down the long hall, leaving the cell door open behind him.

As the light of his lantern faded around a corner, Dorothea sprang to her feet, her right hand cradling the unborn child in her swollen belly. She scooped straw into a pile and covered it with the thin blanket, hurriedly forming a crude sleeping form then ran out the cell door. She ran the unfamiliar, dark streets of Bamberg, praying to make it out of the city before she was discovered.

The determined woman made her way within sight of the city gate. Her adrenaline had run its course and she doubled over in pain. There was a guard at the watch post above the gate. The large carriage gate was built with a small man-gate on one side. That gate was secured with only a simple sliding bolt. She pondered how to get through the small gate undetected.

As she watched the guard for an opportunity, she heard footsteps, the sound of men jogging towards her location. *It's now or never.* She closed her eyes for a moment. *Please, Lord!* She ran for the gate.

Georg went to the city jail to visit his wife.

"She is not here," the jailer said.

"Where is she?" Georg replied.

"The prisoner Dorothea Flock is where she belongs, at the Malefizhaus with the other accused witches."

"Accused witches?"

"Her witchcraft may have helped her escape the city jail but none has yet escaped the Malefizhaus."

Georg returned home. He did not enter his front door. He went to his stable, saddled his horse, and rode to the Imperial City of Nuremberg, a protestant city with an imposing Imperial castle. There were others in Nuremberg who had fled from Bamberg but Goerg headed for the Hoffman house.

For centuries, the ancient walled city was the site of many Imperial diets and was host to one of two high courts of the Emperor. Its strategic importance led the Emperor to paper over religious differences in favor of political allegiance. A council of wealthy trading families ruled Nuremberg and Dorothea Flock was the daughter of one of the leading families, the Hoffmans. Before sunset of the day Georg arrived, Dorothea's father obtained a letter from the Nuremberg Council. Immediately a messenger was sent to the Prince-Bishop of Bamberg protesting the arrest of their citizen, Dorothea Flock. Notice of proceedings was sent to

Auxiliary Bishop Forner, holding him accountable for the safe treatment of the pregnant Frau Flock.

The execution of a pregnant woman was forbidden without exception under church law. Bishop Forner held Dorothea in the Malefizhaus, her wrists and ankles chained to the wall. But he would wait for the child to be born. Dorothea lay helpless, surrounded by the screams and cries of her neighbors being tortured.

While they waited for a reply from the Prince-Bishop, Dorothea's father looked for hope. "Georg, I pray that the baby, my grandchild, does not come too soon. It is her best protection while we pursue every course."

Dorothea's sister Magdalena added, "We have friends in the Catholic Church and among the nobility. I have written to the Guardian of the Order of Friars, Minor Capuchin. He is a good man, known for his opposition to witch trials. He will not stand still for such brutality."

"Influence, yes, people of influence," Georg replied. "My cousin commands a regiment in the Army of Flanders. He is favored by the Infanta of Spain, Isabella Clara Eugenia, governor of the Spanish Netherlands. I shall write to him. A minor Prince-Bishop cannot offend these people. And I shall appeal to the Pope. Yes, even the Holy Father shall hear of this injustice!"

Georg's father-in-law agreed. "All this and more while we pursue the matter in the Imperial court. Tell me, Georg, how does this madness continue in Bamberg? And leading families—they permit this?"

"It started several years ago. The crop failures— superstitious peasants and a madman Bishop whose vision is to cast out evil. He sees witches everywhere and the cause of every calamity. In the beginning, the starving poor accused neighbors with whom they disputed. The Prince-Bishop sent to Wurzburg for the witch hunter Forner. They preached— yes, every mass from the pulpit included a demand to accuse the witches of Bamberg. Soon everyone agreed, whether they believed or not, that Bamberg was damned by witchcraft."

"They agreed? Everyone? And no one objected?"

Georg paused to sigh. "My friend, Georg Haan, vice chancellor of the Hofstift? He went as far as to sue in court at Steyer. But before the case was settled, his wife was burned, and when he returned, he met the same fate. The Prince-Bishop decreed there would be no opposition to the witch trials. Even speaking favorably of an accused was punishable by whipping and banishment, or even being accused as a witch."

Georg paused. "It is a sickness, unstoppable as the plague. A lie is named the truth. Dissent is forbidden and punished. Debate is silenced. Fear reigns. A vicious cycle of accusations and punishment. Once accused and tortured to confess, the condemned are tortured again to name others. Who can they name? Not their loved ones. Old enemies or those they see as persecutors. The more accused are arrested, the more innocent people are accused. It cannot end. Even the council—and the prosecutors—have been accused."

"And you thought it safe to stay there with my daughter?"

"I was a fool. As the last of the council—the only man with a memory of our government—I was convinced that the Prince-Bishop needed me. And I offended no one. Dorothea and I—well, we love each other. We were blinded by the joy of new love. We felt safe when we were alone together.

A LIGHT IN THE DARKEST NIGHT

Forgive me."

Georg Flock broke down and cried.

Auxiliary Bishop Forner advised the Prince-Bishop von Dornheim: "Do not reply. Not to the letter from the Burghers of Nuremberg or the plea for mercy from the Guardian Friar of the Capuchins. They have no authority over you. You are doing God's work! The Emperor—all of Christendom—shall see your righteousness!"

Prince-Bishop von Dornheim nodded. "Yes. It is just as you say. Even so, I shall show mercy to the child. Move Frau Flock to the city jail until the baby is born."

With help from the Hoffmans, Georg filed suit with the Court Council of the Empire, one of two supreme courts. Called the Aulic Council, the court held exclusive jurisdiction over all feudal processes and states within the empire. Within weeks, the court issued a mandate to the Prince-Bishop of Bamberg demanding the easing of detention for Dorothea until childbirth, requiring she be granted the assistance of an advocate in court, and calling for the Prince-Bishop to mediation with the council.

Receiving no response after two weeks, the council strengthened its mandate, demanding the release of the accused until after childbirth and a fair trial under the criminal code. Still, there was no response from Bamberg. Only when the Duke of Furstenberg, head of the council, wrote Prince-Bishop von Dornheim demanding acknowledgment and compliance, did Fuchs von Dornheim defiantly reply to the first mandate:

DAVID MARTYN

Aulic Council
Hofburg Palace, Vienna

The accused, Dorothea Flock, delivered a healthy baby girl six weeks ago. I stand by my decision to try the accused as a witch. The prisoner has been returned to the Malefizhaus for interrogation.

Prince-Bishop of Bamberg
Johann Georg Flock von Dornheim

Upon receipt of von Dornheim's letter, the Aulic Council issued a mandate demanding the immediate release of Dorothea Flock. She and her baby would be free to leave Bamberg at once. The messenger arrived five days after Dorothea confessed, under torture, to witchcraft. The messenger was shown the confession:

> *I, Dorothea Flock, confess that I was seduced by a student in my father's house in Nuremberg. As we continued fornicating, he told me he was the devil and my master. In addition to fornication with the devil, I confess to desecrating the communion host.*

The confession was attested by her mark and signed: Barthol Braun, Prosecutor.

A LIGHT IN THE DARKEST NIGHT

The Vice Chancellor of Bamberg called the messenger to his chambers. Seated, without raising his head or looking the messenger in the eye, he said matter-of-factly, "Dorothea Flock is guilty of witchcraft. She has been sentenced. For denying God and the Holy Trinity, the witch's hands will be cut off, and her flesh torn by hot pincers before she is burned alive. Her body will be burned completely, and her ashes spread in the waste heap outside the wall. You may go."

The messenger replied, "I want to speak with Dorothea Flock before I return."

"Condemned witches may receive no visitors. Denied. You have your answer. Leave Bamberg."

Anticipating von Dornheim's insubordination, the Aulic Council requested and received an Imperial order from Emperor Ferdinand to release Dorothea immediately. Before the order could be delivered, a decree sparing the life of Dorothea granted by Pope Urban VIII was delivered to Bamberg. The papal envoy entered the city gate when it opened at sunrise. Having received notice of Imperial intervention, the Prince-Bishop called his council to a dawn meeting before sunrise.

Auxiliary Bishop Forner pled his case: "Excellency, the woman is a witch. You have made your position clear. Yes, it is rumored that the Emperor is sending a pardon. Until commanded otherwise by the Church, you are within your right to act as the holy shepherd of Bamberg. But you should act quickly. Better to act now than to be seen as weak before your subjects."

The new chancellor of the Hofstift, Pancraz Lorenz, added, "Excellency, we must act quickly. Act before it is too late."

Prince-Bishop von Dornheim nodded. "Yes. The witch must die. But I will show that I am merciful. She shall be beheaded before being burned. And you, Herr Lorenz, will raise the baby girl as your own."

Twenty-two-year-old Dorothea was immediately taken to the yard of Malefizhaus and beheaded. Her body was burned.

The papal envoy made his way to the palace, only to be told that the Prince-Bishop was not in the palace. Spying the spires of the cathedral, the envoy made his way there. A priest brought the envoy to the canon, reluctantly accepting the papal decree, but Dorothea was already dead.

In Nuremberg, the friends of the Hoffmans organized opposition to the Bamberg witch trials. Soon bishops and archbishops condemned the practice. A council of the Electoral Princes met in Regensberg to mandate action against the mad witch hunter of Bamberg. The people of Bamberg no longer obeyed the edict of the commission or cooperated in the trials. Woodcutters refused to cut wood for the pyres. Word was spread that King Gustavus Adolphus of Sweden would send his protestant army to stop the barbaric practice. Von Dornheim's enforcer, Auxiliary Bishop Forner, died unexpectedly. The Prince-Bishop finally succumbed to pressure and halted all arrests for witchcraft.

Ending the arrests did not stop the torture and trials of the unfortunate souls in the Malefizhaus. The Emperor's council, the Hofrat, sent Anton Winter, a prominent opponent of the witch trials, to Bamberg to head the Bamberg Witch Commission. When Winter arrived with his warrant, the

Prince-Bishop fled. Winter's first act was to order the release of every person held in the Malefizhaus. The guards were sent home, and the house of torture was locked. A decree was posted throughout the city prohibiting accusations of any person as a witch. All civil and criminal complaints would be settled through the courts following the Imperial code of law.

The initial relief and celebration of the end of the witch trials were soon followed by anger, remorse, and guilt. The whole of the council resigned. Several priests followed their bishop to Vienna. Herr Winter ordered the city guards to enforce peace. Fighting, assault, and any act of vengeance were to be stopped. Winter needed help. He sent for two people, Georg Flock and Wurzburg's Guardian of the Order of the Capuchin Monks.

Georg Flock returned to Bamberg and took custody of his daughter from council member Pancraz Lorenz. Anton Winter watched Georg take his daughter into his arms, weeping bittersweet tears for the senseless loss of his wife and the gift of his daughter. "Stay, Georg. Stay and help me restore peace and order to Bamberg. God has made you a face for reconciliation and restoration. You have led the city before. Teach, become an example of grace and love."

Georg could not take his eyes off his baby daughter. Tears fell from his face. "Who am I to teach anyone? I was no better than the others."

"All men are weak. But you changed. You have brought justice to Bamberg."

Georg cried. Sobbing, he replied, "I will stay until order has been restored. Beyond that, I make no promises."

Anton Winter smiled. "You will not labor alone. I sent to Wurzburg for the Guardian of the Capuchins. He brings experience in these matters."

An aide to Winter rapped lightly on the door, poked his head in, and said, "Father Francis has arrived."

Winter nodded. "Send him in."

A small man with graying hair and beard walked in. His simple brown robe and bare feet confirmed he was a discalced Capuchin. Father Francis bowed slightly and approached Georg. "A beautiful child! What a blessing from God. May I ask the child's name?"

"Dorothea, in memory of her mother," Georg replied.

Father Francis smiled at Dorothea. "May God bless you, Dorothea, and hold you forever in His love. And may you honor your mother as you grow strong in the Lord."

Father Francis waved his hand over the child in the sign of the cross, then took hold of the wooden cross hanging from his neck and kissed it. He looked into Georg's eyes, smiled, and said, "Georg Flock, I presume. I am sorry for your loss. Today you weep but you will be comforted. What the devil meant for evil, the Lord will use for good. You hold the very promise of God's comfort in your arms. All of Bamberg has much to grieve and much to overcome."

Anton Winter led Father Francis to Bamberg Cathedral. The canon met them in the sacristy. Winter got directly to the point. "Your Prince-Bishop has defied both Emperor and Pope and has fled like the scoundrel he is. Father Francis, from Wurzburg, has come to restore order and, with God's grace, bring healing to our people. As the Emperor's agent, I expect you will assist him in every regard."

The canon nodded. "Your reputation for ending the witch trials in Würzburg is well known. I will assist as I can."

Father Francis replied, "I will hear your confession and

the confession of every cleric and priest in Bamberg. I will hear you in the torture room of the Malefizhaus in one hour."

All color drained from the canon's face. "The Malefizhaus? Yes, as you say. One hour."

Beginning with the Cathedral Canon, one by one, every priest and deacon was silently led through the Malefizhaus to the torture chamber, where Father Francis sat on a stool beside the blood-stained table. He waited silently for the cleric to take in the horror around him before saying simply, "I will hear your confession."

After hearing the confessions, the monk addressed the gathered clergy: "Confession is the first step towards forgiveness which precedes reconciliation and recovery. You are to call the people of Bamberg to confess and remember those who suffered at the hands of their brothers and sisters. Every citizen of Bamberg shall pass through the Malefizhaus before confession. Once every confession is heard, we shall gather at the cathedral for a requiem mass—"

A priest interrupted, "For witches? Surely some were guilty?"

Father Francis stared at the priest. "Surely? Who? Who was surely guilty? Surely not! No! I say, not one was a true witch! Were your eyes closed when you came to confession? Could not your mind hear the screams of the tortured? Truly, only God shall be their judge!"

The priest lowered his head.

Father Francis continued where he had left off. "A mass in their remembrance. Canon, you shall preside, but I shall give the sermon. Let it be known. Two days from now will be Bamberg's day of confession and remembrance."

Two days later, after the people passed silently through the Malefizhaus and stood for the requiem mass, Father Francis walked to the pulpit and addressed them. "People of Bamberg, I have come because of the pleadings of your neighbor, Georg Flock, to save the life of his dear wife, Dorothea. Georg's pleadings moved Emperor Maximilian and the Holy Father, Pope Urban VIII, to command her freedom and condemn the unholy witch trials. The messengers came too late for Dorothea. Help came too late for too many citizens of Bamberg. But be assured God heard their prayers. He heard the prayers and cries of those unjustly burned. You ask: Does He not care? Does He ignore our suffering? I say: Father God suffered with them and suffers with you who have lost loved ones. Our God is well acquainted with suffering."

Father Francis turned and pointed to the crucifix above the altar. "Did God the Father not hear the prayers of His son Jesus? Did He take the cup of suffering away from our Savior? Was not Jesus falsely accused? Was not our Lord unjustly murdered? Is God blind to injustice? No! God is just. Just and loving. He is a rewarder of those who love Him. Where is the reward? Where is the justice their suffering demands?"

Father Francis paused, his gaze passing over the silent citizens of Bamberg. Every mouth was silent. Every ear was attentive. He continued: "Perhaps the Father's justice is held back in mercy. Mercy for the guilty. Oh, we all know someone guilty. Not all of the guilt can be laid upon the Prince-Bishop and the Auxiliary Bishop. Bamberg numbers many thousand, far too many for two men to stand against. Yes. God has mercy on the guilty just as He hears the prayers of the falsely accused.

"It is written, 'He is slow to anger,' but is He slow to save? Never say such a thing! His word is unchanging; His promises unbreakable. What shall we say, then? Is God not sovereign? Why did He not act? Why did he permit such atrocities for so long? God has stood by and watched all of Christendom fight a war for more than a decade.

"We have suffered famine and plague, and God does not intervene. Our God, who created all that is, who divided the sea for the people of Israel, who moved back the sun from its ordained path, has chosen to wait. Perhaps, He waits for sinners to repent. Or He waits for His church to rediscover its faith, love, and works of mercy to the widow, the orphan, and, yes, the suffering. I do not know why He waits. Who can know the mind of God? No man sees beyond the veil.

"But God sees us through the veil. He sees us here and sees us in eternity. Perhaps it is a trial, a test of faith. I trust His love continues. I trust His rewards always come. And I trust justice will be done. I ask: Do you trust Him? Repentance is not enough. You must trust Him and obey—and begin to live again."

Father Francis turned and pointed to Anton Winter in front of the congregation. "Herr Anton Winter comes to Bamberg on the commission of the Emperor. Know that he is a good and righteous servant. All should know him. Please hear what he has to say. I have asked him to pray for you. Herr Winter?"

Anton Winter came forward, stopped short of the altar, turned, and spoke: "People of Bamberg, you have suffered more than most through this era of war, famine, and pestilence. Your Prince-Bishop failed you and added great burdens and unjust fear, persecuting the innocent. Your Emperor has heard your cries. I am here to restore peace. Now hear as I pray to God for you and those you have lost."

He bowed his head and prayed: "May God, the Father of all mercies, end the darkness and shine new light on our city and Hofstift. Make us all, in our daily toils, useful tools in our ordained service. And Father, in your due time and most merciful way, bring us eternal peace and happiness. Amen."

More than a thousand innocent people were burned as witches in Bamberg—nine hundred in the short reign of Prince-Bishop Johann Georg Fuchs von Dornheim alone. The protestant Swedish army of Gustavus Adolphus occupied the city in 1633, preventing Prince-Bishop von Dornheim from returning and ensuring there was no resurgence of witch trials.

The bloody war between Catholics and protestants, begun in 1618, continued to ravage Europe in a time that saw a mini-ice age bring famine and its partner, plague, to the continent until it finally ended with the peace of Westphalia in 1648.

SEARCHING FOR DAVID LIVINGSTONE

The torrent began to let up. The downpour slowed to a steady, soaking rain. Branches, green with leaves and large brightly-hued blossoms swirled, adrift in the muddy flow over the remnants of the pathway. The rain and humidity made the hot air thick to breathe and mixed into sludge with the heavy, salty sweat on his skin. It was an imponderable truth to the Scotsman—as quickly as the clean rainwater washed away his sweat, it stubbornly returned. The relentless rain could not cleanse or comfort his overheated, emaciated body.

A skilled physician, he knew the cholera and pneumonia that racked his body were releasing their grip. His headache and muscle cramps were almost gone, and the morning passed without diarrhea. He knew his strength would return if he could keep down some food without vomiting. He swung his hand over the bowl of food in front of him in a futile attempt to chase away the flies. Insects swarmed around him and he avoided eating them when he could. He managed a few bites of fruit and gulped down a gruel-like manira corn porridge before he put down the bowl, smiled at his audience, and offered a "thank you" in the Tswana language.

Beyond his roped-off, open thatched-roof hut, the men of Bambara watched the curious white man eat. It had been weeks since Doctor David Livingstone was found near death by Arab slave traders and taken to Bambara. The Bambara empire extended across a large swath of central Africa. They were a Mandinka people but as skilled traders, they undoubtedly understood a little Tswana from their neighbors to the south. With his supplies exhausted, Livingston was given medical treatment by his rescuers and left to recover in Bambara. He was fed in return for providing entertainment—a living exposition for his new benefactors.

The year was 1869. It was three years since he began his third expedition to Africa. No longer a missionary for the London Missionary Society, Livingston was on a search for the source of the Nile for the Royal Geographical Society. The Royal Society received his first and last message shortly after he arrived. Two years later, it was reported that his bearers from the Comoro Islands said Livingstone was dead. In truth, only two trusted team members remained with him, James Chuma and Abdullah Susi, former slave traders. The Nile expedition was approved grudgingly after Livingstone's Zambezi expedition in search of a cross-continental water trade route proved an embarrassing failure.

A hero or a goat, the public wondered what had become of the great missionary turned explorer. While the Royal Society remained silent, the *New York Herald* funded the reporter, Henry Morton Stanley, to find Doctor Livingston. And while the naked white primate sat out the rainy season in his Bambara zoo enclosure, his son, Doctor William

Livingstone, made a house call on Sir Roderick Murchison.

Number 15 Whitehall Place was London's address for adventure and exploration. What began as a gentleman's dinner club in 1830 was now the world-famous Royal Geographical Society, and Sir Roderick was the Society's president.

A stern secretary outside of the president's office told William that Sir Roderick was busy and would be unable to see him. "If you leave your card, Doctor, we will send for you when the time is convenient."

William replied, "Aye, I shall indeed leave my card. As for a convenient time, there is no time like the present!" William walked past the surprised secretary and burst through Sir Roderick's door.

Sir Roderick put down the newspaper he was reading, jumped to his feet and exclaimed, "Who are you to barge in here unannounced? Preposterous! Get out or I shall call for a constable!"

"I am Doctor Livingstone...."

Sir Roderick's face flushed with confusion.

"...William Oswell Livingstone, son of Doctor David Livingstone, whom you have abandoned in the jungles of Africa. Not a word from you or the Society since my father left on your expedition nearly three years ago. It seems the whole civilized world asks after my father—everywhere except the sumptuous halls of the Royal Society...."

"Now see here, Livingstone, you can't just storm into my office...." Murchison paused. He took a deep breath and said softly, "Please, sit down, doctor."

Both men exhaled their passion and sat down. Sir Roderick began: "We met, you and I, many years ago. You were just a lad. Your father was speaking at the Society. It was his first presentation. He had returned from the field to bring your mother and siblings home to be raised in the safety of Britain. He introduced you as his little 'Zouga,' named after the river beside which you were born."

William sat down. "My family calls me Zouga to this day."

"I, we—the Society—has not abandoned nor forgotten your father. We have received only one report from him, and that was two years past. He knows where dispatches may be posted. Good men wait for word. And then there is the account from his bearers...."

"Runways! In no way trustworthy. The scoundrels were caught leaving for their homeland in secret. Separate them, and each would give a different account! What of his team members and trusted men? No word. Are you not embarrassed that an American newspaper takes more interest than the Society? They hired the vainglorious self-promoter, Stanley, to mount a search."

"What are you asking? Do you wish to follow in the footsteps of your brother, Robert? He, too, searched for your father when word was lost in his previous expedition. This is not the first time he failed to contact the outside world. Your brother, Robert, searched and found nothing. Was it not his guilt and allegiance to your father's anti-slavery passions that led Robert to join the Union cause in the American Civil War that cost him his life? What did Robert accomplish?"

"My brother gave his life to a noble cause...."

Sir Roderick continued, "Or your brother Thomas, in Egypt, badgering everyone going up the Nile to take him along."

William shook his head. "My father has brought fame, prestige, and contributions to the Royal Geographical Society. I want the RGS to send an expedition to find—to *rescue* my father. Yes, you ask what I want—I seek my father!"

Sir Roderick gazed into William's face. "You search for what you do not know." But then again he paused. "All right, yes; I will help you. Every son should know his father. I have someone in mind. Come back tomorrow. We shall see if he will agree."

After William left, Sir Roderick told his secretary, "There is a gentleman, Lieutenant Dawson, staying at my club. Send a messenger for him. I need him at once."

The ambitious young Lieutenant Dawson stood in front of Sir Roderick Murchison at rigid attention. Sir Roderick looked up at Dawson and said, "You have been pestering the members of this Society for the opportunity to join an expedition. Well, I have decided it is time to find the good Doctor Livingstone. We can't have the propagandists at the *New York Herald* writing the story of Britain's greatest explorer. I'm offering you the greatest opportunity of your life. I want you to lead the expedition. Well, man, what do you say? Others come to mind as well."

"I am your man, Sir Roderick! Mister Stanley is on his way to Africa. If I am to find Doctor Livingstone before Stanley, I will need a good team and a fast ship. I know the right men to ask—"

Sir Roderick interrupted. "You may choose *one* man. The two of you will accompany Doctor William Livingstone and see no harm comes his way. You will go where he asks but see it is done safely."

"I don't understand. William Livingstone will choose the route?"

Roderick sighed. "He is David Livingstone's son. He searches for his father. Your mission is to assist him. You will keep the Royal Society informed and maintain a journal. The Society will determine what is published—the great accomplishments and good faith efforts of the Society. Your reputation, Dawson, is joined with the Society's. I expect you to protect both reputations. Do you understand?"

"You send me to nursemaid a son looking for his father. I am the evidence of the Royal Society standing by its man. You worry Stanley will find David Livingstone to the great embarrassment of the Royal Society...."

"Look at it as insurance. Perhaps Doctor Livingstone is already dead. But just maybe, Stanley will fail, and you become a hero. Regardless, you lead an expedition of the Royal Geographical Society. Others may follow. Now, who will be your second?"

"A friend, Lieutenant Henn."

Sir Roderick nodded. "Only if he is immediately available."

Murchison picked up the newspaper on his desk and scanned it. "Yes, here we are, voyages to Africa, East Africa—port calls—yes, this will do, Zanzibar and Bagamoyo, German East Africa, headquarters German East Africa Company. Banks, good communications, and near the Great Lakes. P and O's newest ship, the SS *Peshawur*, is sailing from Southampton via Port Said, then Suez Canal, Zanzibar, East Africa, and India."

Dawson replied, "I say, the Suez? That will take weeks off the voyage. I heard the first convoy through suffered several groundings."

"That was nearly a year ago, Dawson. First-time stumbles are not unusual. You want to be an explorer yet you fear a passage on a luxury ship through a straight canal? Stanley has a strong start on you. You must take every opportunity."

Sir Roderick stared at Dawson, wondering if he'd chosen the right man. He shook his head the started writing. Dawson's face flushed with the fear that he'd failed before he even began.

Murchison put down his pen and gave the note he'd written to Lieutenant Dawson. "Take this to the Bursar. He will arrange passage for three and give you the appropriate credit documents to use along the way. Please ask my secretary to show Doctor Livingstone into my office."

Dawson stepped out and returned with William Livingstone. Sir Roderick stood. "Doctor William Livingstone, this is Lieutenant Dawson. He will lead the expedition to find your father. There will be three of you. You sail from Southampton for Bagamoyo one week from today. Good luck, gentlemen. That will be all."

William's head was swimming: *What do I need? So much to do. It never occurred to me to prepare if he said yes. Father's friend and companion on his first expeditions, William Cotton Oswell, he will know what I need and how to prepare. His home in Groombridge is only forty-five miles from London. Not too far by train. Yes, I shall call on him at once!*

William Cotton Oswell greeted his namesake warmly. "Zouga! How good it is to see you! You have grown into a man! Studying medicine, like your father, I hear. Come in! Yes, come in and tell me all. How is your father? Any word? Has he found the source of the Nile? Agnes, young Zouga Livingstone has come. Set a place for him at the table, and....." Turning to Livingstone, Oswell asked, "You will stay the night? You'll find no comfort at the local pub. Let me take your coat. Children, come meet the great Doctor Livingstone's son."

William took off his coat and stepped in. "Thank you for your kind welcome. No. There has been no word from Father. That is why I have come. I'm off to Africa to find him. I depart in one week. I have come seeking your advice."

Sitting in William Oswell's study, the experienced explorer gave wise counsel: "Our first adventures took us across the Kalahari desert, quite a different trek than the rain, mountains, and rivers of central Africa's great lakes. Yes, preparation. First, you must stay covered no matter the heat. Always a hat, and do not ignore your neck, arms, and legs. Sweat as you will, good clothing is a must against the sun. And your feet. Bring three or more pairs of boots. Dry feet! Every night wash and dry your feet before you sleep. Begin every day with dry boots. Medicine, a year's portion for each party member doubled or tripled, carried separately to ensure against loss. Malaria and dysentery will surely ail you. Cholera, typhoid, and poison are also great threats. Rifles with plenty of rounds for each of your key men. Don't expect one or even two shots to stop most big game."

Zouga nodded. "Father told the story you survived not one but two rhinos tossing you overhead by their horns."

"Indeed. Your father's prayers were heard and our Lord preserved me for the blessings of a loving wife and children. No doubt you have heard of your father's recovery from the jaws of a lion. Shot three times before the vicious attack." Oswell paused then: "But most importantly, carefully select your laborers and bearers. But even wiser in selecting their overseers. Abide no corporal punishment and treat them with respect. Earn their trust, for your life will be in their hands."

Agnes Oswell stepped into the study. "Dinner."

Over dinner, Zouga asked, "How did you and Father meet? You weren't a missionary."

Oswell laughed. "No. I have been called many things but never a missionary. Please don't misunderstand me: I hold the greatest admiration for your father, his faith, and his service. No, another of his friends—Captain Steele—recommended me to your father. In 1847, your father had established a mission in Kolobeng on the edge of the Kalahari. They were hard times—a bad drought. He brought the entire mission population from Chounuane, the Baakwena tribe. Their young chief, Sechele, converted under the patient ministering of your father. Well, the Boers would have none of it. They feared a new tribe, one being taught irrigation and modern ways. They determined to attack before it became too strong. You must understand that England had won control over all the south of Africa, but the Boers—Dutchmen and some Huguenot French—did not hold to the anti-slavery laws or believe the tribes could be civilized."

Zouga interjected, "Their views have not changed to this day."

Oswell continued, "Aye. Well, threats of reports to Europe cautioned the Boers, but your father decided to move—across the Kalahari, into the unexplored interior and away from the Boers."

Zouga nodded. "And you joined him in his trek across

the desert in search of a new homeland for his mission."

"Some trek! Nearly died of thirst. But we were the first white men to lay eyes on Lake Ngami. Went as far north as Linyanti. When we returned, your father sent word to his London Missionary Society superiors in Cape Town requesting to move his mission. I remember his words: 'I will go where I am sent as long as it is forward!'"

"But the Baakwena tribe, they remain at Kolobeng. There are times I wish my father were not the first to find Lake Ngami...."

"Why say such a thing?"

Zouga replied: "The gold medal awarded him by the Royal Geographical Society. It drew him away from his calling as a missionary for Christ."

Oswell leaned over and patted the arm of his friend's son. "There are missionaries beyond the London Missionary Society. The Doctor Livingstone I know believes he serves Christ and the Church in Africa. *Always forward*, he would say. Now, he had disagreements with other missionaries, but for certain, he was not one to till in another man's garden. David Livingstone is a man of prayer and deep faith, convinced he is doing God's work. You have read his books and heard his speeches and sermons. You must know this."

"His books speak of exploration and the marvels of sights unseen by white men. His speeches beg for support for yet another expedition. I cannot forgive him for his glowing reports of the Zambezi valley—a paradise for settlers and farmers. His exaggerations led to my poor mother's death and the death of the bishop and others who eagerly sought to join him. The land proved to be grassy swamps, a place fouled by malaria and every sort of disease. He wrote for fame and money, not for saving souls."

"You judge your father too harshly. Yes, he wrote for profit. Profit to give you, your brothers, and your sisters a better life than he had. It is something every father wishes for his children. Were you, Zouga, at age twelve, required to work twelve hours a day, seven days a week, in a cotton mill to support your family? No. Nor did you work your way through the University of Glasgow for your medical degree. And your mother, God rest her soul, knew the risks. Your parents heard the whispers—that your mother was a crude and vulgar woman. No, she bore the pain of libel and separation for her children. Theirs was a deep and affectionate love, and their efforts were to bring Christianity to the interior of Africa through commerce and civilization."

Zouga shook his head. "Yes, his great failed philosophy—Christianity, commerce, civilization. Somehow, opening up the African interior to commerce with Europe would miraculously spur the slave traders to abandon their evil practice. And Europeans, with their missionary schools and skills in agriculture, mining, and technology, would civilize the tribes into good Christians. What is the record to date? Easier access for the slave traders! My father's journals tell of large swaths of vacant land depopulated by slave traders. The great states of Europe compete for lucrative ivory, copra, and mineral wealth. They take, they do not give, and most damning of all, they deny the African his due respect as a man created in the image of God, in all ways equal in the sight of our Lord."

Zouga sighed then and lowered his eyes. He felt the heat of his passion tingling on the top of his head.

Oswell replied softly, "Must a man persuade with

words? Are we not moved by a life well-lived? Cannot character reap results? My faith was renewed by walking alongside David Livingstone. What other white man is trusted by so many tribal chiefs? Don't take my word; ask for him among the tribes. Seek out Chief Sechele. Hear what a disciple has to say."

"My father said Sechele lapsed."

Oswell smiled. "Visit the chief. And I pray you find your father and hear his defense."

A knock on his door disturbed William Livingstone's thoughts as he completed packing another trunk. He opened the door, exclaiming in surprise: "Grandpa Robert!"

Robert Moffat stepped into the room. "I heard you are going in search of your father. I came to pray with you before you depart."

"Of course, Grandpa, I would like that very much." William cleared a stack of medical supplies from a chair for his grandfather.

"I would also urge you to visit your uncle John in Kuruman, where he continues the Lord's work at the mission. John and your mother were very close. Both were skilled in the Tswana language. With the Bible in Tswana, now John continues the work in the language of the Ndebele people."

"I have considered visiting Sechele, Chief of the Kwena, thought to be in Kolobeng. I must pass through Kuruman. Of course, I will visit Uncle John. I will gladly carry letters and packages."

Robert smiled. "What a blessing Sechele has become—the Barnabas of Africa."

William replied: "Barnabas? Why do you call him a

Barnabas? Father said he lapsed."

"When you meet him, you will understand. But let me say this about Chief Sechele: No man has done more to introduce our missionaries to the tribes of Africa than Chief Sechele. Lapsed? Perhaps he does not accept all our rules for living—the man was unwilling to give up his wives and some ancient customs—but he claims faith and speaks boldly for our God."

William nodded. "Grandpa, do you think Father abandoned his calling? The way he walked away from the mission field."

"Is this why you seek him? Because the newspapers and the Royal Society portray him as England's greatest explorer? You fear he has abandoned God's call on his life. And you blame him for your mother's untimely death." The gray-bearded missionary sighed. "Sit down, Zouga, and listen. I have overseen the work of many missionaries in Africa. I knew the day I met your father he was different—he would challenge the established order. I was away with my family on leave in England when your father arrived. He wasted no time in quarreling with the Boers and questioning the work of our missions. He had already journeyed in-land from our station. Realizing I would receive reports on his unprecedented behavior, he chose to meet me when we arrived in country. He met us at the ship and arranged an ox cart to carry us and our belongings the four hundred miles to Kuruman."

Zouga interjected, "Yes, that is how he met Mother."

Moffat continued: "For eighteen days he talked; he poured out his heart with his vision for Africa. In his honesty and passion, he could not see how others, well-intentioned, good people, could be offended by his words. So clear was his vision, so pure his motives. I did not doubt his calling or that he would not fit the mold of our current work."

Grandfather Moffat shook his head and laughed. "He once said to me—after all my years of labor—and without a hint of malice: 'You have planted more fruit trees at the station than converts to the faith.' It hurt but it was the truth. We had made Kuruman Station a comfortable outpost for the missionaries. We had good orchards, irrigated fields, and healthy herds. We built a fine church, and a few local laborers attended a small school. I was happy studying their language and translating the Bible. Well, your mother listened to his passion and saw the same vision—taking the gospel to new tribes and people. Not those who came to the mission for work, but Africans who would hear the Good News and spread it among their people. You have heard him say he would not tend another man's garden, but he picked precious fruit from mine—my beloved daughter, your mother. I will not hear any word against their marriage. They shared a deep and abiding love. They were of one mind and one spirit.

"Once their intentions were known, I decided they should open a new station, but it proved too close to a Boer settlement. He tried a second, and again there were troubles. As I said, your parents were of one mind and determined to go beyond the Kalahari, beyond the reach of any white man's footsteps—"

Zouga interrupted. "I know how his trekking began. You spoke of his troubles with others and his vision for Africa. It had to be more than planting mission stations."

"The slave trade and the treatment of the people. He saw the Boers, who viewed the tribes as a threat to colonization, and he saw the Crown authority's appeasement of European settlers, as overlooking injustice and the oppression of the very people we were sent to evangelize. All people are equal in the eyes of God. His vision was to make that truth evident in the life of every African—and acknowledged by every European. Like the key points of a sermon, he summarized his vision: Christianity, commerce, and civilization. Christianity changes the heart and puts men right with God. Commerce determines how people deal with each other. Trading brings prosperity and raises people out of poverty. If the continent's wealth could be brought out to the ports and traded with the world, prosperity on trade goods would end the evil prosperity of the slave trade. But more than that, commerce builds an economy that raises esteem and confidence built on merit and achievement. Commerce pulls along its little brother, civilization. And civilization—equality with worldwide respect—is a civilized Africa built faithful to Christ and Christian values."

Robert closed his eyes in memory and prayer. "And your mother was born and raised in Africa. She stayed in Scotland only to benefit you children. Her happiest days were in Africa. And her heart was always with your father."

Zouga sighed. "It is true Mother would hear no word spoken against father. And she, indeed, was happiest in Africa. But I don't see any fruit from Father's efforts."

Robert smiled. "God commands us to go and make disciples. The command is open—we do not own the fruit of laboring for Him. We are mortal. As Solomon said, our lives are like leaves of grass here today and gone tomorrow. Zouga, know this: God takes a long view. What Israelite welcomed slavery in Egypt or captivity in Babylon? Our love commands us to trust and obey."

A LIGHT IN THE DARKEST NIGHT

Zouga nodded. "It seems everyone knows my father but me. I miss him and want to know him before he is gone forever. Will you pray for me, Grandfather?"

William Livingstone made his way along the busy Southampton wharf until the long black hull of the new steamship *Peshawur* came into view, its tall black smokestack rising just forward of the middle of three masts. William had never seen such a large, magnificent ship. He soon recognized Lieutenants Dawson and Henn standing beside a large wagon filled with crates. "Good day, Mister Livingstone! Keep only your steamer trunk for the passage with you. Put the rest with these. We'll see that they are safely stowed. I have your ticket. Henn and I will join you on board shortly."

William took his ticket while a porter came to take his steamer trunk. An immaculately uniformed officer examined his ticket at the gangway. "Welcome aboard, Mister Livingstone. You'll find your cabin on the starboard side on the main deck."

The officer whistled and a porter scurried down. "Cabin Three." Then turning to William he said: "Follow the porter. Then feel free to take refreshments in the salon. We sail at five o'clock."

William followed the porter down the wide, covered main deck. It was not POSH (Port Outbound, Starboard Homebound) but in every other way first class. His cabin would face the afternoon sun the whole journey down the Suez Canal and the East African coast. The wide covered deck was meant to offer protection from the sun, but the heat would still be felt inside. The positive was that he would enjoy unobstructed views of the Egyptian desert and the African coast during the long voyage south.

Lieutenants Dawson and Henn joined him soon after and they sat in shaded deck chairs outside William's cabin. The three men spent the time reading David Livingstone's reports to the RGS and his books. The most recent maps were laid out as they pondered the best routes to possible locations, knowing Livingstone's theories of the headwaters of the Nile. Dawson agreed to William's destination decision within the bounds of safety for which he was responsible. William's role in-country would be advisory. All orders would come from Dawson. Henn would monitor their supplies and the logistics of the expedition.

The ship arrived at the Eastern Mediterranean entrance to the canal at Port Said in the late afternoon. The ship docked and loaded fresh fruit, vegetables, meat, and fish for the voyage south. There was no intention of docking at Suez at the canal's southern end. The ship would continue the long transit through the Gulf of Suez, the Red Sea, around the Horn of Africa, and into the Indian Ocean for far off Zanzibar. The following morning the transit began. William wrote in his journal:

> Began transit at six o'clock. French and Egyptian pilots are directing navigation. Passing through the dig, the canal is sufficiently wide for one ship at a time. I believe I could safely jump ashore from either side of the ship! The ship's Master tells me passing is only possible in the several lakes along the route. Sitting on deck, it feels like driving through a sandy desert. Uncanny to see caravans of laden

camels walking along the canal. Anchored overnight in Great Bitter Lake while northbound ships passed. So many stars. I wonder if Father is watching them with me. At Port Suez, they loaded fresh fish from a dhow that came alongside. Slowed but did not stop. Most skilled seamanship I have ever witnessed. The time from Port Said to Suez was forty hours.

Life aboard the ship fell into a routine. Breakfast, followed by exercises in the cooler morning while the crew swabbed the passenger deck. Then studying maps and reports, lunch, a nap, and sitting in the deck chairs watching the coast of Africa slip by. After dinner, drinks, and conversation into the night. The hours and watches were announced by the number of rings on the ship's bell. William's sea legs adjusted to a gentle roll, pitch, and yaw as the screw propeller drove the riveted iron hull at a steady twelve knots. The rhythmic heartbeat of the reciprocating steam engine was a gentle reminder that all was well.

Days turned into weeks. A month passed, and the African coast was still fixed in sight of William's stateroom window. Staying close to the shore provided a light sea breeze from the convergence of the cooler ocean beside the scorched land. In the fifth week, the ship altered course just a bit offshore. The island of Zanzibar appeared ahead.

The ship docked alongside a wharf in Stone Town, in sight of the old Portuguese Fort and the palace of Sultan Barghash bin Said. The people of Zanzibar primarily submitted to the Islamic faith of their Omani Arab rulers. Still, a Roman

Catholic Cathedral and Anglican church announced the significant presence of Europeans in the trading capital of East Africa. William, Dawson, and Henn would disembark for a coastal trader to carry them the twenty-odd miles to Bagamoyo on the mainland. The *Peshawur* would load stores and continue to Bombay.

While Henn arranged the transfer of their baggage and equipment to the coastal steamer, William and Dawson made their way past the slave market and the Anglican church to the British Consulate. Lieutenant Dawson produced a sealed diplomatic pouch to Consul John Kirk.

Kirk broke the seal, unlocked the bag, and read the contents. Looking up, he said, "Her Majesty's government directs me to assist the Royal Geographical Society's mission to find Doctor Livingstone with goods, contracts, transportation, visas, and funds up to ten thousand pounds. It continues, 'If upon finding Doctor Livingstone, he determines to continue his explorations, additional funding may be requested.'"

Kirk put down the document. "Lieutenant Dawson, the determination of requirements is left to you. But I must say, a large stockpile of supplies remains at a warehouse in Bagamoyo. Supplies intended for his expedition but languishing for lack of direction from Doctor Livingstone."

Dawson replied, "Excellent. We shall start there. And our laborers, bearers, and reliable overseers?"

Kirk replied, "All available in Bagamoyo. There is a trader, Tippu Tib. He will fit you up with men. His palace is here, but he has a man in Bagamoyo. No one knows the trade routes of the interior better than Tippu Tib."

William asked, "He is Arab? Not a slave trader?"

"Yes to both. But if you want to locate your father, you need Tippu Tib's men. They know the path to every village and hut in Africa."

After the two-hour crossing to Bagamoyo, William, Dawson, and Henn walked to a warehouse across the street from the wharf. Above the door, a sign in English and German read: Royal Geographical Society, London.

Reaching for a key, Dawson was surprised to find the door unlocked. He pushed the door open and stepped inside. The darkened room was filled with wooden crates, tops pried off, and clumps of shredded wood packing strewn across the floor. Clothing, blankets, and mosquito netting were thrown about. Dawson called out: "I say! Doctor Livingston's been burgled! There isn't a box that hasn't been opened and its contents rifled."

As William and Henn followed Dawson, a loud thump was heard from the back of the room. An unseen man replied, "Scoundrels took everything of value—no medical supplies left at all."

Footsteps were heard, and a man in light khakis wearing a pith helmet emerged from the shadows. "This is your fault. If you had done your job, this would never have happened."

"Our fault? We disembarked with William Livingston not half an hour ago. We're here to find Doctor Livingstone. We were told to use these provisions provided by the RGS."

The stranger walked closer. "You are not from the British Consulate? My apologies. Which of you is William Livingstone?"

William stepped forward. "I am he. And you, sir?"

"Sir, your father is safe. I left him on the shores of Lake Tanganyika not a month ago. My name is Stanley. Henry Morton Stanley, reporter for the *New York Herald*. I came to the warehouse looking for your father's supplies. Nothing has reached him in three years. The medical supplies are most urgent. Doctor Livingstone is in declining health—malaria, fevers, and stools. He is determined to continue his work; I have promised to see him properly supplied."

William stammered, "Alive! You have found my father? He is safe—but very sick? Is he dying? Lake Tanganyika, you say. I have brought medical supplies with me. We are preparing an expedition. Yes, relief. We must bring him relief!"

Lieutenant Dawson spoke, "Stanley, if that is who you are, what is your proof? How do we know you found Doctor Livingstone?"

Stanley faced William as he replied to Dawson: "Come to my lodgings. I have your father's journals, maps, and letters, too. Rest easy; he is safe. And you, William, he will be most happy to see you. Yes, you shall carry his relief supplies. I will take his journals to London."

William snapped: "You have his journals? Why would my father give them to you, a penny-a-line reporter? He despised journalists!"

Stanley ignored the insult. "He was kind. He freely shared what he had learned. I accompanied him on his trek to a river, the Ruzizi. No father could be more patient with a son. Come, you'll see."

William felt his legs waver beneath him. *A better father to Stanley than to his true son.*

In his room, Stanley produced David Livingstone's journals of his search for the Nile. Stanley opened a map and pointed to the village of Ujiji on the northeast shore of Lake Tanganyika. "Here. This is where I found him. He has determined the lake is not the headwaters of the Nile. The Ruzizi River—" He pointed to the top of the lake. "—flows into the lake. The elevation is wrong: Two hundred feet; too low to pass the highlands. He now suspects the Lualaba River will take him to the source. But this is a good place for you to start. They will know where he has gone. And—"

Dawson interrupted. "The Lualaba is far to the west and flows north towards the Congo—"

Stanley snorted. "Don't interrupt with what you don't know. No one has followed the river to the sea. And Doctor Livingstone intended to finish mapping all the lake's tributaries before moving on. He is still along the lake; I'm sure of it. It will take time. Its many sources and tributaries are marshy."

William replied, "Marshy. They will be ripe with malaria and every disease."

Stanley nodded. "Just so. Some would say a death trap."

William picked up the journal and read page after page. Finally, he put it down. "It is my father's hand—and most painful to read. You mentioned letters...?"

Stanley replied, "Yes, to the Royal Society seeking patience and continued support and another to Agnes—"

"My sister. Always my sister! First my brother, Robert, his disobedient firstborn, and now my sister. Never a word for me, Thomas, or Anna."

"Isn't Agnes the oldest now? She and Robert remembered their days in Africa. You were young when you were sent to safety in Scotland. Because your father knows Agnes more does not mean he loves you, Thomas, and Anna, any less. He often spoke of the hardship he placed upon you. Go to Ujiji, ask after your father, and be reconciled with him. But do not delay. He is not a healthy man."

Stanley folded the map and put it in a leather pouch with the journal. "Take my men. I have fifty-six good and able men ready to depart. Twenty-two have made the trip with me to Ujiji. I have flour, oil, sugar, coffee, tea, and hundreds of yards of cloth. And rifles and ammunition. Enough for each man. You say you brought medicine. Good. Take what I have prepared—yes, it is better you go."

Through the thick jungle, the five-hundred-mile trek from Bagamoyo to Ujiji took longer than the seventy-five-hundred-mile sea voyage from South Hampton. Lieutenants Dawson and Henn proved capable leaders and good companions for the ill-suited William. Young Livingstone's constitution did not match the African river Zouga for which he was nicknamed. Repeated bouts of malaria and dysentery took their toll on his already thin body.

His African carriers took special care of two milk cows, having learned from Doctor Livingstone that milk is the best food to combat dysentery. William could barely sit upright on a donkey's back when the column reached Ujiji.

The chief told them, "Go south. Along the eastern shore of the lake you will find the Doctor. Take canoes. If he lives, you will find him at the far end."

Dawson broke the news to William. "Four hundred miles. At the south end of the lake. We can save time if we go by canoe. But if your father has gone inland again, we will be without pack animals. A water passage is not without risk: Storms, beasts frequent the shore, and the sun. The rivers and streams that feed the lake are marshy. Hard to see someone in the reeds, not to mention the flies and disease. Even so, the open waters are clean and healthy, with a good stock of fish. I'm told we can make the southern end in a third of the time. Sadly, they cows cannot join us but we can bring milk goats."

"By all means, we take to the lake!"

Dawson traded the pack animals and some of the cloth and most of the sugar for canoes. Once on the water, it was easy to see the difficulty walking the shoreline. The lake was rimmed by steep, rocky hills spiked with tall boulders, all encased in thick jungle. The clear waters of the lake and the beauty surrounding him refreshed William's weary soul. He watched the rocky bottom as they paddled offshore heading deeper and deeper. Old logs were still visible fifty feet below the surface. There was no lake so crystal clear in all of Britain. The men soon fell into a rhythm, paddling the long, sturdy lake canoes.

One week into their voyage, a north wind began to build. As it grew stronger, waves grew. The north-south orientation of the lake meant a long fetch and tall waves. Dawson directed the expedition to a small beach below a rocky shoreline. One by one, the canoes ground onto the sand.

"Quickly, carry them off the beach onto the rock shelf above," Dawson shouted through the howling wind. They set up camp behind a tall outcropping that shielded them against the fierce gusts.

"The Rukuga," an African guide explained. "No more than two or three days."

Twenty hours later, the wind subsided but the small beach was gone. Every grain of sand was carried away by the storm. The men carefully lowered the canoes, loaded their precious supplies, and paddled south. After two weeks, they reached the bottom of the lake. There was no outflow. The canoes beached in front of a small fishing village. Dawson and a guide sought the chief. "We seek a white man. He travels along the lake with helpers?"

"The white medicine man—yes, he was here. He has gone on towards the Chambeshi River. He travels to Lake Bangweulu. He is not well but he would not rest. If you hurry, you will find him."

Dawson said through the interpreter, "Will you lead us to him?"

The chief replied, "For the goats, someone will guide you."

Hearing the price, William nodded yes.

The fifty-six bearers loaded the supplies on their backs and followed the guide on a well-worn path up the steep hill behind the village. In less than an hour, the view of the lake was lost in the forest and the refreshing breeze was a memory. Heat and humidity sucked at their lungs.

On the second day, William's dysentery returned. There was no goat milk to soothe his stomach.

The path continued up. The grade changed from moderate to steep.

On the third day, they climbed out of the forest. A peak loomed ahead. By afternoon a flat summit appeared and a camp was visible, filled with men busy with their activities.

At the center, a tarp shaded a man sitting at a table.

Dawson, Henn, and William strode forward. The white man looked up and said, "Zouga? It is you, my son! You have come! Please forgive me if I do not stand to greet you. I feel poorly today. Sit. Yes, sit here and tell me all!"

William stared at his father, shocked by what he saw: An old, grizzled, pale, emaciated man. Finally, William uttered, "Father, Lieutenants Dawson, and Henn. They have brought me here under the authority of the RGS. You sent no word. The whole world wonders...."

David Livingstone replied, "That other fellow, the American, Stanley...?"

"Yes, Father, I met Mister Stanley at Bagamoyo—he carries your journals."

Doctor Livingstone nodded. "A good fellow. I miss his company." Lifting his arm and sweeping it across the horizon, he continued. "Look at the great lake below. Have you seen a more beautiful sight? I have explored it and now I sit here finishing my map. Perhaps, it can take me to the source of the Nile. There is a river flowing out from the western shore. The Lukaga. It flows west to the Lualaba, which flows north, perhaps around the heights. But I must know for certain."

William cringed and nearly doubled over. He sprang to his feet and said, "My pardon, Father." He rushed away.

Dawson explained. "Dysentery. Would you have some milk for him? The jungle does not favor him. We traded our milk goats for a guide from the fishing village at the foot of this mount."

Livingstone chuckled. "Their chief is an honest man. You did not question him thoroughly. He answers truly but only what is asked. Now you must trade for him to return the goats."

Lieutenant Henn spoke: "We have brought supplies gathered by Stanley. Your warehouse in Bagamoyo was pilfered. And we have medicines from London."

"My lead men, Chuma and Susi, will see to what you have brought."

William returned and stood in front of his father. "We shall pack everything and leave tomorrow. The weather is good. The canoes are sufficient, and our pack animals remain at Ujiji."

"Sit down, Zouga. This is my camp, my expedition and I follow my calling. Go if you must. I am not returning with you. When I complete my map, I move south to Lake Bangweulu."

"You are too sick to continue. And why Bangweulu, a hundred miles south, if you wish to follow the Lualaba north? Your sickness clouds your reason."

"I should finish mapping the great lakes before following the Lualaba to the Nile and Egypt."

"You sit on your mountaintop and declare the beauty of the land. You see it like a colonist would. There was a time you would have seen the people, God's children hungering for the Good News of salvation and the joy of knowing God's love. Is your mind so clouded that you forget even our Lord's calling on your life, just as you have forgotten your wife and children?"

David Livingstone's face flushed red. He slammed his hands down on the table. William winced and bent over again in pain. He rose and ran off again.

Dawson began to speak, "He ails, Doctor Livingstone. Dysentery and malaria from the beginning. He doesn't mean what he says. He is—"

David interrupted. "He is angry. He judges me. He cannot remain here. I could not bear the pain of his death. You must see him safely back."

Dawson replied, "He seeks answers. Answers and the love of his father, whom he fears will die before giving him his love and approval."

David considered this all in silence but when William returned, David hugged him. "Zouga," the father began. "I will always love you just as I do your brother and sisters and as I loved mother, Robert, and Elizabeth, whom proceed us to our reward. But know that I put my calling above me and all earthly comfort. What is my calling? There was a time I believed my calling was to persuade men to follow Christ. Two years of prayer and gentle persuasion brought the conversion of but one man, and after three months, he returned to his heathen ways. But my vision remains clear: Africans will join the brotherhood of believers with the respect and honor due every man. The wealth of their land will save them from the slaver's trade."

William replied, "Your theory of bringing Christianity through commerce and civilization is a failed vision. And now you search for the headwaters of the Nile for glory and to open the interior for England."

David disagreed. "You do not see the long view. The headwaters of the Nile are a means to my ends. It is the great question that keeps Africa in our government's minds. And why not England? Who better for the good of the African nations? The Arabs and the Portuguese seek only slaves. The Boers seek the land and, in their greed, see the Africans as impediments to be removed or bonded in service. The French build their empire, and the Germans desire only the wealth of untold resources. Britain stands alone in the fight against the slave trade. England offers the best hope to protect, educate and lift the Africans as equals in the sight of God and the nations. So, if England seeks the headwaters of the Nile, I will find it and trumpet the needs of the African people. And if some stipend comes my way, I shall gladly see my children saved from my neglect and safe from poverty."

William sat silently, staring at his father. No one spoke. William sighed. "You are wrong about Sechele. He loves our Lord and serves Him faithfully. Grandfather Robert told me Chief Sechele had done more to place missionaries in Africa than every mission board in Europe. The African church is alive and growing."

Tears welled in David's eyes. "Is that true? Praise God! It is right that Africans tend the flock that they labor to build."

William smiled. "After we find the Nile, I promised Grandfather I would call on Uncle John in Kuruman and travel to Kolobeng to meet Chief Sechele."

"Zouga, you cannot stay with me. Your health—"

"My health? Father, you look like death warmed over!"

"The Lord directs my journey. No, Son, you have succeeded beyond your knowledge. You have lightened the heart of an old man. Go to your uncle John and to Sechele. Take my blessings with you. But I will stay the course."

William spent a week with his father listening. David traced his journeys on a map and his eyes brightened as he told what he had seen, experienced, and learned as he opened up the interior of Africa to Europeans. At last, William understood that despite the pain and injustice the white men brought to central Africa, the people could not remain isolated; if not his father, then it would be someone else. If not imperfect and paternalistic England, it would surely be a less tolerant power. William considered his father's words: *You do not see the long view.*

As David's soft voice continued his tales, William closed his eyes and prayed silently. *Lord, pour out your grace on your children in this land. Open their hearts to your love. Give them a Spirit of comfort and shorten their days of injustice.*

Lieutenant Dawson led William safely back to Bagamoyo. They crossed to Tanzania and caught a ship for Port Elizabeth. Coaches now carried travelers the four hundred miles north to Kuruman. No longer transporting missionaries and their families but men seeking their fortune in the newly discovered diamond fields.

William visited Uncle John whom oversaw the mission John's father had founded. His printing press produced Bibles and tracts in the Tswana language and textbooks for the mission schools. John was actively establishing new missions in Matabeleland. He confirmed what William observed: The Cape Colony was drawing white settlers, and they were pushing further and further north. Africans were struggling to adapt.

"Uncle John, I have just come from my father's expedition in the great lakes region. I promised Grandpa Robert I would see you. He was well when we met and sends his blessings. He prays for you and the mission daily."

"So, your father is found. I am heartened by the news. So much has changed here since he left. Most surprisingly: Our missionaries sent to new villages return to us saying the villagers already serve the Lord, having heard the Word from King Sechele. They do not worship as we do but profess Jesus Christ as their Lord and Savior. Sechele's sons attend the mission school—always the best students, knowing the expectations of their father. Come, you must meet them."

"You say they do not worship as we do. How so?"

"You must meet him. He will explain far better than I am able. By my understanding, Sechele is a serious student of the Bible, not the protestant or Catholic church. He is African and would build an African church."

William said goodbye to his uncle and journeyed by cart another three hundred miles north to Kolobeng. When William was presented to Sechele, Kgosi of Bakwena, king of thirty thousand Kwena people, the great chief rose from his throne, stepped down and embraced William. He said in perfect English: "Welcome, Zouga Livingstone. I share your grief in the passing of your father—my father in the faith—Doctor David Livingstone."

Panic flashed across William's face. "My father is dead? But I just left him—"

"You have not heard? Forgive the pain I bring. But it is true. He is dead. I received news two weeks ago. Yes, he died two months ago in the village of Chief Chitambo. His servants, Chuma and Susi, carried his remains to Bagamoyo then his body was sent to London." Sechele called to an attendant. "A chair for my young friend. And cold water to refresh him."

William wound up taking Schele's offer of a room and rest and, after a few hours, the king came to see him there.

At William's urging for more details, Sechele shared: "Your father was a man of great faith. It is reported he was found kneeling beside his bed. His hands folded and his head lay peacefully, in prayer. It pains me that I could not see him one more time. He called me a backslider because I would not put away my wives. One wife is perhaps a good rule in England. I studied the Scriptures; they called me to Christ and to love others. Is putting away my wives, love? And then there are our traditions. My people have superstitions—must these be ignored? Cannot they linger while faith grows?"

William replied, "My father's last words to me were to bring you his blessings. When I told him how Robert Moffat commended your good works, tears fell from his eyes, and he praised God for you. Be sure, King Sechele, your good works, multiplied thousands of times over, were more treasured than all the medals and honors the British bestowed upon him."

"It is my great disappointment that we did not walk as brothers. I took from the English what I valued: The ability to read and write; to irrigate and husband crops, and most importantly, from your father, the truth of God. But we do not worship as one. Perhaps I must look again and find a new vision."

William smiled. "My father would agree with all that. He said something else: *We must see the long view.* We must look to the future and see how God works through trial and tribulation for good."

Chief Sechele nodded. "Like the Israelites in Egypt."

"Amen."

ANNUNCIATION
OF THE MAGI

She stood outside her door staring into the night sky, her eyes fixed on a bright evening star. She did not hear the footsteps of his approach. When she felt the gentle touch of his hand resting on her shoulder, she softly placed her hand over his. She did not turn. Her gaze remained fixed on the star. Unseen soft tears fell on her cheeks. She sniffled lightly and murmured, "I'm going to have a baby."

The man replied softly, "I pray it will be so! Many sons to care for you after I am gone, and daughters, sweet daughters, to share their mother's great love."

Mary turned around and wiped away the tears. "Joseph, I am with child *now*. An angel... I am with child by the Holy Spirit."

Joseph was stunned to silence, his heart broken. "With child?" he finally stammered.

"The star...." She pointed into the night sky. "It is Gabriel. He brought me the message and now returns to the heavenly hosts."

Joseph dropped his hand from her shoulder. The pit of

his stomach turned. He could feel his fingers tighten into a fist. "What do I know of stars? I am a carpenter." His heart crumbled as he closed his eyes in silence. *I must put her away. She carries the baby of another. Yet still... I love her. No harm must come to her. Yes, secretly; I must put her away in secret.*

Mary looked into Joseph's eyes. She saw the hurt and disbelief. "I will go to the house of my cousin, Elizabeth, in Judah. I will not see you disgraced."

Melchior stood on his Babylon rooftop, studying the night sky. A bright flash low near the hazy indigo horizon surprised him and his thoughts raced: *A comet? Soaring upward from the horizon? Yes, and it grows stronger as it soars. But wait, it pauses, and yet it shines bright—steady now, it forms four points! Strange how the lower resembles a pointer fixed over the earth. A heavenly pointer in the black sky. Most unusual! A ball of fire shooting forth in a cross! Brighter than the evening star—more brilliant than any star, smaller than only the moon. Such the intensity! A new star! Yes, I am certain of it! A new star has joined the heavens! A new star? Where has it come from? What can it mean?*

"Salek!" Melchior called. "Come at once."

A young turbaned man in the robe of an apprentice hurried out into the darkness of the roof observatory. "Here I am, Master Melchior."

"A new star. See it in the east? You cannot miss it for its brightness—the one with four points. I must stay and observe it. But I recall a great magnus of the past who wrote of looking into night visions, of streams of fire from the Ancient of Days, whose throne was a fire of flames upon burning wheels of fire. Of course, there were more recorded visions of the heavenly realm. His name was Belteshazzar.

"Among my scrolls, you will find his chronicles. Put them out for me and then go and search the King's Chronicles; yes, I recall, from Cyrus back to Nebuchadnezzar. Bring me any mentions of stars or reports of Belteshazzar, the Grand Magnus, and Royal Governor."

"The day is done, Master...."

"Take my signet. They will allow you entry. I want them all before sunrise. Belteshazzar; repeat his name."

"The Grand Magnus, Belteshazzar."

"Yes. Now go!"

Hours later, as the pale light of dawn slowly extinguished the stars, Melchior made his way into his chamber. Baskets of scrolls filled the room. A large scroll was laid out on Melchior's table.

"Very good, Salek. I shall begin with his journal. Then I will start on the chronicles from his first recording to his last."

Salek found the earliest scroll and asked, "Belteshazzar was more than a magnus, more than the ruler of the magi. He was second to the King. How is it I have not heard of him? The magi teachers do not mention his name."

Melchior did not look up from his scroll. "It is because he was different. I believe Belteshazzar was the greatest magnus of all time. But he never considered himself one of the magi. He used no spells or divined magic of any kind. He was more of a seer and interpreter of dreams. A humble man, he attributed the magic of his survival in a den of lions—and all his gifts—to his god. But to be chosen by not one but *three* kings in succession speaks to his gift. And he was a man of unquestioned integrity and competence. Yes, he exercised authority with honesty and justice. As for his reputation among the magi? He had but three friends, all fellow captives from Judea, worshippers of that same god."

"A captive? A slave like me?"

"Perhaps to a Greek, you are a slave, but among Medes and Persians, you are a captive. Yes, required to live among us but given the opportunity to serve and prosper. Let Belteshazzar be an example to you."

Melchior and Salek studied the scrolls each morning thereafter until the noon sun topped the sky. They took a midday meal and then slept until dusk, rising after sunset to observe the wondrous new star.

Joseph tried to sleep. Mary would go away and have her baby in Judah, perhaps never to return. The betrothal would be forgotten in Mary's absence. There would be questions, of course, but with the rabbi's support, he could convince another father to offer a daughter in marriage.

The hours passed slowly as he tossed and turned. He lay awake on his bed and saw a star through his open window. How it twinkled, and its light refreshed his weary soul. Was he asleep? The star grew, and then a fiery light came through the window! He must have been dreaming, for soon Joseph saw an angel of the Lord standing before him.

Joseph squinted his eyes and looked away from the bright light, but the voice was both commanding and comforting. "Joseph, son of David, do not be afraid to take Mary as your wife. For the child conceived in her is of the Holy Spirit. She will bear a son; you shall name Him Jesus, for He will save His people from their sins."

Joseph sat in his bed, speechless. He said nothing as

the angel left as suddenly it had come.

Mary traveled to Judah to the house of her pregnant cousin Elizabeth and her husband, Zechariah. Stepping through the door, Mary called out, "Elizabeth! Elizabeth, it's me, cousin Mary. I've come to visit you."

When Elizabeth heard Mary call, she felt the baby in her womb jump. Elizabeth felt a strange energy pass through her body. A tingling of excitement coursed up and down her back and out through her arms and legs to her fingers and toes and up through the top of her head.

Filled with the Holy Spirit, in ecstasy, Elizabeth cried out to Mary in prophecy: "Blessed are you among women, and blessed is the fruit of your womb. And why is this granted to me that the mother of my Lord should come to me? The baby in my womb leaped for joy when I heard your greeting. And blessed is she who believed there would be a fulfillment of what was spoken to her from the Lord."

Young, innocent Mary, overcome with joyful peace, radiant in the Holy Spirit, replied: "My soul magnifies the Lord, and my spirit rejoices in God my Savior, for He has looked on the humble estate of His servant. From now on, all generations will call me blessed; for He who is mighty has done great things for me, and holy is His name. And His mercy is for those who fear Him from generation to generation. He has shown strength with His arm; He has scattered the proud in the thoughts of their hearts; He has brought down the mighty from their thrones and exalted those of humble estate. He has filled the hungry with good things, and the rich He has sent away empty. He has helped His servant Israel, in remembrance of His mercy, as He spoke to our fathers, to

Abraham and to his offspring forever."

When Mary finished, standing silent in glowing beauty, Elizabeth embraced her. The decades of age difference melted away and the two expectant mothers bonded. The Spirit knit their hearts together. Now sisters in faith, full of grace, wisdom, and steadfast love, they united as obedient servants of God in His perfect plan of salvation.

Mary stayed with Elizabeth for three months then returned to Nazareth, pondering where God would lead her. She prayed for Joseph, a good and loving man. "Please, God, prepare him for what is to come."

Balthasar of Arabia soon joined Melchior and Salek. "When I first saw the star, I decided at once to see my friend and teacher Melchior. It is a star, not a comet? I saw it rise the first night like a shooting star. I wondered: Has a new star ever been recorded? And I said to myself: Melchior. If any man knows, it is Melchior of Babylon."

Melchior bowed politely to his friend and said, "Balthasar, you do me too much honor. Yes, a new star, just as you say. My young friend, Salek, assists me in our study. We search the chronicles and the journals of a Grand Magnus of old, one Belteshazzar—"

"The Jew? Also called Daniel?"

"The very man. You remember him?"

"It would be a poor student of Melchior not to remember that great man, Grand Magnus, and Royal Governor."

Melchior nodded. "Visions. Belteshazzar was a man gifted by visions. Some were meant for the king, and others for his people. Riddles. His visions were like riddles in need of interpretation. But every interpretation proved true. I search his chronicles for the star. I recall but have not found, a report of living stars of a heavenly realm. This new star—different from all other stars in the vast night sky—speaks to me as one of these living stars. A messenger of the heavenly realm."

Balthasar replied, "The writings you speak of were those of his fellow captive, Ezekiel, a prophet and a priest of the god of Abraham, Isaac, and Jacob. Ezekiel and Daniel served the same god. The Jews remember both as prophets of their god to this very day. If you search the scrolls Belteshazzar kept, you will surely find their god's prophecies. The Jews are fastidious keepers of their holy book to ensure careless men never corrupt it."

Melchior smiled. "Yes, I recall, many years ago, I came across the saved scrolls of Belteshazzar. That is where I came to see his greatness and the greatness of his god. Salek, gather the scrolls and bring them to me! We shall begin with the accounts of Ezekiel."

That night, the two richly-robed magi watched as the new star climbed from the horizon. Like each night from its first appearance, it moved higher and westward across the clear night sky. At about midnight, the star was directly overhead. The magi watched with amazement as the star's tail flashed and appeared to descend upon them. The star stopped its steady course and hovered.

Melchior broke the silence. "It calls to us. We must follow. It will lead us west to something or someone of great importance."

Balthasar replied, "Yes. My heart tells me it leads us to a great king, unlike any born to man. Yes, I, too, must follow."

A LIGHT IN THE DARKEST NIGHT

Melchior spent the morning arranging for camels, provisions, and guides. Balthasar directed the servants as Salek carefully packed the baskets of scrolls retrieved from Belteshazzar's effects. After one meal and a short nap, Melchior led the small caravan through the western gate. A few miles west of Babylon, the road intersected the trading road north to Asshur and Nineveh. Another small caravan was waiting for them. Balthasar called to Melchior, "It's Gaspar. He journeys from India. Permit him to join us."

As the two caravans came together, Gaspar called out. "Melchior! Balthasar! You follow the star! I looked for you in Susa. Not finding you there, I sent my servant into Babylon. I thought I was too late. But here you are!"

"Gaspar, welcome! Yes, we follow the star. It called to us—"

Gaspar interrupted, "The tail—it reached down to you too! Yes, it calls us to follow. It leads us west, around the Arabian Desert. We have been called to a great event!"

Joseph put down his saw, brushed the sawdust from his sleeves, and walked the few steps across the courtyard to the water pitcher beside a basin outside his door. Hearing the giggles of a girl, he stepped inside. Mary was standing beside the simple table preparing their supper. She turned and, smiling broadly, said, "Joseph, he kicked me! The baby kicked me for the first time. Isn't it amazing? Come here and feel him move."

Joseph stepped beside Mary. She took his hands and gently placed them against her womb. "Did it hurt?" he asked.

Again, she giggled and chirped, "I felt it more in my

heart than in my womb. It was firm yet gentle. It felt like love."

Mary beamed as she looked up at her husband. She laid her head back against his shoulder and sighed. "Blessed. The angel called me blessed. And I am. God has given me a loving husband to walk with me. Handmaiden to the Lord but not left alone; I also have the strength of your love and presence."

Joseph's voice came close to a laugh as he replied, "Mary, you are the stronger of us. Your peace, your faith. I am overwhelmed and unsure of what lies before us."

Mary replied, "Joseph, what did the angel say to you? Was it not: 'Do not fear taking Mary as your wife'? Husband, you, too, are called. You are a good and righteous man chosen by God to lead our house and raise the Holy Child. What prophet, called by God, believed himself worthy? God who calls us blesses, guides, and strengthens us to do His will."

Joseph sighed. "Our neighbors talk. The betrothal was cut short. The wedding celebration was modest, and so soon you are carrying a child."

Mary shook her head. "What they may believe will never change what we know to be true. Now, go outside and wash while I finish supper." She kissed his cheek before he went out the door. Mary sang softly as she prepared their simple meal.

The magi followed the star until dawn. They made camp in a grove off the side of the caravan road. Servants prepared a hot meal, and Salek brought a basket of scrolls to study.

"Belteshazzar has made many comments regarding the scrolls of his acquaintance, or perhaps good friend,

Ezekiel, a prophet of their god." The others accepted the elder Melchior as their leader and listened intently as he spoke. "Thank you, Salek. We shall begin with the scrolls after breakfast. Tell me, Gaspar, what might the star lead us to?"

Gaspar poured a cup of wine. "It must be a king. A great king who will deliver the world from the Angra Mainyu. Ahura Mazda, in his wisdom, will for once put an end to evil thought which brings calamity on all people."

Melchior nodded. "You give new power to the god of Zoroaster. The prophet spoke of an endless battle between good and evil. But the good Ahura Mazda gives only wisdom to his followers—a knowledge of the good. But knowing what is right and good has proven insufficient to live life without straying from the path of righteousness. And what proof has Zoroaster presented to his authority? Only his reasoning— reasoning which can be faulty—having fallen from the way of wisdom in his battle against Angra Mainyu."

Melchior turned to Balthasar. "What do you think we shall find?"

Balthasar replied, "Zoroaster aside, it may lead us to a king or great leader, unheard of before this time. There have been many great kings and conquerors, but never one announced in this way. This supernatural announcement must mean he is greater than any king before him, or perhaps not a king but a holy man, a prophet, or a true priest of the divine."

Salek mumbled softly, "I think Daniel, a prophet, was greater than the kings he served."

Melchior chuckled. "So, the student would school his teachers?"

Salek bowed his head and blushed.

Melchior urged him on. "Speak up, young Salek, make

your point."

Salek looked up and took a deep breath, "It seems Daniel—"

"You do not call him Belteshazzar?"

"He writes in his given name. He is honored by his people as Daniel."

Melchior nodded. "Daniel then. Continue."

"Was he not greater than Nebuchadnezzar? Did he not prophesize all that occurred? And in the end, did not Nebuchadnezzar worship the god of Daniel? Daniel administered the empire during the reign of three great kings. Your kings each did as he advised. And Daniel's people were protected all the years of their captivity until they returned home during the time of Cyrus the Great. But greater still was Daniel, who did not seek riches. He gave all the glory to his god."

Balthasar replied, "Yet the prophet you call Daniel looked to his acquaintance, also a prophet, Ezekiel—"

Salek interrupted. "Both a prophet and a priest."

Balthasar continued, "To the Jews, only a priest can bring atonement to the people through sacrifice. Not even a prophet can make them righteous."

Melchior replied, "Balthasar, you say Belteshazzar's— excuse me, Daniel's—people are ruled by a king and yield to the warnings of their prophets but must make atonement through a priest. So, if Daniel, our great magnus and a prophet of Judah, is our guide, we may find a king, a prophet, or a priest. But even so, no ordinary man; his star tells us he is greater than any who have preceded him. Now, Salek, show us where Ezekiel speaks of living stars of the heavenly realm."

"Ezekiel begins with his calling, by the river Chebar,

among the exiles. 'The heavens were opened, and I saw visions of God—'"

"The Chebar? We all know the place. In Babylon! The god of Daniel came to Babylon!"

"He came to both Ezekiel and Daniel in Babylon many times."

Melchior smiled. "So you see, we are connected! Our greatest magnus connects Babylon to the god of the heavenly realm. It is his star we follow!"

Salek continued. "Yes, first a vision of a living, fiery chariot in the night sky, and amid it, something like burning coals of fire—living beings darting to and fro, like bolts of lightning. And there is more."

Melchior was emphatic. "We must search them out! Reading Belteshazzar's visions, each one—given to a king of Persia or the Medes—has come to pass. He foresaw Alexander and the Greeks and the Romans as well. But his last vision—a vision of the end has not yet come to pass. He speaks of an anointed prince who shall bring final judgment upon the evil one. An anointed prince.... We must search his scrolls for this anointed prince to come."

A Roman centurion led a column of soldiers into Nazareth. A shofar called the villagers to assemble in the square. The centurion unrolled a scroll and read in Latin. Two temple guards stood by a richly-robed Sadducee who translated first into Greek and then Aramaic. "Caesar Augustus decrees that every man should be counted and taxed. All men shall return with their wives and children to the city of their tribe and family lineage to be counted and pay the tax required by the appointed tax collector. Any man who does not present his tax token two months from this day will, with his full household, become slaves of Rome."

Joseph hurried home to find Mary waiting anxiously. "It is as we heard from our friends in Capernaum. We must return to Bethlehem to be taxed. We have two months."

Mary replied, "The baby. Perhaps, we can wait until he is born?"

"How long can we wait? We still must travel to Bethlehem. The rains are coming. No, sooner is better. The journey will only get harder for you and the child. Two days. Yes, I can close things here and make arrangements tomorrow. We leave in two days."

Mary took a deep breath and gently felt the baby sleeping quietly in her womb. "Two days then. Perhaps we can visit my cousin Elizabeth while we are in Judah."

"Perhaps. But first, I must see about a donkey. It is too much to ask you to walk. Two donkeys; I will bring along my tools if I must find work during our stay. Yes, it should take no more than a week if you are strong and the winter rains hold off."

The small caravan made its way up the western side of the Euphrates River along the fertile crescent. Few travelers dared cross the Syrian or Arabian deserts. The desert routes followed wadis, or riverbeds, dry most of the year but subject to flash flooding during winter rain.

At Thopsacus, they turned onto a trade route from the north and continued southwest toward Damascus. The long nights allowed good progress, often covering more than thirty miles a night. By day they studied Daniel's scrolls. Salek went through them first. Daniel was careful not to damage his

Torah, the Kings and Chronicles, the Psalms, and the Prophets. His habit had been to make notes on separate parchment and roll them into the scroll atop the passage with his comments. Salek unrolled the scrolls and found Daniel's long-hidden commentary.

Gaspar sat listening as Balthasar read notes from the prophet Isaiah. "He speaks of one to come... but this anointed one appears more a slave or servant, at best a humble priest, not a king coming in power to topple evil for all time. It is hard for me to believe. You say trust this Daniel, for his prophecies were proven—but how can he be trusted when the prophecies of this anointed king or prince are so varied? Zoroaster does not ask us to wade through so much inconsistency."

"Cannot a great king be both powerful and merciful? Can he not impose justice and beneficence on his people? I think you have it backward, my friend. A simple explanation cannot do justice to a great and powerful god."

Balthasar replied, "The Holy Scrolls name anointed kings, and all priests are anointed. What of their great prophets? There is no record that Daniel was anointed. Can a prophet be anointed?"

Salek nodded. "One of their great prophets was anointed. Elisha, the prophet who followed their great Elijah, was anointed. And there is another connection. Elijah was taken up into heaven in a chariot of fire like the one that came to Ezekiel at the Chebar River in Babylon. And there are writings that prophet Elijah may return at the end times to preach again in power."

Salek gazed off for a moment before adding, "Anointed in the Spirit. The prophets speak of the Spirit coming over them before their visions and prophesies. Even Daniel spoke of it."

Melchior nodded. "So, the prophets are anointed. And this prophet, Elijah, is said to return someday. The star... it could be the announcement of his return from heaven. Prophet, priest, or king, we must find this anointed one. We must learn the truth of his coming."

Seeing the white walls of Damascus rising before them in the moonlight, Melchior called to his companions. "Gifts. We should not come without gifts for the anointed prince. Gifts fit for a king. We must visit the great market of Damascus before we continue."

Joseph carefully secured two baskets counterweighted equally over the shoulders of a donkey. The expensive tools of his trade were carefully wrapped against sand, dust, and water. Two bundles of clothes and blankets were secured behind the tool baskets. A second, smaller donkey stood alongside the first. Skins of water, wine, and pouches of flour and oil were carefully strung in place.

Joseph stood back and surveyed his small and tidy compound. The shop was empty except for lumber drying in the rafter racks. He walked the few short steps into the house. Everything was put away, neat and tidy. Mary was sweeping the floor.

"Mary, you shouldn't be doing that. Everything will be fine. It's time. Come. I'll help you on the donkey."

"We didn't pack much food."

Joseph replied, "We will call upon the hospitality of our countrymen along the way."

Mary leaned the broom against the wall. "It is shorter

if we go through Samaria."

"And seek hospitality among the Samaritans? And the law? The child you carry is holy. I will not disobey the Law of Moses and enter the house of a Samaritan. You know this. Have you traveled through Samaria? No, never. Forgive me, Mary, I only mean...."

Mary nodded. "You only mean to be a good and righteous husband and father."

Joseph carefully lifted Mary onto the young donkey's back. He reminded her, "Hold on to the strap. Tuck your hand underneath. We can't have you slip off."

Mary laughed. "Joseph, my feet barely clear the ground. How far can I fall?"

Joseph blushed. "We can't be too careful."

He took the leads of the donkeys and led them off. Once outside the village, on the road south, Mary asked, "What will our son be like? How will we raise him? The angel—in your dream—did he say how we should raise him?"

"No. He only said not to fear taking you as my wife and that I should name the boy Jesus for he shall save his people from their sins. Did the angel, Gabriel, give you instructions?"

"No. Only that I would have a child—a child of the Holy Spirit, and that...." Mary blushed, almost embarrassed to say. "And that I will be called 'Blessed.' God must trust us and we must trust God to give us the wisdom to raise him in the, in the...."

Joseph understood. "We will raise him in the Law of Moses, trusting God to direct our paths."

Mary began to sing softly from the Psalm. "Bless the Lord, oh my soul...."

Joseph joined her, his baritone voice rising in praise, "Bless His holy name! Bless the Lord, oh my soul...."

They followed the Roman road south onto the plains of Esdraelon. Having decided not to enter Samaria, they turned onto a well-worn path outside Jezreel, leading them east to the Jordan Valley. Their journey took them from the hills of Galilee, through vistas of Mount Hermon and Tabor, to the rift that cradled the Jordan River.

While Joseph watched with concern, dark clouds gathering to the west. Mary sang softly as she pondered the mysteries that had changed her life forever. A Psalm of Solomon welled up from within her:

"Give the King Justice, oh God,
And your righteousness to the Royal son!
May He judge your people with righteousness
Let the mountains bear prosperity for the people,
And the hills in righteousness!
May He defend the cause of the poor people,
Give deliverance to the needy,
And crush the oppressor!"

Joseph heard Mary but he looked again at the gathering storm clouds and ahead to the Jordan Valley. *God save us! Please, Lord, hold back the storm. Do not let the way become treacherous or the flood waters overtake us! Bring us safely to Bethlehem. Bless and keep your servant Mary and her holy child.*

Mary was still singing. Joseph tried his best to focus on her words.

"May the kings of Tarshish
and the coastlands render Him tribute!
May all kings fall down before Him,

All nations serve him!"

Joseph's worries passed away. *What amazing faith my Mary has! Blessed? Oh yes, and a great blessing to me! A blessing to all people. She has no fear, no doubt, only peace and joy wrapped in strength. What does she know that I must learn?*

Mary was finishing the Psalm:

"May His name endure forever,
His fame continue as long as the sun!
May people be blessed in Him,
All nations call Him blessed!
Blessed be the Lord, the God of Israel,
Who alone does wondrous things.
Blessed be His glorious name forever!
May the whole earth be filled with His glory!"

Across the Jordan, on the trade road through Decapolis, the magi continued their nightly travels. The daytime clouds broke and separated during the night, and the star continued to lead them.

After a hot breakfast, the magi sat on their rolled-out rugs. Salek read from the scrolls, and Melchior opened the discussion. "I am struck with Magnus Daniel's title of this god, 'Ancient of Days.' For since creation, he seeks to make his will known among men. How many people seek their gods' attention, desperate for rain and fertility? The chosen people of Israel and Judah hear their god's words through their law and prophets but choose to ignore him."

Gaspar replied, "His admonishments never end! So much judgment!"

Salek could not remain silent. "That is not at all the god of Abraham, Isaac, and Jacob—the law-giving god of

Moses, the praiseworthy god of David and Solomon, and the god of Daniel and the prophets! No! He is the most patient and merciful god! Forgiving! Always yearning for his people to return to him. He is rightly addressed as 'Father,' for his heart is for his children. And when waiting does not accomplish his will, he acts with mercy.

"Look how he sent his people into captivity—not once, but twice! Each time they were protected. Their numbers multiplied, and their needs were met. You three look to study this god, to know of him and his peculiar ways among other people's gods. But you err. These scriptures speak to me of a god who asks for my love and for me to love others. That is his law. That is what I hope to find beneath the star—a gift of love from surely an Almighty God."

The three magi sat silently. At last, Melchior replied: "I have rightly named you Salek or 'Seeker.' Wisdom is better than knowledge. I pray you have found what you seek. You have opened my eyes to my error."

Salek mumbled, "Forgive me for my impatience. You have treated me with respect and fellowship. I do not mean to—"

Gaspar reached across and put his hand on Salek's shoulder. "Do not apologize—your testimony convinces me. I will worship him."

Salek's face brightened. "I did not find the True God. He found me."

Melchior spoke for all three: "Wise Salek, Magnus Salek, he called all of us. Yes, he found us. But for what purpose?"

In Peraea, the sky grew cloudier. The star came and went, its position steady now to the west. Jericho lay before them across the Jordan.

"We will cross the river here and continue west," Melchior declared. As they passed Jericho, the star was cloaked by heavy clouds. "There is a fortress ahead where the road enters the mountain. We ask what lies ahead."

At the mouth of a wadi, a deep cleft in the red rock with water flowing out to the Jordan, King Herod built a fortress against invasion to protect the road to Jerusalem. Melchior called out to a guard: "We travel from the east. Tell us what lies ahead?"

"The road is dangerous. Very steep and narrow. It is unwise to travel by night. But it rises to Jerusalem."

Salek asked, "The great city of David?"

The guard laughed. "Perhaps long ago. Today it is the city of King Herod the Great. He built this fortress and many others. Travel in the morning. It will be safer. Many will be traveling. Jews from the north returning for the census. Many eyes are good protection from bandits."

Melchior asked, "How long to Jerusalem?"

"A soldier can make the march in a day."

Melchior nodded. "And on a camel?

"Six to eight hours."

Melchior looked up into the dark clouds. "We'll make our camp here. Where more likely to find an anointed prince of the god of Israel than in Jerusalem, its capital?"

Mary had settled in close to the warming fire. Joseph draped a blanket over her shoulders and gently kissed the top of her head. "Tomorrow. Eight hours up the ascent to Bethany and then two or three to Bethlehem. The donkeys are surefooted.

We will be safe at the inn with a hot meal and a good night's rest, the Lord willing. I will immediately arrange for a midwife to attend to you."

Joseph and Mary set out at dawn on the road to Jerusalem. The donkeys were strong. It was Joseph leading them who set the pace. The sky was covered in thick clouds, but the rain held off. The cold temperature preserved Joseph's strength, and they reached an inn at the halfway point in less than four hours. Joseph stopped and looked up and down the road. "It is better we rest here, eat and drink. I see a caravan climbing behind us. Let them pass here where it is safe."

Joseph lifted Mary from the donkey. She cradled her belly as she waddled to the inn. "I feel strange; the child pushes against my stomach. Perhaps I will not eat. Just water."

Joseph was alarmed. "Is it time? Should we stay here? Will it be safe?"

Mary drank water from a skin and took a few steps. "We should go on. Give me bread to carry. If my hunger returns, I will eat."

"Lie down for a few minutes. Let the camels pass then we will continue. Yes, there is surely a midwife in Bethany."

Joseph sat beside his wife and watched as richly-robed men in strange, foreign clothes rode silently by the inn.

The magi entered Jerusalem at dusk. They found an inn and stabled their camels. Melchior asked the innkeeper, "Where can I find the baby, the prince born to be King of the Jews? For we have seen his star and have come to worship him."

The innkeeper stared back. "Baby? Born King of the

Jews? I don't know what you are talking about. Herod is King. He has sons. But a baby? I know of no new prince."

Melchior and his companions walked to the market near the temple's steps and asked all they met, "Where is he who is born King of the Jews?"

Their questions were answered with blank stares. Finally, a palace guard approached them. "You ask to see the King of the Jews? Come with me."

The magi were led to Herod's palace and asked to wait. Herod was meeting with his council and the Chief Priest. Herod asked impatiently, "Where is this anointed one, the Christ, to be born?"

The priest answered what was common knowledge to any Jew who heard the Scriptures read: "In Bethlehem. It is written: 'For you, Bethlehem, land of Judah, are by no means least among the leaders of Judah. For out of you shall come forth a ruler, who will shepherd my people, Israel.'"

Herod turned and walked out. He went directly to the waiting magi and asked, "Whom do you seek?"

Melchior answered: "We seek the child born King of the Jews. We have seen his star in the east and have come to worship him."

Herod asked, "When did you see his star?"

"Nine months ago. I saw it in Babylon."

Balthasar added, "And I in Arabia."

Gaspar said, "And I, in India. Yes, nine months."

Herod smiled. "Go to Bethlehem, not far south from here, and find the child. When you find him, report to me, and I, too, will come and worship him."

When the magi left, Herod paced in anger as he determined what to do.

It was late by the time the magi returned to the inn. They ate a meal, loaded the camels, and departed the city.

The early dark curtain of a cloudy December evening was falling over Bethany as Joseph stepped into the inn.

"No room tonight," the innkeeper informed him. "But Jerusalem is only an hour's walk."

Joseph asked, "Is there no one in Bethany who will offer hospitality to a woman heavy with child?"

"Friend, the city is filled with other Galileans and northerners returning for the census. Jerusalem, or you can walk two hours to Bethlehem."

Joseph returned to Mary. "We can go to Jerusalem if the two hours more to Bethlehem is too much."

Mary looked up. Her face weary, she grimaced in pain. "I will eat the bread, and then we will go to Bethlehem. What is an hour or two more after coming this far? I will have my baby in Bethlehem, not Jerusalem."

Mary ate the small loaf and drank some of the wine Joseph insisted she needed. She looked at Joseph and said, "The darkness. Can you find our way to Bethlehem? My stomach turns, and the baby carries badly. Can we...? Yes, in the strength of the Lord, we will go on."

Joseph helped Mary back onto the donkey, and they made their way out the gate to the road southeast of Jerusalem. Only yards out the gate, a small patch of the deep black sky appeared through a hole in the cloud cover. Stars appeared as the clear patch grew. The clouds moved away, a bright star appeared, and soon after, the moon brought light to the path. The small cloudless patch marched with them south, a steady beam of light cheering them along.

A LIGHT IN THE DARKEST NIGHT

Mary's pain left her. She felt strong and safe. Her good cheer was undiminished when Joseph told her, "The only room is in a stable hewn from the rock. But it is well-protected and dry with new straw. With our blankets, we will be warm until I search for our kin and find a room for us."

Mary smiled then looked up at the star. "It seems right to me. Our Father has sent us to this very place."

The Magi made their way south as they were told. The heavy clouds in the sky above were beginning to break. Perhaps the star would appear but where?

A few miles along, the road ahead of them was blocked by sheep. A shepherd was busy directing his flock into a night fold. Salek rode ahead and asked, "Is this the right road to Bethlehem? We have come from the east, seeking the child born King of the Jews."

The shepherd leaned on his crook, looked up, and said, "Yes, this is the road. Go to Bethlehem. Beneath the star, you will find the child. Choirs of angels sing and glorify Him as we speak. Hurry! It is a sight not to be missed!"

As the sheep cleared the road, the sky above cleared of every cloud. The star shined more brightly than ever before. Its long tail came almost to the ground. Hurrying their camels, the magi came to the stable amazed by the light and awe-struck by a host of heavenly angels singing, "Glory to God! Glory to God! Glory to God. Peace and goodwill to all men! Amen and Amen!"

The angels repeated the song over and over as the magi sprang from their camels, found the gifts that they carried, and made their way to the stable.

They entered and stopped just inside the door. Setting

their gifts down, each bowed down and kissed the ground in front of the radiant Mary lying beside a manger. Joseph sat beside her. Both had eyes only for the baby wrapped in plain cloth, lying in the manger.

The other magi followed as Melchior went forward and said, "We have come to worship the child born the Messiah, the anointed holy one of Israel. We bring gifts. First is Balthasar of Arabia."

Balthasar came forward. "Gold for the anointed King of the Jews."

"Now Gaspar of India."

Gaspar came forward. "I bring a gift of frankincense for the anointed priest and king."

"Young Salek has come to worship. He travels as a servant but has become a student of your scriptures."

Salek walked forward and presented a pouch. "I bring a gift—or rather, I *return* a gift—from God: Belongings of the prophet Daniel. Your holy writings, and notes on the anointed prince of God."

Melchior smiled. "I am Melchior of Babylon, I bring a gift of myrrh. My heart tells me this is a fitting gift for a savior, one who will free the world from sin."

Mary smiled. Joseph nodded. "Thank you. It is too much to behold."

Melchior gazed upon the infant. "Too much, indeed. We shall leave you in peace."

The magi bowed and backed away as if standing before the throne of the king. They decided to set their tents outside Bethlehem and spend the remainder of the night.

Melchior smiled at Salek. "The scrolls—the word of God! What better gift for a prophet anointed by

A LIGHT IN THE DARKEST NIGHT

God Almighty!"

Gaspar's face showed his concern. "King Herod. Can he be trusted?"

That night, an angel appeared to Melchior in a dream. "Do not return to Herod. Go in peace to your home, knowing that God's blessing is upon you."

In the morning, the magi packed their belongings on their camels. They once more visited the holy child and worshipped him. Melchior told Joseph of his dream and warned the man: "Do not trust King Herod. You must not stay in Bethlehem, for he means to harm the holy child. Now we will leave you in peace. May the blessings of the Lord be upon your house this day and forever."

The magi traveled around Jerusalem and returned to their lands by a different route. That first night they studied the stars. The bright star was not seen.

Salek shared his disappointment. "The star—the bright living star of the heavenly realm—it is gone."

Melchior stood beside his young friend and put his arm over his shoulder. "No, my friend, the light still shines. Don't you remember? You worshipped the light. It shines in the holy child; He is the true light. And in His coming, every person will be able to walk in the true light forever."

A LETTER TO
MY CHILDREN

I dipped my pen into the ink well in my small desk and wrote:

Tegel Prison, Berlin
June 1943
To Eberhard Bethge

My Dear Eberhard,
You are my dearest friend and have become my confessor. As I share with you my thoughts and prayers, I have a small request. I have begun another letter—not to you, Maria, Hans, Klaus, or Mama, but still to someone special. Someone I have never met but have always loved. You know how I love children. My time as a youth pastor in Portugal and, even more rewarding, my time teaching Sunday School in Harlem, New York, has brought me more joy than any theological debate. Perhaps it is Maria's youthful optimism that so captures my love. How much I desire children of my own! Perhaps, by God's intervention, the blessing may still be mine. If not, I will remember fondly those children whose lives I touched.

A LIGHT IN THE DARKEST NIGHT

My mind races at the possibilities. I would like a large family. My mother raised eight of us, and none felt neglected! What a model she was. You know, my friend, she taught us at home for years before permitting us to attend school. Mama used to say: "We Germans have had our backs broken twice: once at school and once in the military." Mama saw that we pursued music, art, and life skills in addition to academics. And she taught us to fear God. Yes, a large family: sons, Walter, after my late brother, and Eberhard, too, after you, my friend. And daughters Paula, after Mama, and of course, Maria.

So, my plea is that you pass on this letter, or perhaps it will become a journal, to whomever may be my children. I want them to know who their father was and how I came to such an ignoble end.
Dietrich Bonhoeffer

The lengthy letter began:

Dear Child,
Every child should know who their father is or was. And you should know that you are loved, even if from afar or beyond the veil. Parents, no matter how loving to you, have made choices in life, good and bad. And we all must endure the consequences of these choices. But our choices alone do not guide our destiny. We live in God's creation—a creation He declared "very good," but now it has become Satan's playground, and we are caught in a great struggle between kingdoms, the Kingdom of God and the kingdom of the flesh and sin. I write this letter in the hope you will understand why I am not with you today.
Your Loving Father,
Dietrich Bonhoeffer

I heard a gentle knock on my office door. No need to look up; I knew my secretary would be entering. I lifted my gold-rimmed glasses to the top of my head, rubbed my tired eyes, and stretched my neck.

"Herr and Frau Hahn to see you, Herr Doctor. They have no appointment. They say Hans sent them."

"I will see them. Send them in. That will be all today, Christine. You have time to make the Lenten service. I will lock up."

"Thank you. Good night, Herr Doctor."

A middle-aged couple quietly stepped into the room. The man removed his hat, which he held by the brim in both hands, and nervously rotated it through his fingers. "It is good of you to see us at this late hour, Herr Doctor. Hans sends his greetings."

The words confirmed what I'd expected. I took off my glasses and reached for a polishing cloth. "Hans should come himself."

The man gave the counter-reply: "*Ja*, always too busy, always too busy."

"Sit down, please, Herr and Frau Hahn. Your real name?"

"Yes. Hahn."

"Good. A common name—doesn't sound Jewish. No need for a false identity. Just the two of you? Where would you like to go?"

"Just us. We have family in America. Tacoma, Washington."

"America is not accepting German Jews. I can get you to Portugal. From there, perhaps other arrangements can be made."

Herr Hahn sighed. "Yes, the Gestapo spy, Friedrich Bahr, was captured, and now, in America, all German Jews are considered spies."

I nodded. "Yes. Or it is a convenient excuse. Your passports, please." Opening them, I commented: "No 'J' for Jew. Not on either one—how?"

Herr Hahn answered, "Our neighbor—until the bombing—"

"Say no more. It is better that I do not know."

I reached into a drawer and pulled out two sheets of paper. "You are about to join the Abwehr, the German Military Intelligence Agency. Fill them out and sign them. I will take photographs and have them approved. Come back at noon tomorrow. Go to the quartermaster's office. You will be approved to attend a symposium at the University of Lisbon on forced labor in the Amazon. The Fatherland believes that rubber producers are shifting to synthetic rubber. Though they will defend their interests in the Amazon, your Abwehr mission is to learn their synthetic rubber production capacity."

The couple looked at each other, then Herr Hahn asked, "We are to attend this symposium?"

"And spy on rubber producers?" Frau Hahn added.

"That is your story for the Abwehr quartermaster, only if asked. There, you will pick up your tickets and papers. To be safe, ask to see only Captain von Haeften. Do not use my name. The shepherd—remember, the shepherd. He will meet you in Lisbon as soon as you arrive. He will help you disappear."

I took face and profile photographs of them and bid them Godspeed.

The following afternoon I took a phone call from Captain Werner von Haeften. "Gestapo are going through the books. Looking at the U-7 accounts."

"The recruits I sent today?"

"They came. I was called away. Meyers was told to handle them."

"Did he say anything? Were they processed?"

"No, they left before Meyers came."

"I pray we see them again. Destroy their file. We can always rebuild it. Just the accounts? Nothing about our special project?"

"No. Nothing else. They are watching Hans. I thought you should know."

"Yes, thank you for telling me. It's in God's hands."

I hung up the phone and walked to the door. "I'm going home, Christine. Call me there if you need me. Better still: why not call it a day? You may go home as well."

I walked the streets of Berlin past bombed-out buildings. The city, under the military command of my uncle, General Paul von Hase, was quick to put out fires and clear the streets of rubble. Families with relatives in the countryside sent wives and children to safety. Yet life went on. Work continued, and the Nazi war machine steadily produced the material of war: young men, arms, and ammunition. So much death and destruction that it tore at my soul.

I turned onto Marienberger Allee and walked to number 43, my father's large stately house shaded by budding Linden trees. I made a phone call to my brother-in-law, Hans von Dohnanyi. The call was answered after several rings with a simple, "*Ja.*" in a stranger's voice. I hung up without saying a word. *I am too late. The Gestapo. I am next.*

Then I joined my father having lunch. I said nothing of the events about to unfold. I went to my room and waited. I opened a false diary and set it on my desk. I hid the thick folder called, The Chronicle of Shame, containing proof of Nazi atrocities, in a compartment above the ceiling in the rafters.

I was a double agent. I used my travel assignments with the Abwehr to meet allied agents. I pled with these agents for allied support for a dedicated group of German officers and officials plotting to overthrow Hitler. I used my position as an internationally regarded theologian to meet with my British handler, Bishop George Bell, Dean of Canterbury, and Bishop of Chichester. Two attempts against the Fuhrer had already failed. A bomb smuggled aboard Hitler's official airplane failed to detonate. And two bombs strapped to a brave German officer, willing to give his life to end this tyranny, had to be defused after Hitler departed the event early. My role in the conspiracy was to convince the British that the plot would succeed. I showed them proof of Hitler's atrocities against the Jews and asked for British support and assurances of favorable surrender terms for a new government. I reminded them in no uncertain terms that the reparations demanded by the treaty of Versailles ending World War I led directly to Hitler's rise. I suspect Bishop Bell withheld what he knew: that Churchill had rejected any notion of support and would accept only unconditional surrender, even from a post-Hitler German government. Even so, he eagerly accepted what intelligence I provided, and I took comfort that it aided the allied war efforts.

At four o'clock that afternoon, my father called to me:

"Dietrich! There are two men here to see you."

I took my Bible and a copy of Plutarch and met the men. I was arrested and taken to Tegel prison.

For two weeks, I was fed only bread and water and given only one urine-fouled blanket. I was not questioned during the first week. I lay in my bunk and considered my arrest.

The Gestapo has been following Hans for several weeks. Could they have made the connection to the airplane bomb? Surely, it was found, and it is solid forensic evidence. But we have heard of no arrest of Lieutenant Colonel von Schlabrendorf, the adjutant officer who placed the bomb on the plane, but then von Schlabrendorf did not construct the bomb, and a connection still could have been made to Hans and me.

But what of others who knew of the plan? Not Herr and Frau Hahn? No, the arrest came too quickly after our meeting, and why would they still meet with von Haeften then?

Then there was the Gestapo review of the U-7 accounts. Hans arranged the payment from my Abwehr account to the Swiss government to support the fourteen Jews we sent there with forged documents. I left no money trail directly to the people we rescued. It was all accounted against my travels. But it was Hans who first learned that the passports of all Germans with any Jewish blood were to be marked with a 'J' and their travel prohibited.

They wait to question me—why? Do they suspect me without proof? But why Hans and me?

When my interrogation began, the questions did not betray

the reason for my arrest. My interrogators wanted to know why I betrayed the Fatherland and who shared my beliefs. *Strange, I thought, they do not question me about Hans. They must know he is my brother-in-law.*

Only after the warden learned that I was the son of the famous Doctor Karl Bonhoeffer, a government official, University of Berlin professor, psychiatrist, and neurologist, and that I was also the nephew of General von Hase, did my treatment improve. Slowly, my thoughts moved from the why of my arrest to my new surroundings and my fiancée, Maria Wedemeyer.

I was thirty-six when I'd met Maria a year earlier. She was eighteen. To my surprise, I—the pastor, theologian, and spy, who had rarely dated or considered dating—fell madly in love. How bright and energetic she was! My love, Maria, displayed an open and curious mind laying a path straight to my heart. Our age difference worried Maria's parents, so we agreed to wait a year before marrying. *Keep her safe, Lord. Preserve and protect her. Surely, she knows I have been arrested. Give her peace and comfort. Let me find a way to assure her I am safe in your hands, loving Father.*

Pacing my cell, a poem began to form in my mind:

> *Stretched out upon my prison bed,*
> *I stare at the empty wall.*
> *Outside a summer evening,*
> *Regardless of me,*
> *Goes singing into the country.*
> *Soft ebbs the tide of the day*
> *On the eternal shore*
> *Sleep awhile!*

DAVID MARTYN

Refresh body and soul, head and hand!
Outside, people, houses, hearts and spirits are aflame.
Until the blood-red night
Dawns upon your day—
Hold your ground!

As the weeks passed, I adjusted to life in prison. I had time to think. I listened to the nighttime cries of my fellow inmates and prayed along with them. I remembered my youthful summers at church camp with silent hours set aside for prayer and meditation. *Let me again feel your presence, Oh Lord. Let me know your peace and love.*

Several months passed. I was surprised by a visit from my uncle, Paul. To the warden, he was his superior, General von Hase. Uncle Paul entered my cell with two bottles of champagne and sat with me for five hours.

"Nephew, are they treating you as well as they tell me? You look healthy." He lifted the two bottles. "I brought champagne. I am sure they do not treat you to champagne!"

"Uncle Paul, thank you! Champagne, really? Yes, they treat me well. Why have you come?"

"I promised your mother I would look in on you. I will try to get them permission to visit. In the meantime, is there anything you need or want while you wait here?"

The general, so distinguished in his dress Wehrmacht uniform, sat down on the bed beside me. I replied, "Paper, pen, and ink. I should like to write letters and continue my work. I have had time to think, to learn. I have been contemplating ethics. It is becoming clearer."

"Paper, pen, and ink? Yes, I can arrange that. Anything else?"

"I find time to sing. I miss my piano."

Uncle Paul laughed. "Your piano? Yes, we all expected young Dietrich to succeed in the concert hall, but you chose a different path. If you had pursued your musical talent, you would not be in a prison cell today."

I smiled. "In uniform, no doubt, or already dead like my brother Walter."

"Your brother died an honorable death, serving the Fatherland. What death can be more honorable?"

I replied, "Dying in service to the Father, our God."

Uncle Paul shook his head. "I promised my sister, your mother, I would do what I could. But no piano. You must train your choir to sing acapella. Let's taste this champagne."

I asked, "Uncle, I do not know the charge against me. Can you tell me?"

"Crimes against the Fatherland. You surprise me, Dietrich. I never thought you were interested in money."

"I'm not. Not in money or accounting of money. I leave it to others."

But I was relieved. *Crimes against the Fatherland. Not treason—not against Hitler. It is the accounts they question.*

My uncle looked at me and said, "In the future, you must more carefully choose those you trust. Now, what shall we toast?"

Much relieved, I smiled. *I still have a future! He is telling me this will soon be over.*

I lifted my glass and said, "To freedom. To be free in Christ is free indeed."

Uncle Paul replied, "To freedom."

With pen and paper freely available to me, I threw myself into writing. I began with letters to my parents, my brother Klaus, and my sisters. I wrote to my closest friend, Eberhard Bethge, and I wrote to precious Maria: *I am safe. This will soon be over. Continue with the wedding plans. Our marriage must be a yes to God's Earth!"*

That night, with thoughts of Hans and my fellow prisoners, I continued my poem:

> *We come before thee as men,*
> *Confessing our sins.*
> *Lord, after the ferment of these days,*
> *Send us times to prove us.*
> *After so much wrong,*
> *Let us see the day dawn.*
> *As far as we can see,*
> *Let thy word prepare ways for us.*
> *Until you have washed away our guilt*
> *Hold us in quiet patience.*
> *We will prepare ourselves in quietness*
> *Until you call us to new times.*
> *Until you still the storm and abate the flood,*
> *And your will works wonders.*
> *Brothers, until the night is past,*
> *Pray for me!*

Days turned to weeks and then months. There was no progress on my release. I was interrogated but never tortured. I repeated my story. "I am a pastor. My duties at the Abwehr were to report on information from international churchmen—any information helpful to the Reich. I was never familiar with the internal workings of the Abwehr."

Returning from interrogation, I would visit my fellow

inmates. Addressing each by name, I would ask, "What shall I pray for? I have pen and paper. I will write to your family. I will include your letters with the letters to my mother. She will send them on. Let me pray for you now. God is listening."

I poured my heart into those prayers for the other prisoners. I took time to write their letters, doing my best to preserve each man's unique position as a son of God, loved by the Father. Though I struggled with thoughts that God had withdrawn His sustaining power from the Earth, leaving it to Satan's will, I never stopped praying. I never stopped believing God heard my prayers. And the other prisoners were surprised when they received mail—letters of encouragement in my hand mailed from Paula Bonhoeffer.

My life fell into a routine. I wrote to my pastor friend Eberhard Bethge:

I've been doing a good deal of writing lately, and for the work that I have for myself, the day is often too short. Sometimes, comically enough, I feel that I have no time here for this or that. After breakfast, I read some theology and write until midday. In the afternoon, I read, then comes a chapter in Delbruck's World History, some English grammar about which I can still learn all kinds of things, and finally, as the mood takes me, I write or read again. Then in the evening, I am tired enough to be glad to lie down, though that does not mean going to sleep at once. Confinement produces opportunity.

When my detention was relaxed, I was permitted an hour a day to walk the outside prison yard, sometimes in the company of my parents or even the warden. I found comfort in the everyday sights, sounds, and smells of God's creation.

The simple song of a thrush would inspire me and guide my pen in a poem, or a play, or expound a new truth of God in the exegesis of a Biblical text.

Imprisonment did not stop the war outside. Bombs fell on Germany and Berlin. The resistance to Hitler continued. My mother carried encrypted messages to and from me between cardboard seals in the lid of her homemade jam. Paula was no spy, but she knew Klaus, Hans Dohnanyi, and I somehow got our sister Sabine, her Christian husband of Jewish descent, Gerhard Leibholz, and their two children to safety in England via Switzerland. My parent's longtime Jewish servant went with them to safety. In her heart, Mama was proud of her children and their efforts in helping Jews escape Nazi Germany. Conversations with her brother, Uncle Paul von Hese, and the warden, convinced her that the Gestapo did not suspect me of helping Jews escape Germany.

Christmas has come. There is no Tanenbaum to cheer my cell. No carolers walk the cold stone halls. But throughout the advent season, I maintain my advent devotions. I wrote in another letter, "A prison cell like this is a good analogy for advent. One waits, hopes—does this or that, ultimately negligible things. The door is locked and can only be opened from the outside."

I meditated on old advent sermons. I remembered Moses standing on Mount Nebo, gazing at the Promised Land. Moses would die on Mount Nebo, never entering into the Promise. *I must be like Moses and know that the promise has been fulfilled. It is a season of death, judgment, and repentance. We all must pass from death into new life. Our death and judgment must occur before we enter the Promised Land due to*

God's victory. God is with us, and we are no longer homeless. A piece of the eternal home is grafted unto us.

I lay on my bed and took slow, deep breaths, letting my body sink into the thin mattress. *And there is Joseph. He trusts God and takes pregnant Mary as his wife. Oh, the promises of God! And the choirs of angels singing, praising the newborn Savior. But then the angel sends them to Egypt to wait. And when the waiting is over, they return to Nazareth. It was for Joseph—as for all the world—incomprehensible that the little-regarded Nazareth should be the destination for the Savior of the world.*

And there is Mary. Who better knows what it means to wait for Christ than Mary? She experienced in her own body that God does wonderful things with the children of men, that His ways are not our ways, and that He cannot be predicted by men or circumscribed by their reasons or ideas. So, I shall wait. Wait expectantly in the freedom that comes knowing God's promises are already being fulfilled.

I learned that on July 20, 1944, Captain von Haeften drove Lieutenant Colonel von Stauffenberg to Hitler's bunker on the eastern front, the Wolf's Lair. Von Haeften waited in the car while von Stauffenberg entered the bunker and set his briefcase under the map table. A few minutes later, Hitler arrived and sat down at the map table to be briefed. Before the briefing ended, von Stauffenberg, an injured officer who lost his lower arm in combat, excused himself and left the meeting. As he reached von Haeften in the waiting car, an explosion destroyed the map room. The two drove off, not knowing that Hitler had survived.

I am still in Tegel prison. Everyone calls me Pastor

Bonhoeffer, not prisoner, but pastor—prisoners and guards alike. I eat the same food from the same crockery as the guards. I move freely, trusted—I feel cherished—as chaplain and pastor to all inside the walls of Tegel. The eastern front is crumbling, and the bombings are more frequent. Hardly a soul in Berlin is untouched by the indiscriminate ravages of war.

Today, I was praying with a patient in the prison hospital. Bent over a dying inmate, whispering a prayer, I heard Hitler's voice on the hospital radio. "...the cowardly assassination attempt has failed. Know that your Fuhrer is well. I see this as a sign from Providence that I must and, therefore, shall continue my work."

My head dropped, and my knees wobbled. *Why Lord? Why do you preserve his life? What will become of us? Good men—men of integrity and goodwill—die but the monster lives.*

I learned that churches across Germany had removed their crosses and statues. The altars now stand beneath the swastika. The State Church is the Reich Church, and it lifts its prayers and allegiance to the Fuhrer.

From the radio, I learned that two days after the attack, von Stauffenberg and von Haeften were captured and immediately executed by a firing squad. The Gestapo arrested Admiral Wilhelm Canaris, Chief of the German Intelligence Agency, the Abwehr, a key member of the conspiracy. A raid on the Abwehr headquarters found diaries and documents identifying most of the conspirators. Fortunately, Hans had safely hidden The Chronicle of Shame elsewhere.

It is September. Mama wrote to me. A few of the items collected by Hans von Dohnanyi were found at a German army base. A search of his house found the master file of The

A LIGHT IN THE DARKEST NIGHT

Chronicle of Shame. Hans was arrested and sent to the Sachsenhausen concentration camp. When I heard of the arrest, I found myself reciting a stanza from one of my prison poems:

> *Death.*
> *Come now, highest feast on the journey*
> *To everlasting freedom,*
> *Death. Lay waste the burdens of chains and walls*
> *Which confine our earthly bodies and blinded souls,*
> *That we are at last what here we could not see,*
> *Freedom, we sought you long in discipline,*
> *Action and suffering.*
> *Dying, we recognize you in the face of God.*

The Gestapo has begun questioning me. "You and your brother-in-law, Hans von Dohnanyi, have betrayed the Fuhrer with your lies. Who are your contacts? Who else has these documents? Your parents and your fiancée? They will be made to talk if you do not. Tell us everything—every conspirator, every contact, every plan."

Last evening, after a brutal Gestapo interrogation, the guard returning me to my cell looked over his shoulder before whispering, "Pastor, we know you serve God. You have brought His love and mercy to Tegel. Whatever you have done, I—no, we— are certain it was God's will." The guard looked both ways down the hall before continuing, "If you can arrange for someone to meet you outside the wall—if you can escape Berlin, there is a way. A mechanics uniform—one that will fit you well. Just tell me when your arrangements are made, and you can walk out of Tegel. We will miss you, but you must go soon before it is too late."

Before my parents could complete arrangements, my brother Klaus was arrested along with another brother-in-law, Rudiger Schleicher. I told the guard, "I thank you for the risk you took in helping me and for the encouragement you brought to my troubled soul, but I cannot go. It would only make things worse for Klaus and Rudiger."

Discouraged and convinced that any future was now lost forever, I lay sobbing in my cell.

"I want my life back," I whispered. "I demand my life back!" I screamed.

When I managed to compose myself, I at once wrote in my last letter to Maria: *My past life is brim-full of God's goodness, and my sins are covered by the forgiving love of God crucified. I'm most thankful for the people I have met, and I only hope they will never have to grieve for me, but they, too, will always be certain of, and thankful for, God's mercy and forgiveness.*

Several days had passed when the door to my cell opened. Two Gestapo officers stood outside. One said brusquely, "You will come with us."

I was handcuffed and led down the hall. Prisoners watched as I was led away. One said, "I will pray for you, Pastor."

Then another, "You have my prayers. God will surely reward you!"

All down the hall, prisoners repeated, "I will pray." and "God have mercy."

A car was waiting in the courtyard. I was shoved into the back seat and driven to an underground Gestapo prison

A LIGHT IN THE DARKEST NIGHT

on Prinz Albrecht Strasse in Berlin.

Autumn has turned to winter, and Allied bombing has increased. The guards complain that there is nowhere to move the rubble. The now-narrowed, often only one-lane streets of Berlin are covered with ice from countless waterline breaks. Open fires burn the rubble and heat the survivors. I have no way of seeing the lengthening darkness of night. Mine is a cold world of constant harsh, unshielded electric light. But I hear the rumbles and feel the walls around me shake as the bombs detonate nearby. I lay on the bed in my solitary cell, my mind lost in music, my hands conducting an invisible orchestra. Guards hear me softly singing Bach's *Saint Matthew's Passion*. I think about Maria and despair that I will never see our wedding day. I expect to die celibate.

A massive Berlin bombing raid, I'm told, conducted by over one thousand Allied bombers destroyed the building above my cell block on February 3, 1945. I was moved to Buchenwald concentration camp. On the drive to Buchenwald, I saw what every German knows in their heart. The war is coming to an end—defeat is inevitable. I arrived at Buchenwald with new hope. At any moment, we might be liberated, or the guards might abandon their posts allowing an escape.

At Buchenwald, I am imprisoned in a special wing with other prominent prisoners: captured politicians, nobles, business leaders, writers, artists, spies, and even Princess Mafalda of Savoy, the daughter of the King of Italy, has been here, though she died of a botched amputation after an air raid before I arrived. I know from The Chronicle of Shame that Buchenwald is one of the first and largest Nazi concentration camps built. Its first inmates were communists, Poles, Slavs, Romani, dissidents, spies, Jews, and homosexuals. As the war progressed, prisoners of war were added, swelling the population. All prisoners are required to work in an ammunition plant adjacent to the camp. The prisoners of war and the 'prominents' are fed better than the 'subhumans' the prison was built for. The slave laborers are fed survival rations only, and their fate, when worked to death, is a foul, black smoke-emitting crematorium.

One 'prominent' does not work in the ammunition plant. A Catholic priest, Father Joseph Thyl, is the prisoner in charge of the crematorium. When I introduced myself, Father Joseph replied with an unlikely smile, "I have read your work, Doctor Bonhoeffer. Passionate. You do not write like a theologian. Theologians are usually scholarly and systematic. Your only system is to ask questions. The hard questions few dare to ask. I admire your faith that God is not troubled by our questions, but do you think the transcendent God can be constrained or explained to a finite creature? Like a Jesuit, you are driven by questions, but you are bound to fall short and seem to find answers within yourself—contradictory answers. Tell me, Doctor, are you still on your quest to know Jesus?"

"God reveals to us all we need to know. It is the quest of everyone He calls—to know him and love him. But contradictions?"

Father Joseph nodded. "You question the Bible's historicity, even its inerrancy, yet you claim it as God's revelation whether accurate or not. And you call for the end of religion as if the Church has outlived its mission to join Christians in worship and good works. And most contradictory of all, you accuse God of turning his back on the world, leaving us all to fight our battles and bring about His Kingdom by our efforts alone. Yet you pray. You do pray, Doctor? Pray to God believing He hears your prayers?"

I looked into the sparkling eyes of the emaciated man before me and said, "I do not see these things as contradictory. I write of them as they appear to me. Yes, I follow Jesus. I love Him and seek to know Him even as I suffer and question Him. And yes, I find the Bible the very Word of God. No matter its origin, He willed it. And somehow, I know He hears my prayers even when they go unanswered.

"My objection to religion is that, too often, it stands in the way of a relationship with Christ. What church welcomes Christians to be open with their struggles and sin? We are taught dogma and obedience, not love and discipleship. We hide—from the people we should trust the most—our struggles with sin and temptation. There is no accountability.

"My happiest worship was at a church in Harlem, New York. The poor, mostly black African Americans, worshiped with exuberance and joy. Their worship was filled with trust and love for our Savior. They knew each other's struggles and shared in God's forgiveness. No, we must rebuild our churches from the hypocrisy of hidden sin into a haven for finding God's love."

"Perhaps, you have forgotten the healing ministry of confession."

"Perhaps. But I ask you to let me minister with you here where the need is so great. Tell me, Father, how do you minister? How can I help?"

"Do what you do best—pray! Pray without ceasing. I have been given a ministry to the dead. Know, when you see the black smoke—no need to see it, you will certainly smell the dead as they are burned—I will be there repeating the last rites for them, acknowledging them as beloved children of our heavenly father. But you will work among the living. Hear their cries, pray with them and show them the love of God."

I closed my eyes and said, "Father Joseph, you remind me that we are commanded to confess our sins to our brothers. It has been my practice to confess my sins before a friend, Pastor Eberhard Bethge, but his letters and assurances of forgiveness are withheld from me. Would you hear the confession of a brother in Christ outside the Catholic tradition?"

"We shall hear each other's confessions."

I began: "I confess that I do not care that God loves even Hitler. I confess I do not pray for his salvation or even a change in his heart. I confess I aid those determined to kill him. Three times, yes, three times, we have penetrated his security with bombs. Werner von Haeften even offered to shoot Hitler when delivering an Abwehr brief. I regret not encouraging him! And no, the Wolf's Lair was not the first. It was the last!

"And now, most of those I worked with are dead or imprisoned, awaiting execution. I have convinced myself, against all that I have learned and taught others, that murder is right. I have concluded that God will not act, so I must! I convince myself that God, in His grace and mercy, has forgiven all my sins by His atoning death on the cross. I convince myself that this forgiveness will avail even though I do not repent of this sin. All this I confess, still loving Jesus and trusting He is my Savior and Lord."

Father Joseph replied, "The sacrifices of God are a broken spirit, a broken and contrite heart, oh God, you will not despise. Take heart, Pastor: God forgives you. He is a rewarder of those who diligently seek Him. You do not count your suffering as loss—you have written on this in your work, *The Cost of Discipleship*. But have you considered that God was willing to let His Son die? Can He not let us suffer in His cause—for His will, in a manner yet to be revealed? Or perhaps never to be understood this side of heaven? You are not the first to anguish on this issue. Surely you have read the church father's writings on a just war. Do you not preach that your faith has saved you? God sees your faith. His arms are open to you. Continue to love God and continue to love those who need to know of His love here at Buchenwald."

I tried to smile, but my heart still ached.

Father Joseph added, "Now hear my confession. I confess that I have become immune to the sights and smells of death. I am unmoved by the harvesting of the clothes, belongings, gold fillings, and prosthetics of the dead before their naked bodies are piled before the ovens. I confess my tears have dried up. I confess that I eat while others slowly starve, and I sleep at night unconcerned with what awaits in the morning. I confess my prayers for liberation are based on my selfish desire to live."

I closed my eyes and prayed silently before replying. "God knows we are flesh. Jesus reminds us, 'God did not send His Son into the world to condemn the world, but that the world through Him might be saved.' Father Joseph, you are a faithful servant of the Lord. He forgives you of all unrighteousness. You do not persevere alone. Recall His words to Joshua: 'Have I not commanded you? Be strong and courageous. Do not be afraid. Do not be discouraged. For the Lord, your God, will be with you wherever you go.'"

DAVID MARTYN

The two of us hugged and wiped away our tears.

As spring approached, the sound of American artillery shelling joined the thunder of the bombing. On April 1, 1945, Easter Sunday, the guards told us political prisoners among the 'prominents' to prepare for evacuation. Days passed. The shelling continued. The hope of liberation and the fear of death from the bombs and shelling strained every soul in Buchenwald.

In the darkness of the night, between the explosions, I heard a prisoner praying. I softly led the frightened prisoners around me in the evening prayer, the Lutheran Compline: "The Lord almighty grant us a quiet night and peace at the last."

A voice whispered, "Amen."

I continued, "It is good to give thanks to the Lord."

Several voices responded: "To sing praise to your name, Oh Most High."

And I said, "To herald your love in the morning."

The others replied, "Your truth at the close of the day."

Then I said softly, "It is good to silently confess your sins to God. I will give you a moment."

The room was silent. Even the shelling seemed to pause.

After a short time, I concluded: "The almighty and merciful Lord grant you pardon, forgiveness, and remission of all your sins. Amen. Into your hands, oh Lord, I commend my spirit."

A small congregation responded: "Into your hands, oh Lord, I commend my spirit."

A LIGHT IN THE DARKEST NIGHT

Peace descended on me and my fellow prisoners. But sleep had not yet come. I whispered: "Friends, shall I tell you how my Sunday School children prayed in the poor of Harlem in America? A very good little prayer:

"'Now I lay me down to sleep.
I pray the Lord my soul to keep.
If I should die before I wake,
I pray the Lord my soul to take.'"

Someone replied, "I have heard it prayed in the Air Corps during nights like this."

Another asked, "And what does the airman pray when flak and enemy fighters open fire?"

The first man responded, "The shortest and truest of all prayers: 'Save me, Jesus!'"

It was a very special time of prayer.

Nearly another week has passed. This morning a truck drove in front of my cell block. I and a dozen other men and two women were hastily thrown into the back. Father Joseph Thyl called out to me as I passed, "As you have written, so have you prophesied: 'When Christ calls a man, He bids him come and die!' Well done, thou good and faithful servant! Pray for me, Pastor! Pray for us all!"

We prisoners were driven through the rural countryside. We stopped at a small farm where the farmer's wife brought us a pail of fresh milk and loaves of freshly baked bread. It seemed a picnic lunch before we continued on to the small town of Schonberg, to the schoolhouse where we spent the night. I could not sleep. *Why move me? Why not just kill me at Buchenwald? A trial, yes, the Gestapo is taking me to my trial, then my execution.*

DAVID MARTYN

Restless, I shuffled through my belongings until I found one of my poems to help me collect my thoughts:

Who am I? They often tell me,
I step out from my cell,
Composed, contented and sure,
Like a lord from his manor.

Who am I? They often tell me,
I speak with my jailers,
Frankly, familiar and firm,
As though I was in command.

Who am I? They also tell me,
I bear the days of hardship,
Unconcerned, amused and proud,
Like one who usually wins.

Am I really what others tell me?
Or am I only what I myself know of me?
Troubled, homesick ill, like a bird in a cage,
Gasping for breath, as though one strangled me,
Hungering for colors, for flowers, for songs of birds,
Thirsting for kind words, for human company,
Quivering with anger at despotism and petty insults,
Anxiously waiting for great events,
Helplessly worrying about friends far away,
Empty and tired of praying, of thinking, of working,
Exhausted and ready to bid farewell to it all.

Who am I? This or the other?

A LIGHT IN THE DARKEST NIGHT

Am I then, this today and the other tomorrow?
Am I both at the same time? In public a hypocrite
And by myself, a contemptible, whining weakling"
Or am I to myself, like a beaten army,
Flying in disorder from a victory already won?

Who am I? Lonely questions mock me.
Who I really am, you know me, I am thine, oh God!

Sunday morning found us gathered in a classroom. My fellow prisoners asked me to conduct a prayer service. I was assured by the Catholics among us that this was acceptable to them. Again, I was both pastor and Sunday School teacher. I led them in a simple service of prayer. I read from Isaiah 53:4 and 5: "Surely, He has borne our griefs and carried our sorrows; smitten by God, and afflicted. But He was pierced for our transgressions; He was crushed for our iniquities; upon Him was the chastisement that brought us peace, and with His wounds, we are healed."

I put down my Bible, took off my glasses, and instinctively cleaned them with the cuff of my shirt. Smiling, I said, "Friends, we are healed. By Christ's suffering death and His triumphal resurrection, you have been healed! And even more so, with His healing, Christ brings peace. Not man's peace. Not an absence of bombs and shelling. Not an armistice and talk of liberation, but God's peace—a peace that passes all understanding. Peace to know that God loves you and calls you into His presence as His adopted son or daughter for all eternity. We fear what we do not know. But we can have peace without fear, knowing that we are healed. Our souls are reconnected to the Father through the Son. And in the hour when we will need it the most, His Holy Spirit will comfort and guide us in perfect peace."

I paused, smiling, my mind savoring the promise of peace. I said, "Join me in the Lord's Prayer."

When the small congregation said, "Amen." two men came in. One of them said, "Prisoner Bonhoeffer. Gather your things and come with us."

The room was silent. Every prisoner knew that meant only the gallows. I turned to my fellow prisoners and said, "This is the end. For me, the beginning of life."

It is here that the handwriting changes. These accounts are no longer crafted by Bonhoeffer. A new hand noted:
This ends Dietrich's writing. I find it my duty to add what my investigation has determined what occurred after Dietrich departed the schoolhouse.
Eberhard Bethge

Captain Payne Best, a captured British spy, wrote in his journal of that day: "Dietrich Bonhoeffer is, without exception, the finest and most lovable man I have ever met."

In the back of the transport, Bonhoeffer must have smelled the foul, acrid air of the ovens of Flossenburg concentration camp long before he was driven beneath the sign that read: There is a path of freedom, and its milestones are obedience, hard work, honesty, order, cleanliness, sobriety, truthfulness, a spirit of self-sacrifice and love for the Fatherland.

Pastor Bonhoeffer was taken to a small, single-story white building that housed political prisoners. He joined his Abwehr superiors: Admiral Canaris, General Oster, and Fabian von Schlabrendorf (the officer who had placed the bomb on

Hitler's plane).

The next morning, April 9, they were read the verdicts and sentences of their court martial. The camp doctor wrote: "On the morning of that day, the prisoners were taken from their cells, and the verdicts of the court martial were read to them. Through the half-open door in one room, I saw Pastor Bonhoeffer, before taking off his prison garb, kneeling on the floor and praying fervently to his God. I was most deeply moved by the way this lovable man prayed, so devout and certain that God heard his prayer. At the place of execution, he again said a short prayer and then climbed the stairs to the gallows, brave and composed. His death ensued after a few seconds. In the fifty years that I have worked as a doctor, I have hardly ever seen a man die so entirely submissive to the will of God."

Hanged naked, Dietrich Bonhoeffer's body was cut down and thrown onto a bonfire along with the bodies of his coconspirators. No marker identifies the resting place of his burnt remains but his soul lives on in eternity.

THE RECOVERY OF MISTER SMITH

The receptionist took the clipboard I handed her and returned my ID and insurance card. She picked up a wrist band and asked, "Left or right?"

"Left," I said, and she snapped the band loosely around my wrist.

A side door opened, and a nurse said, "We're ready for you now, Mister Smith."

I took a deep breath and turned to my wife, Hope. "I love you," she said as she kissed me.

"This is one Labor Day I'll remember," I replied, trying to smile.

I walked to the door. The nurse smiled professionally and said, "Are you ready?"

She turned to Hope and said, "It should be about an hour, Mrs. Smith. Why don't you go and have a cup of coffee? We'll call you when he goes into the recovery room."

This was not my first time in surgery, but the thought of general anesthesia still made me nervous. I tried to relax as my gurney made its way down the corridor towards the operating room. The door swung open, and they wheeled me under the large bright light in the center of the room. *Why are operating rooms always so cold?*

A LIGHT IN THE DARKEST NIGHT

Four, no, five doctors and nurses were waiting, each hidden behind masks, surgical gowns, and caps. One of the green gowned team walked to the IV bag hung beside me. I recognized the same smile through the mask of one as she said, "This will put you to sleep. Please count down from five to zero." And she painlessly injected the drug.

I looked up at the bright light over me. It was so bright. Staring at it, I could see nothing else. "Five, four, three..."

My eyes opened, and there was the light—only the light. My eyes could not move from its intensity. *I feel it is searching my very soul.*

Sound. I could hear the sound of my gurney rolling along. Breathing—not me. Someone else was beside me. I listened to their breath. "Are you're back with us, Mister Smith?" a voice asked.

The voice, now reassuring continued, "Rest, Mister Smith. You need to recover."

"I can't see—I mean, I only see a bright light."

"You are on your way to recovery. Your condition is normal. My name is Gabriel. I will be with you through recovery."

"It's strange. I don't feel anything. I can hear you—but the light..."

"Close your eyes and rest. I will be here to take care of you—just rest until its time. And I will take you through."

"Take me through? Where? I am tired. Yes—tired. The light is so bright."

"Close your eyes. You can close them."

I closed my eyes, and the burning stopped. I opened them again, and I was overwhelmed by darkness—darkness I have only heard about but never experienced—only blackness. My eyes were of no use to me.

I screamed, "I can't see! I'm blind!"

I heard the soft voice of Gabriel penetrate the still darkness. "Which shall it be? Light or darkness?"

"The light is too bright and the darkness too dark! I wish to see, but not be overwhelmed."

Gabriel replied, "You choose a world of gray, neither light nor dark. It is a compromised world where you do not see the truth of the light and hide from the despair of darkness. You have made yourself comfortable in your gray world, yet you remain truly blind. But I will show you even in your world of gray a vision of the truth."

I blinked once, and I could see the curtain surrounding my hospital bed. I saw the blanket neatly folded and tucked over me. A subdued light shone over my bed. I scanned all about and saw a young man sitting in a chair in the far corner against the blue curtain. "Gabriel? I asked.

The young man smiled and nodded.

"It's just not right. I must be dreaming."

Gabriel asked, "What's not right, Mister Smith?"

I tried to sit up but only managed to lift my head. "The light, the darkness, this room, and you. You are not right, Gabriel. You don't look like a nurse."

Gabriel kept smiling. "What's wrong with the room?"

"Well, for one thing, I should be hooked up to a monitor..."

Before I finished the sentence, a monitor appeared beside me, beeping softly in time with my pulse. I could only wince and shudder as I stared at the machine. I was sure it wasn't there before.

A LIGHT IN THE DARKEST NIGHT

I looked closely at Gabriel. "You aren't a nurse! You have no mask or hair cover and your clothes, they are very bright white but not like hospital scrubs."

Gabriel folded his arms. "You mentioned a dream. Do you dream, Mister Smith?"

"Everyone dreams—of course, I dream. But not like this."

Gabriel took a breath and asked, "Do you find that your dreams can be a patchwork—a quilt of your life joining past events and future fears into one fabric? In your dream, it all makes sense only to fall apart when you wake? Why is that? Do you control your dreams, Mister Smith? Did you place the hospital bed beneath you, the curtains around you, and the monitor beside you?"

Exasperated, I sighed. "You're confusing me."

"The dream was your explanation, not mine. Try sitting up for me. You must be able to walk before you leave."

I sat up and took a breath. I was neither dizzy nor sore. I lifted the blanket from across me and swung my feet down. "Let me sit here on the edge of the bed for a moment."

"Don't forget your slippers."

I looked down and saw soft slippers now on my feet. "If this is a dream, I guess I just go along with it."

Gabriel stood up and walked beside me. "Stand up and take hold of my arm. We are going to walk. You were right about one thing, Mister Smith. I am not a nurse, really more of a guide. Before we start, let me check your wristband."

Gabriel smiled. "Just protocol," and took my left wrist. He read aloud, "Name, John Smith, correct date of birth, and religion—hmm—atheist. Tell me; you have never been baptized?"

"No—not something done in my family."

"No confirmation?"

"No."

"Never prayed? Never worshipped God?"

"No. That's my wife's department. She's religious enough for both of us. Oh, I've been to church for weddings and funerals, but never felt any need to worship what doesn't exist."

Gabriel looked into my eyes. "It never seemed arrogant of you to deny the existence of God? How could you know? Have you searched the universe? Yet you say you know? And if God were outside the universe, then what?"

I stammered, "Well, it not that it's just... "

Gabriel replied, "Not an agnostic—someone who says they honestly do not know—but this says 'atheist' you have declared there is no God."

Gabriel asked, "Are you a betting man, Mister Smith? Have you never been awed by the beauty of the earth—the resilience, the balance? What are the odds?"

I mumbled, "Well, no, I am not a gambler and the odds?—again, it just happened."

"It just happened? Really? You say you are not a gambler, yet you stake your very soul on what you could never prove!"

We both stood in silence. Gabriel looked into my eyes. I could only see tenderness. He smiled and held out his arm. I linked my arms through his. He glanced at my face and said, "Pay attention—you will find this very enlightening," and Gabriel brushed the curtain open.

The late afternoon sun burned hot on the back of my neck. I stood outside the door of a stone villa. It reminded me of the villas of Pompeii I once visited, but everything appeared new. Bright paint and mosaics made it welcoming and luxurious. Inside I could see a fountain and a garden. I could hear the gentle splashing of the water and smell its sweetness mingled with the pleasant scent of lilies. At the far end under a portico, a group of men reclined on cushions around trays of food. One man, sitting in the center, was speaking softly.

Gabriel whispered, "We will wait here for Master Luke. You have chosen a gray world. You only see what your weakness allows."

A man in a white robe with a gold sash and gold crown walked out of the garden. Gabriel bowed to him and said, "Master Luke, I brought a dead soul, one who has denied God."

Luke looked at me and said, "You have refused the Master's invitation?"

My heart sank when Gabriel called me a dead soul, and I pleaded, "What invitation—I never..."

Just then, I heard the man seated in the garden say, "Blessed is everyone who shall eat bread in the Kingdom of God."

Luke put his hand on my shoulder and said, "You are given sight and hearing to a living simile of what is too bright for you to see."

Confused, I asked, "Is this real?"

"Not all that is real is physical."

Luke clasped my arm and said, "Come with me. See chapter fourteen."

Instantly I was inside the great hall of a mansion, filled with tables and decorated with flowers. Servants were setting golden goblets, golden bowls of wine, and silver plates. The aroma of roasting meats, sweet and savory foods enticed me away from the visual. My senses were overwhelmed. I closed my eyes and breathed deeply. Spoken words broke my bliss. Opening my eyes, a saw a richly robed lord speak to a servant. "Gather the invited. Tell them to come, for everything is ready now."

I don't remember blinking, but I was no longer in the mansion. I was above the servant at the door of a country villa. A man was at the door, speaking to the servant: "I have bought a piece of land, and I need to go out and look at it; please consider me excused."

Instantly, the servant was at another door. A different man was speaking: "I have bought five yoke of oxen, and I am going to try them out; please consider me excused."

Again the servant was at the door of a compound in the city, and I heard a man say, "I have married a wife, and for that reason, I cannot come."

I was transported back to the banquet room in the mansion. The servant reported what he heard from those invited. The master became very angry and told his servant, "Go out at once into the streets and lanes of the city and bring in here the poor and crippled and blind and lame."

The servant said, "Master, what you have said has been done, and still there is room."

I watched the servant as he went out onto the highways, and along the hedged roads and fields and compelled all who he found to come to the banquet of the great lord. But few came.

When the servant reported to his master that there were no more to be found, the master replied, "I tell you, none of those who were invited will taste of my dinner."

A LIGHT IN THE DARKEST NIGHT

At once, I was standing in the garden of the villa watching the man seated at the dinner. Gabriel took my arm and said, "Not yet."

Bright light blinded me. I closed my eyes for a moment and slowly opened them again. I was in the operating room. I was at the ceiling looking down. I could hear the steady, unbroken beeeeeeeeep of the heart monitor. The doctor and nurses were beside me, intent on their work. A nurse shouted, "I have no pulse!"

I think it was the doctor who grabbed two paddles and held them against my chest, who called out loudly, "Clear!"

I saw my body jolt up from the bed. The doctor looked at the monitor and the faces of the nurses. He lifted the paddles and placed them against my chest once more. Again, he shouted, "Clear!"

Again the shock sent my body up off the bed.

I blinked, and I opened my eyes to the bright light. *So bright! So very, very, bright!*

But slowly, the brightness began to fade. I could make out the overhead lights of the corridor. I could see where the yellow walls intersected with the drop ceiling. I could hear the wheels as they rolled softly against the polished floor. I bent my fingers and wiggled my toes. I breathed a sigh of relief and closed my eyes. *It's over. Thank God. Was it all a dream? A warning? Not now—I can't think about it now—just rest. Hope will be here soon, and she will take me home.*

I could feel the breath of the orderly pushing my bed down the corridor. I could hear his soft footsteps. I listened as the electric door swung open and felt the gurney turn into the recovery room. The curtain hooks squealed as the curtain was pulled closed behind me. The monitor was rolled into position, and I relaxed, *it's over.*

The voice was soft, but still, I was startled. "Here we are again, Mister Smith. Sorry for the interruption. It happens."

My eyes opened wide. "Gabriel?"

Gabriel was standing beside the monitor. "Is the light better—the correct shade of gray? Do you prefer lighter or darker? I think a little darker this time. I remember the sun was hot on the back of your neck."

I stared at Gabriel in fear. "Am I dead?"

Gabriel smiled. "You still haven't learned. You convinced yourself it was just a dream."

"I never—I mean, I did not know..."

Gabriel smiled. "The invitation has always been there for everyone to see. You are the one that claimed there is no God despite the revelation in creation. If creation's revelation was not enough, and truly it is, the Word has gone out—messengers, prophets, the Son of God Himself! You could not miss it! His Spirit called to you in your heart. You chose not to hear."

I could feel my heart sink and my chest deflate. I whined, "The vision, the master was so angry. They say God is love. It isn't fair."

"The invitations were sent in love. It is His love that you reject. His love, far deeper than you understand—a costly love. He offers you love, yet you choose instead what he hates and cannot abide."

I sat up in the bed, looked down, and watched as sandals appeared on my feet. I heard Gabriel say, "Come with me."

A LIGHT IN THE DARKEST NIGHT

The curtain slipped open again. I found myself in the dark beneath a night filled with bright stars and a shining crescent moon. I was at the door of another Mideastern villa. I heard again the gentle splashing of a fountain somewhere in the shadows. A cool evening breeze carried the fragrance of rose of sharon mixed with the aroma of roasting lamb and the smell of sweet dates.

Gabriel spoke softly. "Master Luke has the warm and caring heart of a healer. But now you shall meet Master Matthew, once a tax collector; he comes from tougher stock."

Matthew appeared out of the shadows and greeted Gabriel. "Another dark one, Gabriel?"

Gabriel bowed before the white-robed, gold crowned Matthew, who turned to me and said, "Declare this in the house of Jacob; proclaim it in Judah: Hear this oh foolish and senseless people, who have eyes, but see not, who have ears but hear not. Do you not fear me? Declares the LORD. I placed the sand for the boundary of the sea. A perpetual boundary that it cannot pass; though the waves toss, they cannot prevail. Though they roar, they cannot pass over it. But this people has a stubborn and rebellious heart; they have turned aside and gone away."

Gabriel looked into my eyes and said, "It is darker, but still, you shall see, and you shall hear Matthew's lesson of chapter twenty-two.

I gazed into the open courtyard to the feast inside. I knew it was Jesus speaking his parable in the company of the wealthy. "The kingdom of heaven may be compared to a king, who gave a wedding feast for his son."

Matthew took my arm, and immediately we were in a palace so vast the ceiling was not visible, the walls beyond the horizon. Even in the darkness, my eyes struggled by the brightness of the King of Majesty. I watched as he sent out his servants to those invited to the wedding feast.

As far as I could see, host upon host of servants bowed and flew off into the sky—countless servants all unquestioning in their obedience.

A single blink of my eye and they had all returned, each with the same report: "They are unwilling to come."

The king spoke, and every servant in the endless palace could hear his voice. "Tell those who have been invited, 'See, I have prepared my dinner, my oxen and my fat calves have been slaughtered, and everything is ready. Come to the wedding feast.'"

Matthew whispered in my ear, "Come, see what they say."

We appeared over the door of a house as the servant's knock was answered. The man shook his head no. "I'm off to the farm." The man glanced up into the sky. *Do I recognize that face?*

We were over a man walking down the street. He did not stop or turn to the servant. He said, "I have business" and kept walking. After the servant left, he turned for a glance. *He looks familiar.*

Next, we were above a vineyard. A group of men crushing grapes saw the servant approach. When the servant told them to come to the wedding feast, one called out, "It's the king's servant!" They surrounded him and came upon him. I could see one of them hold the servant's arms behind his back as others beat him. Again and again, they struck him and kicked him until he fell to the ground, unconscious. They threw him outside the wall of the vineyard.

The face of the one who shouted burned in my memory. "Please, let's go," I begged.

Matthew said, "Not yet, another servant has come."

I watched this servant beaten to death.

"Now, can we go?" I pleaded.

Matthew shook his head. "Wait. Here comes the son of the king."

I looked and saw a fair and pleasant man walk into the vineyard. *Surely, they will respect the son of their king.*

The outspoken worker shouted, "This is the heir! Let us kill him and seize the inheritance!"

I could not speak. I was dumbfounded by the brutality of what I witnessed. Fists, clubs, and stones flew against the gentle young man until his broken and bloodied body was thrown on the garbage pile outside the vineyard wall.

Matthew asked, "How will the king respond to such brutality?"

I mumbled, "They should receive a severe judgment."

Matthew pointed, "You shall surely watch and see they receive what they deserve!"

As we watched, a vast army approached from every direction. With shields chest high and spears held out before them, they marched steadily towards the men in the vineyard. The soldiers said not a word as they maintained cadence marching in on the trapped men. I heard the screams as the vineyard workers fell in front of the army one by one, only to be trampled and cut again by the sword. Once they were all dead, the king's army marched off, burning the vineyard and burning the village. No one was left alive. I stared at the body in the center of the vineyard, the man who spoke out. His eyes staring up in death, looked back at me as if in a mirror.

Once again, we were in the endless palace of the king. The hall was filled as far as the eye could see with servants—too many to count. The king spoke, and every ear heard clearly, "The wedding is ready, but those who were invited were not worthy. Go, therefore, to the main roads and invite to the wedding feast as many as you find."

Matthew and I were gone with the servants. Immediately I found myself standing in the center square of the city. People all around me were being herded, directed through the city streets to the palace. *Where is Matthew? Why am I among the people? I am only an observer—I don't belong here!*

I stumbled along, and soon I was in the palace. I was no longer hovering above. I was walking on the beautiful white marble floor. I was pushed along, further and further inside. I passed table after table of wedding guests—each table decorated differently. I never imagined so many varieties of flowers and unique dishes existed. I could smell the food—my mouth watered in anticipation. The sights, the smells, and the sounds too! Glorious music—captivating melodies. My fears drained away. First, I felt peace, and with each step closer to the center of the hall, my spirit grew in joy.

I came to another aisle, no it was a river of water, gleaming and sparkling like crystal running to the center of the palace. I followed the river deeper into the palace.

At last, I arrived at a table with an open place. A servant pointed to a chair, and I sat down. I inhaled the enticing aroma. My eyes wandered over indescribable decorations. I lingered over the place setting—each piece encrusted with precious jewels. When my senses could accept no more, I smiled and looked at the others seated at the table.

A LIGHT IN THE DARKEST NIGHT

Each face shined with joy. Every wedding guest smiled, enraptured in the moment. Time did not exist—an eternal present, only the joy of the moment.

As I sat, I saw the king walking down the aisle, smiling as he looked over each guest. I smiled as he approached. He was magnificent!—handsome, gracious, resplendent in blinding white robes with jewels sending rainbows of colors around him. His crown was crowned with crowns. Words fail me. I cannot describe the glory of his presence.

The king came in front of my table. He stopped and looked at me. His eyes burned through me, and I felt ashamed. His eyes looking into mine, he said, "Friend, how did you come into here without wedding clothes?"

I looked at my clothes—the green hospital gown I was wearing. I looked at the other guests, each one in a white robe. My tongue stuck in my throat. I could not speak. I sat dumbfounded.

The king turned to the servant walking behind him and said, "Bind him hand and foot and cast him into the outer darkness. In that place, there will be weeping and gnashing of teeth. For many are called, but few are chosen."

I was shocked as Matthew took a rope and began to bind my arms behind me. I pleaded to Matthew, "No! Wait! I will put on the robe! Give me a robe! Please! Where can I get a wedding robe?"

Matthew kept wrapping the rope around me, pulling the cords tight as he knotted the ends together. He spoke as he bound me. "Did you not hear? The Son of Man will send his angels, and they will gather out of his kingdom, all who cause sin and all lawbreakers, and throw them into the fiery furnace. In that place there will be weeping and gnashing of teeth. He who has ears let him hear."

I heard Gabriel whisper in my ear, "Only those, who by faith have been washed in the blood of the Lamb, the redeemed, made righteous in the sight of God, are adorned in the white robe of a bride of Christ."

I began to weep, and soon I was wailing in despair and grief. I covered my eyes as they filled with tears. When I opened them again, I was instantly blinded by the bright light. I let the light engulf me. It penetrated my body and soul. My tears dried, and my crying stopped. The brightness dimmed, and the body in the operating room came into focus. The monitor was screaming its flat line alarm. The doctor held the paddles against my chest. I heard him shout, "Clear!" I felt the shock as I watched my body jump from the bed. I listened to the nurse cry out, "I have a pulse!"

I opened my eyes and watched the lights in the drop ceiling pass overhead. I saw the gap where yellow walls met the suspended ceiling. I heard the gurney push the doors of the recovery room open. I listened to the wheels and the breath of the orderly as he said, "Are you with us, Mister Smith? My name is Gabe, and I will sit with you through recovery.

I watched the blue curtains close behind the foot of my bed. I listened to the monitor beside me. I heard myself say, "I just want to rest awhile, Gabe, with my eyes closed."

Gabe replied, "You do just that, Mister Smith. Your wife has been waiting. If you don't mind, I will let her come and sit beside you."

My eyes closed; I smiled and said, "Yes, please."

A few moments later, I heard the curtain slide open as Hope came in. She came alongside me, leaned over, and kissed me. "You gave us quite a scare. The doctor said you had a cardiac event on the table. I prayed so hard! Thank God you're alright. I was so afraid I lost you."

She sat beside me and took my hand. I opened my eyes and smiled, "I remember seeing myself. I was above my body looking down. And there was this bright light. It was so bright."

"What else do you remember," she asked.

"Nothing. Just floating and watching them shock me—but mostly the light."

I closed my eyes again and squeezed her hand. "You prayed? I'm glad you did." Hope bent down and kissed me gently. I felt her tear against my cheek. My eyes opened to see her love.

I gave out one deep sigh, and I relaxed in her warmth. "Tell me—tell me again—how you love Jesus? When I get well, you must take me to church. I want the faith that you have found."

Another tear welled up in Hope's eye. She sniffled and quickly wiped it away. "How long I have prayed for this day!" She leaned over and kissed me. "Darling, John, don't you see? God's love and grace have always been there—waiting for you. Faith? You need only to ask Him. Pray with me...."

THE WITCH OF ENDOR

A low hiss filled her ear. She tried shaking her head and even clearing it with the tip of her little finger, but the soft hiss continued. "Where are we going, Father?" The barefoot girl asked as she followed along the rocky path up the Hill of Moreh. The Jezreel valley opened below them as a flat plain between the low Hill of Moreh and its towering brother to the north, Mount Tabor.

"If you are thirsty, Kerem, we can stop. Drink some water and rest. It is another hour, daughter. I want you to be rested. Look, over there, that is our village, Endor. Look closely. Remember where it is."

Kerem looked down on her home and out towards Mount Tabor. "Father, I can see Mount Tabor and beyond, mountains even greater! And in that direction, I can see a great sea. What lies beyond the mountain, father? Have you been beyond Mount Tabor? Have you been to the great sea?"

A LIGHT IN THE DARKEST NIGHT

Micah slowly turned and absorbed the view. "I have not been beyond the mountain. But my people have come from the end of the great sea. Our patriarch Issachar son of Jacob, called Israel, was given this land. Given?" He reconsidered the word. "We had to fight the Canaanites to take it and fight to keep it. But your mother, her people are of Canaan—from Hazor, beyond Mount Tabor."

"You and Momma were enemies? Papa, did you love Momma?"

"Come along, Kerem, the sun is getting high in the sky. Soon it will be hot. You will burn your feet."

The two started back up the mountain. Kerem did her best to ignore the growing hissing in her ears. "I can't wait to tell my brothers. I am sure they have never seen such a sight. Why did they not come along, Papa?"

"They have work to do."

"You told them to feed the orphan lamb? The one no ewe would accept. It is such a sweet little lamb. You told them, Papa?"

"They will care for the lamb. You will do as you are told when you meet the priest. Do not pester him with questions. Do you understand?"

"I can ask you questions, Papa?"

"Of course, but not the priest. He is not a patient man."

Micah and Kerem continued up. They entered into a thicket of terebinth trees. Kerem asked, "Why are there trees here, but not below us? And what are these tall poles?"

"The others have been cut down. These are holy trees.

They surround the poles of Asherah, the mother goddess. We are almost there."

The hissing grew louder, and as Kerem passed an Asherah pole, it seemed to whisper to her softly, "Kerrrremmm. Kerrrremmm."

Coming out of the woods, Micah led Kerem into a small compound somewhat like a village. They walked past long dwellings, a well, and a kitchen. In the center was a tall, stone building with an imposing golden statue of a bull guarding the entrance. Behind the bull was an altar with a blazing fire atop it. For once, Micah did not wait for Kerem's question. He saw amazement in her wide eyes. "That is Baal, lord of the heavens. This is his temple. Come, his priest is inside."

It was dark inside the temple. Out of the bright sunlight, it took time for their eyes to adjust, even with lamps and sconce torches lit. It was hard to see the walls and ceiling through the hazy smoke that floated in the air. And a smell, like burning wet grass, but sweeter, filled their nostrils. A hand grasped Micah's shoulder, "You have brought her to the priest? This way."

A man in a white tunic with a golden bull emblazoned on the front led Micah into the smoke.

The voice grew louder. "Kerremm."

"Why is there so much smoke, Papa? It is hard to see, and it smells. Has something caught fire?" Uneasy with the voice, the smoke, and the smell, she sought to assure herself as she added, "The men do not seem alarmed."

"It is incense. It is for Baal. It cleanses everything in

the temple, and it is pleasing to him. You will soon find it pleases you as well."

They were led to a man in white robes with a golden helmet, standing in the center of the room swinging a censer and chanting. They waited. The man made a complete circle, swinging his censer high into the air and chanting. When he finally stopped, he handed the censer to the robed man who brought them into the room.

"Who brings this woman to Baal?"

"Sssssss Kerrrrremmmmm."

"I am her father. That is, she is the daughter of my dead wife. My wife was devoted to Baal, Asherah, and the gods of Canaan. This, her daughter was born to her after one of your many festivals. I call her Kerem, Vineyard, for she was fathered in a vineyard or under an Asherah pole. My wife played the harlot, so let her daughter live here as a temple prostitute. She is of no use to me."

The priest looked at Kerem and then spoke to the man. "She is young. And your words show contempt for the gods."

"I am a son of Israel. Baal is a god of Canaan. We are commanded to have no dealings with Canaanites. My wife beguiled me, and I married her. But I worship no god. I will take the price for the girl and be gone. She is of age."

The voice teased, "Kerremm?"

Kerem cried out, "Papa, what are you saying? Papa, please!"

The priest turned to Kerem and said, "Remove your robe."

Kerem stood dumbfounded, her eyes wide and her jaw agape. She muffled a sob but dutifully opened her robe and dropped it to the floor.

The priest took one look and turned to the man. "No man would have her. The mark on her chest, like a serpent crawling down to her stomach. She could please no man. Her coupling would not entice Asherah. I will give you no money. Take her to the priest of Moloch. Perhaps they will buy her to pass through his fire."

Micah stared at the mark. He remembered a birthmark, but when did it grow large? He turned to the priest. "I have watched your festivals. After much wine and your sacred food, both men and women in their frenzy, they show no regard for who pleases them."

Kerem picked up her robe and covered herself. As her father argued, Kerem's head fell back, and her eyes opened wide. She began to chant—words, words her father had never heard. The priest listened as Kerem chanted louder, and she began to dance. Her body writhed rhythmically, almost like the desert cobra moving and stalking its victim. First her chin, then her shoulders. Now her chest, her small body thrusting. The undulating serpentine motion moved lower to her hips and then her knees, all the while she chanted.

Kerem lifted her arms and spun in a circle. Her head, now bobbing, her back bent, her knees lifting, she danced in place chanting louder and louder, till at last, she fell in a heap at the feet of the priest.

Her father and the priest stared in amazement at what they had seen. Then, slowly, Kerem lifted her head and rose to her knees. She clutched her robe in front of her as she stood. "Where is she?" Kerem asked. "Where did she go—I will go with her."

The priest asked, "She? You had a vision. What did you see?"

"Mother. She was here. She came out of the smoke and spoke to me. She told me I am her voice, and she is my strength."

Her father said, "Your mother is dead. Dead and buried. Come with me, Kerem. I will sell you to the priests of Moloch."

"You will not sell me to Moloch. I am free of you. Mother has freed me. You are less than a pig to her, and now to me. I am free!"

The priest asked, "Tell me all that you have seen. Your mother, you say. Was she alone? What else did you see and hear?"

"My mother came to me from others. She was wearing rings. Rings around her neck, her wrists, and her ankles. Beads hung from her hair, and her eyes were circled in black. She wore only a golden belt and the image of Asherah on a necklace. There was laughing and singing. Others were coupling like rams and ewes in the field. When she came to me, she said, 'Sweet daughter Kerem, you have the gift. Power to enter and the power to leave. Submit to no man. Least of all, the pig who sells you. You will be my voice from sheol. Tell them. Tell the priest of Baal you have the gift."

The priest scowled at Micah. "Leave her with us. She is

holy to our gods. Go!"

Micah said, "The price for a temple prostitute is thirty shekels."

The priest replied, "You have said she is not your daughter. She will stay with us. Go."

"I fed her and clothed her for thirteen years. I deserve something. Pay me the price."

"Clothed her? She does not even wear sandals! Take what I give and be gone!" The priest reached into his pouch and retrieved a silver coin. "She is not to be a temple prostitute. She is a seer. Take this and leave."

Micah took the coin, turned, and disappeared in the smoke, not taking a last look at the young woman he raised.

"Papa! Papa! If you leave me, you are dead to me! What is to become of me?" The smoke around her began to spin.

"Kerrremmm, Kerremm, Kerem, you are my voice, my ears, and my eyes to those living. Grow strong, Kerem. Grow strong!"

Kerem awoke the following day in a strange bed in a strange place, and her eyes fixed on an unfamiliar ceiling above her. Slowly the memory of being bathed, clothed in a clean white robe, and fed strange new foods dispelled the shadows of fear and surprise. She sat up and saw a woman standing over her. "Good morning, Kerem. You slept well. No time to linger in bed. Get dressed, come to breakfast. Today you begin your journey!"

Kerem joined others at breakfast, all women. Kerem

smiled as she scanned the faces of the others. *Young and old. There is no distinction of age, But I appear the youngest.* The woman who stood over her when she awoke took the seat of honor and spoke. "Sisters of the priesthood, today our sister, Kerem, joins us. We all must guide her in our ways and duties. I remind you of what we witnessed. Kerem's vision came to her before the ritual meal. She has shown uncommon clarity. Now we must instruct her more fully as she opens her path of intercession with the gods. We must teach her to gather and prepare our food, drink, and incense and our secret words to call our guides from beyond. But first, give her our welcome."

The priestesses replied in unison, "Welcome Kerem, priestess of Mother Asherah, she who eternally conceives but does not bear. May your pathway be open before you!"

Kerem shook her head. "It has been more than a year. I tell you, I do not need the roots and mushrooms, the incense, and the spells. They only blur my mind. No, my mother comes to me when I clear my mind and call for her. It is best when I am seated before the pit, my eyes closed but seeing the flames through my eyelids."

The Chief Priestess smiled. "But you see only your mother. There are others. We speak to many who have gone before."

"Yes, I see others, but they remain away off. Only my mother speaks to me. She tells me she speaks for Asherah. It is enough."

The sound of a shofar interrupted Kerem's session

with the priestesses of Asherah. They rose and looked down from the hill of Moreh. Soon another shofar sounded across the valley from mount Tabor and then from the village of Endor. Finally, a warrior on the back of a donkey rode to the top of Moreh and sounded his shofar.

A priest of Baal approached the warrior. "What is the message?"

The warrior replied, "Our King Saul calls all Israel to join him at Gilgal. The Philistines. A great host has camped at Michmash. All are to come. No exceptions, priest. Leave the tending of your idols to the women. The tribe of Issachar is gathering at Endor and the cities of the valley. Gather your wooden staffs, pruning hooks, spikes, and hoes, and go to Endor. We march from Endor to Gilgal tomorrow."

The priest of Baal replied. "It is better we remain and make sacrifices to Baal on behalf of our King."

The warrior drew a bronze sword, a rare sight in Israel as the Philistines did not permit the Israelites to work in bronze. "Come or die here, idol worshiper. The prophet Samuel will come to Gilgal and make sacrifices to the Lord God of Israel."

The priest bowed. "We shall come and do our duty."

After the warrior rode off, Kerem sat beside her pit. She closed her eyes and cleared her mind. She began to hear a familiar hissing in her ears. She slowed her breathing and concentrated. The hissing increased as the form of her mother moved towards her, her body swaying beneath her head. Her mother's eyes focused on her. The apparition hissed loudly and said, "Kerrrremmm. Kerremm. Kerem, my sweet. It begins for you. Saul—Saul will be in your hands. Tell no one. And beware of Samuel. Leave this place. Go to Endor. Tell the people you are their seer."

"Where will I stay? Papa left me here—he sold me to the priest."

"Go home. Your father and brothers are dead—a happy coincidence!"

"Not happy for me. I loved them. My brothers were always kind."

"Kerem, no one loves you but for me. No one else will ever love you. You have only me. Now go. Tell the priest it is the word of Asherah. You are her seer, and you go to Endor."

"And what shall I tell the elders and people of Endor if they ask?"

"Let them ask what they will. I will tell you what to say. Go, Kerem. Go and watch the men of Endor march to war. Many will fall. Many will come to you to speak to the fallen. Go, my sweet!"

Saul arose from his chair and stepped into the cool air. The morning sun was above the mountains of Gilead to the east. Saul, a head taller than any man in Israel, with broad shoulders, a trim black beard to match his raven hair, stood in front of his tent and stared to the west. Impatiently he turned to a servant and bellowed, "Bring the priest to me. Now!"

The servant bowed and scurried backward before standing tall and running off. In just a few minutes, the man returned with a young man wearing an ephod of a Levite, a priest of the God of Abraham, Isaac, and Jacob. The young priest bowed and said, "Your servant, my King."

Saul's eyes remained fixed on the road west. "Prepare the altar. I will make the sacrifice to the Lord, myself."

The priest did not lift his head. "Were not the instructions to wait for Samuel—that Samuel would make the sacrifice?"

Saul turned to the young priest. "Samuel also said he would return in seven days. Do you see him? I don't. The men grow impatient. They begin to sneak away by night. I will make the sacrifice. Has not the Lord chosen me? Has not His Spirit come upon me when I joined the prophets and prophesied myself? I will wait no longer. Make the preparations—the burnt offering and the peace offering. I will come within the hour."

As soon as Saul finished making the burnt offering, Samuel, a wild-eyed old man, a Nazarite who neither shaved nor cut his hair, arrived. He wore only skins of wild animals and neither ate nor drank of any fruit of the vine. Samuel was a prophet of the Lord God. He led Israel for many years before granting the people their wish for a king. It was Samuel who anointed Saul. Samuel was the only man in Israel with no fear of Saul, the mighty warrior king. Saul went to greet his mentor, but Samuel said, "What have you done?"

"I saw the people scattering in fear. You did not come at the appointed time. The Philistines grow stronger every day, and I had not yet asked for the favor of the Lord, so I forced myself and offered the burnt offering."

A LIGHT IN THE DARKEST NIGHT

Samuel scolded, "You have acted foolishly. You have not kept the commandment of the Lord your God. The Lord would have established your kingdom over Israel forever. But now, your kingdom shall not endure. The Lord has sought out for Himself, a man after His own heart. And the Lord has appointed him as ruler over His people, because you have not kept what the Lord has commanded you."

Saul was silent at Samuel's rebuke. But Saul turned his attention to the Philistines and his son, Jonathan, led Israel to victory.

Kerem stopped a group of men returning to Endor. "Tell me of the fallen. Just a name, and I shall bring comfort to their families."

"You are Kerem, the orphan sold to the priest of Baal. What have we to do with you?"

"I am a seer. I have returned to my father's house."

"You are a seer and you do not know? None from Endor has fallen. Saul has won a great victory! The Philistine dogs or those who remain of the Philistines have returned to their land—to their homes—to lick their wounds!"

Kerem stood stunned. *None have fallen? But mother said there would be many.*

"Wait! Tell me about the battle, about our King Saul and his great victory."

One replied, "We have returned after a hard march. Gilgal is two days each way. Our families, our flocks, and our fields all await us. Ask your spirit guide!"

A man too young for a beard turned around. "I will

tell you."

Kerem said, "My house is nearby. Come, I will give you refreshment."

In her small house not far from the well, Kerem offered the man wine, dates, and small cakes fried in oil, "Be refreshed, And tell me all that you have seen."

"Saul is a mountain of a man. Taller than any I have seen. Strong! Broad shoulders. A man of action—war. He fears no one. His brothers—they are the sons of Kish of the tribe Benjamin, warriors all. But Saul's son, Jonathan, now there is the man I would follow. Brave, strong, cunning in battle but not haughty—no—Jonathan is pleasant company to every soldier and son of Israel."

Kerem nodded. "It is Saul that I am curious about, our king."

"Saul is mighty in battle. Strong and fears no man—no man but Samuel. The prophet chastised him severely. The King's pride was wounded, and his commands became rash. After the victory, Saul determined to pursue and destroy all those fleeing. He made a careless oath—no man was to eat or drink until every Philistine was dead. When it was discovered his son Jonathan innocently violated Saul's oath, it was the people, his warriors, who insisted Jonathan be spared."

Kerem poured the young man more wine. "Samuel. You say the prophet chastised Saul. Saul fears Samuel?"

The young man drank his wine and said, "You do not know? All of Israel fear Samuel. He is a great prophet of the Lord God Almighty. Even now that he is an old man and feeble, Saul fears him. There is no one like him in all of Israel."

Kerem sat down. "His words…"

"Not just his words, but signs and wonders." The young man looked into Kerem's face. "See for yourself. He lives in Ramah but goes to Gilgal to make sacrifices at the Tabernacle. Even the priests obey all that he says. Now, I must leave. Thank you for the food and wine."

Kerem did not get up as the man left. She sat staring down. She closed her eyes and began to think. *Samuel. Saul fears him. The priests of his God fear him. And the people— perhaps I should seek him out.*

Sssssssss. Sssssss. The sound in her ears surprised Kerem. Instantly she was alert in the other realm. She saw a hooded figure sway, a cobra, no, a person. The person turned and moved towards her. The hissing died away, and now she heard the familiar Kerrrremmm, Kerremm, Kerem. Kerem recognized her mother's face, her hair now down and spread wide around her neck like a collar resting on her shoulders and falling over her breasts, her earrings appearing as the hood eyes of the cobra. "Kerem, my sweet, do not be fooled by Samuel. Though men and kings fear him. He shall soon follow his father to his tomb. Saul will come to you. He will bend to your power and our will."

"Samuel serves only the Lord God of Israel. Followers of this God are most adamant. There is no other god."

"Boasting, my sweet, mere boasting. You are a seer. What do you see? Many gods war among themselves. This

God of Israel—just empty boasting. But do not seek out Samuel. I am your guide."

As time passed, Kerem became known to the people of Endor. They sought her out as their seer. They paid her well for her service, and she became wealthy, but no man would take a seer for his wife. One day, Kerem heard a knock on her door. She opened her eyes to the dimming light of dusk. "I am coming," she replied as she stood up. "Let me light my lamp, and I will answer."

Kerem lit the small lamp on her table and opened the door. A man stood there waiting. His face tortured with urgency. "Are you Kerem? I have heard you can help me. Kerem, the seer?"

"I am Kerem, the seer. What is it you need?"

"I must know—they are dead, and no offerings were given. I must know they are not punished for my guilt."

"Come in and tell me all. What is your name? Who is dead? Do you wish me to call them?"

The tortured man stepped in. Kerem pointed to a chair. "Please sit at my table. Have you eaten? You look gaunt and hungry. I was about to cook cakes for my supper. Tell me your story as I prepare the meal. I will listen. I am an excellent listener. You have not told me your name."

The man sat down. Kerem poured a cup of wine and set it before him. "My name is Dav. It is my father and mother who have died. I am the eldest son. It was a fire. My mother's robe caught fire. My father went to help her. He was a very old man, much older than my mother. He fell dead upon her. I buried them in haste. What else could I do? I could not leave them to the birds or the dogs. But my neighbor came to me, looking for my father. The neighbor said my father owed him money, and his debt was due. I told him my father was dead. Still, he took our seed grain. It was all we had left. As he left, he asked where I buried them and if I had made an offering to the gods. I knew nothing of such offerings. My father taught me that the Lord is God in Israel, but others say worship the gods of Canaan as well. Have I offended the gods? Are my mother and father being punished for my guilt?"

Kerem replied softly as she prepared the meal. "You loved your parents, Dav? Yes, I am certain you did. Take comfort that they knew your love. Surely, all is not lost. I will help you. I will ask after them. But first, we shall eat. Yes, warm food and wine will calm you. Here, it is ready."

When Dav had eaten and was calmed by Kerem's soft assurances, Kerem uncovered the pit in her house. With only the embers of her cooking fire lighting the room, Kerem closed her eyes and softly chanted, "Mother Asherah, you who eternally conceive but never bear, I seek Caleb and Nediva. Their eldest son, Dav, would hear from them. Mother Asherah, I seek...."

Soon Kerem heard a familiar hiss. The sound grew louder until, at last, she heard her name, "Kerrremmm." Dav heard nothing but the soft chanting of Kerem.

Kerem said, "Mother, guide, I seek the parents of the man Dav."

"I heard your call, Kerem, my sweet. The man Dav, the

eldest son of Caleb and Nediva, why does he disturb their sleep?"

"He is a good and loving son, worried that his parents are punished for his guilt. They were buried without offerings to our gods."

Dav stiffened and felt a strange sensation in the hair on the back of his neck as he listened to Kerem speak.

"No offering to our gods? Evil indeed! I shall guide you—yes, yes, Asherah has shown them to me. They are here. Beggars in our world. Already they are hungry. They were sent with nothing! Nothing! This evil son, Dav, must make atonement!"

"Mother guide, Dav is not an evil man—just ignorant of our ways. And he is poor. All that his father owned was taken for debt. What can he do? Will Asherah help his parents whom he loves?"

"Sssssss. Surely, he has something?"

Kerem turned to Dav, her eyes still closed, "Dav, you must not withhold anything from Mother Asherah. Tell me. You must have something?"

"I am a widower and have only a small house for my son and daughter. Our sheep and our grain is gone. My kinsmen live far off. I have nothing."

Kerem began to speak, "Mother guide...."

"Ssssss, Has nothing he says? Liar! Let him sell his daughter to the priests of Baal and buy a proper offering. Only then will Caleb and Nediva be free from begging!"

Kerem again turned to Dav, "You have a son and daughter. She has value to the priests of Baal."

A LIGHT IN THE DARKEST NIGHT

Dav cried, "My daughter is not of age. I could do no such thing! She is most precious to me! Anything else!"

Kerem focused on the pit. "The girl is young and precious to her father. Too young for the thirty shekels the priest would pay."

"Ssssss. Kerem! A price is due. His evil must be undone. The priest of Moloch will pay twenty shekels and pass her through the fire. She may even join her grandparents. Yes, yes. Asherah will accept an offering costing twenty shekels. Tell him! Asherah loses patience—I will go to her. Tell Dav twenty shekels for his parents' comfort. Tell him!"

The spell was broken. Kerem looked up. She bit her lip, unable to smile. "An offering must be made—soon. Your parents are hungry. They will spend eternity as beggars. Twenty shekels. You must pay twenty shekels for the offering. It is the price the priests of Moloch will pay for your daughter. She would be offered to him, a sacrifice, and pass through the fire on his altar."

Dav cried, "You ask what is evil to take away what is evil."

"Your daughter for your two parents is what Asherah asks."

"I fear even my mother and father would not wish their comfort come at the expense of my daughter."

Kerem shook her head. "No. Not if they love her as you do."

Kerem looked up, "Asherah demands a cost—twenty shekels. That is the wage of a hired man for a month. I may have twenty shekels—I will loan you money. You must promise to repay me. If repayment is not made, the cost is not paid. Do you understand?"

"And your fee? I must pay your fee as well."

"I ask no fee. I desire to help. Do you agree to a loan?"

"I agree! Thank you, Kerem, thank you!"

Saul led Israel to victory over the Amalekites. Samuel had commanded Saul to utterly destroy the Amalekites. As descendants of Esau and cousins to the Israelites, their attack on Israel when they first entered the promised land was a grievous sin against God. As Samuel made his way to Saul at Gilgal, he pondered the word of the Lord: "I regret I have made Saul king. He has turned his back from following Me and has not carried out My commands." This distressed Samuel, for Samuel loved Saul as a father loves a son. Samuel cried unto God all night on Saul's behalf.

Samuel could only shake his head in despair as he passed the monument Saul had built for himself at Carmel. When Samuel arrived, Saul called out to him, "Blessed are you of the Lord! I have carried out the command of the Lord!"

Samuel replied, "Then what is the bleating of the sheep and lowing of the oxen I hear?"

"I have saved the best to make an offering to the Lord, but the rest we utterly destroyed."

"You did not obey the voice of the Lord but took spoil and did evil in the sight of the Lord."

Saul replied, "But I did obey, and I brought back King Agag and have utterly destroyed the Amalekites."

A LIGHT IN THE DARKEST NIGHT

Samuel spoke loudly so that all the host of Israel could hear. "Has the Lord as much delight in burnt offerings and sacrifices as in obeying the voice of the Lord? To obey is better than to sacrifice and to heed than the fat of rams. For rebellion is as the sin of divination, and insubordination is as iniquity and idolatry. Because you have rejected the word of the Lord, He has also rejected you from being king."

Saul cried out, "I have sinned. I have feared the people and heard their voices. Pardon my sin and return with me that I may worship the Lord."

Samuel walked away, saying, "I will not return with you, for you have rejected the word of the Lord, and the Lord has rejected you from being king."

Saul reached out and grabbed Samuel's robe as he passed. The robe tore. Samuel turned to Saul and said, "The Lord has torn the kingdom of Israel from you today and has given it to your neighbor who is greater than you."

Saul begged, "I have sinned but honor me before the elders. Go back with me that I may worship the Lord your God."

Samuel went back with Saul, and they worshipped the Lord. Then Samuel said, "Bring me Agag." Samuel slew King Agag with a sword and cut him into pieces. Samuel left the sword, Saul, and the dead King Agag, and returned to Ramah. Samuel grieved for Saul but did not see him again.

Samuel did not remain in Ramah long. The Lord had another task for him. Samuel was sent South a few miles to the fields owned by Jesse of the tribe of Judah near the village of Bethlehem. There he secretly anointed a shepherd, David, son of Jesse, King of Israel. God had searched David's heart and declared David: "A man after my own heart." The Spirit of the Lord left Saul and filled young David.

The sun was setting when Kerem left her house and walked to the village well. Dav was entering the gate, returning from the fields. He was talking with a stranger when he noticed Kerem. "Kerem, how fortunate you are here! I have the money you loaned me plus a little extra for your help. This is Seth, traveling north to Dan. He brings news from Gilgal of continued victories and Israel's new champion, David."

"Thank you, Dav. There is no hurry to repay the loan. Please do not take from your family on my account."

"It is no hardship. I have been blessed. A new agreement with a neighbor—my labor in return for wages and seed for my fields."

Kerem smiled and turned to the traveler, Seth. "It is late, friend. I have prepared an extra portion if you are hungry, and I have a room if you need one."

Dav said, "Seth can stay with us. No need to..."

Kerem shook her head. "Dav, you have, but one room for the three of you, and the little one does not sleep through the night."

Dav nodded. "It is Kerem's habit to come to the well at sunset looking for those in need of hospitality. It is true. She prepares an extra portion of food."

Seth looked confused. "Surely, there would be talk!"

A LIGHT IN THE DARKEST NIGHT

Dav laughed. "They dare not! Kerem is a seer. And all in Endor know her to be a good, chaste, and generous woman."

Seth looked at Dav and then Kerem. "I shall accept your hospitality—the meal, but I shall sleep outside. Perhaps a barn or pen?"

Seth washed at the well and followed Kerem to her house. Kerem listened as she finished preparing the meal. Seth spoke of David. "A most unusual man! He is young and handsome, full of good cheer and life. It is no surprise he is a musician and sings like no other, but most amazing is his fearlessness in battle. He believes, no, he knows, God is with him. And the people too, everywhere they sing: 'Saul has killed his thousands and David his ten thousands.'"

Kerem turned and said, "I have heard of this man David. It is said he slew the champion of the Philistines, Goliath. Some have sworn Goliath a giant and David but a shepherd, slew him with his sling—a single stone to Goliath's forehead."

Seth replied, "It is as you say. David slew him and cut off his head with Goliath's own sword."

"And Saul? What does Saul say of him?"

"Not only did Saul make David his armor-bearer and captain of a thousand, he offered David one of his daughters in marriage. But Saul has changed. He is no longer the humble man and fearless warrior. He Leaves the fighting to others. He is sharp in his rebukes and indecisive in his commands. There is talk that Saul hopes David is cut down in battle and worse—in his dark moods, he plots against him. But Jonathan stands with David. There are no finer men in all of Israel than David and Jonathan."

Kerem asked, "And Samuel? Does not the prophet comfort Saul?"

Seth thought before he answered. "Samuel does not leave his house in Ramah. It is said he prophesied against Saul—that the Lord has torn the Kingdom from Saul. No one speaks of Saul, only David whom Saul, in his madness now pursues.

When Seth had finished his meal and gone outside to sleep in the goat pen, Kerem sat in her house thinking. Her thoughts were disturbed by the hissing sound in her ears. She opened her eyes and uncovered the pit. "Kerrremmm, Kerremm, Kerem. What have you done? Sssssss. The girl has not passed through the fire! Sssssssss, you deprived the gods and disobeyed me!"

"No, mother, the price has been paid. You said the price is an offering worth twenty shekels. He has made the offering!"

The vision of her mother swayed side to side. Her eyes, black as night, were flashing reflections into Kerem's eyes. Kerem watched and saw her mother's face scowling. For a moment, her mouth opened, and a thin forked tongue tasted the air. Kerem shuddered at the sight, and the vision became still, and the face calmed. "You lent him the money. Ssssss. Kerem, my sweet. What need has Asherah for money? Now the girl, the daughter, she is what Asherah desired."

"But you said…"

"I know what I said! Now hear me, my sweet, you have

been given the gift that you may be feared, not liked, not admired, and never loved! Fear, fear, and doubt—that is your strength and your weapon."

The apparition shook its head. The rings and necklace of Asherah shook. Her mother smiled and turned to watch the orgy beyond her, her black hair falling away from her breasts as she moved. She was smiling when she turned back to Kerem. "Soon, my sweet, soon Saul will be in your hands. You heard the news; the kingdom will be torn from him. He will fight David. Yes, my sweet, first Saul whom Samuel has abandoned, and soon Samuel will die, and then we take David."

The apparition appeared to sway a dance, hissed, and then said, "Kerem, make them fear you!"

Kerem could not sleep that night. Her visit to the other realm haunted her. *"Make them fear you!"* her mother commanded. But it was Kerem who feared. Feared her mother, *or is she really my mother? Is an evil spirit appearing to me as Momma? What do I remember about Mother? Very little. I was only four years old when she died. And my older brothers, they would better remember, they are now dead. Papa said hard things against her, that she played the harlot. When she appears to me, she is naked and lives in a world of sexual debauchery. Was Momma evil? Papa cared for me growing up—but then he sold me. Was it need? Did he ever love me? Was it guilt—all a story to make me hate him? Papa insisted he was of the tribe Issachar—surely someone would know his family. Yes, there must be some relative who can tell me more.*

The next day, Kerem sought the elder, where he sat

inside the city gate. Kerem bowed and approached. "Elder, I have come seeking..."

"Woman, it is our custom that a husband or father speak on your behalf."

"I have no husband or father. Does not your law demand justice to the widow and orphan?"

The elder stared at Kerem. "I know who you are. You are Kerem, the seer. And you, an idolater, and voice for Asherah, speak of our duty under the Law of Moses?"

Kerem bowed. "I seek only to know the truth. My father was a son of Issachar. He lived under the law of Moses. He sold me to the priests of Baal at their high place on the Hill of Moreh. Perhaps he made me who I am. For in truth, I do not know who I am—who my people are and who my god is. As an orphan, I ask you, who are my people? Who are my kinsman in Endor?"

The elder stared at Kerem and then stroked his beard. "Your father, Micah, never shared his story with you? No, I suppose it was too painful."

He paused and then continued, "I have heard of your kind heart and your hospitality to the stranger. Not like the priests of Baal and Moloch or the priestesses of Asherah. Though Micah doubted he was your father, he doted on you like a daughter he loved, until you became a woman. Micah trusted no woman. It was your mother he saw in you. He never forgave her though she begged his forgiveness. It was well known in Endor—she ventured to the Hill of Moreh to watch a festival. She confessed she drank their wine and ate their sacred food, and she was beguiled and coupled many times with strangers. She sinned. Only the Lord knows for certain, but to me, your face favors Micah. Shame. Shame fell upon Micah. But kinsman? Yes, you have a kinsman, a son of Micah's uncle. But you know him. It is rumored you lend him money and lead him into idolatry. I speak of Dav."

"Dav is my kinsman?"

"Dav is your near kinsman. Take your questions to him."

Kerem mumbled, "Dav is my kinsman? And he never told me?"

The elder cleared his throat. "Kerem, go your way. Give up your idolatry, and may the God of Abraham, Isaac, and Jacob have mercy on you."

Kerem's head spun as she walked to Dav's house. *Why has he said nothing? I have been kind to him. I trusted him and helped him. I thought we were friends. Is Dav ashamed of me? Is there anyone who is not ashamed to know me?*

Dav's son answered Kerem's knock on the door. "My father is away. Come back later."

Kerem asked, "It is me, Kerem. A friend. May I come in? Away? Where?"

"Go away. I will not let you in. My father has gone to Ophrah to see a man about a field. Now go away. I will not allow a witch and an idolater in our house."

Kerem felt her chest fall as she gasped for air. Her mother's words played in her mind. *"No one else loves you. Kerem, my sweet, no one will ever love you."*

Kerem waited by the well and watched people come and go through the city gate. Dav did not come. Kerem sat, her head bowed, afraid to return home but no longer interested in the comings and goings of her neighbors. She had resigned herself to a world of loneliness. Her consciousness stirred when she overheard a man say a name: "Samuel, Samuel protects David. They are at Naioth in Ramah. Saul sent messengers to Samuel, but when they arrived, they fell before Samuel, and they prophesied. So then Saul went to Samuel at Ramah, and Saul also fell before him and prophesied. The King stripped himself and lay naked and prophesied a full day. The saying is everywhere in Israel—Saul is among the prophets!"

Kerem spoke up. "Rumor—gossip and rumors! Tell us truly how you know this."

"Ignore the woman. She is a seer, a witch, and an idolater. She whores after Asherah."

The man replied, "I do not fear her or any idolater. I know what I say is true, for I am a witness. I was there, I am a priest to the Living God, and now I return home to Daberath in Zebulon after my duty at the Tabernacle is complete."

Kerem felt shamed. "Forgive me, priest. I meant no harm. I have heard of the prophet Samuel. Please, come to my house. I shall give you refreshment. I would hear more of the prophet and your God."

"I take only water in Endor. I am anxious to journey on to my home."

As Kerem walked home, she stopped and stared at the gate. *I shall go to Ramah. I shall seek Samuel. Yes! Samuel is a great prophet. The God of Israel is with him. He will tell me the truth!*

A LIGHT IN THE DARKEST NIGHT

Kerem closed the door behind her and turned to her kitchen. A snake, a cobra taller than Kerem, swayed before her. Kerem's eyes locked on the eyes of the snake and the eyes of its hood. Slowly the face of her mother appeared on the head of the snake. "Sssss. You will not go to Ramah. You will never seek Samuel."

"You are not my mother! You are evil. You will no longer guide me. I will not call upon you again!"

The forked tongue of the snake tasted the air. "I could take you now. You are mine, my sweet. But I am not finished with you."

Kerem turned for the door but stumbled over a chair she did not see. Kerem fell to the dirt floor. She could not see her way to the door. She could not see anything. Kerem was blind. Slowly light, a dim light returned. Kerem began to see her mother, naked but for the golden belt and earrings, wearing the image of Asherah. Kerem saw others afar off, still coupling like animals in the wild. She heard their chanting, "Mother Asherah, you who eternally conceive but never bear, mother Asherah watch what we do! Let us entice you as you entice us—conceive! For to conceive is everything!"

Their chant was interrupted. "Kerem. My sweet. You are blind to everyone but me. You will do as I command. When I am finished with you, you will join those who you now watch. Those who forever conceive and forever chant."

Dav returned several days later and called upon Kerem. Kerem heard him knock, but she would not answer. "Kerem, It is me, Dav. You called at my house. I have come. Did you need something? No one has seen you in days. Answer me, Kerem!"

"Go away. I need nothing. I need no one! Why shame yourself calling upon an idolater?"

"Shame? You are my friend. You bring no shame."

"Your son tells a different story. And so does the elder. You are my kinsman but ashamed to say so."

"Kinsman? You say I am your kinsman? This I have never heard."

"My close kinsman. The son of my father's uncle."

Dav was quiet. He thought and then said, "In truth, I did not know. But I do remember my father saying we were to have no dealings with Micah and his whore wife. Kerem, I am sorry. I did not know. Kerem, you are kind and gentle, my truest friend. Kerem, you are hurting. Let me come in."

"Do not come in. I am cursed by an evil spirit. I have wronged you, Dav. You came to me, and I commanded an evil of you, an offering to the gods. They deserve no offering—they bring only evil. Stay away from me, the cursed daughter of a whore."

Kerem no longer offered hospitality to the strangers. She did not welcome Dav into her house. Kerem went to the well after dark. She recognized night by the cool air and silence. Now blind, day and night made no difference to her. Her grain, oil, figs, and foodstuff were left at her door, where a pouch for payment hung.

Kerem sought out no one, but her gift was well known, and men and sometimes women, widows, sought her services as a seer. Once Kerem was satisfied it was only a seer they sought, she would crack open her door and receive them. She would need to be reminded to light a lamp after dark, and she offered no refreshment. "Who do you seek?" was all that she would ask before gazing her blind eyes into her pit.

Kerem repeated what her guide said and added, "The guide has spoken. Ten shekels." It was her business. She worked for her spirit guide, not the frightened people who crossed her threshold. She decided it was easier not to care, even when it meant crying for them when she lay awake at night.

Dav had long ago stopped calling at Kerem's door. So, it was some surprise to her when his familiar voice called out as he knocked. "Kerem. Are you there? Of course, you are. I know you only sneak out at night to go to the well. I know, I watch—for your safety. Kerem, if you won't open your door, listen to me. You must listen. King Saul has issued a decree. No one may practice divination. No one may play the seer in Israel. Did you hear me, Kerem? You are known. There are some in Endor who would gladly betray you. You can no longer conjure the dead. Hear me, Kerem, it is on pain of death! Let no one come to you seeking your gift. Tell me you have heard my words."

Dav waited. Finally, he heard a soft reply. "You have accomplished what you have come for. Leave me in peace."

"Kerem, how will you live? Let me help you."

"Go away. I will live as I have always lived. Now leave me. I will say no more."

Not many months later, Kerem was awakened late at night by the loud knocking of a staff on her door. Surprised, she got up and stood behind the door. "Who disturbs me from my sleep?"

King Saul, disguised in the robes of a merchant, replied, "Call for me one from the dead. Bring before me the one I shall name."

Kerem replied, "You know what Saul has done, how he has cut off the mediums, the seers and the conjurers from the land. Why do you lay a trap for me to bring about my death?"

Saul replied, his voice strong through the closed door. "As the Lord lives, no punishment shall come upon you for this thing."

Kerem opened the door. Saul stepped inside the house, followed by two servants armed with swords and spears. Kerem listened to their footsteps and discerned the breathing of the two silent men. She walked to the pit and asked, "Whom shall I bring up for you?"

"Bring up Samuel."

"Samuel is dead?" Her eyes widened, and she screamed, "You are Saul! Why have you deceived me?"

"Do not be afraid. What do you see?"

Kerem's eyes focused on the pit. She heard a strong wind and did not feel the scales falling from her eye, only the wind blowing her hair back off her face. She saw a bright light moving like a cloud and then a shadow coming from the light. "I see a god coming out to the earth."

Saul said, "What is his appearance?"

The shadow came closer, the bright light behind it made it difficult to see, but yes, she saw a man, an old man.

"An old man is coming up. He is wrapped in a robe."

Saul cried out, "Samuel!" And he bowed his face to the ground and paid homage.

The man from the cloud, Samuel, said to Saul, "Why have you disturbed me by bringing me up?"

Saul answered, "I am in great distress. The Philistines have come to war against me, and God has turned away from me and no longer answers me, either by prophets or by dreams. So, I have summoned you to tell me what to do."

Samuel replied, "Why do you ask me since the Lord has turned away from you and become your enemy? The Lord has done to you as he spoke by me. The Lord has torn the kingdom out of your hand and given it to your neighbor, David. Because you did not obey the voice of the Lord and carry out his fierce wrath against Amalek. Moreover, the Lord will give the army of Israel into the hands of the Philistines."

Saul fell to the ground upon hearing Samuel. Kerem felt the wind reverse as Samuel was drawn back through the cloud into the light beyond. She turned to Saul, still laying on the ground beside the pit. As he lifted his head, she saw the terror in his eyes. She said softly, "I am your servant, O King. I have obeyed you. I have put my life into your hand and have listened to what you have said to me. Now, obey your servant. Let me set bread before you. Eat that you may gain strength when you go your way."

Saul sobbed, "I will not eat."

His two servants finally spoke. "You have had nothing to eat all day. The woman is right, O King. Eat and be strong."

Kerem said, "I have a fatted calf in my pen." Not

waiting for a reply, she went out, killed the calf and roasted meat. She took flour and oil, kneaded it and baked unleavened bread. Kerem served the meal to Saul and his servants. When Saul arose from the table, he stood tall. He stood strong. His eyes burned with the determination of a man who knew his duty and knew it meant death. Then Saul and his servants departed into the darkness.

Kerem stepped out into the night and looked at the stars in the sky. Her sight now restored, she said to herself, "The Lord is God." When she returned to her house, she heard only silence. She walked to the pit. Still silence, not a hiss. Staring, she saw only dirt at the bottom of a hole in the ground. When Kerem opened her robe to bathe, she saw that her birth mark which had grown into a serpent, was gone. Her skin was clean and smooth as a young child's, without a blemish of any kind.

A week went by before the first report came to Endor. "Israel is defeated! The army has fled. The Philistines have taken Shunem, Jezreel, Harod, and many villages in the Jezreel valley. It is best to flee, north to Naphtali or better across the Jordan to Gilead of Gad or Ashtaroth of Manasseh."

Kerem asked, "What of our neighbor Dav and his son?"

The man replied, "Many have fallen. I do not know the fate of Dav or his son. If you are wise, you will leave now!"

Kerem waited for Dav. Two days later, he returned with his son. Kerem ran to meet them. "The Lord has preserved you. I prayed, and he heard my prayers. I am going to the Tabernacle to make offerings for my sin and offerings of thanksgiving."

Dav was surprised. "You follow the Lord? We thank you for your prayers, but—but the Philistines stand between Endor and Gilgal."

Kerem shook her head. "The Lord will be with us. He will shield us on our way. I go. Do you come with me or flee across the Jordan?"

Dav froze and stared at Kerem. "Marry me, Kerem. Marry me, and I will gather my household and go. We shall follow the mountain road south on the other side of the Jordan."

"You ask me to marry you?"

"I am your near kinsman—it is my duty to redeem you. I have always loved you, Kerem, but before I learned that we are kin, I had no money to support you. And when I learned I was your kinsman-redeemer, you would have no man. But the Lord has shown me that it is right that we marry."

Kerem stood stunned. Neighbors were running past. Donkeys brayed under their heavy loads. The air was filled with dust and the sounds of panic. Tears fell from Kerem's eyes. She pointed at the people rushing to the gate of the city.

"We must hurry. I will help you gather your household."

Dav waited. He just stared at Kerem.

Kerem turned to Dav. "Yes, I will marry you. It is a wondrous thing to be loved."

Three days later, Kerem approached Zadok, the High Priest, and made her burnt offerings, a sin offering, and a sacrifice of thanksgiving on the Tabernacle altar. When Zadok completed the sacrifice and brought Kerem her portion, he looked into her eyes. "You have been forgiven much, daughter. Know that the Lord has searched your heart, a heart filled with love for the Lord and love for your neighbor. He smiles upon you and makes you His. Tell me, daughter of Israel, your city and your father's name."

"I am Kerem from Endor. The man Micah of the tribe Issachar raised me, though he said I was not his. My mother, a Canaanite, played the harlot when she worshipped Asherah. I, too, served Asherah for many years. I conjured Samuel for Saul. It was Samuel who showed me the truth."

"Kerem, the Lord always accepts the sacrifice of a clean heart. Know that you are a true daughter of Issachar of Israel."

"Truly, the Lord has blessed me. He has saved me from becoming Baal's prostitute, from being sacrificed in Moloch's fire and enticed as Asherah's seer. The Lord sent my kinsman-redeemer to be my husband who loves me. I will love and worship only the Lord. He has saved me. For the Lord is the God who loves. It is a wonderful thing to love and to be loved."

Zadok paused. "It is as you say, beloved of the Lord. Tell me, Saul went to you? You were a conjurer, a medium? Samuel came up when you called? Tell me, Saul, what did he hear?"

"It is true. I was a seer. I was also blind, but now I see in truth. Saul listened to Samuel. He heard the kingdom was to be torn from him and given to David. The Philistines would defeat the army of Israel. He was told that he and his sons would soon join Samuel. But Saul regained his strength. I saw him stand tall. I saw strength in his eyes. He left like a king to do battle. Tell me, Chief Priest of the Most High God, King Saul, Jonathan, and his brothers, if they are with Samuel, are they not in the bosom of Father Abraham? Has the Lord redeemed Saul?"

Zadok smiled at Kerem. "No one is beyond the redemption of the Lord. He is merciful and gracious towards sinners who repent. The Lord has given the Kingdom of Israel to David, but he has not forgotten his servants Saul and Jonathan, whom David loved. No sin is too great to be forgiven, just as no one is free from sin or the attacks by the evil one. The Lord gives, and the Lord takes away. Blessed be the name of the Lord."

THE COURTSHIP

The sun was high in the morning sky when Rachel shook the man in the bed. "Get up! You promised you would find work. The day is half gone. Get up!"

The man groaned, "Leave me woman. Let me sleep. If the day is half gone, there is always tomorrow."

"Wash your face while I make you breakfast."

The man sat up in the bed. His eyes still closed, he took a deep breath, stretched his neck and then his back. He straightened his arms and drew his shoulders back and yawned. He opened his eyes and sighed. He smiled when Rachel walked by, grabbed her and pulled her onto the bed. Holding her close, he kissed her.

"Come to bed. First pleasure, then breakfast."

Rachel pulled herself away. "You want to please me, find work and marry me."

"I work."

"You steal. Find honest work and let me be an honest wife."

"Marry you? You—an honest wife?" The man began to laugh.

"An honest wife? You joke! How many husbands have you had? Too many for me to count! No husband will make you an honest woman. You will never be accepted by the women of Sychar. Get used to it, Rachel, your whole life has been one man's bed after another. You take our money in trade for giving us moments of pleasure. A leper would be more welcome with the women of this town than you will ever be!"

"Get out! Get out and don't come back!"

The man did not look up. He sat at the table leaning over his meal with an arm wrapped around the plate in front of him. "I'm leaving—after I eat. Then you can sneak about in the hot sun out of the eyes of the neighbors. I will be back for supper."

Rachel walked to the window. "Eat your breakfast and be gone!"

She could see the women returning from the well and said to herself, "I want to go as soon as they are all back, before the sun gets any hotter."

On a dusty road outside of the village of Sychar, a Jewish rabbi and his disciples slowly made their way north from Jerusalem. For most, it was their first journey through Samaria. Good Jews did not travel through Samaria. These men of Galilee would instead add days to their journey to and from the Temple to avoid any contact with this unclean half-breed people.

When Jesus first saw the walls of Sychar on the horizon, he asked Peter, "Simon Peter, tell me the story of your courtship. How did you meet your wife?"

Simon looked up from the dusty path, smiled and said, "I first saw her at the well in Bethsaida. She would go in the morning with the women and maidens. She was beautiful—and such a smile! I knew at once I must charm her and then seek her father's permission."

Jesus smiled. "Charm her? How?"

Peter was nodding his head and smiling brightly, "Well, Master, I was most subtle of course. I would bow deeply as she passed and say, 'tidings to the beauty of Bethsaida.'"

Jesus laughed. "Yes, I see. Very subtle."

Peter continued, "She smiled back! One day she said, 'A handsome, prosperous and wise man would bring a basket of fresh fish and meet my father.'"

"And when did you do so?"

Peter laughed. "That very day. She is a most amazing woman."

Jesus still smiling replied, "She caught her fish—a woman who knows her heart and acts." After a pause, Jesus added, "You love her very dearly. Yet you are here with me."

"Truly rabbi, I do love her. But she knows I love you, as does she. She cannot journey with you, but I can. She is always with me as I walk with you."

"She is a great help to Mary and the others."

Jesus stopped and looked at the village ahead, then up at the bright sun in the cloudless sky above. Turning he looked into Peter's eyes and said, "The Father above has given you a great love. The well—it is a good sign. Jacob met his love Rachel at the well in Haran. It was the same well where Abraham's servant found Rebekah. He prayed for a sign of God's chosen one—the sign that a woman would give him water and his camels as well. Rebekah was dearly loved by Isaac. She was chosen just as Isaac was chosen. And Moses too—Moses met his wife, Zipporah at the well. You see then, my friend, you are in good company."

Peter smiled and walked on silently. As they made their way toward Sychar, Peter spoke up. "We must stay on the road around the town, I dread the thought of encountering Samaritans. It is good that we pass by in the heat of the sun. Few will be about."

"We have encountered Arameans, Greeks, even Romans. Do you fear Samaritans?"

"Rabbi, they have disobeyed God's law. They have married people of the outside. They do not worship at the Temple in Jerusalem but in their idolatrous temple on Mount Gerizim! The Romans never knew our law or the One True God. But they—rabbi, do not forget how Samaritans desecrated the Holy Temple with the bones of men—the Samaritans have offended and abandoned God!"

"Peter, do you hate the Samaritans?"

Peter's eyebrows tightened as he collected his thoughts. "It is written, 'love what is good, hate what is evil.'"

Jesus looked towards Sychar and asked, "What prophet has not called for God's people to repent with warnings of His wrath to come? What prophet was not stoned, thrown down a well, cut in two or murdered? How many times has our Heavenly Father delayed His judgment, waiting that some might repent?"

Peter's face cringed at the words. "But our people were sent into slavery, in Egypt and later Babylon."

"And how did they repay God's salvation from Egypt, the land where they grew in number, with labor, yes but also homes, food and safety? Their faith was weak. They complained to Moses. They doubted their God who led them, and they wandered the desert for forty years."

Jesus turned to Peter and smiled. "Even in His wrath He loved them. Does any father find joy in the misery that rebellion and sin bring to his children? It is the misery of sin that He abhors, and it is the gift of His love that He sends. Should even a Samaritan be punished for the sins of his father? No, let each man or woman be accountable for their own sin. And let each man or woman find the salvation sent to them by their Father in heaven who loves them."

Jesus shook the dust from his head scarf, stomped the dirt from his hot sandaled feet and resumed walking the road. Master and disciples followed the path as it wound its way around the city where they came to a crossroad. To the left the road led into the heart of Samaria. Ahead lay the way to Galilee. To the right was the road to the city gate. A tree was planted by the crossing and near the tree was an ancient well. Jesus walked to the tree, leaned his walking stick against it and sat down, shaded from the blazing sun. The air was still and hung heavy in the heat of the day.

"Judas," he called out.

A lanky man wearing the best robe in the group came over. "Yes, rabbi?"

"Judas, you carry the money, go into the village and buy food. We shall not stop in another city before Galilee. Take your time and find bread, figs, raisins and dried fish. Buy wine, and water and wine skins, for each of us."

"That is much to carry, master."

"All of you are to go. I will wait here."

Turning to Peter, James, and John he said, "Do not fear the Samaritans. Do not call their food unclean. It is not what goes into the mouth that defiles you; you are defiled by the words that come out of your mouth."

Jesus leaned back against the tree and closed his eyes. "Go."

As the disciples trudged off towards the foreboding city of the despised Samaritans, they could overhear Jesus begin his prayer. "Father, send her out to me..."

Rachel scanned the street from her window. It was empty. She glanced at the man at the table, bent over his still warm cakes and figs. She opened the door and stepped out. Seeing the disciples walking towards her she thought, *Who are they? Jews? In Sychar?* She stepped back inside her door. The man at the table did not look up. "I thought you were going to the well. There better be water when I return."

"I'm going. There is a large group of Jews coming in— to the market I suppose. I will wait until they pass. Why would Jews come here?"

"Who knows? A large group? Are they armed?"

"I did not see swords. They are not soldiers."

"For all their sanctimony, Jews are cowards. Perhaps one has come to collect a debt and needs a mob to protect him!"

"They have passed—walking towards the market. I am going."

Rachel stepped out the door, picked up her large water jug, placed it on her shoulder and walked towards the city gate. The narrow streets provided shade, but outside the gate the heat of the sun quickly made its presence felt. Even though empty, the water jar dug into her shoulder and sweat began to run from her brow. *At least there is some shade at the well,* she thought. *Will I ever again be able to draw my water in the cool of day?*

Rachel stopped at the well and set down her jug. She took the rope tethered to a stake beside the well and tied it the jug. She began to lower the jug, careful not to break it against the stone sides of the well. Hand over hand, she lowered the jug waiting to hear the soft splash as it found the water.

"Give me a drink."

The words startled Rachel. She turned and saw a man sitting beneath the shade tree. Another Jew.

"How is it you, a Jew, ask for a drink from me, a woman of Samaria?"

Jesus stood up and brushed the dust from his robe. He smiled and said, "If you knew the gift of God and who it is that is saying to you, 'Give me a drink,' you would have asked him and he would have given you living water."

Rachel stared at Jesus a few moments and replied, "Sir, you have nothing to draw water with, and the well is deep. Where do you get that living water?"

Rachel paused and watched Jesus. He smiled back at her. His smile captivated her. She needed to turn away before—

She turned to the well. "Are you greater than our father, Jacob? He gave us the well and drank from it himself, as did his sons and his livestock."

Still smiling, Jesus said, "Everyone who drinks of this water will be thirsty again. But whoever drinks of the water that I will give him will never be thirsty again. The water that I will give him will become in him a spring of water welling up to eternal life."

His words drew her gaze back to him. "Sir, give me this water, so that I will not be thirsty or have to come here to draw water."

Jesus nodded. His smile gone, he said, "Go call your husband and come here."

Rachel immediately replied, "I have no husband."

Jesus' eyes burned into hers. "You are right in saying, 'I have no husband;' for you have had five husbands, and the one you now have is not your husband. What you have said is true."

Rachel's jaw dropped, but her eyes remained focused on the eyes of Jesus. "Sir, I perceive you are a prophet."

Rachel had to close her eyes and break the stare of Jesus. Then opening them again and looking away she said, "Our fathers worshipped on this mountain, but you say that in Jerusalem is the place where people ought to worship."

His words brought her eyes back to him, "Woman, believe me, the hour is coming when neither on this mountain nor in Jerusalem will you worship the Father. You worship what you do not know; we worship what we know, for salvation is from the Jews."

Jesus paused, and seeing she was listening closely continued, "But the hour is coming, and is now here, when the true worshippers will worship the Father in spirit and in truth, for the Father is seeking such people to worship him. God is spirit and those who worship him must worship in spirit and truth."

Rachel replied, "I know that the Messiah is coming, he who is called Christ. When he comes, he will tell us all things."

Again, Jesus' eyes stared into her soul. "I who speak to you am he."

Both stood silently, their eyes locked together.

The moment was interrupted by the sound of the disciples plodding footsteps as they returned from Sychar. Slowly they encircled Jesus and Rachel. Each of them wondered what was happening. But none, not even Peter could ask 'Why are you talking with her?' They stood there in the hot sun watching Jesus as their dust settled around them.

Rachel turned and walked away, back to Sychar, leaving her water jug behind.

As she made her way to the city gate, her pace quickened. At the gate she began to run. She ran to the market shouting, "Come see a man who told me everything I ever did! Can this be the Christ?"

Once Rachel left, the disciples followed Peter into the shade. "Let's eat," he said, and he opened one of the baskets.

Jesus stood at the well watching Rachel. Peter called out, "Rabbi eat!"

Not turning from his gaze, he replied, "I have food to eat that you do not know about."

One of them asked, "Has anyone brought him something to eat?"

Jesus turned around and walked over to them under the shade. "My food is to do the will of him who sent me and to accomplish his work. They say, 'There are yet four months and then comes the harvest.' Look, I tell you, lift up your eyes, and see that the fields are white for harvest."

Instinctively, the disciples looked out at the valley below, Jesus continued, "Already the one who reaps is receiving wages and gathering fruit for eternal life, so that sower and reaper may rejoice together. For here the saying holds true, 'One sows, and another reaps.' I sent you to reap that for which you did not labor."

A LIGHT IN THE DARKEST NIGHT

The disciples looked at each other in silence, as Jesus said, "Others have labored that you may enter their labor."

Jesus sat down, leaned against the tree and closed his eyes. One by one the disciples began to eat—in silence.

In the market of Sychar, Rachel boldly and urgently recounted her encounter with the Jewish prophet at the well. "He told me all I ever did! I tell you he is a prophet! He knew all about me! He speaks of living water and eternal life. What I say is true! He is still there! If you hurry, surely you will see for yourself! Has the Messiah come to Sychar?"

Some of the women turned and left without a word as Rachel approached. Others pretended to ignore her, keeping their eyes on the fruit and vegetables in the market bins. It was the men who questioned her, "What do you mean, he knew all about you?"

"He said I had five husbands and the man I am with is not my husband!"

A woman counting figs curled her shoulders and shook her head in disgust.

A man replied, "A Jewish prophet? He knows your sin, and yet he speaks to you? I will go. I will see for myself!"

Another replied, "I will go too." Turning to Rachel he said, "Be certain, Rachel. If you are lying, you will pay dearly!"

First the two, then a third and a fourth man walked off. Soon most of the villagers, even the women walked out to see this prophet at the well. As they gathered, Jesus stood up and said, "Friends, there is shade. Do not stand under the hot sun. Sit and listen."

The disciples stood and moved off by the well as the people of Sychar gathered to sit at Jesus' feet. Rachel followed them out and stood a way off. She watched Jesus stretch his arms open, smiling at the people of Sychar.

Jesus began to teach, "The kingdom of God is like a pearl of great value..."

Rachel stared at Jesus and thought, *A Jew, a prophet, here in Sychar? He knows our sin. He knows what we have done, yet he welcomes us? Look how he smiles! His voice is tender. Could it be true? Is that his love I feel?*

The afternoon passed by. The sun was low on the horizon. One of the village elder's stood up, "Teacher, the day is late. We would hear more from you. Please, stay with us this night. Let us show you the hospitality of our village. Come to my house, and your disciples. We will provide for them as well. You must eat and have a safe place to sleep. I know it is not right in the eyes of the Jews to have dealings with Samaritans, but please, do us this honor."

Jesus stood up and lifted one arm towards the city gate. "We will follow. Your hospitality is welcome."

The disciples looked at each other and without word, followed Jesus as he walked alongside the city elder. Slowly the crowd of Samaritans made their way back to their homes. Rachel stood at the side of the road watching her neighbors file by.

The first men who spoke to her in the market stopped and chided her. "It is no longer because of what you said that we believe. For we have heard for ourselves and know that he indeed is the Savior of the world."

At that moment, Jesus stopped and turned around. "Rachel. Are you coming? Draw your water and follow me."

The water jug! Rachel hurried to the well, drew her water jug, lifted it onto her shoulder and walked briskly home.

A LIGHT IN THE DARKEST NIGHT

Rachel had just placed the jug in the door when the man returned. "What was the commotion at the well?" he asked as he took a small pouch of coins and hid it in the bed post.

"Jesus. A Jew and he a prophet, has come to Sychar. He taught at the well and now has come to stay with us and teach..."

"He will not stay in this house," the man interrupted.

"The elder has invited him to stay. I am going to hear him again."

"My dinner!" the man shouted.

"Feed yourself—or come with me. Hear what he has to say. Never has any man spoken like him in Sychar or all of Samaria. He is a prophet! I believe he is the Messiah!"

"I am hungry. I have no interest in your Messiah. Go if you must; but come home quickly. I have strong desires that only you satisfy."

Rachel stopped at the door, turned and looked at the man she lived with. "If you will not come—if you will not change, I have no need or desire for you. This is my house. I don't want to find you here when I return. Things have changed. I have changed. Go."

Rachel took a small water jar, a basin and a towel and went out into the dusk. She hurried to the house of the village elder where Jesus and his disciples were gathered at the door. Jesus was speaking to the elder as the disciples removed their sandals and washed their feet. Rachel came up behind Jesus and gently pulled him to a bench at the door where he sat down. Wordlessly, she unstrapped his sandals, brushed away the manure, dirt and dust caked to his feet. Then she poured clean water and wiped away the mud, pouring a second time to rinse them clean. Kneeling before him she dried his feet with the towel. She then washed his sandals and tied them on his feet.

The elder's face burned red with anger. "Woman! This is not your place!"

Jesus lifted the palms of his hand and shook his head softly while smiling. His voice gentle, he said, "Leave her alone. Allow her this gift."

Jesus looked down, "Rachel."

Again, their eyes met as Rachel looked up into his face. "Your servant, Lord."

"You have chosen well. Do not return to your sin. The kingdom of God is before you." Rachel's eyes remained fixed on his and slowly tears welled up in her eyes as a smile emerged from her lips. She drank in his compassion as he said, "Come inside and listen."

The guests inside stopped talking and watched as Rachel followed Jesus and sat down at his feet. Jesus looked at the guests staring at Rachel and began to teach. "What man among you, if he has a hundred sheep and has lost one of them, does not leave the ninety-nine in the open pasture, and go after the one which is lost until he finds it? And when he has found it, he lays it on his shoulders, rejoicing. And when he comes home, he calls together his friends and his neighbors, saying to them, 'Rejoice with me, for I have found my sheep which was lost!'"

The guests looked at Rachel sitting quietly before Jesus. One by one they gathered around the table set before Jesus and sat down in silence. Jesus was hungry. He took a piece of bread, blessed it and ate his first meal since breakfast.

He took a drink of the wine and glanced to the

wealthy village elder and then looking at each of the guests he continued to teach, "A certain man had two sons; and the younger of them said to his father, 'Father, give me the share of the estate that falls to me.' And he divided his wealth between them. And not many days later, the younger son gathered everything together and went on a journey into a different country, and there he squandered his estate with loose living."

Every ear was listening as Jesus continued, "Now when he spent everything, a severe famine occurred in that country, and he began to be in need. He went and attached himself to one of the citizens of that country, and he sent him into his fields to feed swine. He was longing to fill his stomach with the pods that the swine were eating, and no one was giving anything to him."

Jesus took another bite of bread and a drink of wine, smiled briefly and continued, "But when he came to his senses, he said, 'How many of my father's hired men have more than enough bread, but I am dying here of hunger! I will get up and go to my father, and will say to him, 'Father, I have sinned against heaven and in your sight. I am no longer worthy to be called your son; make me as one of your hired men.' And he got up and came to his father. But while he was still a long way off, his father saw him and felt compassion for him and ran and embraced him and kissed him."

The room was silent. A few guests took a sip of wine while Jesus paused. He continued, "The son said to him, 'Father, I have sinned against heaven and in your sight; I am no longer worthy to be called your son.' But the father said to his servants, 'Quickly, bring out the best robe and put it on him, and put a ring on his hand and sandals on his feet; and bring the fatted calf, kill it, and let us eat and be merry, for this son of mine was dead and has come to life again; he was lost and has been found. And they began to be merry."

Rachel glanced up for just a moment, but quickly lowered her face and wiped a tear from her eye. The guests glanced about nodding politely and returned to their meal.

They were startled by the earnestness in Jesus' voice as he spoke louder. "Now his older son..."

Eyes again turned to Jesus. "...was in the field, and when he came and approached the house, he heard music and dancing. He summoned one of the servants and asked what these things might be. And he said to him, 'Your brother has come, and your father has killed the fattened calf, because he has received him back safe and sound.' But he became very angry and was not willing to go in. His father came out begged him, but he answered his father, 'Look! For so many years I have been serving you, and I have never neglected a command of yours; and yet you have never given me a kid that I might be merry with my friends; but this son of yours came, who has devoured your wealth with harlots, and you killed the fattened calf for him."

Jesus took a deep breath and opened his arms and went on, "My child, you have always been with me and all that is mine is yours. But we had to be merry and rejoice, for this brother of yours was dead and has begun to live and was lost and has been found."

No one questioned Jesus on his teaching.

The guests finished their meal and began to leave. The wealthy elder spoke up. "We would hear more of your teaching tomorrow. Please stay with us and..."

Jesus nodded, "I will stay and teach under the tree by

the well."

Jesus and the disciples were provided rugs and mats and made themselves comfortable in the sheltered courtyard of the elder's house. The young disciple, John, laying down looking at the stars above quietly said to his older brother James, "The master shares the same message with the Samaritans as that he shares with the Jews."

Jesus heard John, whom he loved, and said, "The well is indeed the very one dug by the patriarch Jacob to whom the father gave the name Israel. They have not forgotten. They do not worship in the Temple and they do not follow the law of Moses as they should. Does the father love them any less than their brothers who worship in the temple but also corrupt the law of Moses? John, have I not said, 'God is Spirit and those who worship Him will worship Him in spirit and in truth?'"

John asked, "Will you go to the gentiles too?"

Jesus answered, "There shall be a light to the gentiles. The Father does not wish that any be lost but that all should come to repentance."

John thought about Jesus' words and then said softly, "The woman. Did you come here for the woman or all the villagers?"

John could not see Jesus smile.

Rachel returned to her house, her head spinning, but a radiant smile glowing from her face. When she opened her door, she saw a candle lit on the table and the man seated there with a cup of wine. "You're back at last! Lurking in the shadows outside the elder's house no doubt."

Rachel's smile disappeared. "I told you to leave!"

She stood inside the door and held it open for him. "Go! Get out and never come back!"

The man stared at her for a moment and said, "You're serious." He took a deep breath as anger swept across his brow. "If I leave, I am not coming back!" he shouted.

"Good! Never come back. That is what I have told you. Now go. Take what you have stolen and go!"

The man stood up, went to his hiding place and took several pouches of money. He stopped and looked at Rachel. "You've changed. Do you really think that you can become a respectable woman?"

"Go!"

"It's the Jew. The teacher. What has he said? You will never get him into your bed!"

Rachel stood holding the door, "Go."

The man walked out into the chilled night air and Rachel closed and barred the door behind him.

The next morning, Rachel rose early and went to the well while the morning was yet cool. She smiled as she walked and did not feel the weight of the water jug on her shoulder. Most of the women stopped talking as she walked by and none addressed her, still she smiled, walked to the well, drew her water and returned home.

When the crowd following Jesus and the disciples walked past her house, she opened her door and walked along with them. She sat near the front as they assembled under the tree and Jesus began to teach, "Blessed are you who are poor, for yours is the kingdom of God. Blessed are you who hunger now, for you shall be satisfied. Blessed are you who weep now, for you shall laugh. Blessed are you when men hate you, and ostracize you, and cast insults at you, and spurn your name as evil, for the sake of the Son of Man."

Jesus scanned the crowd and then looked down to Rachel. "Be glad in that day, and leap for joy, for behold you reward is great in heaven; for in the same way their fathers used to treat the prophets."

Looking up across the confused faces he said, "But woe to you who are rich, for you are receiving your comfort in full. Woe to you who are well fed now, for you shall be hungry. Woe to you who laugh now, for you shall morn and weep. Woe to you when all men speak well of you, for in the same way their fathers treated the false prophets. But I say to you who hear, love your enemies, do good to those who hate you, bless those who curse you, pray for those who mistreat you. Whoever hits you on the cheek, offer him the other also, and whoever takes away your coat, do not withhold your shirt from him either."

Jesus paused and looked at a man standing alone at the back of the crowd. The man was not there the first day. "Give to everyone who asks of you, and whoever takes away what is yours, do not demand it back. And just as you want people to treat you, treat them in the same way. And if you love those who love you, what credit is that? But love your enemies and do good and lend, expecting nothing in return, and your reward will be great, and you will be sons of the Most High; for He Himself is kind to ungrateful and evil men. Be merciful just as your Father is merciful."

Only the sound of the light breeze through the leaves could be heard. Even the birds were silent. Every eye was fixed on Jesus. Everyone there felt their heart penetrated by his gaze. Jesus sighed and said, "And do not judge..."

He paused and smiled warmly, "Do not judge and you

will not be judged; and do not condemn and you will not be condemned; pardon and you will be pardoned."

Jesus opened his arms and said with a smile in his voice, "Give and it will be given to you; good measure, pressed down, shaken together, running over, they will pour into your lap. For by your standard of measure it will be measured to you in return."

Jesus taught until the sun was high in the sky and the heat became heavy upon them. Peter said, "Lord send them home that they take refreshment and shelter from the heat, for the sun is high and no one dare draw water while you speak."

Jesus looked up to the sun just as he had as they approached Sychar the day before and he nodded to Peter. "Let us go into the city with them, for my time is not yet finished here."

Peter addressed the crowd. "Please, brothers and sisters go home and take refreshment. The Rabbi has more to teach you."

The citizens of Sychar stood and began making their way towards the city, speaking and debating what they heard as they walked. The elder's wife came alongside Rachel and said, "It is a good thing you told us about the teacher. Truly he is a prophet. What more did he tell you? I feel the power of his words, but there is much I do not understand."

When they reached the gate of the city near Rachel's house, the elder's wife said, "Please, come with me, I would hear more."

Jesus taught again in the afternoon. He spoke of not coveting and not laying up treasures on earth and warned them against greed. He comforted them against worry and encouraged their faith in a loving heavenly Father. He spoke of the power of faith as small as the mustard seed and doing the master's will. He spoke of division and signs of the times to come. Again, and again he shared his vision of the coming Kingdom and the love and joy it would bring.

He challenged them, "When you give a luncheon or a dinner, do not invite your friends or your brothers or your relatives or your rich neighbors, lest they also invite you in return, and repayment come to you. But when you give a reception, invite the poor, the crippled, the lame the blind, and you will be blessed since they do not have means to repay you; for you will be repaid at the resurrection of the righteous."

When Rachel went home that evening, the man was waiting outside her door. "Forgive me Rachel. I understand now. Would you permit me to court you—honorably?"

Rachel looked at the man before standing before her, clean and sober.

"I have returned all that I have stolen—I will never again steal, I... I want a new life—to walk with you and seek the kingdom Jesus speaks of."

Rachel stared in silence while he stood face to the ground. "If you have truly repented... I might allow an honest man—a righteous man to call on me."

That night a great banquet was prepared for Jesus and his disciples. At the table Jesus turned to the those standing nearby and said, "When you are invited to a wedding feast, do not take the seat of honor. Lest someone more distinguished than you may have been invited by him, and he who invited you both come and say to you, 'Give your place to this man and then in disgrace you proceed to occupy the last place. But when you are invited, go and sit at the last place, that when the one who has invited you comes, he may say to you, 'Friend, move up higher. For everyone who exalts himself will be humbled; and he who humbles himself will be exalted."

The guests sat as they pondered this teacher who spoke in parables and contradictions. Mesmerized they listened as he told the story of a wealthy king who persisted with much determination to fill a great hall to honor the marriage of his son. At the end of the banquet, Jesus rose, thanked his host and said he would resume his journey to Galilee in the morning.

Peter said to Jesus in the nighttime quiet of the courtyard, "The people do not understand your parables."

"Peter, do you not remember the parable of the seed which I explained to you? The seed has been planted in the soil of Sychar. It will grow in the good soil. To you and to whosoever's heart where it grows, it has been granted to know the mysteries of the kingdom of heaven. But where it dies or does not sprout, in their case the prophecy of Isaiah is being fulfilled, which says, 'Hearing you will hear and shall not understand, and seeing you will see and not perceive.' But blessed are your eyes and the eyes of all who see, and your ears and all whose ears hear, because they hear. For truly I say to you that many prophets desired to see what you see and did not see it and hear the words you hear but did not hear them."

On the third day Jesus arose and departed the city of Sychar with his disciples. Rachel heard the commotion of the people following Jesus as they made their way past her house. She quickly covered her head with her scarf and was out the door. As Jesus passed through the city gate, Rachel called out, "Rabbi, before you leave, please... please teach us to pray!"

Jesus smiled. He stopped, turned around and opened his arms. "Rachel come, come all of you and listen."

Rachel walked boldly forward, and the crowd followed her. As she stood before him, he spoke loudly but his eyes were on Rachel. "When you pray, say 'Father, hallowed be your name. Your kingdom come; your will be done. Give us each day our daily bread. And forgive us our sins as we ourselves forgive everyone indebted to us. And do not bring us to the time of trial."

When Jesus finished, he turned and walked north towards Galilee. Rachel stood and watched him walk away. Several of the women came alongside her and one said, "I have never met anyone like him. But I wonder... tell us, Rachel, you seem to understand, in all of his teachings, what would he have us learn?"

Rachel did not turn her eyes from Jesus, but answered softly, "God loves me. He loves each and every one of us."

Rachel turned to the women and smiled warmly. "Trust Him. Know that it is His desire that we love Him, and He asks that we love each other as well."

Rachel turned and smiled at the women, "Come, we must draw our water before it is too hot."

Two hours later another Samaritan village appeared on the horizon. Jesus closed his eyes as before, looking to heaven. Peter asked, "Lord, shall we go into the city?"

Jesus sighed. "You may enter if you wish and ask if they will listen, but they will not hear you. They will send you away."

Peter looked into Jesus' face and said, "It was for her. We came to Sychar for the woman at the well."

Jesus smiled and said, "A blessed woman. Her seed will return more than a hundred-fold."

An Interview with David Martyn

When did you start writing and why?

Although I was published in National Scholastic in High School and wrote a story for my college newspaper, I didn't begin to write with any sense of an ongoing preoccupation until after I retired. I found myself with time to think and to compose. I was always active in small groups and thought myself perhaps too forthcoming to share and slow to listen. It occurred that in writing, I could do a better job of sharing without becoming a bore. Many of us use stories to make a point, and fiction moves us away from the pitfalls of discussing current political ideologies.

Which authors or books, or media influenced you the most as a writer?

I enjoy classic literary fiction. Dostoevsky was an early favorite, but also C.S. Lewis, Melville, Thomas Wolfe, Stephen Crane, and others. I enjoy a good story with well-developed characters and rich descriptions. History fascinates me, and Patrick O'Brian's series of Captain Aubrey's fictional career in the British navy (*Master and Commander* is best known) captivated me with its detailed authenticity of both the nautical terms and his rich retelling of the art, music, food, dance, and everyday life in the late eighteenth and early nineteenth centuries. To me, O'Brian epitomizes historical fiction.

Which authors or books or media had the biggest impact on you as a person?

My worldview is distinctly Christian. C.S. Lewis would top the list—not his Christian fantasies, but his other works. Other Christian writers include Tozer, Francis Schaefer, John Stott, and others, mostly non-fiction.

Which of your original twelve *Prompt* stories are you most pleased with?

It seems my current story is always my favorite. My mind is captive to the story when writing. But looking back, I find the Magi story and the Bonhoeffer stories as compelling. My edition of Emerge stories will include a story from *Unconditional* called "The Courtship." It is my retelling of the Bible story of the woman at the well.

Which of your original twelve *Prompt* stories did you find the most difficult to write?

The Bonhoeffer story was difficult because the local resources for my research were inadequate. A sad but true commentary on Western Washington's libraries. Bonhoeffer was a prolific writer who used his two years in prison to write letters, poems, plays, music, and theology. I wanted to use his own words from his letters, not what others had written.

What book on writing do you recommend?

I don't have a favorite textbook. I enrolled in writing classes at the local college. It brought the benefit of a teacher and coach as well as other writers who joined me in my first writer's group. As for a text, my favorite instructor (a retired creative writing professor from the University of Idaho) recommended as a textbook Jane Austen's Pride and Prejudice. Good writing is the best text. Ms. Austen demonstrated character development, plot and sub-plot development, pacing, description, and the highs and lows of storytelling. Balance, pacing, and plot. It becomes instinctive.

What advice would you give an unpublished writer?

Take a class. Enroll in local seminars such as Gig Harbor's Write in the Harbor conference every November, join a critique group (if C.S. Lewis and J.R.R Tolkien found it helpful, perhaps your work could be improved as well), and lastly, connect with other writers to share in bringing local literary creativity to your community. Writers are a collegial group and a great source of encouragement.

Do you have a "dream project" as a writer?

My dream project is to follow my writing where it takes me. I started writing a few psalms, poems that became a short story that grew into a novel, the novel into a Biblical series, and the Biblical series into a general audience mystery series with underlying Christian values in a non-sectarian presentation.

Your stories are published in the seasonal *Prompt* anthologies but also as a collection of just your own work. Did you have a conscious theme for your personal collection?

The prompts for the *Prompt* anthologies speak of a journey, a passage often through darkness to light or life beyond. To me, this mirrors the Judeo-Christian salvation story. We are all God's children on a lifelong journey through a broken world filled with trials, temptations, disasters, and broken relationships. But God steps into this world and brings hope. He saves us time and again. He reconciles us and prepares us for an everlasting reward. I wanted my stories to showcase this Christian hope.

You have a body of work outside your Prompt stories. Share why those other works are important to you and how they differ from your Prompt stories.

I have written two series of novels, one Biblical and one historical mystery adventure. A novel, or better, a series, gives greater opportunity for character growth to mix plots and subplots because life is messy and events are never singular. Schedules and efforts are filled with interruptions and complications, and importantly, good and bad things happen concurrently. A novel can capture the little nagging events that pull us away from the main trajectory of life, altering ever so slightly where we are headed. A novel can paint the background and still focus on a theme--on a driving force of a person, family, or nation.

Who do you write for and how does it drive you to create?

I write to understand. My stories and novels are investigations that help me and, hopefully, others to understand our world. The whys and the hows of life and the answers to questions about one's duties and expectations in a life with a purpose.

Optimally, we're always growing and improving as authors. Talk about how you grew or changed as a writer over the course of the year.

The improvement I have noted is growth, not so much in telling a story but in finding creative ways in presenting who and how the story is being told. It's looking at the frame as well as the painting.

Printed in the USA
CPSIA information can be obtained
at www.ICGtesting.com
LVHW050302131023
760927LV00002B/9